Fantastic Tales
of Time and Space
SIGNET DOUBLE SCIENCE FICTION:

SECRETS
OF STARDEEP
and
TIME GATE

More Science Fiction from SIGNET

SECRETS
OF STARDEEP
and
TIME GATE

by John Jakes

Ⓢ
A SIGNET BOOK
NEW AMERICAN LIBRARY
TIMES MIRROR

NAL BOOKS ARE AVAILABLE AT QUANTITY DISCOUNTS
WHEN USED TO PROMOTE PRODUCTS OR SERVICES. FOR
INFORMATION PLEASE WRITE TO PREMIUM MARKETING DIVISION,
THE NEW AMERICAN LIBRARY, INC., 1633 BROADWAY,
NEW YORK, NEW YORK 10019.

Secrets of Stardeep Copyright © 1969 by John Jakes

Time Gate Copyright © 1972 by John Jakes

SIGNET TRADEMARK REG. U.S. PAT. OFF. AND FOREIGN COUNTRIES
REGISTERED TRADEMARK—MARCA REGISTRADA
HECHO EN CHICAGO, U.S.A.

SIGNET, SIGNET CLASSICS, MENTOR, PLUME, MERIDIAN AND NAL BOOKS
are published by The New American Library, Inc.,
1633 Broadway, New York, New York 10019

First Printing (Double Science Fiction Edition), September, 1982

1 2 3 4 5 6 7 8 9

PRINTED IN THE UNITED STATES OF AMERICA

SECRETS
OF STARDEEP

Contents

One

GHOST OF A LIGHTSHIP

The past, mercifully dead almost seven years now, came back to life suddenly on the first morning of the last quarter. Rob Edison wasn't prepared for it.

He and his friends Byron Winters and Tal Aroon dropped into their seats. The gong rang. There were about twenty boys in the bright underground room located on the Life Sciences Level. The boys were busy adjusting their contoured chairdesks, setting the controls on the automatic note-taking recorders, and checking in.

Rob punched the white attendance button inset into the top of his chairdesk. A plaque in a row of twenty next to the large wall screen lighted up. It read, EDISON, R.

"What happened to Jo?" Rob asked. "I lost track of him after we came out of the cafeteria."

"He's sitting up there with the new guy," By Winters answered.

"Where? Oh, I see him." Rob was big for fifteen, with a squarish jaw, pleasant blue eyes, sandy hair, and a nose that was wide and prominent enough to give him a rugged air. He grinned. "Jo the one-man welcoming committee. With his talent for shaking hands and making friends, he'll stand for Universal Senate before he's thirty. And get elected."

Tal Aroon, a skinny boy with a pointed chin that hinted at a trace of non-Terran blood, said, "Anybody catch this new guy's name?"

"I didn't," By said. "Exate told me we'd have somebody new in the level, though. The new guy transferred in because he wanted this particular course before he took the

1

college entrance exams. The course isn't being offered at any other League Homes this quarter."

By tugged Rob's arm. "There goes the new guy's name now."

Rob watched as the plaque lighted up. SHARKEY, K.

The new student had a narrow face and short-cropped reddish hair. He didn't seem to be smiling much as he talked with Jo McCandless, who sat beside him two rows ahead. He was deeply tanned. That meant he came from one of the surface worlds. Rob reminded himself to say hello at the end of class.

In a second he realized he probably wouldn't have to make the effort. Sharkey, K. was looking back over his shoulder at Rob. His stare was direct and not very friendly. After a minute, Sharkey, K. turned to study the lighted attendance plaques. He asked Jo McCandless something pointing to the plaques.

Jo nodded, grinned back at Rob, answered the new student's question. Rob was almost sure Jo had said, "Yes, that's Rob Edison."

Another glance from Sharkey, K. Outright hostility this time. Rob felt uneasy.

The screen glowed a pale pearl. A human tutor appeared on the screen.

"Good morning, gentlemen. This course is Survey of Cryogenics 414. Anyone not registered had better check his program, his eyes, or both."

A mild wave of laughter from the students, even though the tutor was probably parsecs away on the planet where the course-tape had been prepared.

The tutor continued: "My name is Doctor Wallington. As you know, pioneering research in the science of extreme cold began far back in the twentieth century. We shall spend the first two weeks making a historical survey of . . ."

Rob only half listened. He kept being distracted by Sharkey, K. up front. The tanned boy looked at him every other minute or so. He was making no effort to record key parts of the lecture on his automatic notetaker.

As the hour passed, Rob kept wondering about the new boy's interest in him. He grew impatient for the gong. He did manage to make his notes, though. He had kept his marks high ever since coming to Dellkart IV, and he didn't intend to let down in the last quarter. Too much was at stake.

". . . please withdraw your text cards from the depository," Doctor Wallington concluded. "Review chapters one through four before the next session. Good day." The screen faded. The gong rang. Everyone got up.

"Might as well get the blinking card right now," Tal Aroon said. "The lines won't be any shorter later."

"Here comes Jo with the new guy," said By Winters.

Rob had concentrated on lifting the tiny reel of tape from the note machine. Now he balanced up. Actually Jo McCandless wasn't bringing the new student over at all. It was the other way around.

Jo followed Sharkey, K., who was zigzagging fast between the chairdesks.

"Let's skip the cards until tonight," By was saying. "We can draw 'em all at one time. Why don't we show this new guy the gravball court? We could use a new man at left swing."

The new arrival wasn't interested in anyone but Rob. He held out his hand in a friendly enough way. But his faintly slanted hazel eyes were cold.

"I've wanted to meet you for quite a while, Edison. Didn't know you were on Dellkart IV when I picked the transfer."

Rob grinned. It felt forced. "Have I got some sort of special reputation?"

"With me you do. My name's Kerry Sharkey."

"I saw it on the plaque. Welcome to Dellkart, Kerry."

"Thanks. You and I are going to have to have a good long talk soon."

A few students had stopped at the door, watching the curious scene. Tal Aroon and Jo McCandless exchanged puzzled looks behind Sharkey's back.

"Fine," said By. "You and Rob have a talk, Kerry. Ol' Rob's after the marks. But he still knows the best punchcards to ask for when they send dates in from the girls' branch of the Home on the other side of the planet."

"Girls can wait," said Kerry. "Rob and I are going to talk about FTLS."

"Faster-Than-Light Ships?" Jo said. "You going into Space Service?"

"Most every guy here lost his dad in the service," By said with a frown. "You won't find too many apprentice Lightcommanders in the crowd. Heck, you ought to know that, Sharkey."

Kerry Sharkey nodded. "I want to talk to Rob about one particular FTLS."

"Which one?" Tal asked.

"The fourteenth. Put into service about ten years ago." Sharkey had a way of shooting out his words in bunches, staccato, hinting at barely controlled anger. "The FTLS I'm thinking about was the third one lost in a hyperspace jump. She never came back. No trace of her ever showed up. She was lost with two thousand officers and crew." He paused. Rob's palms were cold.

When Jo McCandless spoke, he was less than jovial. "I don't get this big interest in FTLS, Sharkey."

"Ask Edison."

"Rob, what's he talking about?" By wanted to know.

"Something personal," Rob replied. "I'd like to keep it that way."

Both Jo and Tal Aroon were startled by Rob's tone. Kerry Sharkey chuckled. There was a hardness in his laugh, a hardness about the lines of his face, and an air of tension in the way he carried himself. Still, most orphans of the Space Service matured young.

"Edison hasn't told you guys about it, eh?" Sharkey said. "I'm not surprised. At the Home on Lambeth Omega-O, I got to know one of the tutors fairly well. Seems Rob Edison got into quite a few fights when he was on Lambeth himself. He wasn't keeping the past a secret back then. Obviously he's gotten smarter."

Anger quickened in Rob's eyes. "I'm leaving, Sharkey. We can talk later—"

"No, right now!" Kerry seized his arm. "Let's talk about *Majestica*."

The name rang in Rob's mind like a gloomy bell. All at once the peace and security of the past couple of years melted away.

Sharkey was right, of course. At his first Space League Home on Lambeth Omega-O, Rob had kept no secrets about his father. As a result he had been treated as an outcast by the other boys. He stood it as many years as he could. Finally he asked for a transfer to the Dellkart Home. By not mentioning the past here, he had avoided trouble ever since.

But now there was real trouble.

By Winters sensed something very wrong. He automatically sided with Rob. "You haven't been popping some illegal pills to boost your learning rate, have you, Sharkey? I can't make any sense out of what you're saying."

"No, I haven't been popping pills. I've just been living without a father for about seven years."

"Where's your mother?" By asked.

"Dead when I was three," Sharkey snarled. "Where's yours?"

The harsh words made By flush. He mumbled an apology for his outspoken question, but Sharkey paid no attention.

"About your dad—" Tal Aroon prompted.

"My dad was a hyperdrive stacker, second, on *Majestica*," Kerry Sharkey said. "He was aboard when she went out from Stardeep."

Jo McCandless frowned. "Stardeep?"

"It's a pretty remote planet," Rob said. He sounded tired. "In the Lens End Nebula."

"Other end of the galaxy, huh?" said By.

"What Sharkey's trying to say, for your benefit and probably for mine," Rob went on, "is that seven years ago, *Majestica* vanished after she jumped into hyperspace from the Stardeep launchyard. Sharkey's dad was one of two thousand men lost when *Majestica* never turned up." In a quiet voice he finished, "The skipper of *Majestica* was"—Rob swallowed once—"Lightcommander Duncan Edison."

Jo McCandless gaped. "Your father?"

Rob nodded. His eyes never left the hazel eyes of Kerry Sharkey.

The classroom was silent. The filtered air purred through the high ventilators, smelling faintly sweet with germicidal agents. A few boys still lingering by the door buzzed in sudden conversation.

They had heard it all.

Well, he'd probably been crazy to think he could hide it forever.

"Tell your friends the rest of it, Edison," Kerry Sharkey said.

Rob stepped forward. By Winters saw his anger, laid a hand on his arm. Rob brushed it aside. "What kind of entertainment does this give you, Sharkey?"

"I lost my dad on *Majestica!* So did two thousand others. You dad was in command."

"My father wasn't responsible for—"

Kerry Sharkey's snort cut him off. "I heard you were always saying that on Lambeth. Tell your friends what the Inquiry Commission decided after all the evidence was in."

A muscle in the side of Rob's throat jumped. Sharkey shrugged.

"All right, then. I will. The Inquiry Commission marked Lightcommander Edison's permanent tape C.D.E."

Tal Aroon, whose father had been a Lightadjutant killed in a launchyard explosion, barely whispered, "Command decision error?"

"That's right," said Sharkey. "You can't get anything worse on the record. But I'd say that wasn't half good enough for him."

In a remote way Rob understood how Sharkey felt—understood how the loss of his father must have tormented him over the years. All the boys in the Space League Homes felt more or less the same way.

Yet most of them never looked for vengeance, or scapegoats. Their fathers had chosen the service even though there were tremendous risks in hurling great craft through hyperspace faster than 186,000 miles a second. The men who drove the ships out to explore and colonize whole new areas of the galaxy knew they might die one day and leave their wives and children or—in the case of boys and girls in League Homes, with both parents dead—create wards of the service. But still men served, and some died, and their sons and daughters got along somehow. Most of them were proud of what their fathers had done for humanity.

Now Sharkey stepped in close to Rob. A light film of sweat shone on his forehead. "No, Edison, C.D.E. isn't half good enough for a Lightcommander who made a stupid mistake that killed two thousand men."

That was when Rob swung his right fist.

The blow hit Sharkey's cheek hard enough to bruise it and bring blood oozing to the surface. Sharkey bowled back against one of the chairdesks. He spat out angry, explosive words.

"Hold on, Rob!" Tal Aroon yelled, trying to step between the two. Rob shoved him to one side. Kerry Sharkey bounded up, ducked in, punched Rob twice in the stomach.

Rob doubled, the breath going out of him. Jo McCandless caught Sharkey's right arm and twisted him aside. Furious, Sharkey aimed a fist at Jo, who brought his forearm up to block the punch. Rob lunged forward to help.

A klaxon blatted, deafening. Rob stopped his charge in mid-stride, skidded to a halt. Jo lowered his arm. He let go of Kerry Sharkey, who slumped against a chairdesk.

By Winters glanced at the lighted grid in the ceiling. He looked unhappy.

Several lenses around the grid had uncapped themselves. Suddenly a metallic voice boomed:

"Students! Identify yourselves by last name."

Rob glared at Sharkey. He called to the monitor, "Edison."

One by one the other boys gave their names. The students by the door had faded away at the first sound from the monitor computer. As soon as By had completed his identification, the computer voice boomed out again:

"You will report to your respective tutors at 1815 hours for disciplinary action. Clear the classroom. That is all."

The grid lights faded. The lens caps slid back into place. Rob straightened his tunic and brushed off his tan-colored shorts. Jo McCandless said to Kerry Sharkey: "You haven't exactly made a great start on Dellkart, friend. We all have too much at stake in the summer exams to fool around fighting."

"I'll keep that in mind." Sharkey's sarcasm said just the opposite.

"I don't owe you any explanations," Rob said to Sharkey, "but for the record, I know my dad wasn't guilty."

Sharkey's eyebrow crooked up. "Oh? The Inquiry Commission thought differently."

"I know, but—" Rob stopped. There it was. The old, implacable wall.

Kerry Sharkey wiped his chin and laughed. It wasn't a pleasant sound. "Sure, Edison. He couldn't have done it. He was your dad. But he did. And he killed my dad in the process." Sharkey glanced from Tal Aroon to Jo to By. "Nice to have met all you guys. You pick some first-class friends." And he snatched up his note tape and walked out.

Finally By broke the awkward silence. "Rob, you could have said something to us before this."

"There wasn't any reason to say anything!"

"Don't sound so mad," Tal put in. "Remember who we

are? The guys who share the same bunk level with you. We'll listen to your side."

Rob was still furious. "No, you won't. Because you aren't going to hear it."

"Look, Rob," Jo said. "If the Inquiry Commission wrote C.D.E. into the record, how does that make you guilty? Even if what Sharkey said was true, it wasn't you, it was your dad who—"

"Get one thing straight, Jo! My dad wasn't guilty of C.D.E."

Plainly annoyed at Rob's tone, By said softly, "Just because he happened to be your dad?"

"Yes, that's reason enough for me." Rob turned and stalked out.

Several students spoke to him on the liftstairs up to surface level. Rob was too preoccupied to answer. His behavior produced stares of surprise. From overhead, thin white light leaked down into the automated stairwell. The stairs carried Rob up to the student plaza.

The plaza was crowded with boys hurrying to classes. The transparent dome that covered the plaza was set on a rocky plateau. Eastward, white crags rose like crumpled walls of chalk. A semicylinder of covered service highway ran between the school complex and the double tunnel through the mountains. Out of sight at the far end of the tunnels lay the city. Dellkart IV was a bleached, cold world under a feeble sun.

Normally Rob would have gone straight to the depository to wait in line and draw his various text cards for the quarter. Before his next class, he would have dropped in at the lower level cafeteria for a cup of nutrient broth at the corner table that he, Tal, and the others reserved by right of being senior classmen. This morning he didn't feel up to it.

He took another stairs down to his dorm level. In his cubicle he sat staring at the small platinum-framed fax of his father on the corner of his study table, next to the reader.

There was a strong physical resemblance between the son and the face of the father, including the prominent nose that lent the man in the fax an air of authority only now emerging in Rob's features. Lightcommander Duncan Edison had been forty-one when he died. His hair had been partially gray. The little ship-pins of sculptured gold shone on the collar of his service uniform.

Believe in me, the picture seemed to say to Rob.

I believe, Rob thought. You're my father—that's reason enough for me.

But was it?

Rob simply couldn't bring himself to accept the C.D.E. judgment. Yet, when confronted by someone like Kerry Sharkey, Rob had no real evidence to support his faith. That lack of evidence gnawed at him painfully, as it hadn't since he left the Lambeth Omega-O Home.

Now a ghost of an FTLS had plowed up out of the past, returning from wherever she had vanished in that *other* space between real points light-years apart.

A gong sounded. Rob jumped up. He'd be late for his next class.

He couldn't even remember what it was. Oh, yes. Seminar in Early Galactic Government, A.D. 2175–2250. Taught by a human tutor who had a reputation for flunking half of every class. Rob shook his head to clear it and left the cubicle.

Another student hailed him. Something about a gravball practice that afternoon. Rob paid no attention.

He thought about having to face his tutor this evening. Discipline marks would do his record no good at all. It was certainly starting out to be a bad last quarter.

Two

WARNING FROM A ROBOT

Promptly at 1815 hours, Rob rang the chime at a cubicle on the Tutorial Level.

"Come in."

The voice from inside activated the door. It slid aside on invisible rollers. Rob stepped into the small room.

"Good evening, Mr. Edison," his assigned tutor said. Its voice had an odd ring, produced as it was by machinery. The tutor sounded like a frog speaking Unitongue through a metal funnel. Each syllable was carefully articulated, giving the tutor's speech an even more inhuman precision.

"Hello, Exfore," Rob said. He avoided looking at the two crystal photocells placed in the tutor's head at approximately the position of human eyes. Exfore wouldn't notice this, and Rob knew it. Yet, like most other students at the Home, Rob had grown close to his tutor in the past couple of years and unconsciously attributed all sorts of human traits to it.

Robot Tutor X–4 was seated in a contour seat. The robot had no need to sit. It simply took a chair to make the student feel at home. Rob dropped into the contour bucket facing Exfore. The tutor's hinged cheek plates changed position, pulling Exfore's mouth into a new shape at the corners and forming an approximation of a smile.

"Let us review your first day of classes," Exfore said. With a snap the robot pulled a punchcard from the button-studded sphere next to its chair. "You are carrying a difficult load. Principles of Hyperdrive Theory III is particularly difficult as taught by Professor Bool."

10

"I don't think I'll have too much trouble." Rob wished Exfore would get to the real point.

"Yes, but we want to maintain our mark, don't we? You are presently sixth in your class—"

"Come on, Exfore!" Rob burst out. "How many discipline marks?"

The tutor's photocells brightened. The corners of its mouth snapped down. Exfore laid aside the first card. It touched a blue and then a red button on the sphere beside its chair. A smaller card popped out of a slot. Rob didn't miss the red edging on the card.

"Physical attack upon a fellow student is a highly antisocial activity," Exfore intoned. Artificial lids clicked down over its photocells, then shot up again. The simulated blink indicated the seriousness of the matter. "If I may be indulged, I observe that the human race, which is responsible for creating me, is more capable of building control into its artificial servants than it is of controlling its own emotions."

Rob fidgeted. Exfore asked: "Why did you and new student Sharkey come to blows?"

"I lost my temper."

Exfore blinked again. "Have you no other explanation?"

"Look, Exfore, why don't you just tell me the number of discipline marks? I'm sure you've played the computer tapes. You know what happened."

The robot said something which sounded like, "Ahem." Then it went on, "Very true. I merely wanted to hear your version."

"It's a personal thing. Am I required to discuss it?"

Exfore pondered, touching metal chin with a metal hand. "No. You may accept four disciplinary marks and leave."

"Four!"

"You didn't expect that many?"

"No, I didn't."

"Well, then," Exfore continued, intensifying its photocells, "let us discuss possible mitigating circumstances. If I find them valid, I am prepared to reduce the marks to only two." The robot leaned forward from the waist without a single creak. "I have great faith in you, Rob. You are a fine student—my very best, I don't mind telling you. However, you know very well that discipline marks can affect your entrance standings in the two months of college entrance

examinations this coming summer. Because there are so
many young people in the galaxy clamoring for higher education, a poor exam grade means that your place in college
will be taken by someone else. That would be a shame for
someone of your potential."

"Pardon me, Exfore," Rob said, just a slight edge of irritation in his voice, "but I know how important the exams
are. I've already decided to do an extra seminar tape to offset the discipline marks."

Exfore nodded its spherical head. "A commendable attitude. However, your premise may be faulty."

"What do you mean?"

"You may be assuming that the new student, Sharkey,
will cause you no further trouble. I have served this institu-
tion for seventy-five years, with time out only for sabbatical
overhauls. I know a bit about human emotions."

Here comes another lecture, Rob thought. The tutor
snapped off the recorder in the sphere console. Then it adjusted its tone lower.

"Sharkey's behavior this morning was deplorable. However, his motivation is perfectly understandable. He may
continue to harass you."

Rob eyed Exfore glumly. "Well, don't worry. I won't let
Sharkey get me down."

"Admirable intentions."

"You think I can't stick to them?"

Exfore blinked. "Oh, I am simply saying that we are
dealing with a highly sensitive problem involving human
emotions. Sharkey lost his father in unusual and tragic circumstances. Rightly or wrongly, he holds your father—
and, illogically, you—responsible."

All of a sudden Rob felt his defenses drop. "Exfore, I
just don't know what to do. I know my dad wasn't guilty.
But I'll never be able to prove it to Sharkey or anyone
else."

"Is it necessary that you prove it?"

"It wasn't until today. Now—well, I don't know. I've
lived with this thing a long time—"

"For seven years, to be exact."

"Exfore, how much do you know about what happened
to *Majestica?*"

"Everything that is in the official transcript. It came with
you to Dellkart IV, as part of your record."

"You've never mentioned it before."

"Until today, it had nothing to do with your academic performance." Exfore's photocells brightened again. "It might be well if I spoke to Sharkey's tutor, I believe that's Exnine, Exnine may be able to persuade Sharkey that he is making unfounded accusations."

That's just the trouble, Rob thought. *They might not be unfounded.* Instantly he was ashamed of letting the doubt creep into his mind.

Exfore punched a series of yellow studs on the sphere. A humming sound. In less than a minute another perforated card popped from the slot. Exfore studied it.

"This from the library gives a few facts about *Majestica*'s disappearance."

Rob frowned. "I can tell you all you need to know."

"I am sure you can. However, let me put you to a little test. If Exnine can persuade Sharkey to smooth over the situation for the rest of the quarter, I shall expect you to exercise a similar restraint."

Rob was angry for a moment. But he heeded Exfore's hint and kept from showing it. At times the robot tutors could be—in the fullest sense of the word—inhuman.

Exfore perused the card. "At the time of the fatal launch from the planet Stardeep seven years ago, the Faster-Than-Light Ships had been in existence for only about thirty-five years. Their control technology was still in the development stage and subject to error despite the elaborate failsafe devices. For calculation of the highly critical jump paths through hyperspace, a combination of human brainpower mechanically linked to the FTLS computer was required."

Rob nodded. "It took both a Lightcommander and a computer to work out all the equations. It still does."

"Therefore a Lightcommander was, and is, never wholly responsible for the computations."

"Yes, but the Lightcommander is the only one who could make a mistake."

"Computers can make mistakes," Exfore countered.

"Once in a trillion years, maybe, if all the failsafes break down."

"Granted. Therefore, Rob, the most likely cause of an FTLS jumping to the wrong destination with fatal results is human error. Two FTLS were lost in such fashion before *Majestica* jumped off from Stardeep, I note here. There are no other hard facts except this." Exfore ticked a triple-jointed metal finger against the card. "The automatic Phylex Monitor Station one hundred and ten miles from the Stardeep launchyard tracked *Majestica* until it was five milliseconds into hyperspace. At that time, the Phylex tapes show, someone began to program a course correction. After that the tapes went blank. Silence. And *Majestica* was presumed lost in hyperspace, perhaps disintegrated by the stresses."

"But nobody knows for sure who made the course correction!"

"The Inquiry Commission assumed it was your father, since he was in command of the vessel."

Suddenly Rob jumped up. "You sound like Sharkey. Are you trying to tell me the C.D.E. decision was right?"

"Though it is perhaps cruel to do so, Rob, I have reviewed the facts to reach precisely that conclusion."

"To convince me that my dad was responsible for two thousand men dying?"

"To show you that you must not ignore that possibility."

"My dad was a scapegoat! Someone else made that course correction."

"Who?"

"I don't know. Maybe the computer did malfunction."

"Why do you take that position? Do you have facts to support it?"

All at once Rob felt a moistness at the corner of an eye. He fought it and it was gone. He kept his voice controlled:

"No, I don't have any facts, Exfore. I don't *know* that my dad was blameless. I *believe* he was, because—well, it's just what I said to Sharkey. Because he was my dad. He was a good man. A bright man. I remember—"

Rob stopped. He slumped back into the chair.

"How can I expect a robot to understand? He was all the family I ever had. My mother died when I wasn't even a year old."

"I know," Exfore said softly.

"He had one of the finest records in the Space Service—" Rob began.

And stopped again. He knew his reasons weren't strong enough.

"Your loyalty and love are praiseworthy, Rob," Exfore said. "If I have treated you harshly these past few minutes, permit me to apologize. I subjected you to the ordeal only to make you realize that Kerry Sharkey has valid emotional reasons for his behavior. Those reasons are fully as strong as yours. Neither of you can prove or disprove the C.D.E. judgment. Therefore you must each act with restraint and bury the past."

"Sharkey doesn't show much willingness to forget what happened."

"You are my charge, Rob. Sharkey's tutor will see to him."

Silence.

Deep down, Rob knew that Exfore was right. He would probably have to live the rest of his days with the awful, haunting suspicion that the Commission's judgment was correct.

Exfore stood up with a low whir of tiny servomotors in its trunk and knees.

"Rob, I will reduce the discipline marks on your pledge that you will do your part in the coming weeks to keep your eye on your real goal—success in the examinations. Exnine and I will see what we can do to temper Sharkey's anger." Exfore laid a metal hand on Rob's shoulder. "However, Sharkey's actions whatever they may be, do not affect your responsibility."

Exfore inclined its head to indicate that the interview was over.

Rob realized the wisdom of what the tutor said. He had to keep a level head this quarter. In addition to pursuing his regular studies, he would have to spend every spare minute reviewing all the courses he had taken since coming to Dellkart IV. He would be tested on every one of them. The problem of Sharkey could wreck him if he let it.

Exfore led the way to the door. "The truth is often harsh, Rob," he remarked.

"All the truth about *Majestica* isn't on the record of the Commission."

"You feel that. You don't know it. Don't confuse the two."

Swallowing a protest, Rob left the cubicle. He had gone half a dozen steps when he remembered something. He rang Exfore's chime again. When the door opened, he stuck his head in and said with a sheepish smile:

"Hey, thanks for the discipline-mark reduction."

Exfore's mouth hinges adjusted into a smile. "Rob, you're welcome."

As he headed back to his dorm level, Rob remembered

that he had promised to meet Tal and By Winters in the rec dome for an hour of tri-di chess. He didn't feel like it now. He went back to his cubicle, shut the door, and activated the STUDYING—DON'T DISTURB flasher.

He put his cryogenics text on the reader, dialed the opening page, adjusted the magnification, and dimmed the cubicle lights to reading level. The light from the reader screen spilled white across his face, accenting his worried look.

Exfore was right on every count. He could never prove his father hadn't made the fatal mistake that took *Majestica* to whatever destruction she met.

Come on, Edison, he said to himself. *Page one, chapter one.*

After reading the same three introductory pages five times, he snapped off the reader and rolled into his bunk. The foam adjusted itself to the shape of his body. But he lay sleepless in the dark.

And to think things had been so different only this morning! No sign of trouble. Sharkey, K. had changed it all.

Finally Rob drowsed. Dimly he heard a knock at his door. Tal Aroon, cheerfully ignoring the red flasher, was calling to him to stop the grind routine and play that game of tri-di chess.

Rob made no sound. Eventually Tal want away.

Rob went back to sleep. He had uneasy dreams in which he saw a long, shining FTLS blow up again and again.

He awoke two hours before the morning buzzer. He used the extra time to catch up on the studies he had neglected the night before. When the buzzer sounded, he was already dressed and hungry, so instead of dropping down the hall to see By or Jo McCandless, he took the stairs to the cafeteria level.

The great dome was almost deserted at this early hour. Rob put a glass of red zim juice on his tray. He added a plate of syntheggs cooked to his order in ten seconds by the microwave oven. He picked up a mug of hot nutrient and found a table. While he ate, he plugged in his earplug and listened to his notes from yesterday's Middle Galactic Literature lecture.

The dining hall began to fill. All at once he felt someone watching him. He glanced up. Kerry Sharkey was just starting through the serving line.

Kerry smiled and waved. "Morning, Commander!"

Rob flushed, rising halfway out of his seat. He got control, went back to his food. But he didn't miss the way some of the students in the line snickered.

Fortunately Sharkey decided to eat by himself. Rob lost himself in his notes until someone sat down beside him.

"Well, well," said Jo McCandless. "The cheerful hermit."

By Winters took a seat on the other side of the table. "Abandoned your friends, have you?"

"I didn't feel like tri-di last night, that's all," said Rob.

"And did you take sour pills when you got up today?" Tal Aroon said as he joined them.

"Lay off," Rob growled.

By made a face. "I can see it's going to be a great quarter."

"If you don't like—"

Rob choked off the rest of the sentence. By and Jo exchanged looks of dismay. Then By shrugged. Rob walked with them to class but said little.

As he sat down he heard Kerry Sharkey come into the classroom. Sharkey was talking to some other students. Rob caught one word. *"Majestica."*

Angrily he adjusted his note-taking machine and concentrated on the screen up front, letting the taped image of Doctor Wallington blot out everything around him, Kerry Sharkey and his friends alike.

Three

"YOURS VERY TRULY, HOLLIS KIPP"

The automatic referee, a telescoping arm that shot up from the center of the gravball court, put the ball into play again.

The ball popped out of the padded pincers. With a *whoosh* the automatic referee retracted into the floor. The light gas inside the ball buoyed it higher toward the arched ceiling. In the stands on both sides of the court, boys from the competing dorm levels yelled, whistled, and stamped.

The random-choice lights above the court flashed red.

"Offense!" Tal Aroon shouted.

Rob dropped into backslot position. By Winters was racing down the court at left swing. Playing forward, Tal Aroon led the diamond-shaped formation out under the ball.

Down the court from the opposite direction charged the quartet of Blues. Rob found his spot, planted his shoes hard on the slippery plastic surface. As forward, Tal had to snatch the ball back into offensive play before he could pass to any of his teammates. Rob watched the illuminated chronometer at court's end ticking off the final two minutes of the game. The score read Blues—8, Reds—6.

Rob felt bone-tired. Usually four twelve-minute gravball quarters didn't exhaust him at all. Tonight weariness seemed to make his legs plastic, unsteady.

Warily he watched the Blues left swing maneuver into position a few feet away to guard him. The cheering in the stands slammed and echoed up and down the court. Tal Aroon leaped high, triggered his suction tube by pressing his thumb against the palm latch.

The tube was banded to the back of Tal's right hand. His arm and the tube were parallel, pointing straight up in the air as his jump carried him well off the court floor.

The suction generated by the tube's tiny but powerful motor caught the ball high overhead and began to pull it downward.

The Reds fans howled and stamped harder. Tal sucked the ball all the way down until it bumped the mouth of the tube. Simultaneously he pivoted. As he did so he turned off the suction power. He whipped his arm down to point at Rob.

The ball followed the end of the tube downward almost to the horizontal position. As the suction released, the ball shot toward Rob and then began to arc upward.

Rob lunged forward. He triggered his palm latch. The suction of the tube on the back of his right hand kicked in, caught the rising ball at the last instant. The ball jiggled in the air uncertainly.

"Fall, fall!" the Reds fans yelled.

With a *whaap* the ball attached to the end of his tube. Rob took the six zigzagging steps allowed toward the goal, moving his ball arm in a figure eight to fend off the suction tube of the Blues swing man dogging him. Flashing in the corner of Rob's right eye, Kerry Sharkey zoomed into position to receive a pass.

Rob slid to a halt, pivoted right. He snapped his arm straight out from the shoulder.

As his arm straightened he pressed his palm latch. The ball shot across the floor and upward in an arc. Rob watched it, sweat dampening his singlet and shorts. The Reds needed at least a tie in this one to cinch the dorm level trophy. The way the arm was snapped and the ball released to the other player on a pass was critical. Rob's pass hadn't felt just right. He had delayed the suction turn-off a fraction of a second—

Kerry Sharkey darted in beneath the rising ball. He flung his tube arm upward, turned on the suction.

"Fall, fall, fall!" It was a steady, rhythmic chant from the stands.

The ball hesitated, pulled aloft by the gas inside it, pulled downward by the stream of suction from Sharkey's wrist tube.

Abruptly the ball shot up toward the ceiling. Rob groaned.

Kerry Sharkey and Tal Aroon glared at him. The automatic referee telescoped up out of the court floor, released
a new ball from its pincers. The random-choice lights
changed to blue. The Blues went on the offense. They
scored their goal in the last seconds.

The chronometer lighted up like a display of shooting
stars. Klaxons blared briefly. The final score went up.

Rob's ankle hurt as he walked off the court. He had
twisted it in the third quarter and paid no attention until
now. By Winters passed him, hurrying to the showers.

"Tough luck," By said. All Rob saw was his back.

Rob wiped sweat out of his eyes and kept going. They
were all like that lately—Jo, Tal, and By. They dropped
into his cubicle less often. Of course it was now two weeks
till the end of the quarter. In addition to final tests, the
students had the extra weight of the college exams ahead
of them. Everyone was getting tired.

Kerry Sharkey loped up beside him. "That was a rotten
pass, Edison."

All quarter long Rob had listened to Sharkey's gibes. After the first few weeks he had hardened himself—out-
wardly, anyway—so that he could turn them aside. But
tonight, with the pain in his ankle, he couldn't keep his
temper:

"We all make mistakes, Sharkey. So why don't you just
shut up?"

Sharkey blocked the shower entrance, facing Rob. The
corners of his mouth curled up. "Yeah, but big mistakes
seem to run in your family."

"I got your message a long time ago." With a growl Rob
grabbed Sharkey's shoulder and shoved him aside. Sharkey
banged against the wall. For a moment Rob's face was
ugly. He stalked into the showers.

Kerry Sharkey hung back, startled. Rob's behavior
shocked even himself. He discarded his uniform and
stepped under the intermixed spray of hot detergent water
and skin nutrients, closed his eyes and threw his head back.

The spray soothed him a little. Not much.

That was a lousy trick, losing your temper, he said to
himself. What the social psychers would call antipersonality
violence. Outmoded behavior. Worthy of the twentieth century, maybe. But out of place today.

Finishing his shower, Rob noticed that Sharkey had
skipped the ritual, dressed, and left the intramural area. Tal

Aroon and By Winters had been on the opposite side of the steamy room when Rob came in. They had gone too. Glum, Rob walked into the empty locker hall. He pulled on his shorts and tunic and went back to his cubicle.

He sat on the edge of his bed. He glanced listlessly at his pile of note tapes from the day's lectures.

He should review those. He didn't feel like it.

He wondered whether By and Tal would stop by, as they usually did after a gravball match, to suggest a snack. He wouldn't blame them if they didn't.

They didn't.

Rob puttered in his room for half an hour. Then he walked down to By's cubicle. The tiny light beside the jamb glowed, showing that By had left, but could be found by interrogating the Locater computer via the question-phone at the end of the corridor. A check of Tal's room proved it empty too. Rob didn't bother asking the computer when they had gone.

Shoulders slumping, he returned to his room. What was it By had told him last week? That his whole personality seemed to have downgraded during the quarter? That he'd wrecked his chances of an election to Senior Constellation, the honorary club?

"You growl," By told him. "You sneer. You used to smile. Can't you forget your father's ship for one minute?"

"Sharkey won't let me."

"Ignore him."

"Ignore him when he uses the word 'murder'?"

"Check, check! I appreciate the problem." By had raised his hand and walked away that time too, tired of hearing about it.

Well, Rob was tired of thinking about it. Maybe he could squeeze by the finals with decent grades, then really get down to work during the four-week pre-test holiday and lose himself in study. After all, friends weren't half as important as top marks.

He said to himself several times. But he didn't really believe it.

Finally Rob picked one of the note tapes and threaded it onto the playback. He was just about to slip on the earphones when he noticed the little green message light glowing.

He flipped the green light off and dialed the selector pointer. An instant later the lid of the message chute popped open. An index card with a bit of black film stuck into a slit appeared.

Rob studied the card. The letter, a stamp-size piece of film sent sans envelope, had been forwarded from the Lambeth Omega-O Home by FTLS micromail. Official stamps on the delivery card showed the arrival time at Lambeth eight days ago, the arrival on Dellkart earlier this afternoon.

Rob fed the letter into the reader, illuminated the screen. The letterhead was printed in flamboyant green phosphotype on gray stock. The letterhead said, HOLLIS KIPP. This was followed by a micromail delivery number for the planet Weems' Resort.

A startled expression flicked across Rob's face. He recognized the name. Hollis Kipp was a popular journalist, the author of a good half dozen microbooks. Each one had been a best seller that sent people flocking to the vendalls to slip their cash-cards into the proper slot and receive in return the microcard that carried six or seven hundred pages of Kipp's latest prose.

There's a mistake, Rob thought.

But there wasn't. The letter was addressed to *Mr. Robert Edison, Space League Home, Lambeth Omega-O*. A parenthetical notation read, *Kindly Forward if Necessary*.

Quickly Rob looked at the bottom of the letter. The *Hollis Kipp* signature was a big black flourish. Why would such a famous author be writing him?

Rob had plowed through one of Kipp's microbooks as supplementary reading in a course in recent space history. Kipp did a fair research job, though not enough to be considered a scholarly writer. He presented his facts with a lively style, but was not noted for accuracy. In fact, the course tutor had advised the students to read Kipp only for a quick general survey of the period covered. They were warned to ignore altogether Kipp's analysis of various historical personalities involved in the early days of galactic colonization. Kipp deliberately made controversial judgments of such people, for the sake of increasing sales of what he wrote.

A small cold knot formed in Rob's stomach as he remembered one other thing.

Hollis Kipp's books always dealt with space travel. Frowning, Rob began to read:

Dear Mr. Edison:

Perhaps you are already acquainted with my various works of nonfiction, all of which have appeared under the Solar Press cardlabel. This fall I will be commencing research on my next microbook. I am writing to a number of people in the hope that they may be able to provide helpful background information.

My rough working title will give you an idea of the book's theme and scope—"FTLS, The Early Days, A Definitive Account."

I propose to narrate and dramatize the events of the first decades of the FTLS—the technological accomplishments, the dangers and incredible challenges and—yes, the high price in human life that was initially paid to bring about this fundamental change in travel throughout our galaxy.

A portion of the book will, of course, deal with the three great FTLS disasters that occurred during this period, including the loss of FTLS *Majestica,* of which your father was Lightcommander.

In this connection, I would like to interview you via interplanetary tape-cable at a time and date to be mutually arranged. My publishers will bear all costs of the interview hookup. Your memories, comments, and other information pertaining to your father would be most helpful.

I must tell you, as I tell all those I interview, that I cannot promise to utilize your information in a way that will completely please you. My prime goal is to reevaluate the past with a fresh insight.

Hah, Rob thought. Are you sure your prime goal isn't to malign a few people to get everybody reading your book? Almost dreading the last paragraphs, he went back to the letter.

The Inquiry Commission passed judgment on your father's role in the *Majestica* tragedy. I trust, however, that you will be candid enough to give me your side of it—and that the passage of time has made such an interview possible by removing much of the personal pain you must have felt, even though you were relatively young at the time *Majestica* disappeared. Children often see the truth we adults miss!

I make this inquiry in order to organize my interview schedule well ahead of time, and also to learn which interview subjects are willing to cooperate.

I am sincerely hopeful that you can see your way clear to discuss the Lightcommander of *Majestica* as you remember him.

Please contact me at the above address with your reaction.

Yours very truly,
Hollis Kipp

Incredulously, Rob once more scanned the closely packed paragraphs of ultra-elite type. Hollis Kipp was going to rake up the past completely—and profitably—and spread it out for billions of readers. Further, Kipp would probably indulge in his usual character analysis.

What if one of his targets was Lightcommander Duncan Edison? What if Kipp found him guilty all over again?

Rob had a terrible tight feeling in his middle now. This was worse than the appearance of Kerry Sharkey. This was far worse. Automatically, Hollis Kipp had an audience of staggering size. Automatically, the story of Rob's father's C.D.E. would go into thousands of microlibraries on hundreds of planets, and be preserved there for centuries.

With an angry snort Rob snapped off the reader.

What if he did refuse to let Hollis Kipp interview him in the fall? What difference would his refusal really make? Kipp would get the whole story anyway—or at least the story told by the record books. He'd probably get plenty of interviews rfom people like Kerry Sharkey!

Slowly, the shock of what was happening crept over him. He sat down on the bed again, head in his hands. He sat that way for perhaps five minutes.

Suddenly his head came up.

Some of the fatigue had left his face. His eyes were brighter, determined.

He might be able to do something before Hollis Kipp set to work digging into the fatal launch from Stardeep. He might just have time during the official four-week holiday before the exams. He had to do it, so he could at long last confront the Kerry Sharkeys and the Hollis Kipps with the truth.

New confidence surged through Rob. He felt a little giddy. The plan's details had fallen into place quickly, even though it was not exactly the sort of plan a young man his age thought up. Especially not on the eve of the critical precollege tests.

But he felt a lot better for having made the decision.

He washed up and dimmed the lights in his cubicle. He took one last look at his father's fax in the burnished platinum frame. Then he hurried to the Tutorial Level.

He ran the chime. When he got the voice signal to enter, he rushed inside.

"Exfore, when the quarter's over I'm going to Stardeep. And you've got to help me get there."

Four

DESTINATION STARDEEP

When Rob started explaining his plan, Exfore's hinged cheek plates changed position and formed what could only be called an unhappy expression. The mention of Hollis Kipp caused the robot's photocells to intensity to near maximum brightness. The glow slowly subsided. Exfore sat in its chair with that glum look as Rob finished. For several moments it said nothing.

Finally Rob burst out. "You're acting like making the trip is impossible!"

"It is not impossible in terms of time. You do have the official four-week holiday at your disposal. However, most students at the Home—"

"—will be studying. I know." Rob looked a little lost. "Exfore, there just isn't any point in going ahead with anything, exams included, unless I can go to Stardeep first. All I need is a loan from the Space League Fund for passage and expenses."

Exfore made noises that sounded vaguely like, "Um, yes," while its photocells revolved in their sockets. Rob stood with his fists tight at his sides. At last Exfore's synthetic eyes came to rest. Its head jerked ever so little as though it were emerging from deep thought.

"No problem there, I should imagine. But, Rob—are you certain that you are not merely overreacting to that inquiry from author Kipp?"

Fiercely Rob shook his head. "This has been building up for a long time."

"I imagine so," Exfore agreed. "Probably since long before Sharkey arrived." A pause. "As to your missing the study opportunity afforded by the holiday, your prefinal averages have remained high. You have excellent recall, so even if you didn't study for those four weeks, you ought to do well in the tests. That is not what is bothering me."

"Then what is?"

"The purpose of the trip."

"That's simple. I want to find out all I can about what really happened to *Majestica*."

Exfore continued to stare at Rob with that fixed, glum set to its mouth. It raised one hand, extended a cautionary metal forefinger. "Understood. However, what can you possibly learn that the Inquiry Commission did not? Or, for that matter, that Hollis Kipp will not learn if he goes to Stardeep?"

"Exfore," Rob said, "I honestly don't know. Maybe I won't learn a thing. But at least I can go to the Phylex Monitor Station. I can listen to the last *Majestica* tapes for myself, and ask questions for myself at the launchyard. Maybe there are spacemonkeys working there who were at the yard seven years ago. Sure, it's a long chance. And the whole thing's probably hopeless—But I have to do it. Exfore! I have to!"

The robot scrutinized the boy for some moments. Then it turned both of its hands palm upward. Ceiling light reflected from the smooth, shining metal surfaces. "We are dealing here with an area of human behavior which I find confusing. On an abstract level, I can understand why you wish to go. But I cannot summon the same enthusiasm you possess. Doubtless this is because I had neither mother nor father. In any case, my reasoning sees past your emotional need to the various pitfalls. Failure and keen disappointment for you, not to mention—"

"Will you help me apply for the loan or won't you?" Rob exclaimed.

There were more strained seconds of silence. At last Exfore replied:

"Against the dictates of all my logic circuits, I will."

Rob was disappointed. "Look at it from my side, Exfore! I know it may be a futile trip. But doing nothing is worse. If I don't go, all I can look forward to is a life of listening to accusations from people like Kerry Sharkey. Besides—"

Exfore held up its right hand. Rob stopped, embarrassed. "You have convinced me of your sincerity, Rob." The robot's photocells seemed to glow less brightly. "Against all

logical probabilities, I will not only help you, I will also en-
tertain the hope that you will discover something new and
significant—even if that should be incontrovertible proof
that the record of the past must stand as written."

"I think that would be better than never knowing at all,"
Rob said. But he wasn't sure. It might be torture to live
with that kind of truth the rest of his life. He managed to
add with genuine sincerity, "Thanks for saying what you
just did, Exfore."

Something click-tocked in the robot's polished cylinder
of a neck. The sound faintly resembled a human being
clearing his throat. "Let us get down to practical matters."
Exfore touched a series of studs on the chair-side sphere.

In a moment the sphere stopped humming. An information card popped from the slot. Exfore scanned the card.
"You will be on an extremely tight schedule. The light-
jumps to the Lens End Nebula total almost a week. Only
second-class passenger service is available. You will have
to be satisfied with accommodations on a lightfreighter."

Now Rob was beginning to get genuinely excited. "Fine
with me! What's it cost?"

"One-way passage is fourteen hundred microcredits.
Round trip, twenty-five hundred."

A thick lump formed in Rob's throat. He swallowed it
away. "That much?"

Exfore leaped into the opening. "Perhaps you'd care to
reconsider—"

"No. No, I can't, I'll get the money from the Fund."

Exfore's photocells rolled upward in its head as it calculated. "Allow another two hundred microcredits per week
for expenses while on Stardeep. You will require a sum of
twenty-nine hundred. Let's round it off to three thousand to
be safe. Provided you pass your examinations and do well
in college, your adult earning potential will allow you to repay that amount within five years after taking your first
position."

The robot's meaning hadn't escaped Rob. His whole future, including the computer's willingness to grant the loan,
as well as his ability to pay it back, depended on the exams.

"When can we apply for the loan?" Rob wanted to
know.

Exfore consulted the chron inset in one wall of the cubicle. "Perhaps since it's growing late, it would be wise if we
waited until tomorrow—"

"I'm not tired. And you and the Home computer never sleep. Can't we do it right now?"

Exfore articulated its waist, hip, and knee joints and stood up. "Very well."

The automated stairs carried them up toward Administrative Level, which was below the student plaza. They passed student levels, deserted except for an occasional boy drifting back to his cubicle from a cooperative study session. The robot's metal soles clanged on the porous plasto floor as they stepped off the stairs. They proceeded down a long, empty hall where tiny lights glowed behind the nameplates of the various human deans and staff members.

From the stairwell came a sudden clamor of voices. The weekly dipix feature in the auditorium was letting out. Those voices sounded far away, impersonal. Rob realized again just how his quest had cut him off from the normal routine of student life. When he thought about the awesome distance to Stardeep, he was more than a little apprehensive.

Exfore's photocells lighted the way ahead. They turned into a large arch with an identifying plaque which read STUDENT COMPUTER SERVICES. Three walls of the large chamber were taken up with small open-topped booths soundproofed by a tight sonic field. On the fourth wall, opposite the arch, several thousand tiny squares of transglass flickered with colored lights.

The master Space League computer was located on distant Coenworld. This was merely a massive interconnect, buried in the subground. The display wall was installed for artistic rather than functional effect. Human beings seemed to need some assurance that a hidden supermachine was operating.

Rob and his tutor entered one of the booths. Rob sat down in the bucket in front of the console. He programmed in his name and student ident number. Then he used the keyboard to inform the computer that he was requesting a loan of three thousand microcredits against future earnings.

A rectangular panel set in the curved housing above the keyboard flashed, *State reason.*

Rapidly Rob typed out, *Personal emergency.*

Exfore was busy manipulating a dial in its left side just above its waist. The dial released a small metal plate at the approximate position occupied by the left ribs in a human being. From the opening Exfore pulled a cable with a tiny twelve-prong plug. The robot inserted the cable into a jack on the keyboard housing.

Number of Robot Tutor who will approve request, the panel flashed.

"It is not necessary to key in my name," Exfore advised. "I am already connected."

For roughly one minute Exfore stood without moving. Via the cord, he and the Home computer conversed in silence. Rob's palms began to feel chilly. There was a fluttering in his stomach. What if the computer turned him down?

Exfore unplugged. It folded up the cable, stowed it away, and closed the receptacle cover on its metal skin. The interrogation panel above the housing went dark. Somewhere in the subground, bits of information about Rob were being collected: his scholastic record; his extrapolated earnings potential based upon various models of minimum, moderate, and high college success; probable modes of employment following his six years of higher education. Rob guessed that the computer was considering a hundred or more possible futures for him.

The interval seemed long as eternity. Exfore remained unmoving, its photocells dulled. Only the sound of Rob's breathing disturbed the silence.

Finally the panel lighted. Rob almost whooped with joy.

Request for loan approved. Voucher available at Autobursar 0900 tomorrow.

The message wiped. It was followed by a new one. *Document of agreement already forwarded to your room for signature. Complete and return via chute.* After another wipe, the mechanical brain added one of those thoroughly impractical touches with which the designers tried to humanize their equipment. The panel printed, *Good luck. That is all.*

Rob was a little astounded by the simplicity. It didn't take much these days to mortgage your future. Of course the quick reply was based on the fact that his record was good, and showed every prospect of remaining so. Exfore, however, raised the touchy subject of exams once again as they went back to the stairwell.

"When you make your travel arrangements in the city,

Rob, be certain that you allow plenty of time for your return trip. A week and a half might not be overdoing it."

"The FTLS operate pretty much on schedule these days," Rob countered.

"Yes, but it is wise to give yourself a margin." As they got off the stairs at the Tutorial Level, Exfore maximized its photocells to stress the message. "If for some reason, however good and sufficient, you should not return by the end of the four-week holiday, your place in the examinations will be taken by another student."

"And I'll get a tenth-rate job, and it'll take me the rest of my life to repay the loan. I'll be here in time, Exfore."

"I certainly hope so."

"Exfore . . ." Rob's throat felt clogged. It was hard to speak. "Thanks again for helping."

"I had no hesitation about recommending approval to the computer. I have faith in you. Founded on a solid base of facts, naturally. I would stop you from going to Stardeep if I could. I know I cannot. You are afflicted with human feelings that are important to you. After the quarter is over, I would welcome the opportunity to wish you bon voyage."

Rob thought about this a moment. "That would be fine. But I don't want to tell anyone else where I'm going."

"None of your friends?"

"I think it's best that way." And would save a lot of humiliation if nothing turned up on Stardeep, Rob added silently.

"Whatever you say."

"Good night, Exfore." Rob turned quickly to the stairs.

The robot tutor remained a moment longer. The beams from its simulated eyes probed down onto the softly clacking treads. Then, with a rustle of relays that sounded almost like a sigh, it glided off in the other direction.

The railcar came out of the tunnel with its running lights blurred to purple streaks. The time was well along toward dawn. Rob had chosen this car because those few students leaving for the four-week holiday probably wouldn't be pulling out till morning.

He was right. He and Exfore were the only ones on the platform. The railcar door glided up on silver shafts. Rob picked up his bubblegrip. He felt cold, very much alone. In the grip were his few items of clothing, his passage cards, the fax of his father, and the diary. He hadn't looked at the diary in months. He meant to do it on the trip.

In total, the contents of his grip seemed very little for a journey across half a galaxy.

The purple running lights changed to red. Rob jumped aboard. "Stay oiled, Exfore."

The robot adjusted its plates into a smile. "Safe journeying, Rob. Come back in four weeks."

"In four weeks," Rob called as the railcar door closed and sealed.

Four weeks. The time seemed so short. But he could feel good about one thing. He'd done well in the end-of-quarter tests.

The railcar picked up speed. Exfore dwindled to a blur of polished metal and photocell light. Rob settled into a pneumolounge. He was the car's only occupant.

The railcar shot into the transparent part of the double tunnel. On the level above ran the autoroads for individual vehicles. A heavy service train of footpads could be seen up there, moving in the direction of the Home. Its headbeams were bright in the darkness.

Soon the service train was gone. The railcar hummed on its single track, traveling just over two hundred toward the stark white-chalk mountain. Dellkart IV looked frozen and unfriendly in the pale glow of its three small moons.

Four weeks, the railcar seemed to hum. *Only four weeks, four weeks*. The car plunged into the double mountain tunnel.

Before long Rob glimpsed lights ahead. That was the city. There he would pick up the shuttle rocket to Margoling, the planet where he would board the FTLS. The railcar blazed toward the lights, carrying him forward to Stardeep and back into the painful past.

Five

THE·CURIOUS MR. LUMMUS

FTLS *Goldenhold 2* was in its last lightjump and on schedule. The week aboard the gigantic freighter had dragged unmercifully. impatient for planetfall, Rob lay in the sling-bunk in the tiny cabin which was the most luxurious accommodation the cargo ship offered.

There were a handful of passengers aboard in similar quarters. Rob had eaten meals with them at the spartan autocaf. Most of them were businessmen. Three were getting off at Stardeep. The rest would ride *Goldenhold 2* to its final destination, Blaketower, the capital world of the Lens End Nebula systems.

The slingbunk rocked ever so gently from side to side. Beyond the end of the bunk was the cabin's single port. It was really an anachronism. A passenger could see out of it only during the moments prior to blastoff and touchdown. Within seconds after leaving a launchyard, the ports of the vessel automatically opaqued as the computers and the Lightcommander completed the shift into hyperspace.

All during the long, silent realtime trip through that *other* space, the ports shimmered with weird, oily spectrums of visible light. No human being had ever glimpsed the *other* space through which the FTLS traveled. Nor was it space in the conventional sense. Rather, it was a series of convoluted space-time warps that somehow coexisted at the fringes of reality. These could be entered and mapped by bouncewaves, but never looked on by human eyes.

Trying to comprehend what any FTLS did while bridging between points of the real universe via hyperspace, Terrans applied the verb *travel*. Unfortunately this suggested a

conventional space vessel operating under conventional nuclear power at near lightspeed between closely spaced, conventional worlds.

When the FTLS entered hyperspace, however, it actually
de-molecularized into a near infinity of micro-particles, as
though a rock had been shattered so that its pieces could
pass through a mesh.

But the mesh of hyperspace was twisted, multidimen-
sional, apparently endless. And when the de-molecularized rock—the ship—passed through the portion of the
continuing mesh for an extended time, the particles did not
scatter as ordinary rock particles would have done. Powerful fields kept the ship and its passengers coherent, functioning, during the entire trip. Then, at the other end
of the mesh, which was traversed at faster-than-light
speeds, the ship re-molecularized and emerged, conforming
perfectly again to the known laws of a known cosmos.

In astromathematics Rob had studied some of the fundamental equations relating to this mode of travel—the word
was almost inescapable—and while he could grasp a little
of the theory, it was never so real to him as the metaphor
of the rock. He, and the ship, were this moment scattered
in a trillion tiny fragments. But the special fields made it
seem as though nothing had changed, and he was cruising
at sublight speed along familiar star lanes.

Optical laws were different in *other* space too. Eyes simply did not function as eyes, because—theory stated—there
were no light sources to produce vision. Still, Rob always
wondered what lay outside the ports. Perhaps a few men
had seen, if *seen* was not another misleading term. Men
who rode ships whose systems or Lightcommanders failed;
men who were destroyed somewhere in the awful unknown
dimension that great ships leaped across, making par-
secspanning journeys. Had Lightcommander Duncan
Edison seen that *other* space seven years ago? Rob wondered, staring at the page of the diary he had been reading.

Useless to speculate. He was better off examining the
ideas in the diary his father had penned.

In an age of almost totally mechanized communication,
diaries remained one of the few personally written
documents of the human race. Rob liked to return to the
diary from time to time because it helped him to know
the Lightcommander as nothing else did. The words on the

small ruled pages were inscribed with a deep-blue stylus. They were boldly, forcefully formed.

Rob was rereading an entry dated only six days before the fatal launch of *Majestica*.

. . . and I am in awful doubt about what to do about my second.

The reference was to Edison's second in command, Lightadjutant Thomas Mossrose. The man was little more than a name to Rob. But obviously he had been a man who troubled Lightcommander Edison deeply.

There is no getting around the fact that Mossrose is one of the very few untalented misfits who manage to get into the Space Service. I sensed this when he was first assigned to the ship a month ago. Now I am sure of it. This is his first line command and he simply isn't qualified for it. Should I file a report? I think not, since that is enough to ruin a man for life, both in the service and out. I really believe that the wisest course—from the human standpoint anyway (I wish I could be "wise" like the Machine in the bowels of this monster, that super-smart, all-knowing, hundred-billion-bit-of-knowledge devil that gives me such an inferiority complex)—is to give Mossrose more responsibility rather than less.

Rob's eye skipped from the reference to the FTLS computer to the next entry, apparently written the same day. It was headed simply, "Later."

I thought about it while I ate tonight. I am positive Tom Mossrose is incompetent, especially in astromathematics and intratemporal theory. I am afraid that if he were ever placed in full command of the ship, I would have to be at his shoulder every minute, perhaps plugged into the Machine myself, in a tandem linkup to make certain nothing went wrong. There are too many men on board for me to endanger them for the sake of a single Lightadjutant who somehow got by the Placements.

But maybe I can train Mossross. Sharpen him up. Find areas of extra responsibility to train him bit by bit. It's either that or file a report and ask fo a new man. And in every other way except professionally, Tom M. is likable. Warm, friendly, bright. I can't destroy him. At least not on this voyage . . .

There, in a flurry of asterisks and exclamation marks, the day's entry ended.

The diary itself concluded a page or two later. Lightcommander Edison had been caught up in the final preparations for *Majestica*'s run from Hoggen's Star to Stardeep to Blaketower. The last entry, made on Stardeep, was sad and brief.

What a forlorn place. Much to do. Trying to bring Mossrose along. Uncertain business, that. More asterisks. One large exclamation point. The rest of the pages were blank.

Rob closed the little book on his stomach. Its sonolock snapped shut, to be opened again only by repetition of the Lightcommander's full name.

On the ports the oily light was crawling from cyan to magenta. The intercall rang.

"All passengers for Stardeep," said a scratchy voice. "All passengers for Stardeep, your attention, please. Scheduled planetfall is 1100. Please report to the lounge within one hour of preliminary customs and medical registration."

Frowning, Rob uncoiled his lean frame from the bunk. His blue eyes were puzzled. He had known there would be a customs check, of course. But this business about medical registration was something new. He thought he had completed all the necessary Communicable Disease History forms before boarding on Margoling.

Well, might as well get it over with. He slipped on his tan jacket with its ornamental collar of white myx fur and left the cramped cabin.

Two levels down, the businessmen who Rob had met at meals had already shown up for registration. They were gathered at an oval floating table. The freighter's purser, who doubled as Fourth Mate, was distributing styli and multileaved forms.

"Fill out each one, please," the purser was saying as Rob approached. He repeated the message to each man. The businessmen took the forms to various small floating tables scattered around the metal-walled, harshly lighted chamber. Soon just Rob and one other passenger were left.

The man standing between Rob and the purser was an overweight fellow whose dress boots, breeches, and blouse, though of obviously expensive glitterfabric, were stained and spotted by a miscellany of dust, grime, and food specks. The man had a head shaped like a melon.

"Lot of nonsense, these forms," the man said. His voice

sounded as though it was filtered through a container of pebbles.

"Yes, sir, I agree," the purser replied smoothly. "But the Stardeep Conservancy Patrol insists on them."

"All for the sake of those little beggars," the man complained.

The purser hooked up an eyebrow. "Sir?"

"Those little beggars the Empts."

"That's right, ah, Mister—" The purser hesitated, ran his eye down a checklist. All names but two had been marked off with a bright orange stylus. "Mr. Lummus?"

"Barton Lummus." The man growled, as though he were angry about having to answer.

The purser strove for politeness. "Haven't seen much of you this trip, have we, sir? At least I don't remember you at the autocaf any—"

"Prefer to stay by myself." Lummus snatched the forms and a black stylus. He turned, looked startled to see Rob standing behind him.

Lummus had a face as white as a nutrient pudding. A scraggly little beard decorated his chin. Several rolls of fat formed extra chins below that. The brown pupils of his eyes were huge. Rob had the uncomfortable feeling that those eyes were like lenses, recording everything about him.

"Pardon me, young master," Lummus said in his rattling voice. "Step right up. Your turn to become enfolded in the web of bureaucracy. We'll be manhandled by the Conpats before we're through, mark my word. Stardeep is a regular dictatorship, and they're the dictators." Flourishing the forms for extra emphasis, Lummus moved off to one of the floating tables.

The purser watched him go, smiled. "Odd chap." He consulted his list. "You're the last, so you're Edison, correct? Here."

"What's this medical registration all about?" Rob asked.

"Actually it's pretty much of a duplication. You probably filed most of the pertinent information before departure. But the Empts are extremely susceptible—"

"Who or what are the Empts?"

"The little beasties native to Stardeep. Never heard of them?"

Rob shook his head.

The purser drew on a tablet with his stylus. First he sketched a circle.

"Basically they're gelatinous. Ball-shaped. They're covered with a kind of armor plate—"

The stylus shaded in the plates.

"Two big eyes."

He drew them, with many facets.

"They lay eggs, and they travel by extending pseudopods of their inner bodies. They have a peculiar cry, too."

The purser uttered a squeak that sounded something like *chee-wee, chee-wee*. From the floating table where he was laboring over his forms, Barton Lummus threw a scowl. A couple of the other businessmen frowned.

"The medical exam isn't all that bad," the purser went on to explain. "You'll be sprayed with special germicides and given an ultrabroad antibio injection just in case you're carrying any viral infection. Takes about five minutes. And it helps protect the Empts. Our friend over there made a mountain out of nothing. Just turn the forms in when we make planetfall." The purser picked up his list, touched his braided cap, and moved off.

Carrying the forms, Rob looked around for a place to write. Unfortunately his choice was limited to the purser's station or one of the smaller tables right next to the one at which the fat man sat. The man was chewing moodily on the end of his stylus. There was something about him that Rob didn't like.

He went to the small table anyway, dialed the pneumostool to a comfortable height, sat down.

The back of his neck began to itch. He was being watched.

He concentrated on the forms. Abruptly a voice said, "Ridiculous, what?"

Rob glanced up. Those lenslike brown eyes regarded him with intense curiosity.

"Oh, they don't seem so bad," he said.

"Wait till you run afoul of one of those Conpats. Most of them are young and tough. They're in complete control of the planet, don't you see? They swagger around to show you they know it."

In spite of himself, Rob was interested. "Who are the Conpats? Policemen?"

"Not exactly. They guard the Empt reservations."

"Oh, yes. The purser told me about the Empts."

"Valuable little beggars," Lummus said in a more confidential tone. He waved his stylus flamboyantly. "Did you know that almost the entire planet of Stardeep is their private preserve?"

"No, I didn't know that. I've never been to Stardeep before."

Lummus stroked his scraggly beard. "Neither have I."

"But you know all about the Empts." Somehow Rob felt like laughing.

Laughter was the wrong reaction. Lummus leaned forward in a vaguely threatening way. "It's my business to know a lot of things about a lot of planets, young master. I'm a travel agent. Twice a year I visit various worlds in search of new sights, thrills, and experiences to recommend to my jaded clientele. Bunch of rich riffraff, I'll have you know. But they pay the credits—yes they do. I decided to include Stardeep in my itinerary this trip. Never seen it before. Now I'm wondering if I want to."

To this Rob had no immediate reply. He supposed it was logical for Lummus to brief himself ahead of time on the characteristics of a world he was planning to explore. But it struck Rob as strange that Lummus had already formed such definite and hostile opinions about the Conservancy Patrolmen, who apparently looked after the welfare of some rather helpless-sounding extra-terrestrial Empts. He kept all this to himself, however, because Mr. Lummus seemed angry at everything and everyone. At this very moment he was darting sharp glances toward the men at the other floating tables.

Rob completed the customs information form and tucked it beneath the medical blanks he had already filled out. Uncomfortably, he realized that Barton Lummus was peering at him again.

"Never been to Stardeep, you say? Then what brings you?"

"Family business." Robb stood up, anxious to get away. "My father's estate—"

He muttered the last words while turning to go. He hoped they would satisfy the inquisitive travel agent. They did just the opposite.

"Estate, young master? Settling for a tidy sum of money, are you?" Lummus' eyes shone.

"No, no, just a small piece of property, that's all." Rob strode away so abruptly that Lummus registered complete surprise. Lummus couldn't resist a parting shot.

"If your property is worth anything, the Conpats will

haul you into court and have it devalued. Yes, they will! They'll seize it for part of the infernal reservation. Police-men—bureaucracy—officials—you can't trust any—"

The clang of the sliding hatch cut off the rest of the dia-tribe.

Barton Lummus certainly had an active dislike of all au-thority, Rob thought. But something Lummus had said piqued Rob's interest, and he forgot the stranger, wonder-ing instead about the creatures called the Empts.

There were no references to them in his father's diary. Various planets he had studied in courses at the two Homes were inhabited by equally strange life forms, some quite large. But Rob had never before heard about any kind of extra-terrestrial life that Terran men would label valuable. He wondered about the reason for it.

He would soon find out. Planetfall was still scheduled for 1100 tomorrow.

At table that night—with Lummus nowhere to be seen—Rob tried hard to join the conversation of his fellow passengers. The boring week of lightjumping was coming to an end, and everyone else was in a cheerful mood.

One of the men who was getting off at Stardeep, a tech-nosalesman of giant nuclear-powered pumps, was an excel-lent storyteller. He reeled out anecdote after anecdote about his experiences on this or that out-of-the-way planet. Everybody laughed except Rob.

Later, in his slingbunk, he wondered why. He under-stood quickly enough.

A week of his four was already spent. And he was only now arriving at the place where he might be able to clear the blot from his father's record.

But what if he couldn't?

Rob slept poorly that night.

Next morning, to the accompaniment of ringing bells, the port in his little cabin lost its opacity. He looked out while FTLS *Goldenhold 2* thundered down stern first through the thin cloud layer.

Suddenly the clouds broke. A windy wasteland stretched toward purplish mountain crags. Near at hand Rob glimpsed geodesics glimmering in the light of a pale lemon sun. The city where they were landing seemed to be set down in the middle of the waste, with no roads leading away from it in any direction.

The light-freighter dropped lower. The skeletal black outlines of launchyard cranes appeared against the sky. Then the thrusters of the FTLS cut off in a boil of gray smoke. The stern dropped neatly into its great circular bed. Immense padded rings closed, locking the ship in upright position.

Stardeep. Rob picked up his bubblegrip and rushed into the corridor.

Someone collided with him, stumbled back with an exclamation. Rob started to apologize. A hand clasped his shoulder suddenly.

Despite its layers of fat, the hand of Barton Lummus was strong. It dug into Rob's shoulder until he felt a twinge of pain. Lummus' huge brown eyes shone in the dim corridor.

"Be careful, young master!" Lummus shouted.

Rob apologized somewhat angrily. Lummus let go of his shoulder. He got control of himself, flicked several specks off his coat of glitterfabric. Then he hurried on, lugging a large, floridly decorated bubblegrip.

The man's outburst left Rob shaken. It was all out of proportion to the offense. He wondered whether Barton Lummus was really a travel agent or something else.

Rob shook his head, waited a minute, then moved down the same corridor Lummus had taken to reach the unloading pod.

Six

OF EMPTS AND GREEN JUICE

Travel agent Lummus had barged to the head of the line at the automated customs station. Rob was separated from him by the other businessmen leaving the ship. Rob felt relieved.

From a position near the oval door leading out of the customs room a young, sunburned man with quick eyes and a cool manner surveyed each one of the arrivals. He wore a trim black uniform and high boots. Small gold emblems decorated his shoulders. The man didn't carry any kind of sidearm, but he had an air of tough authority that suggested he wouldn't need one.

A Conservancy Patrolman? Lummus practically confirmed it. He collected his luggage as it popped out of the maw of the radiograph, then glared at the young man in black—while the latter's head was turned.

Lummus rushed out.

Rob slipped his bubblegrip onto the moving belt. The belt carried it under the first inspection scope. A short taped message was repeated over the loudspeakers, courtesy of the local Commercial Association:

"Welcome to the planet Stardeep and the city of Churchill, capital of the North Continent. The atmosphere of our planet is breathable, Terran-4 class. Mask suits are not required. The population of Churchill, largest city on the planet, is 40,000. You will find all types of commercial establishments at your disposal. May we suggest that if your activities will take you outside the city, you check either with the Spacefarer's Aid booth in the lobby or with the headquarters of the Conservancy Patrol. Special permits are required for travel in certain areas of the countryside. When you are finished with customs, kindly leave by the doorway marked with the large green M. You will be processed through medical in the shortest possible time. Thank you for your attention."

When Rob's grip reappeared at the end of the belt, he took it through the indicated doorway. He found himself in a long covered passageway connecting one geodesic dome with another. The walls of the passage filtered out the heaviest rays of the lemon-hued sun while presenting a clear panorama of the surroundings.

Through the right wall Rob saw the domes of Churchill. Aircar ways threaded through the city above the walkways, which were at ground level. To the left, a busy FTLS launchyard stretched out to where the waste began.

By craning his neck, Rob could see back to the *Goldenhold 2*, a huge, sleek cylinder jutting to the sky. Hundreds of men swarmed around the lip of the concrete pit into which the ship had settled. Other, smaller commercial craft were also docked in the yard. With a stinging feeling Rob realized that this was probably the last sight Lightcommander Edison had seen before *Majestica*'s ports opaqued and she went five milliseconds into hyperspace and—*what?*

Illuminated arrows directed him to a small, blue-tiled room where another taped voice instructed him to strip and place his bubblegrip and clothing in a hopper. The hopper promptly flopped back into the wall and sealed itself shut.

Valves in the ceiling opened, bathing Rob in a pleasantly-scented antiseptic mist. A second, colder mist replaced the first. It left him feeling almost unbearably clean. The hopper popped open. His clothes were returned.

They felt warm, smelled freshly laundered. Sonics, probably. He was just tugging on his tunic when a middle-aged tech with a penedermic in one hand walked in.

The barrel of the injecting device was already marked with a piece of tape machine-punched with Rob's name. Medical precautions on Stardeep were certainly efficient.

"This is just a broad-spec antibio," the tech began. "You probably heard about it on board ship."

Rob nodded. "So I don't spread germs to the Empts."

"Correct. Sleeve back, please."

Rob rolled up his cuff. The tech placed the fan-shaped muzzle of the penedermic against his arm just above his elbow. There was a quick sensation of dozens of tiny needles pricking his skin. The wall opened. The tech tossed the penedermic into a chute that sucked it away.

He spread his hands, grinned. "That's it. You're excused."

Rob rolled his cuff down again. "Why so many precautions?"

"Have you heard much about our little friends the Empts?"

"Some. They're armored, oviparous, travel via their pseudopods. And they're valuable. No one's told me why, though."

The tech leaned against the door. "Not because of their intelligence, certainly. That's rudimentary. But get close to one and you'll find out soon enough."

Interested, Rob asked, "What happens if I get close?"

"No one's really succeeded in explaining it yet, but the Empts radiate some kind of mental energy. At close range it exerts a definite psychochemical change in a human being. You forget everything and anything unpleasant in the past. And I mean everything. Psychomedics all over the galaxy use live Empts to treat mentally disturbed patients. The psychomeds call the process Empting, partly because of the Empts themselves, and partly because the treatment literally empties the patient's mind of all his traumatic memories."

"So that's the reason these Conservancy Patrolmen protect them."

A nod from the tech. "Right. All told, the Empt population is small. A very few are allotted to the general population as pets. Maybe a dozen a year. The rest are guarded out on the reservations. Left alone until special hunting teams go in, pick out a few, and ship them to various medical centers around the planets."

Ready to leave, Rob said. "Thanks for the explanation. I can see why they're so valuable. I could use a little Empting once in a while myself."

"Couldn't we all?" the tech grinned and waved farewell.

As Rob swung along toward the lobby of the huge port dome, he thought about the curious little creatures who inhabited the planet. For a minute he wished that he had one of his own. How much easier it would be simply to forget *Majestica*, return to Dellkart IV, and never again be troubled by memories of the past.

Unfortunately it wouldn't work that way. He had to find the answers if he could. His step quickened. Just being on Stardeep after a journey that would have taken thirty-two realtime years in a conventional starship gave him a new sense of confidence.

He located the lobby kiosk with the illuminated sign reading SPACEFARER'S AID. He stepped around to the rear and came upon a robot seated at a rather battered desk.

The robot was a much cheaper model than Exfore, and it had definitely seen better days. Its neck joints had corroded, giving an odd cock to its head. One of its photocells kept blinking on and off.

"Hel-lo," said the robot. "May Spacefarer's Aid be of service, service, service, ser—*rrawk!*"

The robot made a fist and banged its own head. Then it finished, "—service?"

"There's a Phylex Monitor Station about a hundred miles from here. Is that in a restricted area?"

"But definitely," the robot replied. "The station is located behind the electronic barrier." The contraption—Rob couldn't think of it as a person, the way he sometimes thought of Exfore—uttered a series of peculiar metallic coughs. Something noisy took place in its innards, as though a bucket of bolts had been upset. "But definitely. The station is located behind—*rrawk!*"

The robot hit its head again. Things seemed to straighten out.

"Everything behind the electronic barrier is off limits?" Rob wanted to know.

"But absolutely. Only the Conpats are allowed past. You might get special permission."

"How would I go about that?"

"Go to Conpat Headquarters on Avenue Ursus. Speak to the Commander, Simon Ling."

"Ling. Thanks very much."

"Don't mention—*rrawk!*—but definitely—*rrawk!*—but absolutely—" The blinking photocell began to exude a trickle of smoke. The robot's tone sounded almost pitiful. "Service, please. Please call the service department before—*rrawk! rrawk! rrawk!*"

This time the robot clanged its head with both fists, to no avail. It kept emitting raucous cries as Rob raced to the main administration desk on the other side of the lobby and punched in a picphone request. He relayed the plea for service to yet another robot.

By the time he left the building, three shiny repair robots were converging on the kiosk, from which smoke was now belching in quantity.

Rob stepped into the sunlight. The thinner atmosphere cut sharply into his lungs, making him gasp for breath.

Walking slowly, he headed down the broad rampway of the spaceport building. In a few moments his system adjusted to the fresh air. He had been breathing processed oxygen inside the FTLS for so many days that he had forgotten how a true atmosphere smelled.

There were traces of mint and cinnamon in the air of Stardeep, and a dusty tang too. Between geodesics he caught glimpses of the forlorn desert stretching away toward the purple mountains. A brisk, warm wind blew steadily from that direction.

Churchill seemed a pleasant, if not overly modern, town. There were mothers with children on the streets, the usual quota of clerical and service workers, men in coveralls from the FTLS launchyard, and an occasional Conpat walking briskly on some errand. Rob saw nothing resembling an Empt, however.

Overhead, vehicular traffic whizzed on the aircar ways. The ways cut off the direct sunlight and made the walkways below pleasant and comfortable. Since it was nearly noon Galactic Mean Time, Rob decided to find a place to stay and then have lunch before calling on Simon Ling at Conpat Headquarters.

He came to a broad pedestrian boulevard, which he discovered was the Avenue Ursus. He proceeded along it for a block or two, finding a small, comfortable hostel just around one corner. He deposited his bubblegrip in his room and then went out to a central caf, which he had noticed on Avenue Ursus.

The moving belt carried him from the entrance to the head of one of the selection lines. As a tray popped from a chute, Rob noticed an attractive girl just in front of him. She was his own age, or perhaps a year younger. Long straw-colored hair hung down between her shoulders, caught into a tail with a ring of brass. He could only see her face in profile, but it seemed quite pretty, dominated by eyes of a much brighter blue than Rob's own. The girl wore a white single-piece resort outfit. The handle of a shopall was looped over one wrist. In the shopall were several small parcels.

The belt carried cafeteria customers up the line past holograms of the various items offered for sale. With a start Rob realized that the girl and her companion, a shorter, heavier girl, had been busy selecting their food while he had been busy gawking. He had already passed the soups and other appetizers and was just coming up on the nutrient drinks.

Quickly he stepped onto one of the little stationary platforms alongside the belt. He fished in his pocket for a unicredit, slipped the small disc into the slot under a tempting holographic image of a large goblet of bright green vitalime. The door lid flew open. He fitted the goblet stem into the appropriate recess on his tray. Then he stepped back onto the moving platform.

Just ahead in the entree section, the straw-haired girl and her friend were returning to the belt with their selections. At the same time, a worker from the launchyard was trying to get past them to go back to the soups. A wheeled robot hostess buzzed its buzzer at him and demanded that he leave the belt, walk to the beginning, and come through again the regular way.

But the worker was in a hurry. As the belt carried Rob on, the worker squeezed past the two girls and headed his way.

Rob knew it was either step off or get bowled aside. He had one foot on the entree platform, one on the moving belt, and his tray balanced in both hands. The worker rushed past, hitting his elbow. Rob let out an exclamation. The moving belt jerked his left foot, threw him off balance. His tray tipped. The goblet of vitalime fountained out its contents—

Straight onto the back of the pretty girl's resort costume.

The girl's stout companion let out an *"Oooooo!"* Rob watched horrified as the electric green stain spread through the fibers of the girl's white outfit.

The girl spun. Rob caught the blaze of her blue eyes full force. "It feels like I'm an absolute mess, you—you *spaceclod!*"

The stocky girl giggled. "Don't lose your temper, Lyn. But I guess you already have."

"I'm sorry," Rob said. "That man—"

He gaped. Somehow, the hurrying worker had disappeared.

At the beginning belt, the other customers were complaining and urging Rob to get moving. The girl tried to look over her shoulder at the hideous green stain.

"And I just bought this outfit this morning. I should think you could at least say you're sorry!"

Rob's temper heated. "I already did! Look, it really was an accident—"

"Typical offworlder excuse!" the girl cried. She had noted his Dellkart IV clothing.

"Won't you even listen to an apology?"

"When I paid my whole allowance for this—this ruined rag?"

"Now Rob's cheeks were red. "O.K., O.K.,! I'll pay for sonic cleaning!"

The girl's blue eyes crackled. "You certainly will!"

His own anger stoked by hers, Rob snapped. "Where shall I send the money?"

"To me, of course. My name is—" Her friend was tugging at her arm. "What, Beth?"

"Better not give him your home code if he just got off a ship." The stocky girl's melodramatic eye-rollings indicated she suspected the worst of interplanetary travelers.

The pretty girl evidently thought Beth's idea made sense, though. In a quieter but no less firm voice, she said, "You can reach me in care of Conpat Headquarters. My father is the Commander. Just leave the credit voucher for Lyndsey Ling."

Turning, she was carried away up the belt with her friend.

"Belt it or get off, space bum," someone yelled from the caf entrance.

Rob got off.

He stood on the entree platform, looking dismayed. The last of the green vitalime dribbled off the tray he held slack at his side. He stared at the straw-colored hair vanishing down around a bend in the belt. He said, half aloud:

"Her father's the Commander?"

Just how far would he get now with his request to enter the Empt reservation?

Seven

CONPAT COMMANDER

Simon Ling tented his fingers, leaned back in the gray chair hovering just off the floor, and said, "That's a fascinating story, young man. And a most unusual request, I might add. Not exactly in line with Conservancy Patrol policy. You'll have to give me a moment to think about it."

There was nothing else for Rob to say. He sat on the opposite side of a large natural wood desk in the Commander's comfortable office. The office was located on an upper floor of the Headquarters geodesic on Avenue Ursus. It was a cool, shady room, made more friendly by the warm highlights of the hardwood—a rarity in these days of plasto and alloy.

Several sections of the outer wall were transparent sheets of solarscreen, affording a glareless view of the town. Around the office were a number of momentos of Simon Ling's career: a framed scroll of commendation; a Conpat Academy degree; a swagger stick in a glass case; a large color litho showing a small, round, armoured creature with faceted eyes.

An Empt, very likely. The little extra-terrestrial looked almost comical, except for its eyes. They seemed a little sad.

Rob fidgeted. Ling inscribed another note on the tablet where he had written a few comments as Rob explained his reasons for coming to Stardeep. The Commander stood up, scratched the back of his neck as he stared thoughtfully toward a distant crag.

Simon Ling was a massive, big-boned man. He stood nearly six and a half feet tall. Like the Conpat that Rob had seen at the spaceport, he was deeply tanned. He had brown eyes and pleasant, if irregular, features highlighted by a bold hooked nose. His hair showed streaks of white, though Rob guessed him to be only about forty. He wore the black Conpat uniform and high black boots. But the gold emblems on his shoulders—intertwined letters, C and P—were inlaid with tiny rubies.

At length the Commander said, "The Phylex Monitor Stations are the joint property of the space lines. Strictly off limits."

"That I understand," Rob nodded. "But I was hoping for special permission—"

He halted in midsentence. Ling studied him. Rob had the uncomfortable feeling that the girl named Lyndsey had already communicated with her father. He was beaten before he started. And all because of a clumsy mistake.

Simon Ling sat down again. He tossed one boot up to rest on the desk corner. "On the other hand, you've come a very long way through hyperspace. At your own expense, I gather."

"Yes, sir."

"And your time on Stardeep is strictly limited."

Thinking of the oppressive deadline, Rob nodded. "I'm holding a return passage on *Goldenhold 2* when she comes back through."

Ling toyed with the sheet of notes. "Do you really think you'll learn anything by interrogating the tapes at the station? I wasn't serving here when the agents of the Inquiry Commission looked into the *Majestica* matter. But I understand they stayed in Churchill for over a month and visited that station nearly every day. They went over and over those tapes."

Rob felt the old futility. Some of his tension showed through as he replied, "Probably I won't find too much, Commander. But I have to try. I have to hear those tapes for myself."

Simon smiled. "Well, I admire your motives and your persistence. I hope you won't be disappointed."

Rob's stomach flipflopped. Did that last remark mean that the Commander was going to grant permission for the visit? Maybe he was living with luck on his side after all!

Perhaps the Commander's daughter hadn't shown up yet. Rob decided he had done the wise thing by rushing directly to Headquarters as soon as he finished his meal at the central caf.

Simon Ling reached into his desk, pulled out a musicpipe. He touched the controls and stuck the pipestem in his mouth. Smoke, fragrant and sweet, puffed from the bowl. The strains of a very old symphony drifted from the tiny speaker.

"You do know," Ling resumed, "that the Phylex Station is one hundred and ten miles out in the waste."

"Yes, sir. But I presume there's a way to reach it."

"The only way is in a programmed Conpat flyer. There won't be one available for a couple of days. I keep my men busy. We have nearly a whole continent to cover, and right at this time of year we're thinning the Empt population. Twice annually we gather up several dozen for shipment to various hospitals and medical installations. This is one of those times."

Again Rob didn't know what to say. The Commander seemed to be encouraging and discouraging him at the same time.

Simon Ling puffed twice on his musicpipe. With each puff the symphony grew louder for a moment. He drew a punch form out of his desk. As he poised his stylus above it, something else apparently occurred to him.

"We wouldn't be able to provide you with a Conpat escort."

"But I don't know how to run a flyer, sir."

"Perhaps you didn't hear me a moment ago. Our flyers are programmed. If I give you permission to make the trip, we'll prepare an electronically coded card. All you do is place the card in the flyer's control slot. The card will activate the flyer onto the right course across the waste. There won't be anyone else aboard. The card will land the flyer and also program it to take off after a specified interval. Two hours, probably. You'll have to be aboard. This is a large continent. I have only two hundred men to cover it. We can't afford to send out extra search parties at thinning time."

"I understand, sir," Rob agreed. "I'll follow orders."

"Ordinarily," Ling continued, "I'd refuse a request for a trip into the reservation right at this time." He waved his pipe toward the faraway crags. "The Empts lay and hatch their young in the caves up in those mountains. At laying time the female Empt can have her hormonal balance thrown off by contact with human beings. As a result, next year's baby Empt population is smaller. When I send my men out to check the waste, they seldom even land their flyers. I don't expect you'll encounter many female Empts at the Phylex Station. But I do want you to appreciate that I have to bend a few rules to let you go."

"It's very kind of you," Rob said.

Now Simon Ling had his stylus ready again. Abruptly, his rather stiff official manner melted, replaced by one of the warmest smiles Rob had ever seen.

"If it were my father, Rob, I'd do the same thing. Now let's see about getting your card made up."

At the instant Commander Ling started to write, Rob heard a noise behind him.

"Hello, Dad. I'm all finished with—*oh*."

Simon Ling laid his stylus aside. Rob stood up. He found himself looking into bright eyes that were full of anger.

"In case you've left the voucher already," Lyndsey Ling said, "you'd better take it back and double it. I stopped at the cleanmat and there's going to be an extra charge for reweaving. That green goo not only leaves big stains, it destroys fibers too."

"I hadn't made arrangements yet—" Rob began.

"Well, you'd better," Lyndsey repeated. "I only bought this outfit this morning."

Suddenly Rob forgot about the danger of angering Commander Ling. The girl's manner struck him as altogether unreasonable. He responded in kind: "Miss Ling, I offered to apologize. You wouldn't accept it. Next I offered to pay the bill and you weren't satisfied with that either. What would you like me to do, synthesize a new outfit by hand?"

In a heavy tone, Simon Ling said, "What in the name of the Empts is going on?"

"This *offworlder*—" Lyndsey cried.

"Your daughter—" Rob said simultaneously.

"One at a time, one at a time!"

Tense silence, then. Rob cast a glum glance at the punch form, untouched, on Ling's desk. The Commander laid his musicpipe aside. A desk receptacle sucked out the glowing coals and ash and the symphony stopped in mid-beat.

Lyndsey flung her shopall down. She turned to show her father the ruined back of her outfit. Rob cringed at the damage. The vitalime had indeed rotted a hole in the white fibers. Their ends looked like charred wires.

"I was in the central caf with Beth," Lyndsey explained, "when this offworlder—"

"Don't use that slang term in my presence," Simon interrupted. "His name is Rob Edison. He's a visitor to Stardeep. Treat him that way."

"But, Dad—!"

"Young lady, I won't warn you again. Mind your manners. Now. I gather this young man spilled something on your blouse?"

Lyndsey glared. "Green, horrible gunk."

"Did he offer to pay to repair the damage?"

"Well, yes. But he's obviously just a bad-mannered space tramp spending his vacation bumming from planet to—"

"Enough!" roared Simon Ling.

The girl huffed, threw another withering glare at Rob, flounced over to a chair, and plumped down in it. The Commander rounded a corner of the desk. Gently he took his daughter's chin in his big fingers, lifted her head.

"I dearly loved your mother, my girl. Finest woman ever born under the Arco stars. But she had a streak of temper I'm afraid you've inherited. Mr. Edison is not a space tramp. He's a student from the Dellkart IV Space League Home at the other end of the galaxy. He's spending what little holiday time he has on a very serious quest. Believe me, his coming to Stardeep isn't frivolous. I think you owe him an apology, rather than the reverse."

For a long moment father and daughter gazed at each other. Then the color in Lyndsey Ling's cheeks heightened. Rob really had to admit she was one of the prettiest girls he had ever met.

At last Lyndsey smacked the toe of her sandal against the floor. "It's just that I saved all my allowance to buy this outfit—"

"And Mr. Edison has offered to undo the damage," Simon reminded her.

"If you've got a blank voucher," Rob said, "I'll sign it with my ident number. Then you can fill in any moment."

Simon shook his head. "Let me take care of it. I know you're willing, but I expect I can afford it better than you. Lyndsey—"

The girl glanced at Rob. She started to smile, but didn't. "Sorry." She looked away.

"My apologies again, too," Rob told her.

Simon chuckled, went back to his desk and picked up the punch form.

"I'll take care of getting this processed, Rob. Just give me your signature."

Rob signed quickly, conscious of the girl watching him. He was relieved when Simon Ling told him that he could simply drop back to Headquarters in the morning and pick up the card.

"I hope we'll have a flyer for you in a day or so," the Commander concluded.

"Thank you very much, sir," Rob said, heading out in a hurry.

Lyndsey stood up, embarrassed. "I didn't mean to call you a space bum."

"Forget it," he said. He meant it. He was glad to be out of a potentially explosive situation.

Rob hummed all the way down the old-fashioned fixed-position staircase to the dome's lobby. Apparently Commander Ling was a widower who understood the whimsicalities of the female mind. Rob's only regret was that he and Lyndsey Ling had started off so badly. In other circumstances, he would like to have gotten to know her. But he hadn't come to Stardeep to find a girl.

As Rob hurried down the front steps leading from the Headquarters dome to the shaded walkways of Avenue Ursus, he noticed a familiar face across the way. Under a yellow-leafed hydrotree, the travel agent, Barton Lummus, sat on a bench.

Next to him sat a male android of Vegan manufacture. The android had emerald-colored hide, completely hairless, and large gray eyes without pupils. As a concession to civilization it wore a pair of neutral-colored shorts. Its face had been formed into a rigid expression that it could never change. But even though the android's mouth was an inflexible slit across its face, it had a vaguely sinister appearance.

Barton Lummus, seedy as ever, was conversing with the artificial human. Rob wondered how a travel agent could afford to rent one of the constructs.

Rob turned onto a walkway. From a corner of an eye he caught a flicker of emotion.

He was disturbed to see that Barton Lummus was watching him. Lummus made no sign of recognition, merely stared hard with those lenslike brown eyes, before returning to conversation with the android.

In the excitement of thinking about his forthcoming trip

to the Phylex Station, Rob soon forgot about the incident altogether.

Next morning, as instructed, Rob turned up at the Headquarters Building on Avenue Ursus.

Commander Simon Ling wasn't in his office. But his robot secretary had the small, embossed plastic card prepared and delivered it into Rob's hands.

He could make no sense of the jumble of electronic characters raised from the gray surface. But he clutched the card like a talisman anyway, slipping it carefully into the inside pocket of his jacket.

"The Commander also left this for you," the secretary said. She passed Rob a note marked PERSONAL.

On his way out of the dome he unfolded the note. It was written in a strong, slanting hand that reminded him of his father's.

> *Dear Rob Edison—My daughter and I talked it over and decided that as citizens of Stardeep, we owe you a somewhat better reception than you received at the central caf. Why don't we make up for that by having a meal together tomorrow? Let's meet for breakfast at the caf, around 0800. Send a message if this won't work out. Otherwise we'll see you then. The meal's on me. Cordially, S. Ling.*

Rob was finishing the note, a grin on his face, as he reached the bottom of the steps outside the dome. Suddenly a heavy weight crashed against his side, spinning him around. The note flew out of his hand and sailed away in the breeze.

"Watch where you're—ah! Young master!"

Righting himself, Rob tried to conceal his surprise. There, flicking specks from his blouse, stood Barton Lummus with his android close at hand.

Lummus patted his pockets as though searching for something. "We seem to have a bent for collision, young master," he said in his pebbly voice. "Like atomic particles, what?"

"This time I don't think it was my fault."

"Even though you had your nose buried in some document which has now blown away?"

"All right, my apologies," Rob growled.

Lummus continued to poke and probe at his pockets. Finally he stopped. His white face pulled downward. "You really should be more careful. You could do serious injury to your elders."

Lummus' several chins quivered. His straggly chin beard danced as he emphasized his words with repeated nods. The emerald android remained just a few paces away, the unnerving, empty gray eyes trained in Rob's direction.

Lummus made a great show of rearranging his soiled blouse into the proper folds. For some puzzling reason, he seemed to grow angrier by the moment. Finally, scowling, he marched over to his android and tugged its arm.

"Come, Blecho, let's move on. Young hotheads make the streets unsafe these days. Someone ought to teach the little beggars some manners." And away he clumped, the perfect picture of injury.

The android swung its head to give Rob another eyeless stare that made him shiver. The two vanished in the crowds along Avenue Ursus. Rob asked himself whether travel agent Lummus was completely right in the head. Did he need a little Empting therapy, perhaps?

That night, in his room at the hostel, Rob discovered something equally odd.

He was piling his clothing on the bed for overnight cleaning in the central sonichute. He had removed all his personal effects and placed them on the small stand. As he folded his shorts, he happened to glance at the gray electronic card.

There was a large, greasy smear on one corner.

He picked up the card, tilted it. Viewed from a right angle, the glistening smear revealed itself to be the print of a human finger.

Suddenly he recalled Lummus blundering into him. Had the man tried to pick his pocket? Perhaps that would explain Lummus' anger. He had failed to net any loot in the encounter. Rob still had all his valuables.

With that android companion, Blecho, Lummus was certainly something besides what he pretended to be.

A petty criminal working the star lanes, maybe? Traveling from planet to planet filching credit cases and jewelry where he could?

Rob tossed his shorts on the pile and shook his head, hoping that he would have no further meetings with that peculiar stranger.

Eight

RUNAWAY EMPT

The breakfast at the central caf next morning was an unqualified success.

Encouraged by Simon Ling, Rob ate a whopping meal. He started with a big goblet of nutriorange. Then he downed a quarter rasher of inhumanly expensive real bacon, plus a small copper pot of a salty delicacy called yoyo eggs. These were imported from a nearby planet, the Commander said, and were a favorite among citizens of the Lens End Nebula. On top of all this, two steaming mugs of morning broth spiced with chicory and lively conversation made it an occasion to remember.

Lyndsey Ling looked even prettier, Rob thought, now that she had her temper under control. Her face was animated. Her blue eyes shone with friendly highlights. She had put her straw-colored hair up in a bun and fastened it with amber-headed pins. The aquamarine one-piece that she wore complemented her coloring.

The girl made no mention of the incident with the green juice. Instead, she asked a great many questions about Rob's life on Dellkart IV and customs on the planets in his part of the galaxy. Nothing was said about *Majestica*. No doubt Simon Ling had coached her to avoid the subject.

The Commander let his daughter do most of the talking. He sat back puffing his musicpipe as it played a Mellofors electronic cantata, and he smiled frequently. Well, even if Lyndsey Ling was being nice on orders, Rob enjoyed it. The meal made Stardeep, and his purpose for coming, seem less grim.

Finally, as the tabletop revolved the magno-bottomed

dishes out of sight, Commander Ling finished his pipeful
and said, "You did get your card, didn't you, Rob?"

He patted his jacket. "Right here, sir."

"Good. I checked our rosters. Two of my men should be
in at sundown. That means a flyer will be available in the
morning. Well, I must get back to Headquarters. Do you
have plans?"

"Just a little sight-seeing, I suppose," Rob replied. "I
want to hear the Phylex tapes before I start asking questions at the launchyard."

Simon nodded. "Lyndsey, if you're not busy, why don't
you show Rob around?"

"I half promised Beth—" Lyndsey noticed her father's
direct stare. "I'd love to."

They left the central caf. Simon accepted Rob's thanks
for the meal and headed up Avenue Ursus toward the Conpat dome. Rob waited until the Commander was out of
earshot before saying, "I appreciate the hospitality, Lyndsey. But there's no need for me to tie you up all morning."

"Don't be silly. Beth is probably busy anyway."

On the edge of exasperation, Rob said, "My impressions
of Stardeep are just fine. Please don't feel obliged to show
me the sights because your dad told you to."

Lyndsey flushed. "To make up for yesterday, you mean?
I need to. I was wretched. I'm sorry."

"Let's forget it. Your father tried to smooth things over
by taking me to breakfast. I enjoyed it a lot. But—what's
wrong?"

Lyndsey looked a trifle embarrassed. "The breakfast was
my idea."

"*Your*—"

"I'm not really a harpy, Rob. True, my mother was
fourth-generation colonial Hispanio, and Dad always says I
inherited her Latin temper, but I really am sorry for what
happened yesterday." Suddenly her eyes crinkled and
brightened. "Now we've gotten past all the formal drivel
and apologies. I know you're not a space bum, and you
know I'm not a complete witch. So shall we go?"

"Deal," he said, laughing as he matched her stride.

They spent an hour in the shopping district, another at
the low, quiet dome that housed the Churchill Civic
Museum. Although small, the museum had a number of
excellent display cases explaining the physiology of the
Empts, and a whole room devoted to an operating di-rama

that duplicated the city's FTLS launchyard. In this room Rob noticed a bronze plaque hanging in an alcove. A pinspot illuminated the raised lettering. His throat thickened as the words flashed their meaning to his mind:

IN MEMORIAM, FTLS Majestica.

He stepped into the alcove and read the plaque. It gave only a few details: the date; the fact that the cause of the tragedy and the fate of the lightship were unknown; the number of officers and crew. His father was shown as Lightcommander.

Lyndsey came up behind him softly. "Dad told me all about why you traveled to Stardeep. I thought you should see it."

She spoke in a soft, intense voice. This was a completely different Lyndsey Ling. The pinspot put reflected lights in her brilliant blue eyes. He realized that she really meant what she was saying. "When I heard the story, well—that's when I became really ashamed of the way I behaved yesterday. You're to be admired for coming to Stardeep, Rob."

Her words warmed him. But something made him say, "Admired? How can that be? Everybody tells me it's a waste of time."

Lyndsey's hair shone as she shook her head. "Admired for loving your father as much as you did. And do."

A relaxed smile spread across his face. "It's nice of you to say that."

Another moment passed. Lyndsey glanced away.

Her tone became more normal as they moved out of the hushed alcove. "If you've seen enough of the museum, how about a more practical visit? Would you like to go see the Conpat flyer yard?"

He said he would. They got aboard walkways that eventually transferred them to the edge of the town.

"There's the yard," Lyndsey said, catching his hand as they stepped off the walkway. In this part of Churchill most of the domes seemed to be devoted to light industry. They crossed a small park built around natural outcroppings of pink-veined rock and approached a compound with a servodome at one side.

A teardrop-shaped craft was parked at a dock built into the dome. The craft was equipped with small fore-and-aft thrusters and ground-effect skids. Two mechs were busy testing the skids with cylinders of compressed gas.

"It looks a lot like the flitters we have on Dellkart IV," Rob told the girl.

He shielded his eyes against the lemon sun. Out past the compound, the air seemed to shimmer. The shimmering effect was continuous into the distance both to the left and the right. It much resembled heat radiation, blurring the waste and the mountains beyond. But Rob knew the weather on Stardeep was too temperate to produce such a condition. Another answer suggested itself.

"Is that one of the electronic barriers?"

Lyndsey replied that it was. "Actually Churchill is right at one limit of the reservation. You can't get past the barrier except in a flyer, and the Conpats have all the flyers. If you tried to get past on foot, you'd be knocked unconscious and your system would be out of whack for a week. It happens now and then. Poachers come here hoping to pick up a few Empts to sell on the gray market. They're never successful, because there is a continuous horizontal barrier too, ten miles up. The reservation is literally inside a protective box."

After taking a closer look at the teardrop flyer with its golden CP enameled into the rigid-resin hull plates, Rob and Lyndsey boarded the walkways back toward the center of town.

They left the ways at Avenue Capricorn, a thoroughfare that ran into Avenue Ursus near the Conpat dome. It was nearing the lunch hour. Shops and stores had disgorged a crowd of people into the shaded streets. Overhead, traffic hummed.

Rob felt good and much less lonely. Up ahead he noticed a dipix palace. Its shining cloud-marquee announced an attraction that had played to a student audience in the Dellkart IV Home auditorium. The galaxy wasn't so huge and forbidding after all—

"I wonder what all the commotion's about," Lyndsey said suddenly.

He followed her pointing finger. The crowds were parting with great haste about a block ahead. Something in furious motion shot past the legs of the men and women who jumped out of the way with great alacrity. Lyndsey and Rob stepped off the walkway onto the mall of brilliant green plasto turf and watched.

The source of the excitement boiled toward them. People were scattering to the walkways on both sides of the mall in near-panic. All at once Rob had a clear view of the cause.

"That's an Empt," he exclaimed.

The small spherical creature was traveling toward them at remarkable speed. It did so by extending three gelatinous pseudopods out between the armored plates of its body, pulling itself ahead and then quickly extending three more pseudopods while the first three retracted. Two large, faceted eyes on the ball-like body caught random beams of sunlight and flashed as the creature sped along. Those eyes were a bright, almost iridescent yellow.

"Someone's pet on the loose," Lyndsey said. "Look at the chain."

A metal ringstaple had somehow been embedded in one of the armor plates on the Empt's dorsal surface. From this hung a short length of clinking alloy chain. The last link was sheared in half.

The Empt was only a square away now and making rapid progress by shooting pseudopods in threes. Rob heard its weird, high-pitched cry—*chee-wee, chee-wee.*

Almost immediately he spotted the Empt's owner. Down the center of the mall a block behind charged a bearded man, waving a wide-brimmed, cone-crowned hat.

"Hold on, critter! Hold on there!"

The man ran with erratic, zigzag steps. As he came closer, Rob saw that his faded blouse and trousers were ripped at the cuffs and incredibly dirty as well. The man's straggly dark hair hung to his shoulders. His beard waved unkempt halfway to his waist. The other end of the broken chain hung from a bracelet on his wrist.

Chee-wee, chee-wee, squealed the Empt. It shot straight toward Rob and Lyndsey.

People on the walkways gaped, pointed. Someone shouted for the Conpats. The Empt's blazing yellow eyes mirrored fragments of the scene around it as it came to within twenty feet of Rob, then ten.

Still in frantic pursuit, the bearded man wigwagged his floppy hat and howled for "the critter" to stop.

Without thinking, Rob stepped straight into the Empt's path.

At the same time he heard Lyndsey say, "Not too close, Rob!"

Instinct made him want to help. He dove at the Empt which was now about six feet in front of him. As he

launched into his dive, he heard Lyndsey's voice rise
higher:

"Rob—don't!"

By that time Rob had landed on his stomach and chest.
He clamped hands on the faintly moist plates at both sides
of the Empt's body. He had a quick, blurred impression of
faceted yellow eyes shining like nova stars. There was a
mild tingling in his palms. *Chee-wee, chee-wee!*

Then and only then did he really remember the peculiar
power of the creatures. By that time, everything around
him was sliding, dissolving, collapsing, as though his surroundings were made of the same translucent stuff as the
Empt's inner body.

The tingling seemed to reach his brain, muddle his
mind. He still had hold of the Empt—his hands told him
that much—but all his other senses registered a wild,
changing montage of sights and sounds and smells. A portion of the lemon sky of Stardeep melted and slipped to
one side. Lyndsey's voice sounded like a whining, over-
worked motor. Blades of the synthetic turf felt huge as
spears against his cheek. *Chee-wee, chee-wee!*

Men shouted for the Conpats. Their voices seemed to
echo and ring through windy chasms. The tingling inside
Rob's head grew more pronounced. Something faintly
slimy touched the back of one of his hands. A thrashing
pseudopod? He tried to focus his eyes. He couldn't. The
world was revolving like a cartwheel of gelatin.

All at once a face thrust in—a wild, bearded, sun-
parched face with eyes like bits of blue grass. The man's
mouth was working, spitting words Rob couldn't comprehend. The mouth wrenched to reveal white teeth in startling contrast to the dark cheeks above the untidy beard.
The man's blue eyes were both frightened and full of another emotion that might be anger, even hate—

Suddenly there was no longer weight against Rob's
palms. He rolled over on his back, gasped for air. Many
voices sounded noisily about him. They all resembled over-
loaded motors. Faces, distorted as though seen in flawed
glass, floated above him like balloons. The *chee-wee* cry
receded a little. The tingling in his mind slacked off.

Rob tried to remember where he was. He couldn't.

He fought to remember. Bizarre colors chased through
his head. Part of the name of the place surfaced in his
mind. Star—

Star what?

Star*deep*.

But was he here?

Something in the past. Some reason he should know—

Try as he would, he couldn't remember.

Words, concepts, memories slipped away just as it seemed he was about to grasp them. He lay panting for breath in the center of the mall, while his brain buzzed and the balloon-faces drifted overhead. He grew panicky, thrashed his arms. He tried to recall where he had come from. He couldn't. His mind operated in slow motion, fogged, full of odd colors and sounds. He grew genuinely frightened.

He tried to raise himself to a sitting position. A tremendous wave of exhaustion swept over him, carrying him down toward billowy darkness.

The last image he held in his mind was that of the bearded man's face. It was a face oddly youthful despite the weather-beaten skin and hirsute covering.

Hateful, the blue chips of eyes burned, blazed, accused him of—what? He didn't know.

Then even that image faded. He stopped struggling and let the billowy dark cover him over.

Nine

MR. LUMMUS INSISTS

Toward the end of that same afternoon Rob awakened in a pale, aseptic room in what turned out to be the dispensary of the Conpat dome.

He discovered that he had nothing on except a pair of coarse hospital boxer shorts. He was lying in the scented slow-moving water of a hydrobed. On the wall opposite, the electronic letters of a diagnostic plaque spelled out:

Edison, R. Inpatient (temp.) Condition: recup/normal.
Release: immed.

From one side of the hemispherical bath-bed, Simon Ling and his daughter watched as Rob came back to full consciousness.

He thrashed the water as he sat up. "What happened?"

"Nothing too serious," Simon answered. "You just had your first experience with an Empt."

Rob flexed his arms, bent his knee in the tepid liquid. "I feel all right. My head aches a little, that's all."

"The diagnosis machines probed you for over half an hour," Lyndsey informed him. "Then they shot you full of a relaxant that made you sleep for two more."

The Commander indicated the lighted plaque. "You're free to go whenever you want. Your clothes are over there behind that floating screen."

Gently Rob eased himself out of the hemisphere. Trailing scented water from his heels, he moved behind the screen. He threw his soggy shorts into a chute and dressed. Once again his clothes were warm from a sonic cleaning. At this rate he was going to be the most germproof visitor on Stardeep.

As he tugged on his shirt, Rob remembered the wild montage of images that had flashed through his mind as he writhed on the turf of the mall.

"I got a strong dose of Empt mental energy, is that it?" he called.

"Correct," Simon replied from the other side of the screen. "You Empted."

"I could remember who I was, and where I was. But it was a struggle. I couldn't remember why I'd come to Stardeep, though."

"Everything unpleasant in your past was masked out of your mind," said Simon. "Now you understand why the Empts are so valuable in treating people who are mentally ill."

Rob shivered. His father, *Majestica,* the reason for his journey here—for that short time it had all been wiped away by the curious tingling emanations from the small squealing ball of life.

"I'll say."

Another memory slipped into place—the angry bluechip eyes of the bearded man.

"Who was that guy chasing the Empt, Commander? His owner?"

Rob thought his ears had tricked him when Lyndsey replied, "Footloose."

"What did you say?"

"The owner of the Empt is called Footloose," the Commander explained. "No one knows his right name. He's a Terran and very likely a lunatic. He's been living out on the reservation for years. You probably didn't notice, but the close association with the Empts has scrambled his speech. Since well before I got here, the Conpats have tolerated him, because he does no great harm. Once we tried to get him to come into this dispensary for treatment. He got so violent we decided it would be better to leave him alone."

Rob moved out from behind the screen, which promptly collapsed and folded itself into a slot in the wall. "And the Empt I caught is his pet?"

"One of the few pets we allow," Simon nodded.

"What was this Footloose character doing in town?"

Lyndsey provided the answer. "He comes to Churchill for supplies every month or so."

Simon grinned at Rob. "Your motives were noble, anyway."

Rob responded with a smile of his own. "Talk about a psychedelic experience!"

In his imagination he saw again the leathery, young-old face of the man called Footloose. He remembered particularly the malevolent glare of those blue-chip eyes. He mentioned this to the others.

Simon Ling pulled out his musicpipe and tobacco ball, which he inserted in the bowl. Pungent smoke and antique Brahms filled the sterile room as he replied, "Footloose showed up here too. He was still raging. By then we had rounded up his Empt for him. Two of my men got knocked out just the way you did while they caught the beastie. There's just no other way to capture an Empt. Drugsprays won't work. That's the reason Conpats have to be tough. It takes something out of a man to go through the Empting experience five or six times a day whenever we thin the reservation. Anyway, Footloose came storming in here. He seemed to think you were responsible for his Empt escaping. It was quite a scene. But I told you what kind of person he was—"

With a shake of his head, Simon used his pipestem to describe the age-old corkscrew sign of lunacy.

"Can I check out now?" Rob said.

"Anytime," Simon replied.

They left the room, headed down a corridor that led eventually to the Commander's office. Simon halted at the entrance.

Lyndsey said, "Dad tried to tell Footloose that you were helping to catch the Empt, and not the other way around. Dad explained who you were, a visitor to Stardeep, unfamiliar with the creatures—"

"Funny thing about that," Simon remarked from behind a soaring string passage and a cloud of smoke. "When I mentioned who you were—Rob Edison, a visitor from Dellkart IV—it seemed to work the poor coot up even more. He turned positively white, and that's not easy for a man who lives outdoors all year. Well, I suppose it was all due to his fear that we'd hurt his Empt or wouldn't let him have it again. We've already mended the chain. Man and Empt are on their way back to the reservation. We have to carry him over the barrier in a special short-hop flyer whenever he shows up. Nuisance."

"You need to be kind to someone like that, Dad," Lyndsey said. "I feel sorry for him. He really doesn't seem like a very old man."

"He isn't. Except inside his mind. Well, Rob—" A thick-fingered hand fell on Rob's shoulder in comradely fashion. "If you're feeling fit enough to navigate on your own"—Rob told them he was—"Lyndsey and I will say good-by for the day. We have some errands before mealtime. Your flyer is on schedule. It'll be waiting for you at the yard tomorrow morning at 0930. You won't find it hard to interrogate the Phylex Station. Complete instructions are spelled out on the station's programmer. Drop in when you get back in the afternoon. I'll be anxious to know the results of the trip."

"Thank you, Commander," Rob said with gratitude. "For everything." He started away.

"Rob?"

He turned back. Lyndsey's smile made him feel wanted. She said, "Good fortune across Stardeep."

Simon noticed his daughter's rapt expression, chuckled. "A localism meaning good luck, Rob." He waved and disappeared into his office.

Rob hurried down the antique fixed-position stairs. He recalled the look in Lyndsey's eyes long after he had gone out into the late-slanting sunlight on Avenue Ursus. The more he thought about her, the better he felt.

He headed for the central caf and a quick meal. His encounter with the Empt had left him tired. He wanted to turn in at the hostel and have a long, sound sleep before traveling out to the Phylex Station tomorrow. Excitement was building inside of him.

That excitement was marred by a sudden feeling that he was being watched.

He turned carefully. He scanned the bustling early evening crowds. He saw no one he recognized.

With a shrug he walked on until he came to the caf, and went inside.

He emerged twenty minutes later. All the way back to his hostel, the feeling that he was being observed persisted. He spent a tenth of a minicredit at a papertape kiosk, even though he wasn't really interested in scanning the day's news on the reader back in his room. He wanted a chance to survey the streets again.

Again he saw no one he could regard as suspicious. He continued on to the hostel.

On the eve of his trip to the Phylex Station, he hoped for a sound, dreamless slumber. It wasn't to be. Squealing Empts chased through his dreams, pursued by bearded young-old men in filthy clothes. They cursed Rob's name and glared at him with blue-chip eyes brimming with inexplicable hate.

As Rob stepped from the hostel next morning at 0845, a voice hailed him.

"Over here, young master!"

With a start he recognized Lummus. The man was waving to him from an adjoining walkway.

Instantly Rob was wary. He shook his head to indicate haste. He turned, started in the opposite direction. Lummus came after him, catching up with a wheeze and a puff.

Rob spun around as Lummus crowded him into the dim arcade entrance of a cosmetics shop not yet opened for the day.

"Get out of my way," Rob growled. "I'm in a hurry."

"But I insist that we have a chat, young master. I do insist." Lummus' lenslike brown eyes were unfriendly. The twist of his mouth could just barely be termed a smile. "If you are thinking of calling for a civil officer, don't. Not if you value the personal safety of the charming young lady with whom you traveled around town yesterday."

The nape of Rob's neck crawled.

The travel agent's fat fingers played a silent tattoo on his heaving paunch. In the cool shadows of the arcade a female voice whispered an advertisement for the shop's cosmetics. The head of Barton Lummus seemed to float like a bearded melon in the gloom, repulsive, diabolical.

"Are you making threats about the Commander's daughter?" Rob blazed.

Again that greasy smile spread across the drooping lips. "Not idle ones, I assure you. Come, come, young master! Let's discuss this like men of experience. It has come to my attention that you have applied for a pass that will permit you to enter the Empt reservation."

"But no one knows that except the Commander!" Rob was completely mystified.

Lummus wagged a yellow-stained finger. "Tut-tut. No one knows except those who were in the Commander's office when application was made, plus those who were outside, armed with a bit of electronic eavesdropping equipment."

"You listened—"

"Quite right. I am interested in gaining entry to the reservation. What more natural than to set up my listening post near Headquarters? Frankly, I had expected to wait days. Weeks! What a stroke of luck, eh, young master? A person with whom I am already acquainted turns up promptly and obtains permission!" Lummus' remarkably strong hand shot out to grip Rob's wrist. "You do have the flyer control card, do you not?"

Now Rob recalled something else. He shot back, "You mean the card you tried to pick out of my pocket?"

"I almost got it, too."

"You left a fingerprint."

Lummus let go of Rob's hand with a wounded sneer.

"What's this all have to do with Lyndsey Ling?" Rob demanded.

"She is merely my little device to ensure your cooperation. This morning, after her father left their domidome, my android Blecho and I slipped inside and—ah—requested her presence. At this moment my green-skinned companion is waiting with the girl at the park near the flyer compound. No one will question us if you have the pass card, you see. Thus we shall all be going out into the waste. Myself, that merciless rascal Blecho, Miss Ling, and you and your card."

"You kidnapped Lyndsey?" Rob was almost sputtering.

"Harsh words. But accurate."

"You're not a travel agent, are you? You're nothing but a cheap—"

Lummus struck Rob's cheek viciously hard. *"Be silent!"*

For an instant the fat man's face showed naked rage. Then he brought his emotions under control. He resumed that insufferable smirking and clamped his hand on Rob's shoulder again.

"Please be clear about it, young master. Unless you do as I say, the girl will be hurt." Barton Lummus sucked in a long, rattling breath. "Shall we go?"

Ten

DANGER FLIGHT

The walkways carried them toward the edge of town. Rob had the feeling that what was happening wasn't real.

Lummus chattered, commenting on the breezy morning weather, the architecture of Churchill which he held in contempt, the provincial mores and attitudes of the residents of Stardeep, and other miscellaneous topics.

Several times Rob asked pointed questions in a voice that betrayed his anxiety. What was Lummus' motive for this scheme? Where did he come from? What would happen when they took the flyer into the waste?

Lummus' response was invariably the same. He would jog his melon head to indicate people riding the other way.

"Privacy, young master! Ask your questions when we have privacy."

A few of the workers on their way into town gave Rob and his companion sharp stares. With his untidy clothing and jiggling chin beard, Lummus was a rather unusual sight. Each time he was noticed, Lummus fixed a smile on his face and nodded fatuously at the curious person on the other belt.

"Must maintain the front, mustn't we?" he said from a corner of his mouth. "Dear old uncle and nephew out for a morning excursion, what?"

Rob felt like snapping back with a sarcastic remark that Lummus wouldn't be mistaken for anybody's dear old uncle. But he didn't. Under the fat man's posturings, Rob sensed a core of ruthlessness.

The walkway carried them past a series of materials-han-

dling domes. Ahead, lemon sunlight glared from the sides
of pink-veined rocks.

On the other side of the park Rob glimpsed a flyer standing in the center of the compound. In vain he searched the
area for a Conpat to whom he could turn for help. The servodome dock was empty.

The walkway bore them relentlessly on toward the platform alongside the park. Rob couldn't see Lyndsey or the
android anywhere in the jumble of rocks.

All at once, as they were about to step off the way, Rob
had an idea. He hung back, let Lummus precede him onto
the platform. For an instant the obese man's back was
turned. Rob stabbed his right hand inside his jacket. He
seized the gray embossed card, yanked it out, started to
drop it into the crack between the undulating belt and the
platform.

Lummus whirled around. He shot out a porcine hand,
dug his fingers deep into Rob's wrist. The gray card
dropped from Rob's fingers. Lummus' other hand was already beneath it.

He caught the card. Then he pulled Rob hard, so that he
nearly tumbled onto the platform on his face.

When Rob got his balance, Lummus thrust the card at
him and glared.

"You dropped this, I believe? If you drop it again, young
master, the young lady will be in for an extended stay in
the dispensary. Or worse."

The point wasn't lost on Rob. Miserably, he shoved the
gray card back into his jacket. He followed Lummus down
the ramp to the park.

Still no one stirring at the flyer compound. His mind
churned. Somehow he had to break out of this trap! But he
didn't know how to do it.

He grew even less inclined to try something rash when
he caught sight of Lyndsey Ling and the android. They appeared from behind one of the huge pink-veined rocks and
came down a winding path. Lummus waved cheerily. Rob's
stomach flipflopped. Lyndsey's cheeks were pale, her eyes
wide and frightened. She stumbled when she recognized
him.

Walking right behind her, the emerald android extended
one hand from beneath a neutral cape that covered him
from neck to knee, caught Lyndsey's elbow, and kept her
upright with a rude jerk. Lyndsey's anger was apparent, but

it melted under the frightening, almost inhuman stare of the android's blank eyes.

Lummus lumbered up to them. "Ah, good morning again, young mistress. How goes it, Blecho?"

"She wants to fight," remarked Blecho in a tinny voice.

"But not too vigorously, what?" To Rob, Lummus said, "I had Blecho put on that cloak for a special reason. Notice that my android has but one hand showing? His other, concealed, is clasped around an antique but nevertheless operative laser beam. In the event that it becomes necessary to combat violence with violence, he is a tip-top marksman."

"At close range," Blecho commented, "it is virtually impossible to miss."

"Quite so. Well, I believe your flyer is waiting, young master. Come along!"

Blecho led the way. Lyndsey fell in step alongside Rob. She whispered almost hysterically, "Do you know what's going on?"

"I wish I did. They want to go into the desert and my flyer card is their ticket." He noticed a bruise on her arm, just below the short sleeve of her pale-gold outfit. "Did they hurt you?"

"They frightened me half to death with that laser beam when they showed up at the dome after Dad left. Otherwise I'm all ri—"

"I find your whispers annoying," interrupted Lummus. "Desist, if you don't mind."

Lyndsey brushed back a lock of her straw-colored hair. She looked flushed now, and more than a little fearful. Rob admired the way she kept that fear under control.

They left the park and crossed the narrow strip of turf that was the boundary of the flyer compound. Blecho marched straight toward the teardrop flyer. Its hatch was open, its boarding ladder down. Suddenly a mech with a checkboard poked his head around the corner of the servodome dock.

"Morning," the mech called to Rob. "You Mr. Edison?"

"Yes." Desperately he tried to think of a way to call attention to their predicament.

The mech noticed Lyndsey. "Miss Ling! You going along too?"

"That's right, Tom," the girl returned with only a slight hesitation.

Lummus continued to smile blandly, as though his presence were perfectly normal. The mech consulted his checkboard, frowned. "The Commander didn't note down anything about other people in your party, Mr. Edison."

A lump clogged Rob's throat. Here was his chance. He was about to speak, when he noticed the emerald android leaning against the side of the flyer.

The craft was between the android and the servodome. The mech could not see Blecho move the hand slit of his cloak aside and thrust out a needle muzzle with a silver ball at its tip.

Blecho's blank gray eyes were turned to Rob, inhumanly sentient. The silver ball moved to point at Lyndsey.

"These are all friends of mine," Rob said. "The Commander knew we were going out together. Maybe—he just forgot about it."

The mech nodded. "Doesn't matter as long as you have the pass card."

"I do." Rob took it from his pocket, held it up.

The mech seemed satisfied. "Just put it in the marked slot. The flyer will do the rest. Good fortune across Stardeep!"

The mech waved his checkboard and vanished back inside the servodome.

"All aboard!" exclaimed Lummus with disheartening joviality.

The forecabin of the flyer was a dim oval. Padded benches curved around the outer sides. Lummus and the android sat on the benches to starboard. The fat man indicated that Lyndsey and Rob should sit facing them on the port side.

In spite of the complexity of dials and gauges spread on the control panel beneath the front viewplates, Rob had no difficulty spotting the place where the card was to be inserted. A red metal housing occupied a central position on the dash. Large enameled arrows above and below pointed to its horizontal slot. With a perspiring hand he slipped the gray card into the opening.

Immediately there was a clicking, a whining. The boarding ladder began to fold up. Rob took his seat beside Lyndsey.

The hatch whooshed shut and sealed its gasket. Thrusters sputtered. Air made a thin screaming sound as it filled the landing skids and burst out through the tiny openings on the undersides, raising the flyer off the ground. The thrusters cut in at full power. The flyer rose up from the yard in a smooth curve.

The craft banked out across the floor of the waste toward the purple peaks. Rob had an oblique view of the electronic barrier shimmering below them. It was quickly gone. The flyer leveled, turning away from the sun. The forecabin smelled of dust and oil.

Barton Lummus searched in his blouse for a sheaf of papers. He unfolded them, fixed his brown eyes on what appeared to be some sort of squiggly blue diagram.

Blecho looked totally uninterested. The tip of the laser beam had disappeared again beneath his cloak. Because his eyes lacked pupils, it was impossible to tell whether he was staring directly at the two prisoners. But Rob had the feeling that he was.

"Rob?"

He turned, startled anew by the raw fear in Lyndsey's eyes.

"Do you know who these men are?"

"Mr. Lummus came to Stardeep on the same ship I did," Rob told her. "He said he was a travel agent. I should have trusted my first reaction—all bad."

"It's a splendid cover, though," remarked Lummus affably. "The bureaucratic clods staffing the law enforcement agencies of the various worlds to which my affairs take me never question it."

"Don't you think it's time you told us what this is all about?" Rob asked.

Lummus shrugged. "I see no reason why not. The answer is Empts."

Lyndsey blinked. "Did I hear you correctly? You said—"

"Empts." Lummus grew sarcastic. "You are familiar are you not, with those little beggars your father and his officious assistants guard so assiduously? People want Empts desperately. Especially neurotic persons who don't wish to bare their intermost problems to a psychomed. With their remarkable facility for obliterating all past traumas, Empts are in constant demand on the various planetary gray markets with which I have—ah—connections. I have come to Stardeep with a group of assistants to help myself to several dozen Empts and thereby increase the size of my computerized financial holdings."

"A poacher!" Lyndsey breathed.

"A good one," observed the expressionless android. "Best that ever hired me."

"Faithful beggar," Lummus said, patting the android's shoulder. "Blecho has a passion for immersing himself in low-viscosity industrial lubricants. It's akin to the human sport of swimming in natural water. Also, Blecho's manufacturer scrambled his enzyme balance. As a result, he has absolutely no scruples about murdering anyone who obstructs—"

"Can we skip that kind of talk?" Rob cut in.

"Oh, I am sorry, young master."

But he wasn't in the least. His thrust had been well calculated to terrify Lyndsey Ling even more. Her expression showed that it had succeeded.

Lummus rattled the sheaf of papers. "These, plus my ability to penetrate the Empt reservation, will be the secrets of my success on this little venture. The electronic barriers around the reservation are plaguing problems, I don't mind telling you. Especially the sky barrier ten miles up. That barrier prevents any ship from coming straight down onto the reservation. It is controlled, however, by ground-based circuitry. These"—again the sheaf rattled—"were obtained at great expense from the gray market on Ketchum's Cloudplanet. Schematics of the circuitry of a three-square-mile area of the barrier in the sky. The power station controlling this part of the barrier is located approximately eight miles overland from the Phylex Monitor installation at which we'll land. Thus I needed to get inside the barrier without detection—"

"So you could reach the power station," Rob concluded.

"How perspicacious you are," Lummus replied with a faint sneer. "As soon as we are down, faithful Blecho and I shall travel to the power station, disrupt the circuits, and thus eliminate the aforementioned portion of the barrier. I have a ship out in orbit at this very moment, manned by an excellent crew of poachers. The ship will come down through the opening in the barrier. We shall round up several dozen Empts and be away no later than nightfall—undetected!"

Beaming with self-congratulation, Lummus sat back and began to dust food specks from his trousers.

Lyndsey shuddered. "I think it's disgusting."

"Disgusting to turn a profit? What a quaint concept."

"Disgusting you'd steal Empts that could help really sick people."

Lummus raised a porky hand. "Spare me the pious Conpat propaganda, if you please."

All through the conversation, Rob had been thinking about possible courses of action. He saw that they were approaching the purple mountains, a saw-toothed, deep-colored rampart. They had been flying not much more than ten minutes, but already the thrusters were changing pitch. A sudden hissing indicated that the landing skid aircushions were going into action.

The flyer lost altitude. The downtilt of the teardrop bow told him they would be landing shortly.

Blecho pointed at the port. "Phylex Station."

Rob saw it coming up among the rocky foothills in a rush: a three-story column of chrome alloy rising from a stressed concrete base. A circular liftstair wound round and round the outside of the column. It led the eye upward to the station itself, a transparent bubble at the column's top. Inside the bubble Rob glimpsed machinery.

Lummus put away his diagrams. "A most pleasant trip, wouldn't you say? You will accompany us to the power station, young master. As soon as my ship lands and we round up a sufficient number of Empts, you will be on your own. We shall leave you in the waste to be rescued by the Conpats at some later time. You won't starve. At least I don't believe you will," the fat man concluded.

"Tonight Dad will discover we're gone—" Lyndsey began hopefully.

"And I shall be gone also," Lummus said. "Happy thought, what?"

"Be very rich," Blecho remarked to no one in particular. "Go to another planet. Bathe in oil for a week."

The flyer was settling in an open area surrounded by large purple boulders. The base of the nearby Phylex tower was hidden by the rocks. Behind the column-and-bubble, the rock-strewn land sloped upward to the sharp angle where sheer purple cliffs began.

There was a tilt, a crunch, as the flyer landed on rocky ground. The thrusters cut out. The hatch unsealed with a whisper. Clanging, the hatch flew back. Lemon sunlight and a warm, dusty-smelling wind flooded in.

The boarding stair unfolded. Carefully Rob stood up. He took Lyndsey's hand, pulled her after him. She forced a smile. But her bright-blue eyes were getting a glazed look. No wonder, with Blecho's laser beam an obvious lump beneath his cloak.

Rob felt hot as he edged toward the hatch. He studied the ground outside. It was covered with a heavy pumice. Here and there lay egg-sized or larger stones, all various shades of purple. He spotted one near the embedded lower prongs of the ladder. A tic began to beat in his cheek. He averted his head as Lummus clumped past.

The fat man was intent on the landscape outside. He surveyed it with a gross, lip-smacking satisfaction. His straggly chin beard blew back and forth in the breeze as he stepped to one side at the hatch.

"You first, Blecho."

The android plodded outside, started down the stairs. Lummus signed for Rob and Lyndsey to follow. Blecho was four steps from the bottom as Rob ducked through and dug his heels into the top step. The lemon sun beat into his eyes. He swallowed hard and jumped.

"*Blecho!*" Lummus howled as Rob sailed down on top of the android and bashed his fist on top of the hairless emerald head.

Blecho uttered a cry in some alien dialect, collapsing under Rob's weight. Rob rolled off to one side. The android floundered. Things happened with confusing swiftness.

"The beam, the beam, you stupid construct!" Lummus shouted. Rob saw a flash of silver in the sun. Blecho had lost his grip on the laser beam. It was on the ground lying in the open.

Barton Lummus bounded down the boarding stairs, knocking Lyndsey aside. The android seemed confused, as though Rob's blow had impaired its thinking. It rubbed an emerald hand back and forth over its brow. All pretense of gentility gone, Lummus booted Blecho out of the way and dove for the laser beam.

Simultaneously, Rob closed his hand around the purple stone he had noticed before. A stone against an old-fashioned but deadly lightweapon was, he realized, not very much of a contest.

Eleven

"A TOUCH OF THE LASER"

Barton Lummus swung the ball-tipped muzzle of the laser beam on a direct line with Rob's stomach. Rob had never been so frightened in his life.

He didn't stop to think. Faster than he could have imagined, he flung the stone.

It struck Lummus in the forehead. The fat man howled. A gash opened in his forehead, leaking blood. Lummus swore and hopped from foot to foot.

Shoulder tucked low, Rob charged.

He dodged in past the weapon and hit Lummus' stomach. The fat man toppled backward, wigwagging his arms. His gasp sounded like a balloon deflating. By that time Rob was racing past the android.

Blecho made an abortive lunge, but Rob's footwork, fast as a gravball court maneuver, helped him slip neatly around behind the green creature.

Lyndsey gaped at him from the boarding stair. Rob reached up, caught her hand, pulled her down toward him.

He braced himself as she tumbled against him. He kept her from falling, wound his fingers tightly around hers, and started to run.

The glazed look disappeared from Lyndsey's eyes. Her straw-colored hair streamed as she struggled to match Rob's pace. Behind, Rob heard Barton Lummus venting his anger with all sorts of swearwords. The fat man interrupted the profanity to screech at Blecho to get moving.

The pumice chopped hard against the soles of Rob's sandals. Lyndsey's breathing was loud in his ear. They reached the large purple boulders behind which Rob meant to take cover.

Rob banged into the first boulder, scraping his shoulder. He started around behind the rock, still dragging Lyndsey by the hand. She cried out. The pressure of her fingers vanished.

Rob spun around. Lyndsey was being dragged backward by the android.

Blecho had his hands locked around the girl's waist from behind. When she started to kick, the android lifted her off the ground.

Panicked, Rob headed back around the rock toward Lyndsey and her captor. He was just passing the boulder when a thin beam of ruby light sliced past his ear and silently disintegrated a section of the big rock.

The circular depression smoked and stank of ozone. There was a brief aftercrackle of sound. Instinctively Rob ducked his head, jumped backward so that the boulder hid him.

Heart beating furiously, he lay with one cheek against the rough, cool stone.

That laser beam could have killed him!

After a moment he managed to calm down. He heard the sounds of a struggle from the other side of the rock, grew furious with himself for reacting without thinking. He should have charged straight ahead, not backward into cover. Now he was separated from Lyndsey, Blecho, and Lummus by the massive rock.

"Young master?" Lummus' pebbly voice was fragmented by the breeze. "Can you hear me?"

"I hear you," Rob called.

"I meant that as a warning. Poaching is one matter, homicide another entirely. I do not wish to have one or more deaths on my record. However"—Lummus panted between words—"you force me to extreme measures. Blecho has the girl in his grasp again. If you persist in balking me—"

Angry, Rob flung a stone over the top of the boulder.

From the other side Blecho croaked in alarm. The stone struck and rattled. Rob shook his head, a savage motion.

This was getting him absolutely nowhere. Lyndsey was a prisoner, and it was up to him to keep a cool head. Losing his temper because he had reacted normally and gone for cover wouldn't help the situation. He forced himself to crouch down behind the rock and await developments.

Almost at once, Lummus bawled, "One more trick like that, and I'll give the young lady a touch of the laser."

A pause. The wind blew in gusts, whining around the boulders.

"Do you realize that I'm perfectly serious, young master? Too much is at stake—"

"All right!" was Rob's reply. "Just don't hurt her."

"What happens to her depends entirely on you."

"What do you mean?"

"You force a change in my plans. I cannot afford to be on guard against your tactics every inch of the way from here to the power station. Therefore, since it seems that I have you temporarily bottled up"—a chuckle—"I believe I will simply leave you where you are."

Another flurry of sound. Rob recognized Lyndsey's voice. Blecho complained, "This girl is kicking me."

"Kick her back, you simpleton," Lummus snarled. Lyndsey's cries subsided.

"Pay attention, you young whelp," Lummus called after a moment. "My companion and I will proceed overland to the power station. We will take the girl with us. Now I warn you, don't come after us. If I so much as see your ear sticking out from behind a rock, I will take steps. Yes."

Lummus' voice lowered. Rob didn't miss the new, more sinister timbre. The fat man was reacting to the frustration of his plan, and reacting in an ugly way.

"If you pursue us, this little lady will get that touch of the laser I mentioned. Nothing fatal. Just enough to cripple her. A foot, a hand—a touch will do it nicely."

Rob's flesh crawled. He swallowed hard, kept silent.

"Did you hear what I said, young master?"

All Rob could answer was, "Yes. Lummus—don't hurt her." *A touch of the laser.* The words made Rob's stomach hurt. He called out, "Lyndsey?"

Her voice was faint. "W—what?"

"I'll do what he says. Don't fight and they won't hurt you."

"We can't let him steal a fortune in Empts—"

"It doesn't matter!" Rob cried vehemently. "You're more important than—"

"Not to me she isn't," Lummus interrupted. "And don't you forget it."

Another pause. The wind blew eerily aroung the boulders. Rob felt hopelessly trapped.

"We're going now," Lummus informed him, above the moan of the wind.

All at once Rob knew that he couldn't allow Barton Lummus to carry Lyndsey off to the power station without making an effort to rescue her. He would give them a good head start. Then, as carefully as possible, he would follow.

He had to do it! Lummus, in his excited state and with a huge potential profit at stake, might dispose of the girl, anyway, if she proved an encumbrance. And Rob knew he would go crazy if he simply sat for hours without doing anything.

Let Lummus think he had won the point. That might throw him off guard. Then—what?

Well, he'd figure something. He had to.

Breathing a little more steadily, Rob settled down to wait.

From the opposite side of the boulder drifted the faint sound of the party setting out. Lummus gave orders to Blecho. The android responded with another complaint. Lummus raised his voice. The android didn't reply.

Rob heard Lyndsey ask the android not to hold her arm so tightly. Lummus grudgingly ordered his companion to treat her a little less roughly. Feet rattled in the pumice— Lummus' heavy, dragging step, the lighter scrape of Lyndsey's sport shoes, the stolid, rhythmic clump-clomp of the android. Soon the keen of the wind obliterated the sounds altogether.

Cautiously Rob crawled out from behind the boulder. He found a rock he could scale, clambered to the top, searched the foothills.

The sun was moving up toward zenith, shedding bright light on the faces of the purple mountains. The bubble at the top of the Phylex column glittered like a jewel. Rob turned his gaze outward—southward, he calculated it would be—from the mountains.

Off to the southwest, an uninterrupted vista of boulderstrewn foothills, a puff of dust rose. Lummus and the others were moving roughly parallel to the base of the mountain chain. At least now he knew the right direction.

He watched for several moments longer, making sure from repeated drifts of the dust that he was right. He was. There was no other sign of life anywhere.

Directly south, the waste leveled off, dun-colored, unfriendly. One hundred and ten miles back there lay help. If
only he could contact—

But he could.

Irritated by his slow thinking, Rob scrambled down from
the boulder and raced to the teardrop flyer.

The forecabin was cool after the heat of the wind. He
started with the ceiling monitors and controls. He read the
nameplate of each. Nothing of significance.

He moved to the starboard side of the complex dash
panel. Again he scanned the nameplates one by one. SKID
P.S.I. FUEL MIX. RIGHT GUIDE VANES. LEFT GUIDE VANES.
He growled in frustration, kept reading.

Suddenly he spotted a green servoswitch over toward the
port side of the panel. The nameplate read DISTRESS
BEACON.

Rob threw the switch to the ON position.

He thought he detected a faint vibration in the hull and
floorplates. He wondered about the nature of the beacon.
An ultrasonic, maybe? No way of telling. But he hoped
that whatever the signal the teardrop craft emitted, it
would be picked up back in Churchill.

As he left the cabin, a sudden flare of light up to his left
caught his eye.

From the top of the Phylex Monitor bubble, a spidery
antenna had extended. Its basketwork dish made one revo-
lution every few seconds. Rob managed a grin. Perhaps the
rescue craft from Churchill would home in on that.

Outside the flyer, Rob checked the ground. He discovered that by leaning his weight into every step, he could
leave definite impressions in the pumice. Therefore he
could afford to wait a few more minutes before starting after Lummus and the others. By taking care to leave tracks,
he would give the Conpats a trail to follow.

He felt a little better. Now he was getting some results.

He sat down in the shade of a large rock to wait five
minutes. He timed the interval by observing the rotation of
the antenna high up on the bubble. Four minutes passed.
He heard a sudden scurrying noise in the rocks.

The palms of his hands turned cold. Could it be an
Empt? He listened harder.

Footsteps. Heavy footsteps. Slipping and scrunching
through the pumice.

Lummus didn't trust him! He had sent Blecho back to spy, or had come himself.

Sweat broke out on Rob's face and arms. He eased himself to his feet, began to creep around the boulder in the direction of the intruder.

All at once he doubted that it was Lummus or his android henchman. Neither one would make so much noise.

He frowned, backed against the rock. In another second, whoever it was would come through the narrow opening between this boulder and the next. Fingers dug tight into his palms, Rob waited.

Scrunch-scrape. Slide-crunch. Someone was humming, off key.

A spindly human shadow spilled across the pumice near Rob's feet. He heard a soft clinking. A smaller, spherical shadow split off from the larger one. Rob held his breath.

Out from between the boulders shot three translucent pseudopods. A second later, the rest of the Empt followed. There was a staple in its back. A light alloy chain clinked against its plating. *Chee-wee! Chee-wee!*

And then Rob was staring into the wild and astonished blue eyes of the man called Footloose.

Twelve

RESCUE PLAN

Footloose reacted instantly. He shuffled backward two steps, fisted his free hand, and raised it over his head to threaten Rob, his face contorted, hostile.

The Empt rushed to its master, cowered against the man's bare, callused foot. *Chee-wee,* the creature cried. Its faceted eyes glowed gold.

For one tense moment the scene held: Rob standing startled while Footloose waved his fist to and from above his head. Beneath the floppy brim of the bearded man's hat, the blue-chip eyes shone angrily.

"I won't hurt you," Rob said. "Don't you recognize me—?"

His words became a mumble. Footloose's face seemed to dissolve like gelatin. The outlines of the boulders, the purple peaks smeared.

Rob staggered back a step. The surroundings distorted even more.

The Empt continued its yelping cry. Rob's head tingled. The tingling spread to his jawbone. All at once he understood. He was in the Empt's zone of radiation.

Things grew more and more blurred. The ground tilted one way, then the other. Rob blinked hard. That didn't help.

Footloose took a step forward. His mouth cracked into a sly smile. He had Rob on the run.

The boy turned. He used all his energy to take a staggering step, then another. Footloose cackled. "Scared, you. I scared you good, didn't I, person?"

The half-maniacal voice dinned in Rob's ears. He

seemed to be sluicing through hip-deep liquid. The air itself showed weird ripples and bends.

Rob plowed ahead. The tingling in his skull diminished. He kept going until he was a good twenty feet from the bearded man, who had stopped in the shade of a boulder and lowered his fist.

Breath came heavy in Rob's lungs. He felt as if he were surfacing from a long underwater dive. Gradually the silhouettes of the peaks sharpened. The waviness vanished from the air. At last the tingling faded altogether.

Rob wiped an arm across his mouth. He tasted the saltiness of his own skin. Sucking deep gulps of air, he turned around.

Chee-wee, cried the Empt. It was still tucked against its master's anklebone. It resembled an armored ball now. No pseudopods were showing.

Footloose grinned even wider. He clinked the length of the light alloy chain rapidly in both hands.

"My critter won't hurt you, person. I will, though."

Rob shook his head, swallowed. He felt almost normal. But he wasn't certain about how to deal with the stranger.

Footloose had one foot planted out in front of him. The posture was almost defiant. He pushed back his cone-crowned hat. Tangled hair on his forehead spilled out. His teeth shone like bits of ivory. His blue-chip eyes crinkled at the corners, unnaturally lively.

Rob tried a simple gambit. "I'm your friend."

"No friends here." Footloose waved the chain at the mountains. "All alone."

"But I know your name."

That surprised the bearded man. "You do?"

"It's Footloose, right? You live out here all by yourself with your Empt."

The statement made the man wary again. "Who told you about me? About my critter?"

"I met you in Churchill."

The stranger considered this even more astonishing. "Where I go for victuals?"

"That's right. Last time you were there, your—critter—escaped."

Emphatically Footloose shook his head. "Never happened, person. I'd remember."

"You don't remember chasing your Empt down the mall? I caught it for you."

"Never happened," Footloose repeated. He took a few steps forward. Rob countered with an equal number of steps to the rear. Again Footloose reacted with that child-like expression of astonishment. "Why you stand away off there, person?"

"Because if I get too close to your Empt, I'll forget what happened just before you showed up." The way you obviously forgot your Empt running away in Churchill, Rob added to himself.

Rob studied Footloose more closely. It was impossible to tell his age. The man's skin, especially his forehead and the backs of his hands, were rough-textured from long exposure to the open air of Stardeep. In the right light, his deep suntan appeared to have an ebony sheen. All that suggested age. So did the gray streakings in his beard. And yet the blue-chip eyes were oddly youthful. Footloose might be anywhere from twenty-five to forty-five years old.

The stranger hooked his eyebrows together, trying to concentrate on what was clearly a serious matter. "Something bad has happened here, person?"

"My name is Edison, not person." Rob was annoyed at having to deal with the stranger's slow mental processes. He gestured to the scuffed pumice. "There was a fight. I came here with a girl whose father is Commander of the Conpats—"

"Conpats are good men," Footloose said with a genuine smile. "They let me live out here. They carry me over the shocking walls and back when I need victuals."

A plan suggested itself suddenly. "Then you should help me, Footloose," Rob said.

"Help you do what, Edison person?"

"Help me get the girl back from the men I was fighting. They're bad men." He stressed it with an exaggerated face. "Very, very bad." The effect drew a response. Footloose scowled. Rob went on: "One of the men has a laser beam. He may use it to hurt the Conpat Commander's daughter. The men are trying to steal Empts—"

Footloose bent swiftly to scoop up his pet. He cradled the armored creature in the crook of one elbow and patted its plates with his other hand.

"Take mine?" he asked, worried.

"They might. They'll take any they can get."

"Not allowed," Footloose growled. "My friends Conpats say no."

"But the Conpats aren't here, Footloose. We're the only ones who can stop the men. They took the girl to a power station over that way. Do you know where it is?"

"Know, Edison person," Footloose nodded.

"Then will you help me? I think you and your Empt and I could get the girl away."

Footloose gnawed his cracked lower lip. "Not sure you're a friend."

"I helped save your Empt in Churchill!"

The bearded man passed a hand in front of his eyes, a vague gesture. "Not sure."

"Because you've forgotten! The Empt erased—oh, never mind."

Rob was conscious of the changing angle of the lemon sun. Minutes were slipping by while he argued with this naïve hermit. He put as much pleading into his voice as he could muster.

"Believe me, Footloose, I wouldn't take your Empt. But those men I talked about would. If they get hold of your pet, you'll never see him—it—again."

Footloose sniffed, disdainful of Rob's ignorance. He stroked the creature's plates. It let out a faint *chee-wee*.

"It's a lady, don't you know?"

"I beg her pardon and yours. Will you help?"

After some deliberation, Footloose asked, "What must be done, Edison person?"

Quickly Rob explained what he had in mind. Footloose did not grasp all the details right away. Rob had to go over certain parts two and three times. When he finished, Footloose still gave no sign of being willing. His blue-chip eyes gleamed suspiciously from under the grimy brim of his hat.

"The Lummus person is the one with the hurting thing?" he asked.

"Yes, the laser beam."

"Will he hurt my critter with it?"

"Not if the plan works right."

"You swear Lummus person means to steal Empts?"

"Dozens of them," Rob avowed.

"You say you helped me in Churchill—" Footloose still looked a little dubious. Then, abruptly, the lines of his face smoothed out. He was less menacing. "I believe you, Edison person. And all the talk about Conpat daughter and stealing Empts too. I'll help."

Weary from the long exchange, Rob almost whooped.

Footloose lowered his Empt gently to the ground. Kneeling in front of the creature, he extended his right hand.

Fascinated, Rob watched a chink appear in the Empt's plates. One pseudopod extended, translucent and quivering. Footloose laid his palm on top of the pseudopod. His beard danced in the wind as he made a face. It was an exaggerated grin, almost as though he were a grandfather trying to charm an infant into smiling. From deep in his throat, he brought forth a sound that was a very close imitation of the *chee-wee* cry.

He repeated the sound in varying rhythms. All at once the Empt retracted its pseudopod and began to roll back and forth. Footloose clapped his hands. He stood up, continuing to make the *chee-wee* sound, which the Empt immediately duplicated.

Listening to the cacophony, Rob blinked. "Footloose, can you talk to that thing?"

The bearded man peered over the shoulder of his sun-bleached blouse. "Isn't a thing. It's a critter. Critters have brains like we have brains!" Footloose exclaimed. Rob was impressed by his depth of feeling for the odd beasts.

"Critter brains are little, so the Conpat persons tell me," Footloose went on. He showed how little by measuring off the ball of his thumb with his index finger, then enlarging the volume threefold by pantomiming with both hands. "But critters think and talk, person. I know it. I have lived with them always." Again that vague, peculiar gesture, as though Footloose were trying to brush cobwebs from his eyes. "Or at least I think always. Maybe part of always. Half. Some." He shrugged. "Anyway, Edison person, they listen to me. Know what I say."

Even better! Rob thought. He moved forward a few steps, carried by his own enthusiasm, but he recoiled sharply when the tingling started in the frontal bones of his head.

Back in a safe position beyond the reach of the Empt's power, he said, "Listen carefully, will you please, Footloose? Remember the plan I told you about?"

Footloose pondered, finally nodded. Score one, Rob thought. At least he doesn't consider that unpleasant. Yet. He continued. "Remember how I said we'd use your Empt against the men who took the girl? Well, more than one Empt would make it a lot easier."

Rob paused to give Footloose time to think it over. The man followed the concept with some difficulty. Even when he nodded and murmured, "More Empts easier," Rob wasn't sure he understood. But he pressed on, anyway.

"Could you round up some more Empts right now?"

"How many, person?"

"About half a doz—this many." Rob held up all the fingers on one hand.

Footloose's lips moved in silence as he counted. "Think so. Take time, though."

"Very much?" Rob was worried about more delay.

Footloose struggled for a way to express the time idea. At last he held up his own hand with three fingers raised. He added his little finger just to be certain.

"This much all right, Edison person?"

"If it's no longer," Rob agreed. He hoped Footloose meant minutes rather than hours or days.

"Be back," Footloose chortled, giving a tug to his Empt's chain. Man and creature vanished among the rocks.

Rob let out a long sigh. He wandered over to a shady place and hunched down.

Already the boulders were throwing off longer shadows. Atop the Phylex Station the spidery antenna continued to turn in silence. For a moment Rob felt very discouraged.

The threat posed by Lummus was diverting him from the purpose of his trip into the waste. He looked enviously at the bubble of the Phylex Station. How soon would he get back to interrogate its banked tapes?

He had to help Lyndsey Ling. But he was already so embroiled in this trouble that his week and a half on Stardeep might run out before he even had a chance to start his search.

It had been an alarming day. And he wasn't so sure he'd done the right thing by inviting the assistance of an obvious lunatic who—

Chee-wee! Chee-wee!

The cry up in the rocks startled him. He realized that it came from a human throat.

The sound echoed strangely on the shifting wind. It was repeated at intervals during the next few minutes. Then there was an answering cry. Another. Before long the slopes above the clearing rang with the squeals.

Was Footloose summoning Empts from the caves that

Simon Ling said were woven all through the peaks and foothills? It must be so.

In another moment, the scarecrow figure appeared along a defile, waving his cone-crowned hat and uttering the strange cry full volume. Footloose grinned so wide that his mouth looked like a porcelain ornament. Behind him, racing along by extending groups of three pseudopods, came six more Empts, four larger and two smaller than the pet that Footloose still had with him on his chain.

"All here," Footloose shouted. "I can get more, Edison person—"

Rob shook his head, which was already tingling. He started walking so as to keep well ahead of the little Empt army. He motioned for Footloose to follow.

"We help the Conpat girl, yes?" Footloose chortled, dancing along behind Rob like a macabre pied piper. "I am only afraid for one thing, person. That the Lummus uses his bad hurting thing on my critters."

Or on us, thought Rob grimly as he led the way from a safe distance.

Soon he, Footloose, and the chirruping Empts were moving through the foothills on a line parallel to the mountains. Footloose was completely cheerful again. Apparently the presence of his little friends relieved him of all worry about the possible peril ahead. Empting certainly had its advantages, Rob thought.

Thirteen

FIGHT AT THE POWER STATION

The trail to the power station wasn't difficult to follow. Barton Lummus had taken no trouble to hide his tracks, preferring, Rob supposed, to move swiftly and accomplish his objective as soon as possible. But covering the eight miles proved harder than Rob expected.

It soon became evident that Lummus had only the roughest idea of the terrain through which he was so obviously hurrying. The trail he left wound back and forth through the foothills. Rob discovered this when Footloose called to him from behind. The bearded man indicated a narrow crevice between two boulders. Rob shook his head, pointed to the footprints ahead. He felt it was imperative to keep to the trail in case anything happened to Lyndsey along the way.

Footloose argued in his half-coherent manner that the crevice was a shortcut. But Rob stuck to his original idea. With a grumble, Footloose squeaked to his Empts, who had a tendency to wander off whenever he didn't keep at them with a *chee-wee* cry every few seconds.

The lemon sun of Stardeep was far down toward the horizon when Footloose again called Rob's name. He was making erratic gestures.

Rob wiped sweat from his eyes. He was worn out from pushing across the up-and-down terrain of the sloping approaches to the mountains. He estimated that they had been on the march some three to four hours, and his sandals had offered next to no protection. His feet bled from half a dozen ugly gashes. To top it off, he was growing a little light-headed from lack of food.

"Not far now, Edison person," Footloose informed him with a wave. "Other side, there."

Rob willed himself to alertness. He was aware of the risk of shouting at Footloose across the intervening distance, so he tried making the traditional finger-to-lips gesture for silence, coupling it with gestures toward the ridge. Footloose seemed to understand.

"We go up and hide in the rocks at the top there, we see them," he said.

"Let me go first. You wait here."

Footloose ticktocked his head in a nonchalant way. His largest Empt started to scuttle away downhill. Footloose let out the *chee-wee* cry. Rob clapped his hands.

The sound reverberated among the rocks, too loudly. But Footloose got the idea. He grinned in a vacant way, sheepishly mimed the finger-to-lips.

Rob tried to keep his patience, returned the smile. Footloose squatted on his heels. He uttered his cry to the Empts again, but this time much more softly. The round creatures, including the runaway, gathered around his feet. He stroked each in turn.

Rob slipped between boulders, crept to the ridge. Here the shadows had lengthened. The constant breeze was turning cool. He found a shallow gully that seemed to offer fairly good footing as it wound to the crest.

As he stepped into the gully, his left foot slid against the edge of a sharp stone. He stifled a cry. Another gash opened, bleeding. He kept his mind on Lyndsey Ling and forgot the pain.

Near the top he dropped down flat on his stomach. He crawled the rest of the way. Slowly he lifted his head.

At least something was going right!

There, in a cuplike depression surrounded on three sides by boulders, stood the power station. It was nothing more than a large weatherproof plasto egg, perhaps eight feet on its long axis. Inside, he could see color-coded circuitry panels arranged like vertical folders on a shelf. The egg was mounted on a preformed concrete pedestal. And there were Lummus, Blecho, and—thank heaven!—Lyndsey.

The girl was between the station and the ridge, sprawled out on the ground with her hair a tangle in her eyes. Her one-piece garment that had looked so crisp this morning was now stained and torn. Lyndsey was on her side, an awkward position. Something that resembled the belt of

Barton Lummus' trousers was lashed round and round her wrists and ankles, pulling them tight together.

Lyndsey paid no attention to her captors. She stared with fixed expression at the natural entrance to the little depression. There, no boulders obstructed the view of the waste that shimmered in the late sun. From the girl's melancholy stare, Rob guessed that she must be incredibly weary and frightened.

Blecho and the bogus travel agent were quite busy. Two of the service doors in the transparent egg had been broken open. Several circuitry panels had been pulled out on extendable roller tracks. One group of panels at the egg's far end had already been fused into a shapeless mass. Now, at the end of the egg nearest Rob's hiding place, Blecho reached inside and slid a second panel out alongside another.

Lummus rattled his diagrams. "Not that one, you chemical cretin! The green-keyed one."

"Looks green to me." Blecho said, rapping his emerald knuckles against the yellow board.

"Just like the color of your hide, what?"

When Blecho nodded, Lummus sneered and reached past the android's shoulder. The fat man shoved the yellow board back inside on its track, pulled out the correct one.

"Someone should have issued a warranty when you were manufactured in that Draconian lab," he grumbled. "The shoddy workmanship is appalling. You've been seeing the wrong colors ever since we got here. Stand aside and let me finish it!"

Lummus' irritation hardly fazed the android. Blecho stood with folded arms while the fat man huffed and snorted and dragged forth two more boards of differing colors. He glanced quickly at his diagrams. Lummus' face was white with an accumulation of dust mixed with sweat. He began to fold the diagrams.

"Where's the cave map I gave you? I'll hang on to all the valuables."

From under his cloak the android produced another folded sheet. This, together with the diagrams, disappeared in Lummus' waistband.

"You fuse them," he ordered, lurching over to a stone and sitting down with a gargantuan puff.

Blecho drew out the laser beam. He turned it on and directed the thin ruby light at the four boards hanging out-

side the egg. The surfaces of the boards began to glisten
and spark.

Lummus picked up a pebble, played with it. "I'd like to
get my hands on the formula for the alloy those panels are
made from. I'd use it to build a sweet little ship so tough
that all the law chasers in the galaxy couldn't burn its
hull." He glanced at the darkening sky. It was streaked in
the northeast by the first gleamings of moonrise. A green
radiance touched the sawtooth peaks.

"As soon as those blasted boards melt, Blecho, the sky
barrier will open. How infernally much longer is it going to
take you?"

The android continued burning the panels. "Five or ten,
now."

"If Captain Ridirigo doesn't put the ship on the ground
within fifteen minutes after we knock out the barrier, I'll
have his hide. We're already behind schedule."

Emphasizing the cause, Lummus lobbed another pebble
toward Lyndsey. The pebble hit her shoulder from behind,
startling her. She let out a low, dismayed cry.

Rob scowled, fought his anger. Twists of smoke rose
from the extended panels now. The air reeked of ozone.
The aftercrackle of the intense red beam was continuous.
He had no more time to waste.

Rob started crawling backward down the gully. His sandal struck some loose stones. The rattling was loud in the
stillness.

He clutched the gully wall, didn't move. On the other
side of the ridge, Barton Lummus took instant notice.

"Blecho! Did you hear that noise?"

Evidently the android replied that he didn't. Rob
couldn't catch the answer above the faint aftercrackle of
the laser beam. But he distinctly heard Lummus, who
sounded relieved.

"Just one of those little Empt beggars, I suppose. My
nerves are in a state. I'm a sensitive person, Blecho. Not
being human, you fail to understand the effect of any dis-
ruption of my well-ordered plans. I didn't anticipate having
to hold that ridiculous girl hostage. Nor did I count on that
young master showing any spirit whatsoever. The youth
these days—its the same on all the planets—"

The rest of the grumping monologue was lost as Rob
continued his scramble back to the base of the ridge.

Footloose saw him coming. He rose. Rob pantomimed

his instructions. The third time through, Footloose seemed to understand.

Hoping the bearded man really did have the idea, Rob turned and began to climb. Near the top he slid into a gully, twisted his head around to look back.

Down below, Footloose had gathered the Empts. He was talking to them. Fortunately he kept his voice down.

The largest Empt, the one that had shown a tendency to wander, began to quiver suddenly. It emitted a quick series of cries. *Chee-wee, chee-wee.*

Rob slid up the ridgeline, peered over.

Blecho had nearly reduced the circuit panels to melted ruin. Barton Lummus was walking up and down. He halted when he heard the cry of the Empt.

"There *is* one of the beggars around here! One more for the bag, what? I'll go see."

Lummus started for the slope. His path would bring him up to the place where Rob was hiding. Rob's palms were slippery again. His heart raced.

Fortunately Footloose had done his job.

To the left, where the ridge sloped to the plain, the half dozen Empts were traveling with amazing speed. The largest Empt reached the natural entrance to the depression and shot through. The others followed.

Lummus gaped. "A veritable flock of the beggars! Fancy that!"

One of the little Empts raced toward the fat man's feet. Lummus blinked. Another Empt joined the first while two more converged on Blecho. And the android's pupilless eyes studied them. Rob watched tensely for a sign of reaction.

Round and round the android's shell-hard green ankles the Empts scurried. *Chee-wee!* Suddenly the ball tip of the laser beam dipped.

Blecho let the weapon drop at a careless angle. The ruby beam played over the plasto surface of the egg, crazing it instantly. The android's head lolled. The Empts had him!

Three Empts frolicked near Barton Lummus now. His chins shook as he chuckled. All at once his face went slack except for that moon grin.

Lummus sat down, legs spread, looking exactly like an oversized child at play.

One of the Empts hopped upon Lummus' left leg, regarded him with its faceted hollow eyes. Lummus giggled. With elaborate gentleness, he patted the Empt's armor.

"Amusing. Ah, yes. Amusing indeed."

Rob waited till he was sure both Lummus and Blecho were completely under the power of the Empts. The android paid no attention to the destruction his laser beam was causing to the surface of the egg. Lummus bobbed his melon head and crooned nonsense syllables at the three creatures near him. Rob visually gauged his course down the slope—a wide loop to the left, to stay out of the way of the Empts. He jumped up and plunged down into the depression on the run.

Blecho heard him first. The emerald head rotated toward him, but Blecho took no other action. Barton Lummus saw Rob speed by and continued to grin in a bemused way. His lenslike brown eyes had difficulty focusing.

Lyndsey was the only one who recognized him. She cried out his name as he dropped to his knees, struggled to unfasten the belt around her wrists and ankles.

"I thought I'd never see you or anyone again," Lyndsey said in a ragged voice.

"As soon as I get this off, we'll get out of here."

Lyndsey's blue eyes darted past his shoulder, fearful. "That awful man! He's *giggling*."

"Footloose rounded up the Empts for me."

"Footloose!"

"I came across him at the Phylex Station. I took a chance that the Empts would make Lummus and his green pal forgot who I was. Obviously I'm not a pleasant memory to that fat crook. Looks like the trick worked, too. Just a second more, Lyndsey—"

Rob's hands were slippery, and the belt had been securely knotted. He bit at the last knot with his teeth, loosening it. He broke a fingernail trying to wiggle his finger into the crack between the strands of the knot. At last he forced his finger through.

He tugged hard. The knot came loose. The belt dropped off.

Rob slipped his right hand around Lyndsey's shoulder. He stood up slowly, drawing her with him. All at once her knees gave out. He supported her for a second as she wobbled.

"Lean on me and walk," Rob whispered with a glance at

Lummus. The fat man was still crooning to the Empts in a wordless monotone.

Lyndsey's breathing was strident, uneven. She was a heavy weight against Rob's shoulder as they started up the ridge. With a loud crack the surface of the plasto egg gave way. Oblivious, Blecho continued to play the laser beam into the interior of the power station. Purple sparks crackled. Smoke fumed.

Half running, half walking, Rob and Lyndsey hurried up the slope, while the Empts kept Lummus and the android busy. All at once, though, Rob became conscious of a peculiar sound.

It came from the sky. A low, steady chuttering. The moon of Stardeep, huge as a small planet, was just looming up over the mountains. It shed a bilious green light that reflected on five specks approaching in the sky from the direction of the Phylex Station.

Rob shielded his eyes. The chuttering grew louder. Abruptly he recognized it. "Those are flyers! The Conpats, I'll bet." He wanted to cheer.

The five specks came on at remarkable speed. They dropped to skim the foothills, took on definition. They were teardrop shaped, with landing skids below. The sputter of thrusters became a roar as the flyers swept on toward the depression. They were the most welcome sight in the world.

An Empt let out a high-pitched *chee-wee*. Rob looked back. His stomach flipflopped.

The Empts were fleeing.

They extended and retracted pseudopods wildly as they scattered up into the rocks around the depression. The sound of the flyers had terrified them.

The last two Empts scampered out of sight. Blecho shook his head, switched off his laser beam. Barton Lummus staggered to his feet. His eyes were no longer bemused. From deep in his throat came a pebbly growl of rage.

"Blecho?" he howled, pointing. "Catch them, Blecho!"

Rob dragged Lyndsey toward the ridgetop. "Run for it!"

The android was remarkably fast now that he had returned to his senses. He sped up the slope past Lummus. The fat man reached out, grabbed the laser beam. Blecho ran on without breaking stride.

Lyndsey was stumbling again. Rob's feet were raw with pain. The dash up the slope had reopened some of the cuts that had clotted earlier. His left sandal was slippery with fresh blood. He heard Blecho churning the pumice close behind and pushed Lyndsey ahead of him to keep her out of the android's reach. Suddenly his foot twisted inside the bloody sandal. He slipped to one side.

He struggled to right himself, couldn't. He hit the pumice in a sprawl.

The android loomed against the darkening sky of Stardeep, emerald cheeks reflecting the green beams of the huge moon. Blecho's blank eyes shone as he groped for Rob's throat with both hands.

Rob picked up a chunk of pumice, tossed it with all his strength. The android ducked. The chunk sailed on down the slope and struck Lummus on the head.

The fat man let out a cry of rage, his melon head shaking, his small beard jiggling. He whipped the laser beam up to fire—

Blecho almost had Rob's neck. Somehow Rob got his footing, started away. Lyndsey cried a warning about the laser beam.

"Out of the way, Blecho!" cried Lummus. The android doubled at the waist.

This gave Lummus a clear target—Rob struggling up the slope.

Lummus aimed the laser beam. Rob jumped to one side just the instant Blecho stood up. He had a wicked piece of pumice clutched in one emerald hand.

The android hadn't heard his master. Blecho flung the rock as Lummus discharged the beam.

There was a blaze of red light, an aftercrackle, a horrible, rasping cry.

Rob's vision blurred as the pumice hit, a corner of it skating across his eye. All at once the left side of his face was warm and wet. The pumice-chunk had opened a wound at the corner of his eye.

Rob lurched toward a small boulder, tumbled against it. Everything revolved at dizzying speed. The roar of the flyer thrusters became a din. Rob shook his head from side to side. His left eye was totally useless.

A Conpat flyer was landing near the power station. Its ground-effect skids blew up clouds of dust. The whole scene crawled with weird shadows—or perhaps that was only in Rob's mind.

Men jumped out of the flyer. Lean men in black boots. Another flyer came down right behind.

There was another cry from along the slope to the left. Dimly Rob knew he had to respond to it.

He shoved himself away from the small rock with both hands. He staggered a few steps, hit his bloodied foot against something slippery-hard, glanced down. A sour choking constricted his throat.

Nothing remained of Blecho the android except a charred strip of cloak and two emerald feet with toes upturned to the moon. Somewhere down in a glassy mass of fused pumice, a blank gray eye seemed to glimmer—

Lyndsey screamed Rob's name.

Shambling, Rob moved toward the crest of the ridge. The girl was struggling with a misshapen, melon-headed thing made out of shadow. The immense moon of Stardeep was right behind them like a giant illuminated screen. The glare blinded him.

The shadow-thing—Lummus!—reached arms around Lyndsey's middle. The fat man lifted her bodily, carried her out of sight down the other side of the ridge.

Rob staggered on. In the depression, all the Conpat flyers had landed. Rob thought he heard Simon Ling's voice bawling orders. Spotbeams rose up through iris ports on the tops of the flyers, began to whirl spears of white light in circles.

The beams flicked across Rob's back as he fought toward the top of the slope. Each time a beam passed over him, it threw his silhouette ahead on the ground. The chaos of lights, shouting, his own pain, became a nightmare . . .

He was aware of cool wind on his bloody cheek. The top of the ridge. He was in the open, dwarfed by the gigantic green-tinged moon. Out in the darkness of the foothills, a little red eye blinked. Somehow Rob knew enough to fall to the side.

The laser beam gouged a trough where he had been. The aftercrackle died. The pumice bubbled and fused into a glasslike glob.

"Young master—the rest of you—" The strangled voice was far away. "I have the girl—and I have a map of the mountain caves—"

Men pounded up the slope behind Rob, thrust around him. He recognized Simon Ling's huge frame, his hooked nose. *Flick-flash* went the revolving beams from the flyers.

"Down!" Simon shouted, knocking two of his men aside as the red eye winked.

The blast missed. More men were spilling to the top.

"Here's the portabeam, Commander."

"Keep that thing off!" Simon snarled. "It just makes us better targets." His voice broke. "That—that lunatic's got Lyndsey."

Rob was on his hands and knees. He felt warm, drowsy, unable to think with coherence. *Flick-flash.* His shadow chased across the pumice in front of him. And before the beam swept on, he saw blood fall from the blinding wound beside his eye and spatter like a red flower on the ground. *Flick-flash.*

"Lummus?" Simon Ling shouted. "Don't hurt the girl!"

"Then don't you come after me!" came the faint, wind-blown voice. "I'm going for the caves. If you so much as set foot—"

The wind shattered the rest. A hand touched Rob's shoulder.

"The boy's hurt, Commander."

Simon Ling said something Rob didn't understand. His wrists were turning to jelly. He couldn't even prop himself up any longer.

Rob keeled over on his side, unconscious.

Fourteen

FOOTLOOSE AFRAID

"How long have I been out?" Rob wanted to know.

Simon Ling was stalking back and forth in front of him like a caged animal. There were pits of shadow beneath his eyes.

"About an hour," the Commander answered.

One of the flyer spotbeams had been adjusted downward to illuminate the area around the power station. There were at least fifteen Conpats present. Most carried sidearms. One approached holding a small plio-covered bar of some dark stuff.

"I broke this out of one of the field kits, Commander."

"Thanks, Gerrold. Want something to eat, Rob?"

"Yes!" Rob was a little startled at the intensity of his response.

He unwrapped the bar, bit into it. Synthetic. But its strong beef flavor made it taste magnificent.

As he chewed he discovered that his left cheek hardly hurt at all. He paused long enough to run a finger up past his left eye. Alongside it he felt a springy, slippery patch where skin should be.

Simon Ling didn't notice. He was staring out past the brilliant light to where the moon of Stardeep was just discernible as a greenish ball. The Conpat named Gerrold told Rob: "We dressed those cuts with aerosols from the medikits. That wound was the worst. What you feel on your cheek is an osmosis stitch. The plasto resin will grow the edges together and be absorbed through your pores in about three hours. Does it hurt much?"

Rob shook his head. His feet, particularly the left one,

were completely free of pain too. He wolfed more of the beef bar. Then:

"Commander?"

"Yes?"

"What about Lyndsey? I tried to stop Lummus—"

"I know you did," Simon said in a bleak voice. "I'm grateful. But I can't make a move in that direction till we get the poacher ship squared away."

"How do you know about that?"

"It got to be pretty obvious by the time we got here, Rob. There's always a ship. There has to be, to transport the Empts off Stardeep. We picked up the distress beacon back in Churchill this afternoon—"

"I triggered that in the flyer," Rob nodded.

"Right. The beacon set off coordinating signals from the nearest Phylex Station. We knew the source of the call immediately. I sent a crew to the yard for a flyer. They talked to the mech on duty. He reported that three other people had gone out with you this morning. I discovered one of them was Lyndsey. I checked our domidome. She was gone, all right. So I came out with my men. Just as we approached the Phylex antenna, we began to pick other signals up indicating power station malfunction. Those installations don't burn out of their own accord. The failsafes are too elaborate. So that meant one thing—poachers, with their ship waiting upstairs for the barrier to break. What about you?"

As quickly and clearly as he could, Rob described all the events after Barton Lummus stopped him outside the hostel that morning. Commander Ling listened without comment. He stood with his thumbs hooked on his black belt, his profile sharp against the glare of the spotbeam.

Rob described the trip overland to the power station. He told how he had used the Empts supplied by Footloose to lull Lummus and the android while he rescued Lyndsey.

"That was pretty fair thinking." Simon meant it as a compliment.

"Only it didn't work. Commander"—Rob strained to sit up, moving from the flyer skid where he had been leaning—"we've got to get her away from that man!"

"I know, Rob. It's"—a fraction's hesitation—"just as heavy on my mind as it is on yours. More."

Somewhere a communicator began to beep. A Conpat ran up.

"We just got word, Commander. They've located the poacher ship."

An almost icy smile etched Simon's wide mouth. "Is she secure?"

"She is, Commander. Boarded and secure, with all hands prisoner. She was right where we thought she'd be. *Moonlet Hopper* is her name. A registry cert from Johnson's Third. The captain—Ridirigo, or something like that—folded his flag immediately. No one was hurt."

Simon gave a sharp nod. "All right. Now let's worry about my daughter."

The Conpat who had provided the beef bar said, "We're breaking out search gear, sir."

"No!"

Rob was taken aback by Simon's intensity. Even the Commander himself was a little embarrassed. He continued with forced calm. "No, don't do that. I want to go in after her with a very small party. That's the only safe way. Too many men and Lummus will know he's being chased. We need surprise working for us, especially in the caves." Simon twisted around. "Where's the man with the beard?"

"Wandering around here somewhere," Gerrold answered.

"Get him."

Soon two of the Conpats returned with Footloose shambling between them. The Conpats already looked faintly glaze-eyed. They backed off to a safe distance and recovered their alertness.

Standing near Simon Ling, Rob felt a faint tingling playing at the front of his skull. He took a step to the rear, another. All at once he remembered his father, *Majestica,* the reasons he had come to Stardeep. But he didn't need the momentary memory lapse caused by Empting to erase those memories. The events of the day were doing a very effective job of frustrating his original plans. He felt a quick, sudden pang of defeat.

Simon was speaking.

"Footloose? Do you know who I am? Don't you remember me from Churchill?"

The man's blue-chip eyes glowed in the spotbeam. His chained Empt nestled against one leg, going *chee-wee* softly.

"Conpat Commander person, you," Footloose replied. Evidently the memory wasn't unpleasant.

"Please listen carefully. The man who took my daughter—"

Footloose shook his head. He smiled that strange, wistful smile to show he had forgotten. But Simon kept right on. ". . . still has her. In the caves, I think. I've been in some of the Stardeep caves many times, but not the ones in this area. Have you been in these caves?"

Footloose surprised everyone by fisting the hand to which the chain of his Empt was attached.

"Don't ask, you Commander person! Don't ask!"

"Footloose, my daughter's life depends on this. Do you know the caves?"

"Don't want to go in there!" Footloose exclaimed. "Won't go there, that place." And he spun, starting to run off.

Three wiry Conpats barred his path. Suddenly Footloose bent down. He pulled his Empt into the crook of his arm. He pressed his cheek against the creature, hiding his mouth against the little beast's armor while he made unintelligible sounds. The Conpat named Gerrold strode to Simon's side. His voice was low.

"He's terrified, Commander."

"Of something strong enough to counteract even Empt energy," Simon agreed.

"That would have to be pretty strong," Gerrold breathed.

"Footloose?" Simon began again. "What do you remember about the caves that makes you afraid to go there?"

The Empt let out a sharp *chee-wee* as Footloose hugged it fiercely. The bearded man was breathing in noisy gulps. Suddenly Rob noticed that there were tears in the corners of the young-old eyes.

"Don't make me, Commander person," Footloose whispered.

"I need a guide, Footloose."

"But—" The bearded man shook his head violently. "Can't. *Can't.*"

Astounded, Rob wondered what powerful memory or emotion could be tearing at the man's dazed mind with enough force to nullify the Empting process. Simon stepped one pace closer. He lowered his voice, spoke swiftly, convincingly.

He reminded Footloose almost the way Rob had done that he, the Commander, had helped Footloose recapture his runaway Empt in Churchill. "And who sent a flyer over the barrier every time you wanted to come into town for what you call your victuals? I did! Commander Ling! I wouldn't ask this of you, but a criminal called Lummus took my daughter as a hostage."

Footloose dragged a perspiring hand across his brow. "All cloudy, person. Something wrong. Did this once already."

"Yes," Simon emphasized, "you did. You tried your best, and so did the young man you helped. The two of you tried to get Lyndsey back. Through no fault of yours, Lummus got her again."

Footloose located Rob in the glare, pointed. "Edison person. He was the one." The man's bright-blue eyes still gleamed with unexplained tears.

"We have to make another try, Footloose. Another one, understand?"

Simon spoke with patience and quiet force. Rob knew that he must be torn with worry, but somehow he kept it almost completely hidden.

"I'm going into those caves myself, Footloose. But I really need an expert to show me the way. Have you been in the caves around here? Give me a straight-out answer."

Footloose clutched his Empt. "Commander person, please not—"

"Answer me!"

"The caves I know. Many times—too many times. But—don't want to go."

"Why not? Your Empt will keep you from being afraid."

"Not from everything," Footloose sobbed. "Not from—from—"

A dazed headshake. Then silence.

"What's in the caves that you fear, Footloose?"

The bearded man simply wouldn't answer. He hugged his squealing Empt and hid his face.

Gerrold and the other Conpats watched their Commander. Simon Ling chewed on his lower lip. He waited.

Finally, struggling against awful emotion, Footloose raised his head. His eyes were haunted. His voice was barely audible.

"Commander person, I—remember good things of you. I don't—want to go. But—for you I—I—"

He turned his back, shuddering. A moment later Rob and the others heard the whispered word. "Yes."

"Thank you," Simon sighed. "We'll move out right away. Gerrold? I want a homing device."

In another moment the Conpat brought one. Simon Ling clipped the small black box onto his belt. He adjusted the controls.

"Set up flyer four as the monitor. See if you're reading."

Another of the Conpats rushed away, climbed up inside a flyer. There was a burst of static, then a sustained warbling tone.

"O.K.," Simon called. "Keep tight on my signal so you can come into the caves right away if I program the distress tone. Now let's see. I'll need a sidearm, a tracker, a torch, some rations—"

While the Commander's men ran to fetch the supplies, Footloose was huddled against one of the flyers, still hugging his Empt to his chest. Rob walked over to Simon.

"I'd like to come along, Commander."

Simon smiled, without humor. "I would have been surprised if you hadn't asked, Rob. I think you've earned it. Just the three of us, then. You and I and our frightened guide." With unhappy eyes Simon studied the bearded man's trembling back. "I hope he can stay coherent long enough to help us find my girl."

Fifteen

INTO THE CAVES

In less than half an hour all the Conpat flyers but one took off. The green moon, an immense shadow-pocked ball in the sky, made the disappearing craft glitter and wink as they sped away over the waste toward Churchill.

Inside flyer four, Commander Ling was checking final details with the two Conpats who had stayed behind to monitor his homing device. Rob sat on the ground outside, gnawing another bar of synthetic beef. His mouth and eyelids felt gritty—the former because of his exposure to the constant wind, the latter because he was exhausted. He knew he wouldn't get a chance to sleep for many hours yet.

Boots rattled in the pumice. Rob ate the last of the bar, got up.

"All set, Commander?"

Simon didn't miss the signs of weariness. "Are you sure you want to come along, Rob?"

"Yes, sir. I have to go."

Simon gave one crisp nod, cupped hand to his mouth. "Footloose?"

The bearded wanderer shambled into the light circle cast by the spotbeam. His eyes were hidden beneath the brim of his battered hat. At least he's stopped crying, Rob thought. His Empt was docile, at the end of the alloy chain.

"I'll go first until we reach the caves," Simon advised them. "We'll follow the tracks with this." He waggled the plasto cylinder strapped to the inside of his right wrist.

The cylinder's pointed end emitted a faint beam of purplish light. Rob had difficulty seeing it clearly. "This is the tracker," Simon explained. "Unfortunately it's only good

107

for a few hours. Then a special sensor cell has to be replaced. We'll have to move as fast as we can. Come on, I'll show you."

The Commander started for the crest of the ridge. Rob followed. The Empt went, *Chee-wee*. Footloose responded with two similar sharp cries. At a safe distance, he started after the others.

They climbed the ridge and went down the other side to the bottom. There Simon stopped. A sizable boulder cast a thick shadow across the open area. Where the pumice glowed under the direct moonlight, Rob detected shallow indentations. The indentations led toward the shadow thrown by the rock.

Commander Ling adjusted dials on the wrist cylinder. "A tracker is sensitive to human tissue. What was Lummus wearing on his feet?"

"Boots, I think," Rob said.

Simon played the cylinder's feeble light into the rock's shadow. A pattern became visible, like a scattering of luminous purple dust.

"Then that footprint belongs to Lyndsey. It's too small for Lummus, anyway. Let's see—yes, I remember. She put on sandals this morning. You see, Rob, the tracker works because human dermal tissue constantly sloughs off in microscopic bits. The tracker's sensitive to the deposits even in total darkness."

He raised the beam. A foot or so ahead, where the land sloped upward again, another eerie purple cluster glowed. By a trick of his tired eyes, Rob imagined a great purple nebula whirling in space.

"Let's go," said Simon.

In silence they followed the glowing skin-prints for nearly ten minutes. Behind them Footloose scrambled along, chain clinking. The young-old man muttered to himself. Though his hysterical mood had passed, he obviously wasn't happy.

The three of them moved in and out of splashes of pale-green moonlight. Twice they lost the trail, had to double back to the last scatter of purple motes that seemed to float in the shadows before them. Each time they located the right way to go by finding the patch of purple dust they had missed earlier.

But each delay cost them time. Before Rob realized it,

the moon was setting. He mentioned this to Simon, who nodded.

"We'll have about two hours of total darkness before false dawn. That's when the tracker really becomes useful. I just hope the sensor cell lasts that long."

"Lummus could duck into the caves almost anywhere, couldn't he? I've seen what looked like two entrances already."

"Yes, he could. But he hasn't so far."

"He does have a map," Rob reminded the Commander.

"I'll wager it's an old copy of one prepared by the first geol team on Stardeep. Tourists get them in gray markets along with phony sales deeds for the mineral wealth just waiting to be picked up in the caverns. When the tourists reach one of the barriers, they discover they've been fleeced. Besides, there isn't any mineral wealth underground. Just vast networks of caves, big ones and small. Interconnecting, it's said, for thousands of miles under the surface."

"And that's where the Empts live?"

"Not quite. They spend most of their time in the open. The females go into the big rooms underground to lay their eggs and hatch their young. A female Empt will stay with her babies for about two weeks. Then she leaves them. About a week later the babies mature. It's a short life cycle. Empts live about four years. All during that time"— Simon's voice hardened—"they're prey for snakes like Lummus. We—oh-oh. Go left, Rob."

Their passage up through the foothills became increasingly difficult once the moon was down. They stumbled often, blundered into boulders, required a longer and longer time to locate a purplish patch and search out the next one. Either Rob's tiredness was catching up with him or the air was growing thinner. He had trouble breathing again.

At one point Footloose cried out from behind them: "High enough, Commander person. We turn back."

"No, Footloose," Simon said flatly.

"Bad things here. Too dark. Too many voices talk-talk in the dark."

Simon swung around. "You mean you heard something?"

"Little voices, person. I hear. *I* hear. Not you."

"What's he afraid of?" Rob whispered.

"Can't imagine," Simon returned. "The poor devil. The

way he's mumbling to himself, we may wind up going into the caves without any guide at all."

"Need to go back," came the sad, unsteady voice. "Go back."

After fifteen minutes of searching for the next telltale patch, the Conpat commander called a halt. They sat down to rest.

"We're losing time, not gaining it, crashing around this way. And the tracker's cell is almost done for. We'll go faster when it's light. Let's wait till false dawn.

"But Lummus might—" Rob began. He stopped, regretting that he had said even that much.

Simon adjusted the lens on the tracker. The purple beam looked feeble as it modulated to a pale blue, lighting the rocky nook into which they had stumbled. The Commander sank down with his back against a stone. Despite the coolness of the predawn air, sweat streaked his cheeks. His eyes were circled with shadows.

"I don't think he'll harm her," Simon said, though without a great deal of conviction. "I think he's bluffing us. Poachers are the low rung on the criminal ladder. Vicious only up to a point. Lummus won't want a homicide to his credit."

"He said as much when we landed at the Phylex Station," Rob remembered. But he wasn't convinced.

Simon glanced at him uneasily. The Commander was plainly worried about the wait. Still, it was the only practical thing to do.

Rob leaned his forehead against a cool stone. Footloose came clattering into the patch of bluish light. Rob watched him through half-closed lids. He kept up a constant mumbling monologue. His hat was pulled far down over his eyes, as if to avoid the glances of the others. Tiny beads of perspiration glistened in his straggly beard.

At long last, a thin sliver of lemon light appeared along the faraway horizon.

"Time." Simon heaved to his feet.

As their surroundings became visible, they had less trouble maneuvering between the jutting boulders. They had left the pumice behind and now clambered upward over smooth slatelike surfaces. Simon intensified the pace as the light increased.

For a man of his bulk, he was very quick, squeezing through narrow places and pulling himself up short, sheer vertical surfaces with apparent ease. Rob had to push to keep up. And the higher they climbed, the grimmer Simon looked.

Presently visual tracking of the runaway and his victim became easy—they spotted a scuff mark on a ledge, a patch of small stones disturbed. The purple peaks loomed above them in the light. As they inched along a ledge with the warming breeze gusting around their legs, Rob glanced down and sucked in his breath.

He hadn't realized how far they had come. The boulder-strewn slope fell away a good mile below them. The power station egg gleamed down there like a cracked toy.

Footloose was noisier than ever. He talked exclusively to himself. The tone was that of an utterly terrified man.

They passed the round entrance to a cave. Footloose moved out to the edge of the ledge, dragging his Empt with him. The Empt wanted to dart into the black hole. Footloose gave a savage tug on the chain. The Empt squealed.

Footloose's face had grown ugly. White teeth glared between peeled-back lips. Rob remembered seeing that ferocious expression in Churchill. It was a terrifying thing to behold.

Ahead, the ledge curved around the rock face. Simon was busy directing the all-but-invisible purple beam on the ledge itself. He missed the sudden flurry of color that Rob saw out past the turning of the ledge.

Straw-colored hair glowed in the risen sun. A melon head jiggled and bobbed. Brown lens eyes stared across an intervening declevity, then were gone.

"I saw them, Commander!"

Simon's head snapped up. "Where?"

Rob pointed. "That cave. I'm sure I saw Lyndsey and Lummus go in there."

"Did Lummus see you?"

"I think he did. I'm not sure."

"Hury it up, Footloose," Simon called. "This is where we need you. We're going in that cave across the ravine."

As if the Commander had set off a triggering device, Footloose reacted immediately. He planted his horn-hard bare feet on the ledge, wrapped the Empt chain around his wrist, began to shake his head from side to side. His blue-chip eyes beneath the brim of his hat were pricked with the sun's highlights.

"No, Commander person. Hear many little voices now. Can't go."

Tension exploded in Simon's voice. "I helped you, Footloose. Now you're going to help me."

"No, Commander person. No, no!"

"Keep your voice down!" Simon's whisper still managed to be a roar. "Look at me!"

Slowly the bearded man raised his head. Tears streaked his cheeks again.

"I wish not. Oh, I wish not."

"Tell me what frightens you, man!"

The wet blue eyes blinked open. "Much, person. The little voices and—much."

"But we're going."

At last, with a gulping sob, Footloose signified his acceptance of the Commander's orders. He bowed his head and started to shuffle forward along the ledge. Simon glanced at Rob—helpless, mystified, not a little angry. He made a sharp, sudden sign to resume the march.

It took them twenty minutes to negotiate the shallow ravine separating this ledge from the one on to which the cave opened. They went down hand over hand, climbed back up the same laborious way. Simon pulled Rob up with one powerful hand. When he clenched his mouth against the Empt power and leaned down to offer the same assistance to Footloose, the bearded man waved him away angrily. The Empt rode on Footloose's shoulders as its master climbed.

At last Footloose was beside them. Simon unsnapped the holster of the sidearm he had put on at the power station—a laser beam, Rob saw. With a last glance at the lemon sun hanging over the waste, he ducked into the cave mouth and flattened against the wall. Rob was next. Footloose came last, making an inordinate amount of noise. The Empt's faceted eyes looked like molten coins in the gloom.

Here the air was sweet, cool and damp. Ahead, Rob saw nothing but a faintly moist rocky floor slanting downward to complete darkness.

Footloose started muttering again. Simon glared. It did no good. He drew the laser beam cautiously up in front of his chest. His head bobbed. He moved out. Rob followed.

They moved downward for about a dozen feet. The damp darkness closed in. Footing was uncertain. Simultaneously, the rattle of a rock echoed far ahead, and Simon hissed a warning. A red eye blinked.

The red beam carved a thin, smoking channel from the cave wall directly above Rob's head. The ozone smell and the aftercrackle were intensified by the confined space. Footloose yelped. Simon dove on his face and so did Rob.

The laser beam spurted again. It touched the Empt skittering on the end of his chain. There was an awful squeal, a puff, a reek like smoldering leather—

The end of the chain swung free. The last link was sheared in half. The link fell off. It dropped into the steaming puddle that had been the little Empt.

"Told you, person!" Footloose howled. His hat had gotten knocked off. His blue eyes were wild.

He blinked several times, shook his head violently. He glanced down at the puddle. Grief made him shudder.

"Didn't I tell you, Commander?" Footloose boomed. His voice was unexpectedly free of all slurring. "I told you we shouldn't go on, and we won't. You won't force me this time!"

Rob thought he heard noise far down the tunnel, scrambled up, turned that way. He heard Footloose move, whipped his head around as Simon rolled onto his back to defend himself.

Footloose held a rock in one hand. He ducked in, churned his arm in a big arc. The rock struck Simon's left jawbone.

Simon shuddered, made a choking sound. His head fell back. His mouth dropped open. His eyes were glazed.

Footloose turned to Rob. He advanced in a tense half crouch. The blue chips of his eyes burned.

"You won't force me into the caves either," he said.

Rock raised, Footloose sprang.

Sixteen

THE METAL ROOMS

Rob leaped back. His sandal slipped on the moist floor. He caromed against the wall, ducked his head as Footloose brought his arm down.

The blow missed Rob's ear by inches. The rock scraped a gouge in the tunnel wall.

The light was uncertain. Only a feeble lemon glow penetrated this far into the tunnel. Maneuvering was difficult.

Rob darted under Footloose's arm. Simon was struggling to sit up, knuckling his eyes. All at once, as Footloose turned and shambled after Rob, the Conpat Commander grasped the situation. He came to life instantly, rolled onto his stomach, shot out his hands.

Simon caught Footloose in mid-stride, just as he swung the rock again. Rob bent backward from the waist. His head hit the other wall of the cave. Simon's hard pull on the bearded man's ankle was enough to shorten the range of the swing. The rock whizzed by Rob's forehead.

On his knees, Simon grappled his arms around Footloose's legs. "Help me get the rock!" he yelled.

In two strides Rob had his fingers on Footloose's wrist. He levered it back and forth. Footloose spat and snarled and swiped at Rob's head with his fisted free hand. One blow connected with Rob's neck. He gasped in pain.

Footloose hit him in the temple. But Rob refused to give up his hold. With a groan, Footloose opened his hand. The rock dropped.

Instantly Simon let go. He leaped to his feet, punched Footloose in the midsection.

The bearded man doubled at the waist. As Footloose

started to collapse, the Commander jabbed his index finger into the tangled hair directly behind the man's grimy ear.

Footloose sighed like a punctured weather balloon. He slid out on his back, eyes closed.

"There's blood on your jaw," Rob panted. His chest hurt from exertion.

"Probably looks worse than it is." Simon wiped his arm over the superficial wound. He rubbed his forearm dry on his black blouse and gazed down at Footloose unhappily. "I hated to maul him that way. No choice, though. He was really after us."

"The death of his Empt must have done it."

A quick nod of agreement. "Did you notice something odd just before he hit me?"

"What?"

"All at once his speech was coherent. More so than I've ever heard it."

"That's right," Rob remembered. "He yelled a couple of sentences that sounded as if they came from an entirely different person.

"Curious." Bleak-faced, Simon shrugged. He knelt down, examined Footloose quickly. "He isn't badly hurt. That nerve chop should keep him sleeping for about half an hour. We'll leave him here."

"Can we go on without a guide?"

"No guide at all is better than one who keeps attacking us. Besides——" Simon rose. His face stood out briefly in the wan light from the cave mouth. He looked savage. "I want to find Lyndsey."

Thinking of Lummus somewhere ahead, Rob shivered. But he said nothing as he fell in behind the Commander.

Before they had taken more than two dozen steps along the sloping rock floor, Simon put away his tracker. Its sensor cell was dead. He unhooked his tiny torch from his belt. He switched it on. The beam was thin, intense. Simon modulated the controls so that the beam diffused, becoming much dimmer at the same time. With its aid they could see more of the way ahead, but less clearly. They kept moving.

They made a turning. Rob glanced back. No light whatever showed behind them.

As they crept along, they stumbled over occasional piles of loose rock. Rob wondered where they came from. Every ten paces or so, Simon stopped to listen for Lummus. The air became sweeter and damper. Unpleasantly so. Rob's skin felt as if it were covered by a thin coating of grease.

The tunnel angled downward more steeply. They made several more sharp turnings. They had been moving for only about ten minutes, but it seemed far, far longer.

All at once Simon growled, "Hold up. There's something ahead."

Rob edged up closer. Simon ran the beam over what appeared to be an obstruction completely blocking their way. He blinked.

His eyes weren't deceiving him, nor was the feeble light. The barrier did have a matte gray appearance, except where it was stained with patches of flaky reddish-brown material. The weak beam picked out an oddly familiar oval outline in the center of the obstruction.

The Commander advanced cautiously. He rapped his knuckles on the barrier. It rang like a bell.

"A metal wall *underground?*" Simon whispered.

"With a doorway in it, too," Rob exclaimed, pointing to the oval.

He reached out, scraped his fingertips across the faintly convex barrier. His hand came away with the flaky red-brown material caked under the nails.

"And rust. Rust all over it."

"What the devil could it be?" Simon wondered. "Some kind of research facility buried down here?"

"Wouldn't the Conpats know about something like that?"

"Of course they would, unless it's been here for more than a hundred years. But that can't be. The metal shows too few signs of corrosion. Get back against the wall in case Lummus is close by. I'm going to see what's on the other side of that opening."

Rob obeyed orders. The moment his shoulders touched the tunnel wall, a portion of it gave way. He leaped across the tunnel as a mound of stones crashed at his feet.

Gradually the clatter died away. The last chunk dropped from the wall, hit the side of the pile, rattled to the bottom.

Frowning, Simon shone the beam across the section from which the rock had crumbled.

"Fragile stuff. We'd better be careful or we'll start a real cave-in."

Rob recalled the other piles of rock through which they had walked. Simon turned the torch toward the rusty surface. He dilated the torch aperture. The beam shot through the oval opening. If it was a doorway, the door had long since fallen off. The beam revealed rusty walls forming a narrow metal corridor.

A low whistle came out between Simon Ling's teeth. "This has to be some kind of underground station. Come on."

The Commander lifted one black boot over the bottom of the oval, then the other. Rob came right behind.

Once past the barrier, Rob reached up to discover a metal ceiling. Simon reduced the intensity of the light. They crept forward ten or twelve steps.

"Another doorway," Simon whispered. "I see something—" Out went the torch.

Gingerly, Rob followed Simon across the sill of the next doorway. Beyond the sill, which was flush with the floor, he could detect weld nodes through the thin soles of his sandals. All at once the entire feel of the surroundings changed.

His fingers bumped a railing on the left. Another on the right. Without being able to see a single detail of this new place in which they found themselves, Rob knew they had left confining walls behind, were on a walkway or railed platform in a much larger chamber. There was more movement of the damp, sweet air against his cheeks, plus an eerie sense of vast space all around.

"Rob!" the Commander whispered. "Look down below."

Far down to the left, a flabby figure recognizable as Barton Lummus crouched over a slumped body with straw-colored hair.

Lummus' clothing was torn. The backwash of the tiny torch he carried in his left hand illuminated a shining swathe of grease on his cheek. The light sketched in something else too—a corner of a massive piece of machinery.

The machine resembled a giant vertical wheel with vanes on its steel spokes. A curving shield ran all around its rim. Lyndsey—the crumpled shape—lay against the dusty base of this incredible and unknown machine.

"Let me reconnoiter," Simon whispered. "You wait here." Then the Commander was gone.

A faint creak of the walkway—Rob was certain they were suspended high above the floor of the huge chamber—was the only tiny sound that marked his leaving. Rob clutched the rail, stared downward. He was fairly sure that he couldn't be seen.

Besides, Lummus was occupied. He rolled up one of Lyndsey's eyelids, swore loudly. Rob's stomach tightened up.

Had Lyndsey simply fainted from fright and exhaustion? Or was it something much worse? He couldn't tell.

The obese man stood up, jammed one fist against a hip, stared in disgust at his hostage. Nervously he raked his fingers through his sleek brown hair. Rob saw no more—a touch on his elbow startled him, swung him toward Simon, who had come back silently.

With his mouth against Rob's ear, Simon whispered his discovery and what he intended to do about it. Rob nodded several times to indicate he understood. Simon faded into the dark again. Rob crept forward, inching his hands on the rail till he came to a vertical support with nothing beyond. He faced about, dropped his foot down to the first rung of the ladder Simon had found.

Holding his breath, he started the downward climb. Somewhere farther on in the blackness, Simon should be moving down a second similar ladder.

A rung beneath Rob's left sandal squeaked, then sheared in half.

Rob's body dropped. His right foot hit the next rung, slowed his fall. He gripped the ladder uprights with all the strength left in his hands. His arm muscles throbbed.

When he realized that he had caught himself, the shock flooded in on him. What about the noise? Surely Lummus must have heard the creak of the fatigued metal giving way—

A low, steady *smack-splat* drifted up to him. He screwed his head around.

In the tiny patch of light cast by the torch that he had put down on the machine base, Barton Lummus crouched beside Lyndsey. He was slapping her cheeks.

"Come, come, young mistress. Enough of this cheap dissembling. We must hurry on." Lummus' voice had an odd, echoing quality, which confirmed Rob's belief that this chamber was of great size. The poacher grew more angry when his hostage failed to respond with more than a groan. *Smack-splat.*

"I won't tolerate this sort of playacting, young mistress. Wake up, you wicked minx!"

Using the sound of Lummus' voice as his cover, Rob rushed on down to the floor of the chamber. His sandals settled on metal, disturbed dust that clouded up around his knees. The dust rose higher, made him want to cough. He clapped a hand over his nose and mouth.

The spasm passed. He waited. Other huge vaned wheel machines were arranged in a long row between where he stood and where Barton Lummus squatted. Lummus had gotten no results with his slapping. He was rocking back on his haunches and scratching his scraggly chin beard as if undecided on what to do next.

Rob peered along the aisle that ran beside the immense machines. He gauged his route of attack—

Out in the dark, there was a piercing whistle. Simon's signal!

Lummus grunted. "Uhhh?" His head swiveled. Rob launched himself into a dead run.

The poacher swung toward the pounding of Simon's boots. He jerked the laser beam from his waistband, fired. Out past the glow of Lummus' torch, Simon appeared briefly. He seemed to hurl away into the darkness as the thin red tracery ate through air where he had been. In the extreme distance the intensified light met a barrier. The aftercrackle blended with a burst of sparks from disintegrating metal.

"Take him from behind!" Simon bawled to Rob, his boots thudding again.

Rob made as much noise as possible. The clang-bang of people coming at him from both sides had the desired effect. Lummus didn't fire again. Instead, he darted out of sight, to his right—Rob's left.

Rob kept running. He kicked his way through a small mound of white, stick-like things that rattled and gave off dust. He and Simon reached Lyndsey at just about the same moment. From the cross-aisle into which Lummus had darted came a yipping cry. It dwindled suddenly. There was a faint, ugly crunching.

Then complete silence.

The Commander and Rob exchanged baffled glances. Rob snatched up the torch Lummus had left. He shone it down the cross-aisle. "There, Commander! The flooring's rotted through."

"And Lummus didn't see the hole. He fell right into it."

Simon ran to the edge of the sizable opening, snapped on his own torch. He held his laser beam ready in his other hand.

When there was no deadly discharge from below, not even the faintest murmur of sound, Simon craned his head out over the opening. He played the torch back and forth.

"Looks like sand down there. No more than fifteen or sixteen feet. I'm going after him, Rob."

Simon jumped feet first.

In a second there was another crunch, followed by another, heavier and more muffled. Rob thought he heard Simon let out a dismayed cry. He edged up to the hole on hands and knees.

"Commander?"

"Here."

Simon appeared with his torch. He held something black and crumbled in his open palm.

"I smashed the homing box, blast it. Now the flyer outside isn't receiving any signal. And the tracker's useless too."

A thrill of fear coursed through Rob. They were lost in these caverns now. Lost.

"This ground is sandy," Simon called. "Seems to be the floor of another cave. Lummus is already gone. I think I see some marks showing that he crawled away."

"What kind of place is this?"

"I don't know," Simon cracked back. "But first things first. See about Lyndsey."

Rob hurried back to the base of the machine. He bent over the girl. He repeated her name and rubbed her wrists. It was a hackneyed technique he had seen in a dozen dipix. But he didn't know what else to do short of imitating Lummus and slapping her cheeks.

Lyndsey's eyelids looked pale and thin as fine plasto. He shook her shoulders, called her name several times more.

The girl's eyes opened, horror-filled until she recognized him. "Rob. Oh, Rob."

She clasped her arms around his neck and held tight. His shoulder grew damp. She was crying.

She hugged and hugged him. At last, gulping for air, she leaned back. "Is Dad with you?"

"He's—uh—down below," Rob said for want of a better term. "Can you walk?"

With his assistance, she could. They went to the edge of the hole in the floor.

"Here she is, Commander," Rob called.

Simon Ling appeared again. "Lyndsey! Lord, girl, I'm

glad you're in one piece. You two come down here. You'll have to jump. I'll keep my light on you. Can you make it, Lyndsey?"

She nodded yes. There was something close to a wan smile on her lips now. The Commander added, "Get Lummus' torch for more light, Rob."

Rob ran back to the base of the wheel-and-vane machine. He snatched up the torch, swung around. The beam swung too, sweeping across the dust-sheathed base of the machine adjoining. Suddenly Rob skidded to a stop. He turned the torch back to what he thought he had seen.

Almost obliterated by the dust. But there it was. He swallowed hard.

He walked to the machine base.

Reached out with a shaking hand.

Scrubbed the dust away with his palm.

Stared uncomprehending at the small metal plate.

The stamped-in letters were squarish, utilitarian, for identification purposes only. The letters spelled out: FTLS *Majestica*.

Seventeen

REVELATION

Rob couldn't believe what he saw. His hand kept shaking, and the beam of the torch wavered across the recessed letters.

From where she was standing by the gap in the metal floor—or was it a deck?—Lyndsey called to ask whether he was all right. He said yes. He wiped his wrist across his eyes, clutched the torch tighter in his other hand, turned toward the aisle down which he had come running at Lummus.

Drifting behind him, the Commander's voice: "Rob?"

"In a moment, sir. Just let me look at something."

He shone the torch on the base of the next wheel-and-vane machine. The beam skittered across dust-coated metal. He didn't see a nameplate.

Perhaps it had been an illusion brought on by hunger, physical weariness, the tension of the chase through the caves. There was no plate on this—

Yes, there was. He had missed it on his first pass of the light. This machine, too, whatever its purpose, was marked: FTLS *Majestica*.

He was unsteady on his feet as he returned to Lyndsey. She noticed.

"Rob, you look sick."

He stared down between his sandals. He was right at the edge of the opening. He noticed something he had overlooked before. There were four separate layers of plating between the one on which he stood and the one in which the bottom of the opening had been torn.

The two inner layers were a ceramic material. The indi-

122

vidual layers had air spaces between and were braced apart by alloy beams. One such beam had been sheared when the hole was punched through all the layers. The beam's end projected about six inches into the opening, knife-like. From top to bottom layer, the plating easily measured two feet thick.

Simon wigwagged his torch from below. "What's holding you, Rob?"

The impatient voice jarred him to his senses. He took Lyndsey's elbow, guided her to the edge of the hole. He said in a hoarse voice, "Try to relax when you jump. And stay to this side. Watch that beam sticking out." He shone the torch on it.

Lyndsey gave him a bewildered, almost frightened look. Her straw-colored hair hung in disarray. She was grimy, tired, miserable—and, plainly, her condition wasn't helped any by Rob staring back at one of the immense vaned machines as though mesmerized. She pushed a lock of hair away from her left cheek. She edged to the rim of the hole. Below, a foreshortened figure with hand over his eyes and torch upraised, Simon waited.

"All right, Dad," Lyndsey called, and jumped.

The Commander darted aside. Lyndsey hit and rolled. Simon bent over her, helped her up, and drew her out of range as Rob followed.

Air swept his cheeks. Its cool, overwhelming sweetness turned his stomach, made him violently dizzy during the seconds of the fall. At the last instant he remembered to unstiffen his knees.

He hit left foot first, buckled over sideways with a sharp exhalation of breath. He flopped on his side, then scrambled up, more than a little dazed. He aimed the torch overhead. He followed its beam with his eyes, afraid of what he would see.

The Commander rushed to his side, said something Rob didn't catch.

Above, the torch picked out a huge expanse of pocked, heat-streaked gray metal. Rob moved the beam to the right, adjusted it for maximum definition. The convex surface ran on and on, well out of range of even the strongest torch setting. The same thing held true when he pointed the beam to the left. The metal stretched above him like a giant ceiling. Exactly where it ended at either side of what must be another oversized cave, he couldn't tell.

"Strangest arrangement of underground rooms I ever saw," Simon commented. "I'd almost swear it looks like—"

"The hull of a ship." Rob's voice was dull. "I think it is."

"A ship?" Lyndsey said. "Down here? That's impossible."

Rob swung around sharply, "Do you know what I found on the machines up there? Nameplates. Unless I've gone crazy—and maybe I have—that's my father's ship."

That stunned Simon Ling to silence. At last he managed to say, "An FTLS underground? How—"

"I don't know how!" Rob interrupted. "But those nameplates say *Majestica!*"

Neither father nor daughter could reply. Simon's eyes were somber, thoughtful. Rob got control of himself, apologized lamely for the outburst. Simon's voice showed the effort he was putting into remaining calm. "All right. Granted that it is a ship, let's see how large it is. Put your torch beam up above with mine, Rob."

Simon's beam angled high, struck the pocked metal. Rob focused his torch on top of Simon's. The three walked left from the overhead hole, following the long axis of the convex surface.

The sand underfoot oozed cool and damp over Rob's sandals. A gash at the base of his big toe was bleeding again. He paid no attention. Lyndsey spoke in a hushed voice.

"The more you look at it, the more it does look like a hull. Half of a hull, anyway."

"Streaked by re-entry friction," Simon added. "Pocked by micrometeorites."

Rob shot his beam ahead. "There's the end of the cave."

They stared, stunned. Like an immense half-round bar of metal, the hull seemed to have been jammed by force into the damp and glistening wall of rock above. They played their torches higher. It was too far to see clearly. The vertical rock face and the impacted metal blended together into meaningless dark.

Rob's stomach ached. *Majestica* here? Somehow rammed below the surface of Stardeep? That meant there must be two thousand corpses, or the remains thereof, in the various parts of the vessel . . .

All at once he remembered running toward Lyndsey in the chamber of the machines, kicking his way through a pile of white, sticklike things that pulverized into dust. His skin crawled.

Were those the bones of two thousand dead?

Questions flooded his mind. Out in the dark, someone screamed.

A rock whizzed by, struck Simon's shoulder, glanced off. "Torches out!" Simon bawled, extinguishing his. "Get down!"

Rob blacked out his beam, dropped to hands and knees as the wild, senseless yelling started again.

Rob slid out prone. He heard Lyndsey breathing close by. Her father was just beyond. Another rock landed with a chunk in the sand. More rocks showered on them. One hit the back of Rob's calf.

The maniacal yells continued. They seemed to come from a different direction each time. But maybe the strange acoustics of this vast underground room were playing tricks.

More rocks clattered around them.

"I'd get the laser beam on him if I could tell where he was," Simon growled.

"He keeps moving," Rob called back.

Another burst of yelling. It was the bay of a sick or wounded animal, a vibrating cry of pain and rage.

"Is it that man—" Lyndsey began.

"Lummus? It must be," Simon answered. "He may have damaged his laser beam when he fell. They're usually pretty sturdy, but—"

Abruptly the fusilade of rocks stopped. The last screech died away, echoing in the damp air.

They lay unmoving for several minutes. Rob listened hard, but detected no sound of movement. The sandy floor of the cave tended to deaden it, he suspected.

At last Simon suggested that it might be safe to get up. They did. Lyndsey lurched against Rob, apologized. Rob's stomach growled. He felt filthy. His gashed foot hurt badly. And on top of everything, there was the terror of being buried down here with Lightcommander Edison's ship and its cargo of dead men, while in the blackness, somewhere a deranged poacher stalked them—

Or was it, Rob wondered with a shock, merely the onslaught, at last, of mental breakdown?

He couldn't believe that. Everything felt real enough, including the pain.

But Commander Ling's homing device was smashed. His tracker was useless. They were cut off from help. *Why had he ever left Dellkart IV?*

In a moment the attack of near-hysteria passed, and Rob was himself again. Weary, baffled, frightened, but himself. He heard Simon's voice.

"Let's try to corner Lummus. If he doesn't have his laser beam, we can do it without too much risk. There are three of us, one of him. I'll turn on the torch. We'll spread out in a line abreast. Get between Rob and me, Lyndsey. Rob, get your torch going."

Simon's light winked on. Rob followed suit. Lyndsey moved into position, casting a long, flickering shadow across the sand.

"Now, let's walk to the far side of the cave," Simon told them. "Scuff your feet so we can see where we've been. That way, we can cover a new stretch of ground on the way back. Sooner or later we should pick up Lummus' tracks."

They moved ahead with slow, shuffling steps. They worked their way across the cave on a line roughly parallel to the gray bulk of the FTLS hull above them.

They passed beneath the ragged hole, kept going. The widened beams of the torches created a feeble swathe of light ahead. Lyndsey was the first to spot the crumpled shape that swam into Rob's beam.

Simon and Rob charged toward it. The Commander was faster. He was on his knees turning the fallen man over while Rob was still half a dozen steps away.

Lyndsey stopped, said, "Oh, Lord," softly. She turned her back and started to cry.

Simon played his torch over the misshapen mound of flesh. The details were all too recognizable.

Shabby, spotted blouse. An oversized belly. A melon head with the sleek hair out of place. The head was oddly bent to one side. The eyelids were shut. The butt of Barton Lummus' laser beam rested in the palm of his dead hand.

Shaking his head, Simon stood up. Slowly he began to shine his torch around the area.

Rob noticed a peculiar troughlike pattern in the sand. He added his light to the Commander's. They followed the trough back to a position just a little to one side of an imaginary line coming straight down from the hole in the hull.

"He must have broken his neck when he fell." The torch in the Commander's hand ranged back along the trough. "He dragged himself as far as he could before he died."

Lyndsey buried her head against her father's chest. Simon slipped his free hand around her waist. Even Rob was moved by the awful death. In a strange, weary way, Rob felt sorry for the man.

Rob's fatigued mind belatedly registered something else. "If Lummus has been dead all this time, who attacked us?"

Simon was grim. "There's only one other person it could be. Someone who knows the caves—"

"Footloose!"

"That must be it."

"Did you bring Footloose with you in here?" Lyndsey exclaimed.

The Commander said yes, described the bearded man's abnormal behavior—his protests about entering the caves, his consuming fear of something or someone underground, how he'd gone completely berserk when Lummus lasered his Empt.

"And another strange thing," Simon concluded. "Just moments after the Empt died, Footloose began talking differently."

"More coherently," Rob agreed.

"As though he'd been living for years with his mind" —Simon groped for a word, made an emphatic gesture— "like mush, because he was surrounded by Empts, and kept at least one close by at all times. The Empts helped him forget something terrible. It was so terrible that, before he attacked, he was remembering it in spite of the Empt. We knocked him out and left him. But he could have wakened in the meantime and come down here to—"

"*I hear you.*"

The three froze as the voice hissed from the darkness behind them.

"I hear you all talking about me!" A rock came sailing at them.

Rob bowled Simon out of the way. The rock missed. Another flashed at them, a third.

Simon dropped his torch, charged into the darkness. Rob followed. Simon launched into a dive. Before Rob reached him, the Commander had caught the bearded man and knocked him flat.

Simon kneeled on Footloose's chest, fist drawn back, face furious. Footloose writhed.

"Stop it, Footloose. I said stop it, or I'll break you apart!"

The threat was understood. Footloose relaxed. Simon jumped up, drew his laser beam, used his free hand to search Footloose for weapons. Then he stepped back.

"What's wrong with you, Footloose? Why the devil do you want to attack us?"

Never on a human face had Rob seen such horror. Footloose whispered, "You shouldn't have made me come back down here. Shouldn't of." Blue-chip eyes glared in the light of the torch Rob had picked up. "It all came back. I knew it would, I knew it! I couldn't help remembering even with the little"—a struggle to recall a lost word—"critter." Suddenly Footloose was crying.

Fat tears rolled down his weathered cheeks and sparkled in his long beard. "The critter got shot. You caused it, you." His tearful glance indicted both Rob and the Commander. "You killed my critter, you. *You made me remember!*"

"Remember what?"

"That." Footloose pointed at the looming hull. "My name."

Simon was puzzled. "Your name is Footloose."

Eyes like blue flames, Footloose breathed, "You made me remember the real one. Mossrose."

The torch fell out of Rob's fingers, its beam flashing crazily.

"Mossrose?" Rob repeated.

Footloose sobbed. "Yes."

"Lightadjutant Thomas Mossrose?"

"Yes. Yes! *Yes!*"

Eighteen

DEATH OF A LIGHTSHIP

The reverberations of the awful cry died slowly. Footloose swiped at his eyes in that vague way Rob had seen before. He took three breaths, each a little steadier than the one before.

Lyndsey stood tense beside her father, alternately watching him and Rob. There was too much confusion in Rob's mind, too much shock, for him to organize a single coherent sentence. Footloose turned away.

The Commander's voice was low and hoarse. "Stand still."

"You haven't—" Footloose gulped. "You haven't got a right—"

"Yes, we have. This boy's father commanded that ship up there."

It took Footloose a while to digest the information. But instead of surprise, his face registered a curious bitterness. He stared at Rob, and for a moment his blue-chip eyes were bright with maniacal rage. Then he returned his gaze to the Commander.

Quite unnoticed, Simon had passed his torch to his daughter. Now he held his laser beam in his right hand. The ball-tipped muzzle pointed to the ground. But its significance, its threat, temporarily banished the antagonism from the bearded man's eyes.

"Edison?" Footloose said. An unsteady nod. "Rob Edison. Yes. I—" Again the leathery face wrenched. "I don't want to remember."

"You have to," Simon cracked out. "This boy came halfway across the galaxy to find out who destroyed the ship."

129

The bearded man fell into a steady monotone as he repeated, "Edison. Edison. You caught my critter in Churchill, Edison. I think I heard your name there."

"I mentioned it," Simon replied. "At the dome. I told you who had saved your Empt and you got excited. I thought—"

"That I was crazy? Crazy Footloose, that's what I'm called. I know it. Well, the crazy man is the man who lets himself remember"—a glance at the looming hull—"that."

"Even at the dome, the past was fighting through the Empt barrier, wasn't it?" Simon asked.

Footloose wiped his lips. "I think so."

At last Rob was able to speak. "You were my father's second."

But he didn't actually believe it yet. How could this be the same Thomas Mossrose his father's diary had characterized as warm, friendly, bright? There was terrible pain in the man's blue-chip eyes, and hatred of every memory Rob represented.

Footloose didn't reply to the question. He merely glowered.

Simon glanced at Rob, squeezed his eyes shut for the barest part of a second. Rob caught the meaning. A bluff.

Footloose was too slow to catch the glance. He shifted his hardened feet in the damp sand, picked at his raveled sleeve in a way that reminded Rob of Barton Lummus.

Simon called Lightadjutant Mossrose by his more familiar name, speaking harshly again.

"Answer his questions, Footloose."

"I don't have to do—"

A raising of the laser beam. This was the bluff. Footloose cringed.

Simon pointed the weapon at Footloose's belly. "Answer."

Silence. Footloose looked through Rob into a past where horror stirred. Slowly he spoke. "From the first day I can remember, watching the interstellars launch from Albemarle, I wanted the service, you see. I studied for the Placements and came in just one below the minimum percentile. Just one. My uncle—I don't remember his name. Ephraim, Efrem—he was high up in service administration."

Rob started to speak. Over Footloose's shoulder Simon nodded sharply, a negative. Rob's stomach hurt. He kept quiet as Footloose went on in that clear, low voice. "You can't know how much I wanted the service. None of you can. The times were right. The first FTLS were going out over bigger distances than"—he faltered, passed his browned fingers over his eyes—"immense distances. The constellations. The nebulae. My uncle used his rank. The test tapes were partially wiped. I was accepted for training. My first command—" A supple movement of his fingers, up in the direction of the ship. "Lightcommander Edison. Duncan, he said. Call me Duncan. There I was, green. Frightened. Wanting to do the best—" Again an abrupt change in mood. Footloose glared. "Don't make me tell this."

Rob swallowed. "You have to. My father died with *Majestica*."

"Not immediately, not right—"

"But he's dead. And C.D.E. has been carried on his record ever since." There was fury creeping into Rob's voice now, controlled but still real.

It took Footloose a moment to interpret Rob's statement. "C.D.—is that error?"

"Command decision error."

Lyndsey watched Rob's grimy, haunted face. She stepped closer to her father, wrapped her fingers around his arm as a bleakness spread on Rob's features, making him look implacable and very old. He felt that way.

"Your father knew—" The beaded young-old man began.

"That you were inept." *Pay them back,* Rob thought. *Pay them all back without mercy.* "He knew there was something wrong with you, Mossrose."

"Are you certain about that?" Simon asked.

"It's in my father's diary. He said his Lightadjutant didn't know astromathematics and time theory and should have been on report." Rob's voice grew more and more caustic. "But he didn't put him on report. He thought he should, but he didn't. He decided to help him. Take a chance. Give him more responsibility." A cruel, giddy excitement filled Rob now, a sense of harrying prey, of closing in on a kill. "My father gave you that chance, didn't he?"

"He was kind—" Mossrose faltered.

"He was too kind. He took the blame." A stab at the

truth, risking all: "Who was plugged into command when you launched from Stardeep?"

"I was."

"Your first launch?"

"Y—yes."

"My father wasn't linked in a tandem setup?"

"N—no, not at first. He let me try it—alone."

"And you killed two thousand men!"

Footloose lifted his gaze and stared at Rob, stared straight at him and really saw him for the very first time. Sweat shone in the scraggly hair above and below his lips.

"I know I did," he said. "God help me, I know."

Rob's nails were curled tight into his palms. The digging brought pain. The pain ignited his smoldering anger. He took a step forward. Simon dashed in front of him.

"Easy, Rob. *You heard me!*"

Rob hesitated. The Commander's eyes were fierce above his hooked nose.

"You want the truth, Rob? Be man enough to listen to it."

"But he killed—"

"Let him tell it!"

Under control again, Rob stepped back to where he had been standing. Tears reappeared at the corners of Footloose's blue eyes. He complained once more that he should not be forced to dredge up the past.

Simon reacted with equal firmness and wrath. "Don't start that. The sooner this is over, the better it'll be for all of us. The boy wants to know about the launch. Tell him."

So Footloose began, a numbed monotone: "It was a computation error. Mine. I had difficulty with the pre-launch program I prepped for the computer. One series of equations didn't fit properly. I didn't know enough to find the error, and I didn't want to admit it to the Lightcommander. So I—I fed the equations into the computer anyway. By then I think I believed they were right. We launched perfectly. We thought we went into hyperdrive for about—I don't know, three or four milliseconds—"

"Try five," Rob breathed.

"All right, five. The Lightcommander plugged into the other chair. The FTLS was creaking, all ports blanked out. We couldn't see—"

"My father programmed the correction?"

"Yes, I think so. He started—it happened too fast—by

that time it was—too late to correct any error. We weren't in hyperspace. We were here. Underground."

"Resistance!" Simon exclaimed softly. "I don't know much about hyperdrive mechanics, but I can imagine what could happen if an FTLS re-molecularized not into hyperspace but into conventional space occupied by solid rock. The resistance would de-molecularize the ship again for an infinitesimal part of a second. And because the space was already occupied, the process would continue to completion. Matter—the ship—would simply cease to exist."

Slowly Rob lifted his head to the pocked, streaked hull. He had difficulty coping with the concept. All he could imagine was an oversimplified image of a tiny metal cylinder suddenly existing, or trying to exist simultaneously with hundreds of millions of tons of rock. In a blinding instant the cylinder would be squeezed, compressed, compacted, obliterated. But if part of the cylinder, a small portion of its mass, arrived in a place in that rock where an air space existed, then perhaps—perhaps—

Rob's head ached. He pointed overhead. "That part of the ship was left?"

Footloose nodded.

"You programmed *Majestica* into the ground of Stardeep?"

"The Lightcommander tried to correct—"

"Where was he when it happened?" Rob wanted to know.

"Right alongside me on the engineering bridge. It's at the top of that huge room up there. You—couldn't see it in the dark. We—were all knocked unconscious by the impact and—half the men left alive were—broken apart inside. I woke up hours or days later. Everybody but your father and one other crewman was dead. Your father was bleeding from his nose and ears. I don't know how it happened but—I was the only one who wasn't seriously hurt. Just a broken arm, some cuts where the command chair ripped loose from its bolts and slashed me. We—found flamecutters in the gyrobal chamber. We sliced our way through the decking, down through and out. We tried to find our way to the surface of the planet. The crewman—I don't even know his name—he died. Then your father—he could barely stand—his face was all red—all red in the light from the last torch we had—"

Rob wanted to yell at the man to stop. He couldn't. In

his mind a specter of a face, awash with blood, blended with and then separated from the fax of Lightcommander Edison he had treasured so long. His ears rang. He heard Footloose reply to some question of the Commander's.

"—yes, buried. Not far—"

"Come on, Rob," said Simon.

In a dizzying nightmare, they crossed the cave floor. Simon's torch lighted the way. The floor rose slightly. Rob's vision cleared. The torch picked out two small cairns built of stones.

"I—can't remember which is the place I buried the Lightcommander," Footloose stammered.

Rob walked forward and stood by himself. His shadow fell across the crude markers.

His light-headedness vanished. His fatigue remained, but he could think clearly again, though tears clotted his eyes. He fought back all sound, but he let the tears come.

This passed. He straightened up. It was as though a cold wind had blown over him. Somehow he had passed a marking-point and changed. For all time.

He turned around to Footloose.

"You made the mistake that sent *Majestica* down here."

"I said so, didn't I? But the Lightcommander—"

"Let you command the launch. So he made a mistake too."

Command decision error. Forever on his father's record. *Belonging* there.

And the Lightcommander's error was the greater. He had permitted his Lightadjutant to have command at a critical time, and thereby risked the lives of his entire crew. It made no difference that Duncan Edison had been trying to save one man. He had destroyed two thousand.

Rob's hunt was over. His faith, his hope, was as dead as the two human beings whose remains had rotted away under those little piles of rock.

Simon sensed the crisis. "Shouldn't we face the more immediate problem, Rob?"

Hollow-eyed, Rob looked at him. "What, sir?"

"Survival. We have to get out of here." Simon eyed the suspended hull critically. "I don't know whether we can reach that opening. Maybe we can if you get on my shoulder. If that's no go, we have to find another way. Can you lead us out of here, Footloose?"

All at once Rob was very frightened.

A queer little smile twisted the face of the bearded man. He looked like someone on the verge of hysterical laughter, or complete breakdown, or both. The expressions on his face were changing as swiftly as a summer landscape on an agriworld.

The Commander repeated his question. "Can you lead us out?"

"You think I would?" Footloose breathed. The old venom was back. "Do you really think so? I lived through this! I buried the last two left alive! Dug graves with my own hands and wandered down here till I nearly lost my mind. Then I found those little critters. They helped me forget. You made me remember it all. You killed my Empt." Footloose swung to Rob. "The Lightcommander made me kill all those men. He shouldn't have let me take over."

"Watch him," Simon whispered to his daughter and Rob.

"The critter helped me! That's why I stayed out here with nobody but the critters. I had my own till you killed it!"

"Stop it," Simon barked. "There's no sense yelling at each other. We'll all die down here if we don't find a way out."

All at once Footloose grinned. "I won't die."

"What do you mean?" Lyndsey whispered.

"You need me to show you the way. There are a hundred tunnels right around this very cave—and most of them go the wrong way!" Footloose leaned forward to giggle. "That's why I did what I did up above. Followed your tracks in the tunnel to the place where you came into the ship. I kicked and banged the tunnel till a big slide started where a little one had already been started before. The top hole in the hull is blocked. You don't think so? Climb back up through the ship the way you came. Try to get out past the rocks. Try!"

While Footloose giggled, Simon stared at him as though trying to guess whether he was bluffing. From Simon's stiff expression, Rob decided that the Commander believed the claim. Well, Rob did too. This new development only added one more defeat to a string of them.

"You won't get out without me," Footloose was chortling. "Not without me, without me!"

"Then you'll take us," Simon answered.

Footloose made a menacing gesture. "I'd sooner kill you!"

The Commander shoved his daughter around behind him, raised his laser beam. "You'll do what I say. No one else knows the right way."

"But you made me remember!" He seized his temples with both hands. "You made me *hurt*."

"Footloose—"

"No!" Footloose yowled and dove for the ground.

Chaos then. Lyndsey crying out. Simon pushing her to one side. Torch beams dipping crazily. Footloose snatching up handfuls of sand and flinging them in wide arcs.

The damp, gritty stuff caught Rob and Simon in the eyes. It blinded them just long enough. Footloose yelled and charged in with both fists swinging.

Nineteen

NO WAY OUT

Rob reached for Footloose. The bearded man eluded him, going after the Commander. His doubled left hand caught Simon in the jaw and made him reel.

The Conpat chief aimed the laser beam, just as quickly lowered it. There was a humanity in Simon that refused to do mortal harm to a poor madman, even though the madman was attacking him.

Simon ducked a second blow. He dropped his torch accidentally. Rob lunged for it. Footloose whipped up his foot. Rob took a powerful kick under the point of his chin. He staggered, fell.

Rob's hand crawled out toward the torch. He couldn't get it. His head throbbed. He saw everything as though underwater. Footloose clamped his hands on the Commander's neck.

Lyndsey darted in, seized Footloose's sleeve. The sun-faded fabric ripped in her hands. Footloose kicked her too, a vicious blow to the ankle. Lyndsey's legs failed to support her. She tumbled away.

Help the Commander, Rob thought. *Get up and help him.*

But he was wobbly. As he stood, the cave floor seemed to tilt from side to side.

Footloose's lips skinned back from his white teeth. He seemed to be laughing as he choked Simon. The Commander still had his laser beam in his right hand. He inverted it. Emotionless, a curious look slid over his face. He became the professional policeman, trained for self-preservation. He bashed Footloose across the bridge of his nose with the laser beam grip.

Then he drove his left hand up between his attacker's arms, jabbed for the region near Footloose's right ear. That ended it, as it had ended the first attack.

This time, however, Simon was more cautious. He rolled the unconscious man onto his stomach. He lifted the tails of the faded shirt, yanked out the piece of fibrous plasto that served Footloose as a belt. He called for the torch at closer range. Rob picked up Simon's light, added its beam to his own, and held the two while the Commander lashed Footloose's tanned wrists together.

Glumly Simon shoved his laser beam back into his belt. "We needed him."

Rubbing her calf, Lyndsey said, "Do you think he did what he said?"

Rob answered. "Yes. I think he told the truth about Dad's ship too."

Seeing the hurt on Rob's face, Simon frowned. "You came a long way to find that kind of answer. When we get out—"

"If we get out," said Lyndsey with a shudder.

"Don't talk that way, girl. Of course we'll get out. I meant to tell Rob that we can come back with exhumation gear. Seven years isn't such a long time. There are scientific tests that can identify the men in those graves. We can find out for certain whether—"

"I don't want to open the graves, sir. I know the truth."

"Grant that Footloose—or Mossrose—wasn't making anything up. Remember that your father tried to help him, not destroy him. That counts for something."

"My father did everything he has been accused of doing. Everything I knew he couldn't do."

"What are you, boy? Some kind of judicial computer?"

Stung, Rob raised his head. "Sir?"

"Your father did what he did because he felt he had to."

"I defended him, sir. Lied for him."

"Your father was a human being! Not a million-cred machine with built-in failsafes. Do you really understand what it means to be a human being? It means, among other things, being imperfect!"

A great weight had settled on Rob, a sense of events drifting from his control. Here they were, buried below the crust of Stardeep, and except for a vague academic interest in his own welfare and that of his companions, he didn't really care. He was drained.

He remembered the years on Lambeth Omega-O. He remembered the cuts on his face, the hooting of a crowd of Home boys when he fought because of, and for, his father's reputation.

He remembered his own exhilaration when he left Dellkart IV, positive that he would discover the *right* truth about the past.

All the pain, the hope, the caring—for nothing.

"Don't chain yourself to the past, Rob," Simon was pleading. "I could tell that the past was making a wreck of you the first time I heard your story. Don't let it. Don't crucify yourself because a man made a mistake."

"Two thousand dead—" Rob began.

"All right!" Simon's voice was thunder in the cavern. "A horrible thing! But it's over! Gone and buried! The galaxy turns. Life goes on."

"I wanted to prove he was innocent. I wanted to prove that more than anything."

"And all you proved was that he was a man like other men. That's your mistake, Rob. Judging him instead of loving him."

"That isn't true. I fought for him because I loved him."

"Don't hand me that rot. You judged him, your own father, the way the rest of the galaxy did. People judged him as a bad Lightcommander. Did that make him a bad father? A bad human being? For you it did. Because that made you less than perfect too. You haven't been trying to save your father's reputation, Rob. You've been trying to polish your own. Into what? I don't know. Something shiny and flawless like one of those robot tutors I've heard about? You'll never be half the man your father was, Rob. He tried to help Mossrose. The outcome was tragic. So you'll never try anything like that. You'll keep busy worrying about yourself all the time. You'll be afraid of living. Afraid of mistakes. Afraid of—"

"Mistakes?" Simon's words had flayed Rob's temper raw. "We're trapped down here. Whose mistake is that? Yours!"

"Rob!"

Lyndsey's cry released the anguish that had been building within him. He felt bitterly ashamed and humiliated. Quickly he attempted to make amends. "I'm sorry, Commander."

"Well, I had no right to talk to you that way, either," Simon returned. "We're all tense. But the situation isn't as hopeless as all that."

The Commander checked Footloose's bonds. The bearded man remained unconscious. When Simon straightened, he was brisk again, calm but not falsely cheerful.

"We have an ample air supply. Food and water are the critical items. We can't last too many days without them. On the other hand, we know there are ways out of here. I believe our sleeping friend probably did block the upper entrance to the ship. With you two boosting me, I might make it to check. But I think we could expend our efforts more wisely."

Simon ticked two big fingers against the crumbled remains of the tiny black box that had hung at his belt. "The homing signal isn't being sent any longer. Flyer four will know something's amiss. My Conpats will come searching for us eventually. But if they have a tough time finding their way, it may be a matter of days or even a week until they reach us. That pretty well establishes priorities. Water and food."

"But where can we find them down here?" Lyndsey asked.

"Footloose must have a cache. He comes to Churchill regularly for his victuals, remember. If we can't find the cache ourselves, we'll have to make him tell us where it is."

"I wonder," Rob mused, "how much more of anything we can force out of him."

"Very little," Simon agreed. "The point is—we have to stay alive, so we'll solve the food and water problem somehow."

"I'll say it's a problem," Lyndsey sighed in a totally hopeless voice. She scuffed her foot in the damp sand. Rob stared vacantly out past the periphery of the torch beams. His weary mind picked up a statement Simon had made, toyed with it. Finally he realized its implications.

If it took the Conpats a week or more to locate them, he would very likely miss his connections back to Dellkart IV. Therefore he would miss the start of the entrance examinations. All of Exfore's dire warnings came back: Someone else in his place in college, his own life potential drastically reduced—why, he'd have to labor until he died just to pay off the loan he had gotten to come here. Failure to return to Dellkart IV on time would simply and effectively wipe out his future. As if he really had any, now that he knew the truth about *Majestica*.

It was all too confusing and disheartening to think about.

"Let's make a start," Simon grumbled.

"How?" Lyndsey asked.

"Take torches. Head for the perimeter of the cave. Try to find tunnels. We could follow Footloose's trail and make short work of it if the tracker cell was still good."

"Come on, Rob," Lyndsey urged.

He picked up one of the torches. But he was just going through the motions. Listlessly he followed Simon's lead. Lyndsey fell in step beside him. They tramped toward the darkness that the torches pushed back little by little. Rob was hungrier than he had ever been before.

"Rob?" Lyndsey said as they walked.

"What?"

"I'm sorry Footloose told you what he did."

"It was only the truth," he returned. "People are supposed to respect the truth, aren't they?"

"All the same, I know it was an awful shock. So much has happened—you must be about to drop over."

"I'm fine."

"There's the wall," Simon called from ahead.

They used the torches to search a wide area for about twenty minutes. They found no openings. Simon directed them to the next section to the right. Once more they searched the cave walls, playing the beams up and down carefully. Once more it was the same, futile story—implacable, unbroken rock.

They searched the next section. The next. Even Simon began to sound upset. "I know for a fact there are tunnels. I've been in them on other parts of the planet!"

"There may be only one or two entrances to this cavern," Rob suggested. "And we've explored just on this side of the ship. The cavern might be bigger than we think. It could take days."

For the first time Simon's rugged face showed hopelessness. "It could. But let's keep going."

They searched for three hours more. They worked their way beneath the hull of the great lightship, out into the part of the cavern beyond. It was huge, as Rob had suggested. Again the rock walls revealed no sign of a break.

Weariness began catching up with all of them. Simon dropped his torch twice.

As they were preparing to move to another section of wall, Rob admitted to himself that they would probably have to wait for the coming of the Conpats—if the Conpats found them. He felt light-headed again. *Well,* he said to himself, *I've lost everything else. What does a chance at college matter?*

Suddenly Simon's alarmed voice broke in. "Where's Lyndsey?"

They swung the torches, crisscrossing the sand. Simon grew pale.

"I didn't see her walk off," Rob said.

"Lyndsey?" Simon sounded desperate as he shouted. "Lyn!"

Lynlynlynlynlyn went the echo, singing away.

From far to their right came an answer, very faint. "Dad. Over this way."

Rob heard a high-pitched sound. It seemed to come from the same general direction as Lyndsey's reply. He thought he should recognize the sound. His weary mind refused to provide the identification. And somehow the squeaking terrified him.

"Lyndsey?" He bolted into a run. "Lyndsey—we're coming!"

Twenty

EMPT TIMES TWO

Simon kept up with Rob as Lyndsey called out to guide them. All at once Rob saw small strange splotches of yellow in the blackness. They glowed, vanished, glowed again like gems.

The strange brilliance was located directly ahead of them now, and somewhat over their heads. The damp sand sloped upward just a little.

"I'm up here, Dad." Lyndsey sounded quite close. "In this little niche."

Her shadow passed between Rob and the yellow spots. He flogged his mind for the obvious answer and all at once he had it. The sound was repeated, *Chee-wee*. Empt eyes! Empts crying!

But why were the cries so high and thin?

As they climbed the sandy slope and Simon directed his torch into the natural recess in the rock, Rob saw the reason. Simon put words to it.

"Babies! How did you find them, Lyndsey?"

"I heard them squeaking," she explained, kneeling beside the two little creatures. Four brilliant yellow eyes were visible in the light of the torch.

One of the Empts, which was about half the size of a full-grown specimen, shot out three translucent pseudopods and tried to scuttle away into the dark. A tingling, not unpleasant, stirred at the front of Rob's skull.

Lyndsey caught the escaping creature and snuggled it against her. She laughed.

"Aren't they darlings? They must be in the last week before maturity. I don't see any sign of the mother. Dad, can we keep them for pets? Let's take them with us."

Lyndsey's eyes were bland discs in the glow of the torches. Rob marveled at her calm. It was a grotesque contrast to the disarray of her hair and her grimy appearance.

When her father didn't immediately reply, Lyndsey pleaded, "Say we can take them, Dad. Let's take them back to Churchill right this minute."

"Get back, Rob," Simon whispered. He clutched the boy's arm. "Back!"

The warning came none too soon. Rob's mind had already begun to blur. He took half a dozen sliding steps down the sandy slope. The tingling lessened.

Simon followed. In an undertone he said, "They've made her forget that we're trapped down here. She thinks everything's fine, as if all that business with Footloose never happened. As if we could just walk out of—"

Simon broke off. He turned to stare over his shoulder the way they had come.

"By heaven!"

"What's wrong, Commander?"

"For a change, nothing. Lyndsey!"

The girl was crooning to the Empt in her arms. The creature no longer seemed quite so frightened. Nor did its companion. The Empt on the ground nuzzled its plated body against her ankles. Nearby, the torch beams revealed fragments that resembled antique china overlaid with an iridescent pink. Remains of the eggs laid by the mother Empt?

"They're marvelous," Lyndsey was murmuring. "Not a bit scared of me. Dad—"

"Lyndsey!" Simon barked. "Put them down and come here!"

The force of his voice penetrated her daze. Slowly she laid the baby Empt beside its brother—or sister. Four round yellow eyes glowed in a row. Lyndsey left the niche, slid down the slope. In amazement Rob saw her face actually change. It lost that look of blithe unconcern. It became haggard, white, fearful.

Lyndsey rubbed her temple. "What—what happened?" A glance into the darkness. She was suddenly aware again. "I forgot everything!"

"Good," said Simon. "That means that together, those little babies may be radiating at almost the level of an adult

Empt. I think we have a chance. Listen carefully, both of you. This is extremely important. Once I pick up those Empts, I'll forget everything too. I won't know what to do—or why—unless you tell me."

And in terse sentences, Simon outlined what must be done.

Rob felt a twinge of hope. He suppressed it quickly. He was all too fearful that it would prove false. Yet he paid close attention to the Commander's instructions.

"Take this." Simon passed his torch to his daughter. "Stay far enough away from me so that you don't pick up the emanations."

"Empting won't hurt you, will it, Dad?" Lyndsey wanted to know.

"No. The combined power of the babies obviously isn't as strong as that of the Empt that Rob caught in Churchill. Its power knocked him out, remember? This is a case of too little, not too much. The Empts affected you. But can they affect—Well, let's stop talking and find out."

He clumped up the slope, his boots stirring the damp sand. Rob held the torch steady. It wasn't easy. Fatigue made his hand shake.

Simon entered the niche, bent down. He picked up both baby Empts and fitted one in the crook of each arm.

One Empt shot out two pseudopods, then quickly retracted them. It settled comfortably into place with a piping *chee-wee.*

Encircled by the light from the torches, Simon stared down at Rob and his daughter. His face was smooth and untroubled.

"Come on, Commander," Rob called. "Walk down here with them."

Simon took time to evaluate the request. His grimy face had a curious air of innocence. For a moment Rob feared the strategy wouldn't work.

Then Simon lifted his right boot over the pink remains of the egg. He carried the babies down the slope.

Without speaking, Simon followed Lyndsey and Rob back beneath the suspended hull to where Footloose lay.

Despite the chill of the cave air, Rob started sweating again. Everything hung on the next few moments. Everything.

"Put the Empts down, Commander."

Simon's movements were slow, deliberate. But he obeyed. Gently he set the Empts down.

"Now take that plasto binding off the bearded man's wrist."

In a minute or so Simon had the knot free. He peered at the fibrous belt in his hand, tossed it away with a shrug.

"Roll him over on his back."

This Simon proceeded to do.

"Now shake him so he wakes up. That's it. Harder, sir."

Lyndsey gripped Rob's arm. "He's coming around."

"All right, Commander. Set the Empts on his chest and get away."

"I'm perfectly safe here," Simon returned. "There's no reason why—"

"Do it, Commander! The Empts on the man's chest. Then stand back."

Obeying but not comprehending, Simon lifted one of the squeaking babies. He set it on Footloose's heaving chest.

The bearded man was beginning to make loud snuffling sounds. He shuddered. The Empt toppled into the sand, landing on the upper curve of its spherical body. It shot three pseudopods into the air, righted itself, engaged its pseudopods in the sand and started to scuttle off.

"Catch it, Commander!" Rob's voice was raw with strain. "Take hold of it."

Simon extended his hands. He seized the baby Empt just before it raced out of range.

Under Rob's direction, Simon cradled the Empt and soothed it with a wordless murmur. Footloose was nearly awake now, thrashing his arms and groaning. His eyes opened. There was sudden memory in those eyes.

"Put the Empts on his chest, Dad!" Lyndsey cried.

Simon responded, dumping one baby Empt onto Footloose's shirt. Then he scooped the other from the sand and deposited it beside the first.

Footloose struggled to sit up. The Empt's faceted eyes were bright as yellow jewels. They squeaked steadily. Footloose gazed past them, recognizing Rob for one awful instant—

Chee-wee, chee-wee. The sound diverted the bearded man's attention.

He examined the Empts perched on his chest. One leathery hand crept up to touch the armor of the smaller baby. His blue eyes turned almost dreamy.

"Critters." His white teeth shone through his beard. "Critters."

"Get away, Dad," Lyndsey whispered to her father.

Rob shared her concern. "Come over by us, Commander. Hurry!"

Simon walked toward them with a stiff, stumbling gait. He stopped between Rob and his daughter. He glanced from one to the other, vacant, uncertain.

All at once his eyes cleared.

Simon pounded the palms of his hands against his eye sockets. He shook his head. Remembered. Swiftly he pivoted toward Footloose, who was gurgling and chortling over the newfound pets that squeaked on his stomach.

The Commander spoke very softly. "Footloose?"

The bearded man turned to the voice. He frowned. "I know you, person."

Lyndsey's hand stole to her father's arm, dug in tightly. Rob fought to steady the torch he held. Simon Ling swallowed a deep gulp of air, continued in a low, earnest voice.

"Of course you know me, Footloose. The Commander of the Conpats."

"Won't hurt me? Won't hurt me, Commander person?"

"You know I won't. But I need your help, Footloose. We seem to have lost our way down in these caves."

Rob marveled at the way Simon managed to say it so casually. As if it hardly mattered.

"Can you help us find our way out, Footloose?" Simon asked.

The man started to stand up again. Both Empts tumbled off. He caught one. The other struck the ground.

Footloose picked it up, crooned over it, rubbed his beard against it. With one Empt in each arm, he frowned a second time. His blue gaze slid past the Commander to Rob.

Rob's stomach turned over. He was sure Footloose remembered him and everything else.

Footloose growled. "That person. Young person. Something bad on his face. Makes me think of bad things. There is something bad here."

He lifted his head. He searched the high darkness for the hull of *Majestica*. Mercifully, it could not be seen.

"His name is Edison person, yes?" Footloose hissed it again, almost angrily. "Edison person bad!"

"No," Simon insisted. "Forget that. He's your friend."

"Need remember why person is very bad," Footloose insisted.

"He isn't, Footloose. He's a friend. We're all your friends."

For one moment Footloose's face mirrored the awful struggle. The past fought against the obliterating power of the Empts. Rob's hand shook harder.

"We'll protect your critters if you help us," Simon offered. "You can have both of those for your own."

A blink of the blue-chip eyes.

"Both?"

"That's a promise."

Once more Footloose lifted his gaze to the darkness at the cavern roof. Slowly, he swung to Rob, and stared.

The Empt in Footloose's arm squeaked loudly. Footloose giggled. He pressed his filthy bearded cheek against the creature to quiet it.

"These are my critters, Commander person?"

"Yes."

Hesitation.

"All right."

Simon breathed with relief. Rob didn't know whether to laugh or cry or both.

Footloose bobbed his head to show that he would lead the way. Two hours later he guided them past a tunnel turning. Ahead, Rob saw a patch of sky washed with the lemon sun of Stardeep.

Twenty-one

"GOOD FORTUNE ACROSS STARDEEP"

"Attention. Attention, please. FTLS *Roger Dunleavy* is now in the final boarding process. All passengers holding space should be cleared through customs and aboard. Repeat, all passengers holding space should be cleared through customs and aboard. Thank you."

Rob's bubblegrip popped from beneath the last inspection scope and bumped toward the end of the moving belt. Another taped message boomed into the dome. It was less detailed than the one Rob had heard on arrival. The automated voice merely hoped that all persons boarding the FTLS had enjoyed a pleasant stay on Stardeep, and would return again.

Fantastic would be a better word, thought Rob. *Come back? Never.*

He carried his bubblegrip toward Simon and Lyndsey. They were waiting for him by the hatch that led into the loading pod. A purser from the *Roger Dunleavy* watched with obvious impatience. Rob was the last passenger who had to be boarded.

Three days had passed since Footloose had guided Rob and his friends out of the caves. Along with Simon and his daughter, Rob had spent one of those days undergoing exhaustive tests in the Conpat dispensary.

The tests proved negative. Massive nutritional therapy plus twelve hours of hypnotically induced rest restored Rob to some degree of normalcy. He didn't feel tired any longer. Only, only—well—changed.

In the dispensary there had been plenty of time to talk. Rob told Simon and Lyndsey everything. That included the

149

incidents with Kerry Sharkey and the question of the interview that author Hollis Kipp wanted in the fall. He had been seven days on Stardeep. Nearly two of them had been spent in the caves. The past had no more secrets. But the future had problems without limit.

Simon offered no advice during the dispensary discussions. He puffed on his musicpipe, putting forth a question now and then, but refraining from any kind of opinion. It wasn't necessary that Simon speak. Rob recalled with shining clarity what the Commander had told him during the awful time in the caves.

But Rob hadn't yet brought himself to the point of accepting that advice. Somehow he couldn't.

"You forgot one package, Rob," Lyndsey said as he approached.

Startled, Rob lifted his bubblegrip. "This is all I have."

She shook her head. Her bright blue eyes twinkled. She looked crisp and fresh in a white one-piece. Except for some lingering shadows under her eyes, the experience in the caves might never have happened.

Simon too was freshly turned out in a black Conpat uniform, the gold emblems gleaming on his shoulder. His musicpipe gave off aromatic smoke and the second movement of a symphony composed by one of the first of the great creative computers.

"My daughter has a somewhat illegal present for you," Simon observed, not pleased.

From behind her back Lyndsey brought a small plasto shipping container. There were several ventilation ports punched into the sides below the carry handle. Official seals all over the surface proclaimed that the parcel had been cleared by Stardeep customs. Puzzled, Rob also saw a special stamp which read STARDEEP CONSERVANCY PATROL RELEASE #11048.

"Take it, please," Lyndsey urged.

"What is it, Lyn?" he wanted to know.

With obvious disapproval Simon told him. "A baby Empt. The container is especially shielded inside. You have to open it for Empting. Lyndsey's idea, not mine. Let's not go into the details of how she got it. Being the Commander's daughter unfortunately lets a girl swing weight in some quarters where she shouldn't. I didn't find out about it until she'd already had the Empt processed and cleared.

Lyndsey looked straight at Rob and said softly, "I

wanted you to have it. I know how bad this visit has been for you. Maybe when you need to forget, this will help."

From the ventilation ports Rob heard a faint *chee-wee*. He looked closely at the container. Emotions swept over him like a storm—doubt, longing, sorrow.

The automated voice repeated its message about the final boarding. Rob continued to stare at the container in Lyndsey's outstretched hand.

He was tempted. That package held a lifetime of forgetting.

"Rob?" Lyndsey said.

"I can't take it, Lyndsey."

Afterward he often wondered how he had reached that decision. It hadn't come consciously. Yet there it was. And he was committed to it—and all it meant—for the rest of his days.

Strangely he felt better almost at once. Simon's glance thawed. Even Lyndsey seemed pleased.

The Commander reached out, gently pried the container handle from his daughter's hand. "I made a little bet with her, Rob. I told her you wouldn't take it. People grow up in different ways and in different places. Stardeep was your place."

Rob wasn't so sure. But Simon's smile cheered him. To his discomfort, he noticed that Lyndsey was crying.

The purser at his elbow coughed impatiently. Lyndsey darted forward suddenly to kiss him on the cheek.

"I'm glad you didn't take it," she whispered.

"Your tickets, if you please," the purser said in an officious voice.

Rob handed over the punched machine forms. Simon waved his musicpipe. "Come visit us if you can, Rob."

He looked at Lyndsey. "I will."

"All in order," the purser was saying. "Into the loading pod, please, Mr. Edison."

"—and send us a beam and tell us how the exams come out," Simon finished. "Good fortune across Stardeep!"

There was much more Rob wanted to say. There was no time.

The purser followed him into the pod. The hatch slid shut. The pod disengaged and began to rise. Through a small port he saw the side of the great FTLS flashing past.

Even now he wasn't sure he understood it all. So much had happened in such a short span. The nightmare in the caves, Footloose, gone back now to his old untroubled life on the reservation with not one but two Empts, the fate of *Majestica*—

One thing was certain. It was over. He had the exams to worry about.

As the loading pod rose, he found himself facing the thought of the tests with fresh confidence. In fact, everything looked much brighter.

He still wasn't sure that he could wholly accept the truth about Lightcommander Edison. On Stardeep he had learned —painfully—that his father was a human being subject to error. Somehow it was an ordeal to think of Duncan Edison that way.

Yet when he did so consciously, as now, a bit of the burden seemed to lift from his shoulders.

He thought briefly of Lyndsey's offered gift. By taking it, he would never have needed to fret about the secrets buried in the ground of Stardeep. Never for the rest of his life.

But as the boarding pod decelerated, it struck him that, had he taken the Empt, he would never have remembered his father either.

Rob stowed his bubblegrip away in the tiny cabin. Then he strapped himself into his slingbunk. Bells rang. The intercall announced launch in sixty seconds. The great thrusters boomed.

Rob turned his head to the small port. Smoke boiled and blew. The pressure of acceleration squeezed against his chest. He had a last glimpse of the planet through the tatters of vapor—windy wasteland, purple crags, the geodesics of Churchill aglow in the lemon sun.

Then the curve of Stardeep's horizon defined itself. The color of the atmosphere darkened. The thrusters cut out. The port opaqued, crawling with magenta light.

Presently Rob unstrapped himself. He opened his bubblegrip. He took out the small platinum-framed fax of his father.

C.D.E., he forced himself to say in his mind. *C.D.E., but so what?*

Empting would have been wrong. In fact, a lot of the past had been wrong.

Not that facing the truth was easy. But he had made his decision when Lyndsey offered the Empt. He had to live with the truth. That was the last of Stardeep's secrets.

All right, he said to himself. *Follow that where it leads. Living with the truth means facing Kerry Sharkey.*

It won't be easy. But I can do it.

What about giving Hollis Kipp an interview?

I have to.

Was this what Simon Ling meant by growing up? Perhaps he could be himself now. Rob Edison, student. Not some extension of himself forever living in the past.

Rob smiled at the fax. Really smiled. And he realized another surprising thing.

He loved his father.

How long had it been since he had looked at the fax without feeling resentment and fear? How long had it been since he had looked at that fax with a smile on his face instead of a knot in his middle?

Too long.

He laughed.

It was a wonderful feeling.

TIME GATE

For my nephews and nieces—
Jim, Chris, Steve,
Dick, Joe, Sara,
Alice Anne, Louise, Hans Luther,
and Faris

That's ten more science fiction
readers right there

Time present and time past
Are both perhaps present in time future,
And time future contained in time past.

—*T. S. Eliot,*
Four Quartets.
Burnt Norton, I

CONTENTS

1

THE RED DOOR

"HAWAII," Tom said. "Marine biology."

Dr. Calvin Linstrum put down his fork and stared across the cafeteria table. That infuriating, superior smile turned up the corners of his mouth.

"You feel you're qualified to make that decision?" he asked.

"Don't be sarcastic, Cal. I'm eighteen. It's my future."

"To waste as you wish," Cal nodded. He glanced at the clock set in the concrete wall. Ten to one. Ten minutes until Dr. Gordon White would begin his preparations for departure into the past.

Tom shoved his plate aside, no longer hungry. Every discussion with Cal ended the same way.

But he tried once more. "The university feel I'm qualified. I got a telemail from them yesterday—"

"You told me."

"But did you get the point? The university will accept me when the new term starts."

"So in two months you'll just hop off to Honolulu, fool around for four years, and *then* decide whether you're going on to grad school?"

"What's wrong with that?"

"Plenty! Education is far too important to be left to chance. We need to sit down now, map out a complete tentative program—"

"If it's not a lifetime master plan, and it doesn' bear the personal stamp of approval of Dr. Calvin Linstrum—"

1

"Now who's being sarcastic? I do have thirteen years on you, remember."

A short, explosive sigh from Tom. Then, "Cal, it's not that I don't appreciate all you've done since Dad died. But why does everything have to be so methodical? Planned down to the last little nit?"

"Method is the key to science, Tom."

"Well, I'm no scientific experiment!"

"True. You're my brother. I'm concerned about your future."

"Let *me* worry about my future."

"When you have the proper experience, the maturity—"

Angrily, Tom flung down his napkin. "It always comes down to that, doesn't it? You're older, you're smarter, you have all the education. Well, I get sick and tired of having you sit in judgment. As if the fact that you're carrying on Dad's work gives you the right—"

"But that's the point," Cal interrupted. "I think it does."

Heavy silence.

Cal didn't take his position out of malice, Tom knew. It was brother looking after brother, because each represented the only family the other had. Yet it was stultifying, especially when Cal's slender, bony face pulled upward into that smiling suggestion of superior wisdom.

"What makes you so certain I'm qualified for doctoral work?" Tom challenged. "You've seen my achievement scores. They're not the highest."

"Any son of Dr. Victor Linstrum can do whatever he wants in science. The name alone will open doors. That's why it's important to be careful." Cal leaned forward, his unruly reddish hair bobbing across his forehead. "You asked me how I can be certain. How can *you* be sure marine biology is it?"

"I enjoyed those field trips to the Gulf with the class—"

"High school summer excursions? Proves nothing." Cal stood up. "We'll discuss this another time."

"Let's discuss it now!"

"No, Tom. Later. When you're less resentful of the fact that I'm only trying to help."

"I'll take advice," Tom exploded. "But not orders!"

Cal picked up his tray and carried it to the load chute, where it was sucked away into the wall. "I'm glad you don't bridle so much at carrying out orders around the department," he said. "We couldn't afford an inexperienced summer assistant who demanded that we operate the Gate his way or not at all. Try to apply that fact to your personal affairs."

And he walked out.

Tom all but flung his tray into the chute. The stainless steel covers clanged as air pulled the disposable dishes and tableware down into the underground.

Why *wouldn't* Cal listen?

Sure, he was brilliant. And yes, it *was* rare for a scientist not long past thirty to be in charge of an installation as advanced as Department 239-T. But that was because—the old bogey again!—Cal was Victor Linstrum's elder son.

Not that Cal wasn't at home with most of the intricacies of the time-phase effect. He was. But scientific expertise didn't guarantee skill in dealing with other people.

And Tom was number two son. *Ipso facto,* not quite bright. He hated the role.

The clock hand reached a minute before one. Tom hurried to the door, displayed his photo-ident to the security cell. The door whooshed back. Tom walked down a concrete corridor, approached a soldier on duty at a massive gray metal door. The guard wore a white helmet and a holstered gun loaded with nerve darts. A sign on the door read: ADMITTANCE TO AUTHORIZED PERSONNEL ONLY.

The door opened to Tom's ident. Halfway down another short corridor, there was an alcove on the left. Under a pin spotlight, an oil portrait of Dr. Victor Linstrum, blue-eyed, spade-bearded, glowed softly. A small metal plaque carried words in a fine script: NOBEL LAUREATE, 1978.

The hall ended at a large concrete antechamber with several doors opening off each side. One led to the costume storage rooms. It was open. Tom saw Donald moving around inside.

Another door, extremely thick, was the entrance to the department's timelock vault, which housed master records of each archaeological mission. The vault controls were located beside the door.

A third, red-painted door led to the Gate. Tom went to yet another door and pushed through.

Inside the brightly lighted ready room, Calvin Linstrum was talking with a stout, florid man of middle age. Gordon White wore his hair long, contrary to current styles. Over the past month he had grown a gray-peppered beard. He was just hanging his shirt on a peg.

Seeing Tom, the older man held up his right hand, palm outward. *"Vale!"*

"What's that mean?" Tom wanted to know.

"You wouldn't ask that of a resident of Pompeii," White grinned. "He'd know you were wishing him good day and good luck."

"Quite the scholar, isn't he?" Cal said.

"I should be," Gordon White harrumphed. "I've practically been sleeping with those instruction machines."

"What do you need?" Tom asked.

"My toga, for one thing."

"I saw Donald in the storeroom. I think he's getting it."

"The camera and recorder, then."

"Coming up."

Tom crossed the antechamber, entered a room in which various small electronic devices were stored. From the bins he selected a matchbox-size camera that took a special hundred-exposure roll of fast film, and a tiny, egg-shaped device.

Next, by yellow light, he loaded the camera. Then he inserted a spool tape inside the tiny egg. He signed his name and ident number to his requisition and fed the punchcard into the inventory machine. The machine flashed lights and rang a bell to indicate everything cleared.

Tom started across the antechamber again. A tall, well-built young man with hair lighter than his brother's and features less sharp, less angular, he was actually taller than Cal by about three inches. Perhaps Cal resented that.

But the quarrel was forgotten as Tom's glance slid across to the closed red door.

No matter how many times he saw a temporal archaeologist depart, he never quite grew accustomed to the idea. In the stillness of the underground, with only the air conditioners whispering, the old feeling of wonder returned.

It seemed remarkable—awful, in the original sense of that word—that in less than two hours, Dr. Gordon White would walk through the red door to the Gate, then emerge on a plain outside Roman Pompeii, four days before the city was destroyed by the eruption of Mount Vesuvius—

Seventy-nine years after the birth of Christ.

Of all the secret departments of the United States Government, none was more secret than the one known by the innocuous designation Department 239-T.

Its modest operating appropriation, passed routinely by Congress every year, was concealed in the budget of the Department of Defense. Department 239-T came under the jurisdiction of Defense almost by default. Government planners believed there might be potential military application for the secret contained in 239-T's underground bunker. But no planner had yet found a way to apply the secret on a risk-free basis.

The White House exercised close personal control over 239-T's operations, to make sure no one tried to employ the Gate for short-sighted gains, because no one really knew what the consequences might be.

Even Victor Linstrum, the man who had put together the mathematical-physical base for the Gate in 1974, had not been able to calculate all possible consequences, though he guessed at many. Concerned about his discovery's ultimate use, he approached the Government with caution. Fortunately, he found an understanding administration. The Government funded construction of the bunker as one of many basic research expenditures. Eventual payoff, if any, was unknown. The then-President was sensitive to potential dangers when Dr. Linstrum explained them. Each of the two succeeding chief executives had been equally perceptive.

Dr. Calvin Linstrum had been in charge of the facility since the death of the elder Linstrum five years earlier, in 1982. Department 239-T functioned solely as a lab for an entirely new kind of research—temporal archaeology. For, by means of the Gate, travel forward and backward in time was now possible.

So far, there had been only limited, and cautious, use of the Gate. No one knew, for example, what would happen if a twentieth-century man appeared in Washington at the end of the War Between the States and prevented the murder of President Lincoln. All sorts of tampering with historical events was theoretically possible. But the hazards were far too great to be tolerated.

Indeed, at the insistence of the President, time-tampering experiments were not even contemplated.

Department scholars traveled back in time to selected historical sites. They were costumed in the style of the period and equipped with a basic knowledge of the language and customs, plus appropriate coinage. Thus they were able to blend into the culture reasonably well.

Temporal researchers were permitted to do only three things: observe; take photographs; and make sound recordings, using unobtrusive, miniaturized gear. Victor Linstrum had insisted on no disturbance of the milieu into which the time traveler ventured.

For this reason, travel forward in time had been tried only in a limited way. A few short trips, no more than twenty-four hours into the future, had been undertaken to prove the idea's feasibility. Even then, travelers weren't permitted to leave the department—no scrutiny of the next day's newspaper was allowed, for example. If Cal had his way, trips to the distant future would never be routine. It was logically impossible for anyone to prepare to blend in, physically or linguistically, with unknown societies of the future.

The temptation was great to employ the Gate for a look at the years immediately ahead. But so far, the President had successfully restrained those members of the military who argued most vocally in favor of it.

Because of the explosive potential of the Gate, the Government had long ago decided that its existence should not be revealed to the public. There would be too many pressures. Until you found the true potential of a weapon that might do inestimable damage, you did not play with the weapon, whether expediency prompted experimentation or not.

As Tom continued across the antechamber, the red door slid aside. A dark-haired man stuck his head out.

"Hello, Dr. Stein."

"Save me a trip, will you, Tom? Dr. Walker and I have finished the checkout. We'll be ready by three."

"I'll tell Cal," Tom nodded, moving on.

The door from the outer corridor opened. Tom saw a lift truck piled with large sealed cartons. The cartons bore the name and address of a New York theatrical costume house. The owners, Tom thought, must wonder why the Federal Government ordered eighteenth-century perukes and American Indian breeches.

The guard pointed to the storage rooms. The lift truck driver—another uniformed soldier—shifted gears and rolled his vehicle ahead.

What was keeping Donald? Tom saw no sign of anyone moving back in the bays where the costumes were racked.

In the ready room, Cal and Gordon White were still discussing the mission. Tom reported the successful checkout of the Gate equipment. A tall, gangly young man entered, carrying a plain gray toga, sandals, and several arm rings.

"You're late," Cal said.

"Sorry," Donald Koop said, though he didn't sound it. "I took five minutes to read the news. Archy's pushing disarmament again. When will he learn that the only way to deal with the Comchins is to punch them, not pat them? He'll have us surrendering yet."

Cal held out his hand. "The costume, Donald. We can do without your political commentary."

Gordon White said, "Lord knows I'm no superpatriot, but it does run against my grain to hear you call President Archibald 'Archy.'"

"His friends call him that," Donald answered. "I've met him, you know."

"Yes," Cal said, "We know."

Behind Cal's back, Donald grinned at Tom, as if to say that the attitudes of older people were beyond comprehension.

Donald Koop was even taller than Tom, and slender to the point of emaciation. He had a high forehead, accentuated by a hairless skull. The college fashion these days was a shaved pate. Donald wore round spectacles tinted blue—the most popular current shade. His white smock looked as though it hadn't been laundered in weeks.

Two years older than Tom, and an Ivy League poli sci major during the winter, Donald Koop had won his position as a summer assistant in the department through the efforts of his uncle, Senator Koop. Cal didn't care for Donald, perhaps because he had been politely forced to add the young man to his staff.

Dr. White donned a pair of coarse woolen underdrawers, then pulled the toga over his head. He slipped on the arm rings and the sandals. A wide elastic belt went around his waist beneath the toga. Special pockets held the matchbox camera and the little egg-shaped recorder.

"You forgot the cloak," White said.

Expressionless, Donald left. He returned with a long piece of wine-red wool, which White draped over his shoulders and looped across his left arm.

"Am I the perfect picture of a Roman citizen or am I not?"

"You will be when you take off your class ring," Cal said.

"Oops." White removed the gold signet.

Donald, meantime, had wandered over to speak to Tom in a low voice. "Did you read about Archy's latest proposals?"

"Haven't had time."

"I tell you, somebody has to do something about that man. Three years in office, and he's forcing the country into a totally defenseless posture. He just made public the disarmament plan he started drawing up last March. He wants to scrap all missiles—"

"That isn't exactly a new idea. It goes back to Eisenhower."

"But this time the Comchins are listening!"

"I happen to like the President's policies," Tom countered. "I guess there are some things friends don't have to agree on."

"I'll bring you around one of these days," Donald said.

Often Tom wondered whether his friend actually believed some of the outrageous ideas he espoused. He always sounded as though he did.

Dr. Walker appeared at the door. "Phone, Cal. The White House."

Cal frowned. "Transfer it in here."

"Can't. They want you to take it on the scrambler in your office."

Cal left. When he returned, he looked puzzled and unhappy. "Ira Hand will be paying us a special visit at three o'clock."

White's brow hooked up. "The Vice-President?"

Cal nodded. "His secretary sounded upset."

Donald and Tom exchanged glances. Ira Hand, liaison between President Benjamin Archibald and all the various scientific programs and departments of the Government, personally oversaw operation of the Gate facility, visiting it regularly. But the visits were always announced at least one day in advance.

White stepped to a mirror and jutted out his chin, applying a comb to his beard. "I'm flattered to have the eminently distinguished Vice-President come down expressly to witness my—"

"Cut the clowning, Gordon," Cal scowled. "Hand isn't coming here for your benefit. The Vice-President's disturbed by rumors that his office has picked up."

"Rumors?" Tom said. "What kind?"

"That there may be a security leak in this department."

2

WHO IS SIDNEY SIX?

"SECURITY LEAK?" Gordon White repeated, stunned. "With things run as tightly as they are down here? Sometimes I get the feeling I can't even tell myself what I'm doing."

The forced lightness was lost on Cal. He paced back and forth. "I don't see how it could happen either. We take every conceivable precaution—"

"Including a week of tests and interrogation just to get a part-time job," Donald said.

"But if even the possibility of a leak exists," Cal added, "we need to know."

Strain was apparent on his face. Tom lost all feeling of animosity. At a time like this, the bond between brothers was strong. Whatever Cal's faults, he took his job of carrying on Victor Linstrum's work with utter seriousness and dedication.

"Hand's secretary said the Vice-President would try to arrive a little before three," Cal told them. "Let's review the Pompeii plan once more, Gordon. Then I want to double-check the Gate, Tom—Donald—that's all for now."

"We can watch Dr. White leave, I hope," Tom said.

Cal nodded in a vague way as he left, with White right behind.

Donald rubbed his shaved head. "Personally, I'll take Hand over Archy any day. Hand believes in a strong defense posture."

10

Tom's mind was elsewhere. "Are we still going to the gem races tonight?"

"Right. Six thirty. My place. How about helping me put those new costumes away?"

"Sure."

In the storage rooms, overhead lights cast pools of yellow in the aisles between the racks and shelves. The pile of costumer's cartons had now grown to three times its original size. Delivery had been completed while they were in the ready room, Tom guessed.

Despite the lights, the vast storage area had a ghostly quality, perhaps because the hanging costumes made Tom feel that he was in the presence of disembodied people from the past: men of colonial times, dandies of Restoration England, lords of ancient Manchu China—

"We'll never get all these put away this afternoon," Donald complained. Using a knife, he slit the tape on the first box and checked the contents against an inventory list. He marked the list with a blue marking pen. Then he scribbled blue letters and a number on the carton's side.

"Mongol. Late twelfth century." Donald tapped the pen against the code scrawled on the box. "There's the shelf position."

Tom picked up the carton. He walked by a cluttered table with a newspaper lying on top. The headline caught his eye:

PRESIDENT VACATIONS AT CAMP LOOKOUT.
Prepares Draft of Latest Disarm Plan.

A paragraph of the story had been encircled. Something about the paper struck Tom as odd, some detail that registered in his mind unconsciously. As he walked down a gloomy aisle, he tried to figure out what it was. He couldn't. He'd have to look at the paper again.

While Donald put the next carton away, Tom returned to the table. The paragraph that had been encircled—with a blue marking pen—related to the probable time of President Archibald's departure from Camp Lookout, his personal retreat in the Adirondack Mountains. The story had a strange familiarity, though Tom couldn't say why. Perhaps it was because the President was always working on some version of a disarmament proposal.

Frowning, Tom scanned the page a second time. He still couldn't understand.

Suddenly, annoying because it was so obvious, he saw it.

The date of the newspaper was March 12. A weekend five months ago. No wonder the story sounded familiar.

Tom remembered the widely publicized mountain sojourn from which Archibald had returned with a first draft of a new set of recommendations for the United Nations. The President had been refining them these past months and was due to present the proposals to the world forum in person in two weeks.

Hearing Donald return, Tom picked up the paper. "For somebody who dislikes the President, Donald, you're keeping a pretty accurate history on him."

Behind the blue lenses, Donald Koop's eyes were unreadable. "Let me have that."

"Sure, but I'm curious about why—"

"I'm writing a report." Donald grabbed the paper, folded it, stuffed it into his back pocket.

"On Archibald? In the summer? On both counts, old buddy, I know you better than—"

"Look, we've got work to do."

"Hey, don't get sore."

"I'm not. I just want to get this stuff put away, so your brainy brother doesn't give me another of his lectures about efficiency."

With slashing motions, Donald used the knife to attack the tape on the next carton. Tom had seldom seen his friend so angry.

They worked in near-silence until a gong sounded. Most of the first batch of costumes had been stored, but the newest cartons hadn't been touched.

Dr. Walker, a tall man, stuck his shaved head in the door, announcing, "The Vice-President and his party have arrived."

"But it's only two thirty," Tom said.

Dr. Walker shrugged. "They want to see everyone in Cal's office, pronto."

Calvin Linstrum's personal office was a cement-block room off the central chamber. Harshly lighted and crowded with files, piles of reports, and government forms, the office barely held all those assembled: Cal, Gordon White, Doctors Stein and Walker, two other department technicians, two secretaries, Tom, Donald, and Vice-President Ira Hand and his party.

The Vice-President was a short, stocky man. He had a heavy jaw and a style of choppy gesturing that made him an effective platform speaker. He had brought a thin young man with a briefcase, who was one of his aides, plus a nondescript man in a gray suit, a stranger.

Vice-President Hand introduced the stranger promptly. "This is Mr. Sloat, my personal contact in the Justice Department. I want him to give you the same story he gave me yesterday."

Cal said, "Fire away."

Said Sloat: "Our sources have come up with a distressing rumor that may have a basis in fact. Are you all familiar with the name Sidney Six?"

Cal balanced a pencil between his fingertips. "The syndicated journalist?"

"The syndicated muckraker would be more like it," Dr. Walker said. "Mister Sensationalism. Specialist in the exposé. Long on headlines, short on facts."

Sloat smiled tightly. "You have the picture. It's possible that Sidney Six has gotten wind of the existence of this department."

"Good Lord!" White exclaimed. "Our affairs could be hanging on the public clothesline in no time."

Ira Hand nodded. "That's why we want each of you full-time employees to double your guard. Sorry, Sloat, go on."

"How Sidney Six could have gotten on the trail of this story, no one knows. How far he's developed his leads—if at all—is another unknown. The real problem lies with Six himself. You see, no one knows what the man looks like."

The stocky Dr. Stein rubbed an index finger across his old-fashioned beard. "You know, you're right. I've read his material. Dreadful stuff. But I've never seen his picture. That's unusual for a reporter with such a following."

"It's deliberate," Sloat confirmed. "Six uses assumed identities—falsified papers—we can't imagine what all—to gain entrance to wherever he wants to go. The fact that nobody knows what he looks like helps him get away with it. Do you remember those holograms of the Darien sub pens that were published a year ago?"

Nods.

"Sidney Six got them. He got into that highly guarded

installation and out again before anybody realized he was
there. To this day, my department has no clear idea of
whom he impersonated, or how he carried it off. That's an
embarrassing admission. I make it simply to emphasize the
seriousness of the problem if Sidney Six indeed decides
that his next target is this department."

Cal looked slowly from face to face, trying to smile.
"Okay, Sidney, where are you?"

There was uneasy laughter. On stumpy legs, Vice-
President Hand walked to the center of the group. "Whatever new security measures are necessary, Dr. Linstrum,
take them. I say again, ladies and gentlemen—until the
Government ultimately hammers out an official time-travel
policy, we cannot afford a clamor in the press. In the Gate
we have a very, very tricky capability. I certainly do not
understand all its ramifications—"

"No one does," Cal said. "We're like cavemen with one
plug, one lamp,—and no knowledge of how far we can, or
should, go in taking advantage of electricity."

"If Sidney Six penetrates this department," Ira Hand
went on, "he would have absolutely no scruples about
publishing the story worldwide. And we'd have investigat-
ing committees, blue-ribbon panels, editorial opinions—
indeed, the President might well be forced to shut the
department down. Our best course remains what it has
been since 239-T was organized by your late father. Careful, considered historical research, taking care to disturb
no milieu into which your people venture. We will make
this facility public knowledge when we have gathered
enough data to prove beyond doubt that the Gate can
safely be used for unlimited travel to the past. That and
only that will forestall public panic."

Cal stood up. "Thank you for spelling out the situation,
sir. We'll be on watch. Though against what—or whom—I
wish we knew. We can start by having a new crew of military guards assigned to the outer corridors. Guards who've
been freshly screened."

"You don't suspect any of the boys on duty now?"
White asked.

"No, Gordon. But evidently we can't be too careful."

Sloat said, "I'll arrange for the computers to select the
men. We'll have them tested, investigated, and on duty the
day after tomorrow. I guarantee Sidney Six won't be one

of them." He paused. "If that's all—I gather there's a departure coming up?"

"Mr. Sloat would like to watch," Ira Hand said. "I've okayed it."

"Fine," Cal said, walking toward the door. "This way."

"To where?" Sloat wanted to know.

"To the eve of the destruction of the city of Pompeii."

Moments later, the red door slid closed behind them.

A dark tunnel showed golden light at the end. The footsteps of the party rang and echoed. Tom's pulses picked up, as they always did when he saw the Gate.

To step into another epoch, walk the strange streets, listen to an ancient language—one day, he'd have that thrill.

The Gate proper was a stainless steel platform one foot above the floor of the circular room at the end of the tunnel. The room was thirty feet in diameter, its wall completely filled with dials and switches. Around a cluster of gold floodlights in the ceiling, computer display boards flashed tiny lights in sequence.

Dr. Stein picked up a clipboard with a sheaf of closely written notes. He began checking readings on the various dials and displays.

"Forgive me," Sloat said, "but is this all there is to it?"

"This is only the operating center," Cal replied, as Dr. White stepped onto the stainless steel platform. His face, hands, and legs were several shades darker than they had been earlier. "Thirty times this amount of gear is buried beneath us."

"A computer does most of the work of relating the two coordinates," Walker said.

"Temporal and spatial," Cal explained. "Time and space. We must locate the researcher in both. And carefully. The computer handles the billions and billions of calculations necessary to make sure Gordon doesn't arrive on the wrong day—or land in the Tyrrhenian Sea. I doubt that you have any idea of the complexities involved, Mr. Sloat. Consider all the various calendars that have been in existence since A.D. 79, each slightly different from the next. They must all be taken into account."

"I'm sure the technicalities are beyond me," Sloat nodded. "My chief question is, How safe is it?"

"I've been to ancient Babylon," White said.

"I watched the battle of Waterloo last week," added Stein.

"And they haven't lost one of us yet," Walker concluded.

"You might describe some of your precautions, Dr. Linstrum," Ira Hand suggested. Tom noticed Donald Koop watching the Vice-President closely, an expression of almost mystic adoration on his face.

"Right," Cal said. "A week prior to a field trip, we begin programming the spatial and temporal coordinates. It can be done much faster, of course. But we like to be careful. We recheck the coordinates upward of two dozen times. Right now, Gordon's coordinates are locked in. The hard work's done. It's a simple matter to send him off."

"Equally simple to bring him back?" Sloat asked.

"We try to make it so. You know about our rules?"

"Only observation via camera and sound recorder? Yes, the Vice-President mentioned those."

"Gordon carries the camera and the recorder in a special belt under his toga. Plus the Gate control unit."

Dr. White fished out a small, shiny box about twice as large as the matchbox-size camera.

"That's our most important failsafe," Cal explained. "Should the researcher encounter an emergency, pressure on the side of that box returns him here instantly. It's preferable that he return from the spot where he landed in the other time. Any other location presents risks, but it's not impossible. Also, only one researcher is allowed to use the Gate at any given time. And he, in effect, controls the entire operation from the moment he vanishes from this room."

Sloat walked around the platform. "How so?"

"Because of certain relays built into the equipment, no one else at this end can go anywhere in the past except where the original researcher has gone. When our controls are properly set, the time-phase waves remain focused—locked—on the first site."

Sloat digested this slowly. "You mean that once Dr. White departs, if I decide I want to see the battle of Iwo Jima—programming all these gadgets accordingly—I'll still wind up in Pompeii?"

"Exactly. We must keep the passage between *then* and *now* open because we have no way of foreseeing what sort of trouble the research man might run into. Despite all his linguistic study, for example, Gordon could still be spotted as a stranger in Pompeii. He's applied that deep-deep-stain makeup, but he still doesn't look precisely Latin. Well—anything else?"

Sloat shook his head. "Amazing."

"Staggering might be a better word," said Ira Hand. "Do you wonder that mere human beings have trouble deciding how the Government should utilize this phenomenon?"

In the ensuing silence, Tom thought of the wonders Gordon White would soon encounter. Strange new sights, smells, sounds that ordinary archaeologists could only speculate about from the evidence of Pompeii's wall paintings and bits of shattered clay.

Dr. Stein started snapping down switches. "Two minutes," Dr. Walker announced.

"When will he be back, Dr. Linstrum?" Sloat inquired.

"In about three days, our real time. Just before Mount Vesuvius erupts. Are you familiar with the Pompeii story?"

"Vaguely."

"She was one of the finest cities of the Empire. Perched on the west coast of Latium—Italy—at the foot of the volcano. Vesuvio, as they called it. Legends say the god Heracles founded the city. A great many notable people had lavish seacoast villas in and around the city. Cicero, for one. Some scholars have called Pompeii the Monte Carlo of old Rome. In A.D. 63, an earthquake destroyed many of the public buildings. The residents were just finishing major restorations in 79 when the real destruction hit."

"The eruption of the volcano," Sloat nodded.

"Thousands died. The city was buried under tons of ashes and cinders. Archaeologists didn't start digging up the remains until the eighteenth century, when—"

"One minute," Dr. Walker called.

A sheen of sweat had built up on White's face, glistening in his salt-and-pepper beard. The top of his head was bathed gold by beams from the ceiling. The sequencing of the lights grew more rapid.

Suddenly Sloat said, "But going back there with a knowledge of the language and knowing what was—is about to happen—couldn't he warn them?"

"And save countless lives," Cal nodded. "Theoretically. The danger is, we have no way of knowing how that would affect the course of history afterward."

Ira Hand said, "And there is no person in this room—in this nation—or anywhere, so far as I know—who is prepared to accept the responsibility for a decision of that magnitude. That is why we cannot allow someone like Sidney Six—"

Cal gestured in warning.

The sequencing lights flashed faster across the blue lenses hiding Donald Koop's eyes. Dr. White started to raise his hand in a farewell gesture—

The stainless steel platform was empty.

Reflections rippled across its polished surface. Cal turned to his visitors. "Now comes the hard part, gentlemen. All we can do is wait."

3

TRACK DUAL

"LADIES AND GENTLEMEN," boomed an amplified voice, "five minutes until the main event of the evening. Twenty laps for a two-thousand-dollar purse—"

"I bet a friend that Geyser Hankins will take it," Donald said, following Tom down the steep aisle to their seats.

"He's a rough driver," Tom said, balancing the cup of iced vitabeverage with one hand while he wiped the mustard off his lip with the other. "He shaves the rules pretty closely."

Donald grinned. "That's typical of you, Thomas. You let a lot of nice little scruples stand in the way of a goal. Geyser Hankins wants to win. He does what it takes to be first around that track."

Donald bit into a chocolate-covered cereal bar. "Sometimes I think there's nothing you want badly enough," he added. "When a normal person wants something, he goes after it. Or has Calvin browbeaten that out of you?"

Tom found himself irritated. "I think I'm as normal as the next guy. But I won't go after what I want regardless of the price. Doing that nullifies the worth of whatever you're after."

"A pretty little philosophy. Lucky for us, the movers of this world think otherwise. Hey! Here they come!"

A gate opened beside the banked oval track below. The track, erected around the rim of the Sportsdrome for tonight's races, consisted of interlocking slabs of a very light but firm blown foam. The gems needed only that

19

kind of resistant surface for their air currents to push against.

The Sportsdrome was Washington's newest public building, a gleaming, air-conditioned enclosed hemisphere. The tiers of seats were jammed with fans, who roared as the first of the small ground-effect machines glided onto the track.

The lime-green racer carried a large yellow numeral 7, plus a decal that identified the helmeted driver, Typhoon McGee. McGee, a black, held up his glove in a fist. His partisans yelled and applauded.

The second gem nosed onto the track. Its supporters let the driver hear their enthusiasm. All the gem jockeys seemed to affect nicknames associated with windstorms or air currents, which was natural, considering that the light, swift racers skimmed along on jets of air blowing from their underbellies. They never touched the special roadbed.

Donald said, "I'm having some friends in afterward, Thomas. Want to come over?"

This was a surprise to Tom. Donald explained that he had arranged the party at the last minute. "So the guy I made the bet with will be there. To pay off."

Tom replied, "Sure. I haven't seen the new place yet. You like it?"

"Living by yourself takes getting used to. I depended on Mom pretty heavily. But I eat over at the Senator's a lot, so that helps." Donald took off his glasses and pinched the bridge of his nose. For an instant his veneer of tough pragmatism dropped away. "I couldn't stand our old place after Mom died. Too many ghosts."

Another gem racer joined the four already at the starting line. The applause and shouting grew louder with each new arrival—the favorites usually made their appearance toward the last. The program said Hankins would be the final driver. He had won the pole position in the draw.

Tom wondered whether the friends Donald referred to shared his political views. If so, Tom was prepared to dislike them. In the last decade, student activisim had swung from the ultraleft to the extreme right. And Donald parroted all the militant slogans.

Donald had first come to work in the department the preceding summer. But it seemed to Tom that his friend's views had hardened since then, or at least he had become more vocal.

Perhaps it was partly due to the emotional shock of his mother's tragic death on an operating table. At any rate, Donald had an intense, even haggard look lately. But he was bright and, in most ways, a pleasant companion.

"Here comes the tiger!" Donald shouted, on his feet.

A sleek black racer painted with jets of red-tinged steam nosed through the gate. Just under the cowl, Geyser Hankins' name appeared in flame-colored letters. Some older fans nearby glared at Donald, then booed. Throughout the Sportsdrome, a chorus of disapproval mingled with scattered applause.

The racers began final maneuvering for starting positions. Giant floodlamps in the 'drome's ceiling poured light onto the lacquered cowls. Geyser Hankins' black helmet flashed with hard highlights.

"You don't seem very interested tonight, Thomas."

"I was thinking about Dr. White."

"Come on, Geyser!" Donald yelled suddenly. "Knock that bum if he won't move!"

Hankins was doing just that, nudging the driver on his right to make more room at the line. The bumped driver looked angry. Hankins ignored him.

The starter began his climb to the metal tower overlooking the track's inner edge.

As the stands quieted, awaiting the start, Donald said, "I'm beginning to think trips like White's are a farce anyway. I could find less trivial ways to use the Gate."

"Such as?"

"Here you have one of the most powerful—or potentially powerful—tools for change in the history of the world. What does Archy do with it? Nothing!"

"Keep your voice down! You know we're not supposed to mention—"

"Ah, these people wouldn't believe it if we diagrammed it. They're lumps, Thomas, just like most men. Squeezed out of the mold that society, and the Government, creates for them. The Government's gotten too big. Too powerful. An individual can't make a mark. He's too far removed from the decision points. That's why I get so infuriated about the Gate. Think of how it could be used, selectively, to change things."

"You mean tinker with the past?"

"Sure! Look. What if, right now, someone traveled back

to Germany circa 1933 and removed Adolf Hitler? No World War II! Millions of human lives saved!"

"My father wrote about that sort of theory," Tom said. "It supposes that time—the past—is like a road that can be made to fork. Here we are, down at the end of a line of history that began—okay, let's say in 1933. But if there hadn't been a Hitler, A Second World War, would we be here? Would the Sportsdrome be here? Who knows? And back in the '40s, would this country have worked so hard to develop the atom bomb, and all the atomic generating plants that have come in its wake? Would we have captured the German scientists who helped us to land Armstrong on the moon? Would we have learned how to mass-produce penicillin? How much or how little would everything change because of your one suggested alteration? No one knows. And my father wasn't willing to experiment to find out. Cal isn't either. Besides, there isn't just one place where the road can fork. There are millions, when you count minor historical events. It would be foolish to try to manipulate the present via the past."

Donald snorted.

"You don't buy that?"

"No. It's a crime for that Gate to sit there, a real means of getting things accomplished—"

"But who would decide on what to change, Donald? You?"

"I have a few ideas."

"Name one."

"I'd go back and make sure Archy didn't get elected in '84. With the Comchins building up strength in Asia, we don't need his brand of mealymouthed pacifism."

Disturbed by his friend's vehemence, Tom countered, "So you'd use the Gate to ensure his defeat three years ago?"

"I'd use the Gate to get him out of office. Period. I—"

A pistol crack whipped their attention to the track. The gem racers shot forward in a glittering row, riding less than a foot off the hard-surfaced track, their airblowers blasting and whistling. In a matter of one lap, Typhoon McGee had taken the lead, skimming over into the pole position an eighth of a lap ahead of Geyser Hankins.

"Catch him, Geyser!" Donald shouted, on his feet, waving his fists. "Knock him off!"

The race quickly became a duel between McGee and

Hankins, obviously driving the two fastest machines. Donald screamed Hankins' name until his voice began to grow hoarse.

During the sixteenth lap, while the other ground-effect machines fought for secondary positions, Hankins at last found the power to edge up on the leading driver. He swung his racer out to the right of McGee as they sped into one of the high-banked curves.

"Knock him out, Geyser!" Donald yelled. *"Kill him!"*

Hankins slotted over to the left, trying for position ahead of McGee. The tail of his racer slammed McGee's right front. McGee wobbled to the left. His left-hand air jets ran off the track rim and suddenly had nothing to push against. McGee fought for control as Hankins zipped into first place in the pole lane.

Hanging half on, half off the edge of the track, McGee's machine slowly tilted. Finally he lost control altogether. The nose of his racer veered sharply to the left.

McGee's machine dropped eight feet to the brilliant green artificial turf and landed belly down with a heavy thud. Smoke began to pour from the power compartment.

All over the Sportsdrome, fans were on their feet, most of them booing Hankins' tactics. Cheeks glistening with sweat, Donald applauded. His ugly expression made Tom wonder again about him.

Hankins now had a full lap's head over the nearest contender.

Donald's blue lenses loomed as he turned to laugh. "See what I mean? When Hankins wants something, he gets it."

"At any price—right?"

"That's the way the movers get things done."

"Then the movers and I don't see eye to—"

"Good for you, killer, you did it!" Donald cried, as Hankins took the checkered flag.

A rescue crew was foaming down McGee's machine to prevent fire. Other men used crowbars to pry open the driver's bubble. Moments later, McGee climbed out. Limping, he waved to the crowd. He received a sympathetic round of cheers—and a raspberry from Donald. Tom decided that he was not in a mood for a party with Donald and his radical friends.

But, watching Donald's ferocious face as he applauded Geyser Hankins pulling in to accept the purse and trophy, Tom changed his mind.

It might be smart to meet Donald's crowd. It might give him a valuable insight into the extent of Donald's rather wild convictions.

"Good for you, killer!" Donald kept shouting above the din. *"Good for you!"*

After the races, the two young men used Tom's small exhaust-free electric for the drive to Donald's flat. Tom had bought the car secondhand, with money from his earnings in the department. In about half an hour, the car brought them to an area where large apartments had been put up as part of urban redevelopment.

The night air was heavy with the threat of rain. They took the lift up to Donald's rented efficiency on the next-to-top floor, where about a dozen students Donald's own age had already gathered.

Uniformly, the young men displayed shaved heads and glasses with lenses of various colors. Tom noticed only three girls, one quite fat. They all had the drab, faintly pop-eyed look that Tom characterized—with a suitable lack of interest—as "intense."

A military march blared from the four-corner sound system. The air smelled sweet. About half the guests were smoking a legal variant of marijuana. Tom never used the stuff, for the same reason that many people, years ago, had avoided cigarettes, now long banned from public sale—he liked to feel in perfect shape, all his faculties sharp, all the time.

"Throw your jac in the bedroom and grab a high in the kitchen," Donald said. Then he shouted into the blue haze pierced by a couple of pin spotlights, "You owe me, Karlberg. Geyser took the race."

In the hall leading past the tiny bedroom, a circular dart board hung on the wall. A news photo of President Archibald had been pasted to the board. Three darts stuck from the hole-pocked photo, one in the chief executive's mouth, one in each of his eyes. Tom shivered.

Carrying a pop-open can of high, one of the girls blocked Tom's path. "Are you here about the demo?"

"Demo? No, I'm a friend of Donald's—"

The girl's face froze. "Forget I asked." She hurried on.

Tom turned into the bedroom. It was sparsely furnished—a bed, a bureau, two chairs. The focus of attention was a huge American flag tacked to the wall above the bed. A rotating multicolored plastic disc, mounted in front of a ceiling spot, cast changing patterns of red, white, and blue over the national emblem.

Tom threw his jac on the bed and headed for the kitchen. There, two bald students were discussing the "demo" the girl had mentioned. The conversation stopped a moment after Tom walked in.

He took a can of a popular brand of high from the fridge, popped the ring, let the sweet, mildly carbonated beverage relieve his thirst. He heard a faraway rumble of thunder.

In about sixty seconds, he began to experience a pleasurable sense of relaxation. High was the nickname for a generic chemical that had been developed in a major research lab a few years earlier. Invented as a substitute for hard liquor, it induced a mile euphoria without impairing judgment or motor performance, no matter how much was consumed. It left no traceable aftereffects. A sort of pop containing chemical mood lifters, it was consumed in vast quantities by young and old—much to the relief of police forces, which no longer had to contend with a high percentage of drunk drivers.

One of the students said to the other, "We plan to leave on a Tuesday. The bus is already chartered. We should be in Manhattan by—"

A nudge from the other student, obviously meant as a reminder of Tom's presence, silenced the first speaker. Both stared.

"Haven't seen you around here before," one said to Tom.

"Right. Friend of Donald's. But I'm interested in the demo. When is it?"

More scrutiny. Thunder rumbled. The military march blared.

At last one of the students shrugged and said, "Archy's presenting his latest disarmament offers to the United Nations in a couple of weeks. He's in for a big surprise when he stands up to speak in the Assembly."

"What kind of surprise?"

"First, there'll be a massive sidewalk demo, marching, singing, in front of the building when he arrives."

"But that's not all," said the other student. "Archy is going to learn that power belongs to the people in this country, or Archy isn't going to be around very long. We have plans that will shake—"

A wagging motion of the other student's head prompted caution again. The second student said, "You'd better talk to Donald."

"Sounds interesting," Tom said. "I will."

In truth, it sounded appalling. The more he saw of Donald's friends, the less he liked them.

Sipping from his can of high, he returned to the living room. His friend was surrounded by five others, all of them shouting above the music. Tom dropped into a corner, propped himself against the wall, drank again. The room had a dim, dreamy quality. Clouds of sweetish blue smoke turned slowly through the slanting light beams.

There's something dangerous here, he thought.

After half an hour of being ignored, Tom got up. Donald was still arguing. Tom slipped to the edge of the crowd.

"Have to move out, Donald. It's late."

Weaving slightly, Donald broke from the group. "Not exactly your kind of rally, eh, Thomas? These people are pretty involved—"

"That is *not* the best corner for forming up the demo," a girl shrilled. "I'll prove it! Donald, where's that map we marked?"

"Top drawer, in the bedroom." To Tom, "So we can't interest you in a little political activisim tonight?"

"Nor any night, thanks anyway." With a forced smile, he told Donald he would see him tomorrow. Donald waved and went back to his wrangling friends.

Tom passed the map fetcher just leaving the bedroom. He found his jac, started to put it on. As he did so, his eyes drifted toward the bureau. The top drawer was half open. Sticking out from under a Harvard sweatshirt was an object whose shape Tom recognized instantly.

He glanced at the door. No one was coming.

He moved to the bureau in two quick steps, and lifted the sweatshirt. Among tangled T-shirts lay a black needle-muzzle laser pistol.

The i.d. plate below the light-amp chamber had been filed bare. Bought illegally, then. Only contraband weapons had the federal registration serial removed.

What earthly use did Donald Koop have for a laser pistol?

Suddenly Tom had the feeling that he was being watched. He whipped his head around.

The hall outside the door was empty.

Quickly, he replaced the sweatshirt, closed the drawer, and left the room.

Driving back to Georgetown, Tom could not push the twin images from his mind:

The lighted flag.

And the deadly weapon.

The August night was still muggy. Distant lightning flickered. Tom finally rolled up the windows and switched on the air conditioning to eliminate the heat and the stink from the befouled Potomac.

Tonight had been illuminating, in a grim sort of way. Just how emotionally stable *was* his friend?

"That's the way the movers get things done—"

Surely Senator Koop wouldn't have used his influence to get Donald a job in a delicate security operation such as Department 239-T if he had been aware of his nephew's radical leanings. On the other hand—

Tom pulled into a parking place in front of the elegant old house. A light still burned up in Cal's bedroom. He locked the car, let himself into the house, started up the stairs.

On the other hand, as Tom had recalled earlier tonight, Donald's swing to outright militancy had seemed to accelerate only after the death of his mother. Completely on his own, with no family besides the Senator, Donald was accountable to no one—except his intense and secretive friends.

Cal's door stood partially open. "Tom? It's a little late."

Tom stifled a retort and said instead, "I stopped off at Donald's. Any report from Dr. White?"

"All quiet. The mission must be proceeding according to plan."

"Cal, I—"

"What is it?"

About to enter his brother's bedroom, Tom stopped. "Nothing."

Cal appeared at the door, wearing his bathrobe. "You want to continue the college discussion?"

"Tomorrow," Tom said, heading down the hall. "I'm beat."

In his room, Tom switched on the window air conditioner and pulled off his clothes. As he headed for the shower, he realized what had stopped him at Cal's door.

A feeling of foolishness.

Surely his suspicions about Donald were just that—unwarranted suspicions. Talk of the kind in which Donald indulged had never hurt anyone, and it was most often nothing *but* talk.

And yet, the laser pistol—

A lot of people in urban areas carried weapons for personal protection, didn't they?

Yes, of course. But—*registered* weapons.

That night Tom had trouble sleeping.

4

SUSPICION

THE NEXT MORNING, the problem of Donald popped back into Tom's head. He considered it in the light of Vice-President Hand's concern about security and decided that no matter how foolish his suspicions seemed, he couldn't in good conscience keep them from Cal.

He raised the subject on the drive to Alexandria. Traffic was heavy. Heat haze obscured the horizon, promising another stifling day. Maneuvering around a slow driver, Cal laid on the horn.

"I told you I stopped at Donald's apartment last night, Cal."

"So?"

"He has some pretty strange friends. All of them are dead set against President Archibald's disarmament policies—to the point of planning a demonstration when Archibald speaks at the United Nation."

"That won't set well with Senator Koop. But it won't cost Donald his job, unless he breaks the law. The dissent trials back at the end of the Nixon administration settled that."

"But that's not the only thing."

Looking tired, Cal reached for his sunglasses. "Well, unless it's vitally important, let's skip it. There's enough to worry about with this security problem. I thought about it most of the night. Every last person in our section passed the very strictest screening before coming to work. And that includes Donald."

"Still, Donald took his tests over a year ago. Since his mother died, he's acted—well—different."

That superior tone edged Cal's voice all at once. "Can you come to the point?"

Instantly Tom felt defensive. Angry. He had an impulse to keep silent. Let Cal suffer the consequences, if any.

He couldn't do it. As Cal swung the sedan onto the beltway leading to Alexandria, Tom said, "Last night, Donald made some pretty outrageous statements. He thinks the Gate should be used for what he calls selective historical change. He'd like to see President Archibald defeated in the last election, for instance."

"I gave Donald credit for more brains."

"He doesn't understand the theory of alternative histories, I guess. Or if he does, he doesn't believe it. I tried to explain it again, but I'm no expert."

"Who is?" Cal snapped. "We're dealing with something incapable of verification except at enormous risk. Who can say how the world would have changed if Rome hadn't fallen? if Christ hadn't been crucified? if Edison had died before he found the right filament for his incandescent bulb? Would another Edison have come along? Would we be lighting our cities with gas to this day? Donald's naïve to think as he does."

"Disturbed people sometimes oversimplify things."

"I see no evidence that Donald's disturbed."

"But you hardly ever talk to him."

"Are you saying you're a better judge of character than I am?"

"I'm saying I know Donald."

"Tom, we have enough problems wrapped up in this security business without manufacturing—"

"I'm not manufacturing anything! I'm only reporting—"

"Unfounded suspicion," Cal finished. "Personally, I don't like Donald. Never have. He was rammed down my throat because of his connection with the Senator. But that doesn't alter the fact that he passed the very toughest scrutiny of his background, plus all the psychological tests."

"A lot of things can happen to a person in twelve months. Ideas—personalities can change."

"I won't argue, Tom. Do you or don't you have any concrete evidence to show that Donald represents a threat to the department?"

Suddenly Tom's forehead began to hurt. The pain was

intensified by the glare from the metal of the cars on the beltway. Why did Cal automatically sit in judgment? Why wouldn't he give others the benefit of at least feigned equality?

Tom recalled the laser pistol, started to mention it. But, noting his brother's expression, he resigned himself to silence on the subject, saying instead, "No, Cal, there's no evidence. Only Donald's talk."

"I appoint you chief monitor of everything Donald says from now on. If he tells you he's going to hop through the Gate, return to '84 and stump for President Archibald's defeat, you let me know."

Tom subsided into gloomy introspection for the rest of the trip.

Shortly they turned off the beltway. Ten minutes later, they reached the parking lot of a plain concrete building on the outskirts of Alexandria. Beside the building's tinted glass doors hung a metal plaque:

U.S. DEPARTMENT OF THE ENVIRONMENT
AIR QUALITY DIVISION

A lobby receptionist nodded good morning. They walked down a long corridor flanked by closed office doors, each with a plastic nameplate. Stopping by a door at the end, Cal took out a key. The plastic plate identified the office as belonging to Dr. Charles Q. Lind. There was no such person employed in the building.

Inside, a few pieces of furniture simulated a working office. From time to time, the papers on the desk were changed, ones with more recent dates being substituted. A folder on top showed the subject of the material to be urban pollutant emission levels.

Cal unlocked a door in the rear wall. He and Tom stepped into a private washroom of unusually large size. Alongside the medicine cabinet was a horizontal slot, wider than the usual one for used blades. Cal inserted his ident, held it there a moment, then pulled it out. Tom did the same with his card.

They stepped to the center of the floor. Suddenly a hairline crack appeared around a rectangular area. Activated by their weight, the rectangle began to sink.

In the bunker, Cal went immediately through the red door. One of the senior technicians was always on duty when a research trip was in progress, and Cal wanted to check on any overnight developments. Tom had filing to do in his brother's office. Because of security, the two girls who worked as departmental secretaries were not allowed to handle certain key documents.

Tom paused at the door of the storage rooms. Having used his own ident, Donald had already come through the bogus office upstairs, been lowered by the sinking floor, and was at work slitting open another of the costume boxes.

This morning he seemed more relaxed. He grinned, pushing his blue glasses up on his forehead.

"You should have stuck around last night, Thomas. We really hung Archy. Figuratively, of course."

"You know, Donald, if you take part in anything besides a peaceful demonstration up at the UN, you could lose your job."

"Forget it. The Senator's made that very clear. And I can't afford *not* to work here. College tuition doesn't come cheap. My friends and I are going to get Archy, all right. But in the court of public opinion. And at the polls."

For a moment Tom accepted the explanation at face value—and with relief. Then he realized how glib Donald had been.

Too glib?

Had his friend become suspicious in turn? Paradoxically, what alarmed Tom most was Donald's broad grin, so unfamiliar of late. Such abrupt changes in mood didn't seem genuine. All at once—dismally—Tom felt he was in the presence of someone he couldn't completely trust.

"When does White come back?" Donald asked.

"Nine tomorrow night."

"Cal planning to supervise?"

"Far as I know."

"I'm not signed on for duty then. Too bad. It's still kind of exciting when one of them returns."

"I'm sure Cal would clear you to come in for the arrival."

"No, I've got plans. I'll read White's monograph later."

"Okay. See you for lunch?"

Donald slid his glasses down on his nose. "Don't think so, Thomas. Unless I keep at this, I'll never finish." He turned his back.

On the way to Cal's office, Tom recalled his brother's

earlier words. Maybe Cal was right. Maybe he *was* a poor judge of character. It was a disheartening admission, because it automatically helped to validate all Cal's other attitudes and supported his contention that his decisions must be accepted without question.

Tom recalled the feeling of being watched when he discovered the laser pistol. Had one of Donald's friends passing along the hallway seen him and reported it? That would account for Donald's attempt to dismiss his own rantings as just talk.

Or was he still reading far too much into the entire situation?

Confused and feeling that he had lost another round in his long fight to establish his own competence in his brother's eyes, Tom entered Cal's office. For a moment he wanted to grab the papers to be filed and toss them helter-skelter, jumbling them hopelessly.

But he didn't.

When Department 239-T officially closed at five the following evening, Tom and Cal stayed behind. Dr. Walker went home. Dr. Stein, scheduled for duty along with Cal, said he would be back after doing a short errand.

The filing had proved a monumental task, because Tom had let it go for three weeks. He was still busy duplicating the originals on the microfiche encoder, setting up retrieval numbers for the timelock vault, and disposing of the original documents down the chute, when Cal looked in at six, suggesting that they eat supper.

Sloat's new guards were already on duty. The burly, phlegmatic-looking soldier on the far side of the thick gray door was unfamiliar.

When Tom commented on it, Cal nodded, and said, "But if Sidney Six lives up to his reputation, I'm not sure a battalion will keep him out."

They showed their idents at the cafeteria door, were admitted, and chose their food—enriched steak plus side dishes—from the cathode-ray-tube display. A smaller CRT lighted up to show the sums that would be automatically deducted from their computerized payroll accounts. In less than five minutes, wall doors popped open and extensor arms shot out the warmed trays. The department's tiny cafeteria was serviced by the larger automated installation in the Air Quality building, above ground.

As they sat down, Cal checked his watch for the second time in minutes. He was always excited when one of the researchers returned.

Tom's mind flooded with potential subjects for conversation. He really wanted to bring up the matter of Donald again, particularly the question of whether his friend shouldn't retake the psychological tests he had passed easily a year before. Then there was the question of college plans. But somehow he didn't feel up to raising either topic, only to have his views knocked down as immature and unworthy.

Toward the end of the meal, Cal said, "I thought Donald would be joining us."

"He's off duty tonight."

Cal frowned. "Last night he asked for clearance to come in. I didn't know poli sci majors were big on Roman history, but he expressed interest in getting a firsthand report on Pompeii. I okayed the request."

Puzzled, Tom said nothing.

They finished their hot vitamin drinks and left the cafeteria at five of seven.

Tom said to the guard on duty at the gray metal door, "Have you seen Koop?"

The name didn't register with the new man. Tom described him. The guard nodded.

"He came in about twenty minutes ago."

"How about Dr. Stein? Stocky man, with a beard?"

"He was back about six fifteen."

Cal slotted his ident, crossed the antechamber to the red-painted door. Tom turned off to the storage rooms. The outer door was ajar.

Inside, he flicked on the lights and looked around. No Donald. Four large costume cartons remained to be unpacked. One of them had a half-dollar-size hole punched in its side.

Returning to the antechamber, he saw the yellow warning light glowing above the door of the photo lab. The department's part-time technician was evidently readying his soup for White's film.

Five after seven. No point in heading for the Gate yet. He might as well go on with the filing—

Suddenly the red door slid back. Cal rushed across the antechamber, looking neither left nor right. Tom had never seen his brother look so worried.

Cal pressed the button that opened the gray door. "We're on alert. No one gets in or out."

The closing door hid the guard's surprised face.

"Cal, what's wrong?"

"Stein's unconscious. I think he was attacked."

Heart pounding, Tom followed his brother down the tunnel.

Dr. Stein lay sprawled in the Gate chamber, groaning. He had a nasty gash on his left temple. A thin line of blood, dry now, had run down his cheek into his beard. Rust-colored spots stained his white coat.

But those were not the only signs of trouble.

The face plate of one entire section of control equipment had been torn off. It lay twisted on the floor. In several places, the wiring in the guts of the wall had been ripped out. A smell of burned insulation clogged the air.

Tom's eyes jumped to certain dials. All red. Circuits had burned out before regulators forced auxiliary circuits into operation.

Like a hurt bear, Stein rose to hands and knees.

"Leo?" Cal said, kneeling beside him. "Can you hear me now?"

"Dizzy—" Stein shook his head with a ferocious motion. "Give me a hand up."

As he did, Cal blurted, "Who hit you?"

Dr. Stein seemed both startled and enraged as he gasped, "Koop. That kid Koop. He came in here a little while ago—I thought he was acting pretty jumpy—" He paused for breath. "Sorry. Give me a minute. I'm not exactly used to being slammed over the head."

He closed his eyes, swaying while Cal held fast to his elbow. Finally Stein signed that he could make it. Cal let go. Stein lurched to the platform and sat down. "As I said, Koop seemed to be acting strangely. But I consider that normal. Never liked him. He started asking inane questions about White's trip. I was too busy to pay much attention. I was working over there—" He pointed to an undamaged section of the wall. "I heard a sound. Didn't turn around in time. He was running at me, and he had a gun. Laser pistol, I think. He hit me with it—" Stein touched his injured temple, where an ugly bruise now showed. "I tried to grab the pistol. He kicked me in the stomach. I fell. He hit me on the head again, then gave me another kick for good measure. He went right to work—he had some kind of tool—" Quietly, Stein finished, "Somewhere in there, I passed out."

Cal had already rushed to the wall. When he turned back, his voice was full of disbelief. "The Gate's been reset."

Stein cried, *"What?"*

Cal's hand touched dials. "New spatial and temporal coordinates."

"For when?" Tom exclaimed. "And where?"

Stein waved to the exposed wiring. "Was he trying to bollix the failsafes, Cal?"

"Obviously, the crazy fool! How could he possibly believe that he could override the mechanisms locking the Gate onto Gordon's site? He's worked here long enough to know that the failsafe systems are three deep. If one's knocked out, another takes over."

"In the state Donald's been in lately," Tom said, "he probably believed he could do anything."

Almost as if he were hoping aloud, Dr. Calvin Linstrum said, "Of course we're not absolutely sure he did anything besides reset the coordinates."

"Maybe he's somewhere in the bunker," Stein said.

"Let's find out."

Cal ran down the tunnel. He returned in several minutes with grim news. "No. And the guard said Donald didn't leave by the main door."

"There's no other way out," Tom said. "Where did he go?"

"You mean where did he *want* to go?" Cal replied. "Regardless of programming new coordinates, there's only one place he could go—Pompeii. Tom, I—I'm sorry about this much. You did try to warn me. I refused to believe you—" Suddenly he raged again. "To work down here and still think he could single-handedly override—he *must* be deranged!"

"Get a reading, Cal," Stein urged. "Find out where he tried to go."

Swiftly Cal punched buttons, flipped toggle switches. Behind the curved wall, a mechanical chattering began. Shortly a paper tape fed from a slot. Cal studied the pricks in the tape.

"It makes no sense! It's programmed for a day last March."

Utter dread touched Tom. "March? What date?"

"The twelfth. What's the significance of—"

"Regardless of the significance," Stein said, "we've got big trouble. That loopy kid's running around Pompeii this minute, wearing twentieth-century clothes, flourishing a laser pistol—who knows what has already happened."

The empty, polished platform reflected the sequencing lights. Cal and Stein stared at it, as if for an answer.

All Tom could think of was the newspaper Donald had marked. A newspaper dated March 12. The weekend that President Archibald had gone into retreat in the Adirondacks—

To draft the disarmament proposals Donald Koop hated.

5

THE UNTHINKABLE

Dr. CALVIN LINSTRUM lifted a red phone and began to dial. In a moment he said, "Arthur? This is Cal. How fast can you get down to the department? There's an emergency. I'll explain when you arrive, but I need you to monitor the Gate, perhaps all night. Right, thanks. And hurry."

"Why all night?" Stein asked when Cal hung up. He waved at one of several synchronized clocks set into the wall. "Gordon's due back in about an hour."

"I expect to meet Gordon before he returns."

"In Pompeii?" Tom exclaimed.

"Yes. I'm going back at exactly ten minutes until nine, our time. I hope to meet Gordon at his departure point. Since he can handle the language, between the two of us maybe we can catch Koop."

Dr. Stein was upset. "Cal, you're too important to the department. We can't risk losing—"

"If things get out of hand back there, Leo, there won't *be* any department. You can count on Archibald to see to that. Don't you realize that this is exactly what we hoped and prayed would never happen? You said it yourself a minute ago—imagine Donald running around the streets of Pompeii, wearing bizarre clothing, waving that laser—it's a disaster!" Again he reached for the phone. "I'll find a doctor to check on that forehead."

"Skip the doctor," Stein said. "If you're set on going

through the Gate, we have work to do. Costume, makeup—"

"Cal?"

His hand still on the phone, Cal turned. "Is it important, Tom?"

"I think I know the significance of the date Donald tried to program. March twelfth—" Even now, in this crisis, he found it hard to articulate the truth, because it was so frightening, so very nearly unthinkable.

Cal reacted with nervous irritation. "Tom, I have no time for speculation about—"

"It's more than speculation. I saw a newspaper Donald marked. A paper from that very same weekend." Rapidly, he reminded them of Archibald's sojourn at Camp Lookout. "Donald especially hates the President's disarmament programs. And up in the Adirondacks that weekend, Archibald began work on the proposals he's planning to present to the UN week after next."

"With a very good chance for approval," nodded Stein.

"The laser pistol he kept in his apartment"—Tom described finding it—"and the newspaper, and Donald's rantings—it all fits together. I never thought he could be that far gone, but—" The magnitude of the idea chilled him to silence.

Dr. Stein put words to it. "Attempted assassination."

Miserably, Tom nodded.

Cal's reaction was typical. "That's ridiculous."

"Don't be too sure," Stein countered. "I've noticed Koop's behavior lately. Erratic, to say the least. If he thought he could use the Gate to remove the President, a place like Camp Lookout would be an ideal spot to strike. Archibald would still be surrounded by security men, but a remote mountain camp would be infinitely easier to penetrate than the White House. There would be times when Archibald would be in the open. Coming out of the lodge to climb into his 'copter, for instance. Donald could position himself in exactly the right location. Hindsight is operating here, remember. He's probably read every published account of that weekend. And you know how a President's major movements are recorded in detail, *after* the fact. He—" Stein swallowed. "He'd have a very good chance."

For one incredible moment, Tom actually believed that his brother's stare signified furious resentment, as if Cal couldn't tolerate one of Tom's ideas being proved valid. Then, ashamed, Tom negated the thought. Cal was showing strain.

"Even if that's all true," Cal said, "it has very little to do with Donald in Pompeii."

"It has everything to do with it," Stein said. "It means Koop is most certainly deranged. We suspected it from the way he tried to override the failsafes. But this ices the cake. Donald Koop is extremely dangerous."

Silence.

Cal's shoulders sagged. Tom glanced at the clocks. Twenty-two minutes before eight. Another idea probed at the edge of his mind, refused to be stifled—

Cal started for the tunnel. "I need to tell the guard to admit Walker—"

"Cal, let me go with you," Tom said.

"Of all the nonsensical suggestions!"

The force of Cal's contempt was almost like a physical blow. But Tom kept on. "Please listen. The idea makes sense because—"

"A crisis like this—and you're thinking about *joyriding?*"

"I can *help!* I know Donald much better than you. If he's out of his head, maybe I can talk to him—keep him from getting angry—when you couldn't. Maybe I can distract him so you can get hold of the laser. You *know* how he'll react to you and Dr. White. You represent authority."

With a sinking feeling, he saw from Cal's expression that he dismissed the idea even before he said, "Impossible. I wouldn't permit—"

"I'd think very seriously about it if I were you," Stein broke in. "Sure, it's a gamble. Tom may not be any more effective than you. On the other hand, as he says, there *is* a reasonable chance that Donald might listen to him and no one else."

Bleak-faced, Cal thought it over. Tom could almost see the interior struggle, as Cal rebelled at someone else's idea. At last he said, "That would put four of us back in time at the same moment. We've never—"

"We've never faced this kind of situation!" Stein exclaimed. "You said so yourself!"

Tom asked, "If Donald really causes havoc in Pompeii, would you report it?"

"I'd be bound by conscience to do so."

"And there goes Dad's work—your work. You admitted Archibald will close the department if he finds out."

"He's right," Stein agreed. "Take him along, Cal. You'll need every bit of help you can get."

Once more Cal measured his younger brother and, Tom was sure, found him wanting. Just as Cal seemed ready to reject the plan a second and final time, he glanced at Stein. Anger simmered on the stocky scientist's face. Perhaps Stein appreicated the situation between the brothers better than Tom had ever suspected.

Finally, Cal said, "All right. But we have to hurry. We're still going through the Gate at ten minutes to nine." And he raced for the tunnel.

The next hour passed in a furious blur. Tom dashed through the bunker, gathering togas, arm rings, sandals, and makeup kit. By eight thirty he and Cal were dressed, their faces darkened with stain.

Call wanted to take person-to-person communication gear in case they became separated, so Tom hurried to the electronics stores and located two tiny talk-receive units that fitted into the special belts they wore beneath their clothing.

Both communicators had built-in recording functions. Tom recalled that he had used one of the devices at home a couple of weeks back to record one of his favorite electronic rock-pop sonatas from FM, intending to transfer it to permanent tape later. Through the unit's tiny window he saw the miniature reel still in place. He was about to remove it when Cal shouted from the antechamber, "Walker's here, Tom. Let's get moving!"

Tom left the reel in the unit and hurried down the tunnel. Both Dr. Stein and Dr. Walker were busy checking the Gate settings. Stein had slapped a bandage on his gashed temple. He seemed to have recovered. Or perhaps he was forcing himself, knowing the extreme emergency.

Tom felt odd in the thigh-length tunic of coarse, drab wool. His sandaled feet were chilly. The clock hand inched toward the hour.

At a quarter to nine, Dr. Walker asked them to step onto the platform.

Busy snapping relays, Dr. Stein nevertheless managed to say, "A pair of noble Romans if ever I saw—"

"Four minutes," Dr. Walker interrupted.

His palms itching, his stomach aching faintly—*he was*

*actually going through time, back nineteen hundred and
eight years*—Tom tried to smile at Cal.

No response. The gold floodlights threw harsh shadows
under Cal's eyes.

Tom watched the multicolored lights blinking faster and
faster. Would he ever see them again? See Washington?
The familiar world?

Dr. Walker barked, "Thirty seconds. Stand by."

With the minute hand at ten before the hour, the sweep
second hand hit twelve. A cool, tingling darkness, en-
veloped Tom suddenly.

Far away, as through windy darkness, a disembodied voice seemed to call, *"Good luck—"*

There was the smell of salt wind. Feeling light-headed,
Tom opened his eyes.

Something had gone wrong! Nothing but darkness—

"Cal?"

"Behind you! And don't shout. There's a cart coming."

Cal dragged Tom behind some boulders. His eyes adjusted to the deep blue night. They watched a fat grandfather pass, driving a little wagon along a road paved with
large stone blocks. Two flea-bitten ponies pulled the cart,
which was loaded with casks.

The road ran along the edge of the sea, at the bottom of
the rocky slope where they had arrived. Beyond the road,
the land dropped away to a beach. The sea murmured.

Overhead—reality was finally falling into place—stars
glimmered in unfamiliar constellations. The night breeze
blew balmy out of the south. At least Tom presumed the
direction was south, since Pompeii was situated on ancient
Latium's west coast.

The wind mingled smells of the salty ocean with another, more sulfurous tang. There was a low rumble, a
tremor in the earth. The cart driver called to his nags in a
strange language, urging them on.

Tom searched for the source of the rumbling, couldn't
stifle an exclamation—

Vesuvio!

Its open volcanic top tinged red, the mountain rose
directly behind a walled city where many lamps burned.
The cart rattled away around a bend.

Cal signed for them to stand up. Tom couldn't keep his
wonder-struck gaze from the city. Its buildings stretched

between the foothills of Vesuvio and a wall fronting the sea. Suddenly his wonder was replaced by a grimmer thought. Tomorrow, the citizens of the Roman city would be fleeing in panic from destruction pouring out of the volcano.

"Gordon should be coming up that road any minute now," Cal said.

"Somehow I thought the Gate would transport him— and us—closer to the city."

Cal shook his head. "The Gate's accurate only within an eighth of a mile, so we have to set it for what we guess to be an open area near the destination. Besides, you can imagine what would happen if a man appeared out of the air in the center of Pompeii."

Tom followed Cal down the rock-strewn slope to the road. "Then Donald would have arrived right here?"

"Yes."

"Where do you suppose he went?"

"He'd probably head into Pompeii. There's nothing else around."

"But he'd realize he wasn't in the Adirondacks."

"Who really knows how he'd react in his state?" Cal replied.

"He has no control for the Gate."

"Right. Gordon's carrying the only one. I checked in the bunker. None of the other control units is missing. If Donald was thinking correctly, he'd have taken one for his own protection. He—Someone's coming!"

They hid behind another large stone. In a moment they saw a man approaching from the direction of the city. He seemed to be about the right height. Tom recognized White's beard, the wine-colored cloak looped across his forearm. He walked slowly, as if footsore.

Cal waited till he was ten yards away, then stood up. "Gordon?"

White's mouth rounded. He crouched as if expecting an attack.

"It's Cal and Tom."

After White recovered from the shock, he came toward them at a shuffling run. "When I heard my name in English, I thought I'd lost my mind. What's wrong, Cal? Why are you here?"

"Donald Koop used the Gate tonight. We think he's in Pompeii."

White seemed able to cope with this second shock. "I've seen no one I know—including Donald."

"You're a little late getting here. Is everything all right?"

"I'm late because checking my infernal watch requires caution. You can't just whip out a modern timepiece in public. And I did encounter one minor difficulty."

He held up his left arm. He no longer wore arm rings.

Tom noticed that White's face was bruised. "What happened?" he asked.

"Quite simply"—an attempt at a smile—"I was robbed. I dropped into a little tavern near the temple of the Fortune of Augustus—Fortuna Augusta, in the vernacular—just north of the forum, to have supper. I've picked my eating spots well until this one. No trouble. Tonight—well, every town has its criminal element. I ran into Pompeii's. They waited outside, jumped me, and stole the arm rings, plus what little money I had left. Luckily, I wasn't searched. If they'd found the control unit—" He touched his waist again. "But what about Koop? When did he arrive?"

"One or two hours ago," Tom said. "He probably disappeared into the city before you left."

White scratched his beard. "Come to think of it, there did seem to be a lot of excitement in town earlier. People congregating on street corners—I wanted to make inquiries, but I didn't. I've tried to stay unobtrusive."

"Excitement about the volcano, maybe?" Tom suggested.

Sadly, White shook his head. "Vesuvio often rumbles. The citizens haven't any idea that destruction's coming tomorrow. Oh, a few temple priests have been predicting dire things in an effort to improve public morals, but no one takes them seriously. Koop, now. Is this his idea of a lark?"

"Far from it," said Cal and explained.

"An absolute calamity!" White said at the end. "We've got to find him."

"Preferably before Vesuvio buries us all," Cal said in a somber tone.

White studied himself with one hand on Cal's shoulder while he massaged his foot. "And I thought I was done with walking. These sandals have given me blisters that you wouldn't believe."

He rubbed a moment longer, then straightened up. "The best place for information is obviously the forum. We'll have to risk speaking to someone. I've tried to keep that to a minimum, because I don't have the local dialect down pat. When my speech produces curious stares"—still limping, he started up the road, Cal and Tom alongside—"I pretend I'm a foreigner, come for a holiday. I tell them I'm from Africa. Even though it's just across the sea, it's the other side of the world."

Tom watched with awe as the lamplit city grew larger ahead of them. Outside the wall, they encountered a party of nobles, the gentlemen riding horses, the women carried in sedan chairs.

White urged his companions off the road. "Those men are *equites*. Knights. Very upper-upper. Being just ordinary citizens, we have to defer. Watch me for cues about when to get out of the way."

At the city gate, a burly soldier in armor stood under a flickering lantern. He recognized White, who whispered to the others, "This could be tricky. I came out this gate only a few minutes ago. Try to grin and act like a couple of rural clods."

Doing his best to look rustic—the effort consisted of a smile that Tom felt must appear patently false—the brothers waited while the doctor greeted the guard in Latin. The soldier scrutinized Cal and Tom. White made another remark. The guard laughed, then waved them into the city.

As they moved down a dark, twisting street, White explained, "I said you were friends of mine whom I'd planned to meet on the road. Farmers, come up from the country outside Rome. For dicing, wine—maybe a girl friend or two. That, the guard understood."

Conversation fell off. Both brothers were enthralled by glimpses of the city through which they hurried—straight, stone-paved streets; small shrines or fountains on nearly every corner; imposing houses, walls unbroken at street level except by locked gates, but opening up to spacious porches and colonnades at the second story. Nearly everywhere, the street-level walls were painted with colorful scenes of daily life. Tom remembered textbook illustrations of excavated chunks of those walls. From the paintings, archaeologists had deduced much about the ancient city.

But the walls also reminded Tom of Pompeii's doom, a doom already sealed and certain.

At this hour, most residents were indoors. From one house, laughter rang out. A dinner party? On an upper porch, a lute sang gently. The few pedestrians they met hardly gave them a glance. Presently White pointed. "The forum."

They approached a torchlit plaza some five hundred feet long and a quarter of that distance across. The forum was paved with great blocks of travertine marble, well-worn. Imposing bronze statues of gods and goddesses thrust up here and there. White enumerated some of the structures surrounding the spacious plaza. "The *macellum*—that's the local meat market. Those are shops. That small building is a temple for worship of the emperor's family."

Next he indicated a building at one end of the forum. The building was fronted by a portico and six great columns. "That's the Capitolium. A temple where you can pay your respects to Jupiter, Juno, or Minerva. Hold on—" Gripping Tom's arm, he indicated a half dozen loungers conversing near the temple steps. "You stay here. I'll see what I can find out."

White limped toward the group of citizens as Tom and Cal dropped back into the shadows of a shop portico.

White approached the citizens with his right palm upraised. The Pompeians, all rather shabbily dressed, gave him cool looks. But White maintained a friendly smile. Vesuvio rumbled. Red light washed over the statues and buildings. Then it faded.

"It seems inhuman not to tell them what's coming," Tom whispered.

Cal looked at his brother with a strange expression. "For exactly that reason, Dad very nearly destroyed all the papers in which he'd written the theoretical base of the time-phase effect. Before anyone so much as thought about constructing a Gate, he understood the agony of a situation like this."

"I didn't know. What changed his mind?"

"He was a scientist. He felt the truth couldn't be hidden, or suppressed, no matter what the consequen—Here comes Gordon."

As White limped rapidly in their direction, one of the men in the crowd stared after him, suspiciously. White darted into the portico, unsmiling. "Donald Koop is the subject of all the commotion, right enough. At least I'm reasonably sure it's Donald. It's unlikely that two—to use their words—*strangely dressed barbarians speaking a wild foreign tongue*—would appear in Pompeii on the same night."

"Have those men seen him?" Cal asked.

"No, but many others have. Apparently he made quite a stir before he was seized."

"Seized?" Tom exclaimed. "By whom?"

"The watch. According to those fellows, the watch worked up the nerve to corner Donald about an hour ago. They surrounded him and carted him off at spearpoint. For some reason, he didn't use the laser. Perhaps he was too frightened. At any rate"—White sounded despairing—"He's been imprisoned."

6

MUSIC FOR ESCAPING FROM A ROMAN PRISON

INSTANTLY, Cal asked, "Do you know where?"

White nodded. "Just a few blocks beyond the *thermae*—the public baths. Donald's in a building where the watch collects drunks and other undesirables and holds them overnight till they can appear before a magistrate. The place is next to a baker's."

He stepped from under the portico, but Cal hauled him back. The loungers by the Capitolium steps were staring in White's direction, their expressions decidedly suspicious.

Abruptly, three of the group started walking toward the portico.

"My dialect must be showing," White whispered. "This way!"

They raced along the shadowed portico. Tom glanced back. "They're coming!"

White dashed into a sour alley between shuttered shops. Following at top speed, Tom stumbled over refuse. White signed them to the left. Distinctly, they heard the pounding sandals of their pursuers.

The three kept a fierce pace along dark streets, then finally stopped to listen.

"I think we've lost them," Cal said, breathing hard.

"There's still the problem of reaching the jail," White said. "Now it'll take longer. We'll have to circle wide around the forum."

It actually took about an hour to locate the building. They got lost twice, White failing to remember a detail of Pompeii's street geography. At last they approached a corner where a bronze fountain bubbled. White raised his hand to check their advance.

Looking both ways, he crept to the fountain. In a moment he signed them forward and pointed.

Halfway up a narrow, sloping street, a canopy supported on two poles hung over the paving stones. From the lamplit doorway drifted the aroma of hot bread. Beyond the stop a small, one-story structure showed light behind barred windows. Tom thought he heard an angry yell, though from which building, he couldn't be sure.

White said, "Let's walk past the open door of the jail and check the situation as we go by."

Doing so, they attracted no notice from the noisy bakery. Somewhere at the back, men shouted at each other in some sort of dispute.

The situation at the jail wasn't encouraging. Inside, a heavyset Roman soldier, armed with sword and spear, dozed on a stool under a lamp. He presented a direct threat to anyone attempting to sneak in by the front way.

Cal discovered a narrow passage along the far side of the jail. He darted into the passage, signaled them to wait, and disappeared.

Directly above Tom's head, a barred window shed dim light. Beyond the bars, a man sang in a low, drunken voice.

Soft footsteps alerted them to Cal's return. "Bad news. I went nearly all the way around. There's no other door."

White scowled. "Then we'll have to bring him out the main door."

"First we'd better be sure he's in there," Tom said.

Carefully, Cal reached up, grasped the lower edge of the barred window, and raised himself for a quick glance.

"He's in there, all right. With two drunks. One's asleep, the other's singing. Donald still has the laser pistol in his belt. The watch must not have recognized it as a weapon."

"All we have to do is to lure that one guard outside—" Tom began.

"It's tougher than that," Cal said. "There's a small office on the far side of the building. Through the window I saw an officer. At least he's wearing a fancier helmet than the guard is. He was writing on a tablet. We'll have to get both of them out."

"A commotion in the street?" White suggested.

"That would bring the guard. I'm not sure about the officer." Cal glanced around. "We need some kind of unusual diversion—"

Right then, Tom remembered an object concealed in the special belt. "I may have—yes. Here."

"That's only a communicator." Cal sounded annoyed.

"I was using it at home a few days ago. I returned it to the stores, but I forgot to take the reel off the playback. I recorded a rock-pop sonata. Wild stuff. Electronic. Something the Romans have never heard. We could play it full blast—"

"Just what we need," White said.

Cal chewed his lip. "Those men in the bakery would certainly come out too."

"If you can handle the first guard," White said, "I'll take care of the bakery. Then I'll come back to help with the officer. Tom, you open the cell."

"Do you suppose there's a key?"

"Probably just a bar."

"I need a weapon—" Cal prowled off down the passage, returned with a large stone. Tom's stomach tightened. He wasn't accustomed to violence. Neither were his brother and Gordon White. Their tension showed on their faces.

Tom pushed a control on the communicator, advancing the music reel to about the center. One flick of another small switch and Pompeii would be blasted with a clangorous, bleeping music that would make Roman hair stand on end. He hoped.

The three crept into the street and crossed to the far side, moving around the oblong of lamplight falling through the door. White stole down to the baker's shop as Tom and Cal recrossed to the jail, keeping to the shadows on either side of the lighted oblong. Cal flattened against the outer wall. Tom peeked at the guard.

Still dozing.

Tom bent, placed the miniaturized communicator against the worn step. He swallowed, saw Gordon White signal his readiness.

Except for the argument in the bakery, the street remained eerily still. Cal surveyed it one more time. Abruptly, he nodded.

Tom pushed the switch.

With a screech and a wheep, electronic music blared. It sounded even more cacophonous than usual through the communicator's small speaker. White kicked the poles supporting the canopy. It tumbled down over the bakery's front door.

Inside the jail, the guard let out a yell. Boots slammed on stone. A burly shadow, a man with a spear, fell across the street.

Cal edged forward. The soldier rushed through the door. Cal whipped his arm over and smacked the rock against the side of the guard's head.

Cursing, the guard dropped his spear. He staggered. Cal grabbed the spear and flung it away. From the bakery, there was louder yelling, as the bakers tried to fight their way through the canopy. White came on the run.

Enraged, the guard lurched to his feet. The earpiece of his helmet had protected him from the full force of the blow. He grabbed the hilt of his short sword. From behind, White pulled the guard's chin back, but the man was large and strong. He shook White off, leaped at Cal.

Fortunately Cal was ready. He drove his fist into the man's belly.

The punch took the wind out of the guard. White chopped the blade of his hand against the back of the man's neck. By then, Tom was through the door and racing for the jail room on his left.

Sure enough, only a bar secured the door. Tom had forgotten about the officer, though. The man came charging down a short corridor, drawing his sword.

Tom seized the nearest weapon, the guard's stool, and flung it.

The stool sent the officer reeling. By that time, White burst in the front door, followed by Cal with the rock. Tom heard sounds of scuffling and furious oaths as he yanked up the bar and hauled the screeching door open.

"Donald? Donald, come on!"

Seated against the wall, his glasses pushed up on his forehead, Donald Koop regarded Tom with a dreamy expression. A curious smile played over his lips.

All at once Donald's eyes cleared. He lurched to his feet, his expression instantly suspicious.

"Who's with you?" he demanded.

"Cal, Dr. White—What's the difference? Come on!"

"They'll just lock me up again—"

"Donald, do you know what's going to happen in Pompeii tomorrow? The volcano will erupt. The whole city will be buried! If you prefer that to getting out of here, you—" Tom held back the final words. *You must be out of your mind!*

He started dragging Donald by the arm. A couple of hard tugs seemed to restore Donald's reason. "All right. Let's go."

White and Cal had gotten the officer down on the floor. White sat on his armored chest while Cal punched his head. Three blows, and the officer was too groggy to move.

As the four plunged toward the door, Cal snatched the laser pistol from Donald's belt. About to protest, Donald suddenly wilted under Cal's furious stare.

First outside, White shouted, "Trouble!"

To the left, at the low end of the street, four soldiers appeared around the corner, a staggering man in tow. Two of the soldiers carried lanterns. Reacting instantly to the wild music, the two without lanterns pulled out their swords.

"It's the watch!" White exclaimed.

All four soldiers forgot about their inebriated prisoner and sped toward the jail.

As they began running, White shouted, "We have to reach the city gate before they do—"

Tom wondered how. The Pompeians all seemed to be powerful men. They ran at incredible speed, considering the street's upward slant. But luck worked for Tom and the rest.

It took the form of the bakers, who finally freed themselves from the canopy and rushed into the street, howling and waving their arms.

The first two watchmen collided with the bakers and tumbled. That gave Tom and the rest the needed edge.

They used it to maximum advantage, racing up the hill. Even Donald seemed aware of the danger. He kept pace.

At a corner, Tom gasped, "Cal, can't we use the Gate control from here?"

"Too risky. Keep going!"

Of the long, wild race to the gate of Pompeii, Tom remembered little, except for impressions of wall paintings streaking past the corner of his eye. White frequently led them in a new direction. Finally, a block from the gate by which they had entered, they slowed down.

Tom's chest hurt. He was sweating, dizzy. Puffing, White and Cal seemed to be in even worse shape.

"Keep walking," White wheezed, limping. "They can't be far behind."

Watching for signs of pursuit, the group reached the gate. White threw his torn cloak over Donald's shoulders, concealing the gaudy shirt and trousers as best he could. The guard didn't notice Donald until the party was directly under the lantern that hung outside the gate. Even then, his reaction was slow, for Donald was partially hidden by the others.

The guard's eyebrow hooked up, the start of a question. Behind, the watch cried warning. White and the others broke into a run.

By the time the guard yelled, they were well away from the city wall.

Tom felt he could not drive himself much farther. Even though he was in good condition, the long run had been grueling. Yet somehow he kept on. Vesuvio gave off a deep ominous sound, showing reddish light brighter than before.

As they raced around the first bend in the coast road, Cal fell. White and Tom helped him up. Cal's cheeks were pale with exhaustion. Back at the city gate, the watch appeared, swinging lanterns, and brandishing spears and swords. The party had grown to some ten men. They charged up the road at top speed.

"Get—" Cal fought for breath as they staggered on. "Get your control ready, Gordon. We have to go through the Gate the instant we reach the area—"

Of them all, only Donald Koop seemed to run without losing strength. Perhaps it was desperation, an awareness of what had almost happened to him. Ahead, Tom recognized the hillside where the Gate had deposited them earlier.

He looked back. The watch was gaining. Their lanterns bobbed wildly.

Suddenly he remembered that he had left the communicator behind, to be buried under tons of ash when Vesuvio erupted tomorrow. Would the tiny device be destroyed? Or would some archaeologist in the far future discover a melted lump of metal that, among all the other relics found in the ruins, completely defied classification?

"Can't—make it," White choked, suddenly dropping to his knees.

Panicky, Cal struggled to pull the doctor to his feet. The watch was steadily closing the distance. They would be caught, taken back—they would die in tomorrow's devastation!

Vesuvio thundered so loudly that the watch broke stride, turning their faces toward the mountain. Tom suddenly felt intense pity for the men. Doing their job tonight, they had no idea of what tomorrow held.

"Not far, Gordon," Cal gasped, supporting White. "We turn off just ahead."

The roadway shook. The red light brightened, faded. The watch resumed pursuit, but again the distraction had provided the narrow margin between capture and escape. They reached the hillside, huddling together as Cal fumbled with the small, shiny box.

He dropped it. He searched for it in the dark as Tom fought to keep from keeling over with dizziness.

Finally Cal located the box, thumbed the side. Cool, tingling darkness began to drop across Tom's mind.

He had a last vivid impression of a belch of red from the volcano. The light reflected from Donald's glasses. On the road below, a member of the watch bawled a command to halt, flung his spear—

Tom watched the spear arc through the starlight, sure it would strike one of them—

Pompeii vanished.

Exhausted, Gordon White sat on the stainless steel platform. Not looking much better, Cal stood nearby, the laser pistol in his right hand.

Tom leaned against the wall. The shock of their experience had finally hit him. Only Donald remained unmoved, seemingly nerveless.

Five minutes earlier, the four had found themselves back in the Gate chamber. A clock showed the local time as ten past one in the morning.

Cal said to Donald, "Take off those glasses. Stop hiding."

Donald obeyed, trying to smile. "Look, Dr. Linstrum, would an apology—"

"*Apology!* You incredible fool! Do you think words can begin to compensate for what you did? For what you *might* have done?" He indicated the gutted wall. "Repairing that damage will cost thousands of dollars. Beyond that—" For a moment, Cal couldn't go on. "You need help, Koop. Your reactions—they're simply incredible!"

Stein and Walker appeared from the tunnel. Walker carried a tray with a pot and coffee cups. The break was welcome.

Tom gulped coffee and began to feel a little better. But Cal still looked furious.

"Shall I ring up security now?" Stein asked him.

"Not till we hear his explanation. If any! You didn't expect to wind up in Pompeii, did you, Koop?"

Donald simulated embarrassment. "I admit I tried to cancel the failsafes—"

"Endangering Gordon's life!"

Donald said nothing. Tom wished he could read his friend's thoughts. He had an eerie feeling that Donald was keeping a mask carefully in place.

Finally Donald replied, "I thought I could override the failsafes without harming anyone. I've studied some electronics on my own—"

"You not only think you can play with this equipment as though it were a toy," Cal exploded, "you apparently believe you're competent to change history. Anyone who thinks that is extremely sick."

Donald let that pass, saying instead, "I'll admit I got a bad fright on that hillside when I realized where I was."

White asked, "Why did you go into Pompeii?"

"I hoped I'd find you. I was pretty scared. Not thinking clearly—"

"You make it all sound so casual! You tried to tamper with the very fabric of the past! The risks—" Again Cal bit off the words. He added, disgusted, "I honestly question whether you're sane enough to understand all I'm saying."

"Well," Donald offered, "when those watchmen caught me, I did wave the pistol at them. Thought it might scare them off—"

No one spoke. Donald finished lamely, "It didn't work."

"Did you seriously expect Roman soldiers to recognize that kind of weapon?" White demanded. "The very fact that they let you keep it should have told you—"

"I know, I know. That hit me pretty fast. Once I was in jail, I decided to use the laser to destroy the door. Late at night, when everything was quiet."

Again heavy silence. Again a weak afterthought. "I couldn't think of anything else."

Cal said, "We have a readout on the destination you tried to set on the Gate."

That, at last, produced a reaction—a visible start. Recovering quickly, Donald said, "Oh?"

"We know you were heading for March twelfth, this year. Tom told us about the newspaper you marked."

Donald glanced at Tom and Tom saw something new and terrifying in his eyes.

Hatred.

Cal was relentless. "You wanted to return to March twelfth. To Archibald's retreat in the Adirondacks. To kill him? To wipe out not only the President but his disarmament proposals?"

"Where's your proof?" Donald snarled.

"Do you deny it?" White shouted.

Blinking, Donald shriveled a little. Then he straightened up, almost proudly. "All right. I don't deny it. Archy deserves to die. He and his milksop ideals are destroying this country."

"You do need a doctor," Walker said. "The sooner, the better."

"Let's go to my office," Cal said. "I'll ring Sloat."

Walker and Stein volunteered to remain behind for a few minutes, shutting down the system. Cal gestured with the laser gun. Donald preceded him along the tunnel. Tom and Gordon White followed.

They had just cleared the red door when they heard a crash from the storerooms. White ran to the door, flung it open, froze. And Tom wondered whether his sanity had collapsed under the night's strain.

One of the costume boxes had been ripped to pieces, the contents scattered. Hovering unsupported in the air, three feet above the litter, was an incredible apparition.

It consisted of a silver metallic cube about a foot and a half square. Across its face were small dials with jiggling needles, and two rows of winking lights. From the sides of the floating box, a pair of metal stalks projected, waving gently. At the end of each glowed a hemisphere of pale green glass mounted in a metal cup.

While all their heads were turned toward the incredible sight, Donald Koop leaped.

He smashed his fist into Cal's head, knocking him sideways. Donald's fingers clawed Cal's wrist. He kneed Cal viciously. Crying out, Cal doubled over.

Donald tore the laser pistol from Cal's hand and pushed him. Cal crashed into the wall. The metal box waved its stalks in an agitated way. The green glass hemispheres pulsed with light.

Gordon White rushed forward. Donald's growl drove him back. Donald backed to the far wall, covering them with the needle-tipped gun. His glasses had fallen back into place, blue mirrors. The set of his mouth said he was desperate.

"Stand still," Donald ordered. "Otherwise I'll have to kill you all."

7

WHAT THE BOX REVEALED

DESPITE THE WARNING, Tom said, "Donald, whatever you're thinking—"

"Thinking, Thomas?" A strange smile. "I'm thinking that, of all these people, you'd be the hardest to kill. But I can do it. After all, you're an Archy sympathizer. So don't force me."

White couldn't take his eyes from the floating box. "What *is* that thing?"

Donald shrugged. "I don't know. But it's obviously metal. And metal burns." He moved the laser pistol ever so slightly. "Just like the rest of you."

At this, the dials on the box jiggled more wildly. The stalks whipped back and forth. Tom had the feeling that they were suffering from a collective nightmare.

"Now listen carefully," Donald ordered. "I want you to move. But very slowly. You first, White."

"Where?"

"In there."

Their eyes swung to the thick door. Cal gasped. "The vault?"

"Don't worry," Donald told him, "I'll turn on the air supply. But I want you where you can't interfere."

"Koop, if you tamper with the Gate again—"

"Dr. Linstrum, your theories about the so-called consequences don't interest me."

"Irreparable damage to the flow of history is more than theory! It's an extremely likely possibility."

"How do you know? Who has used the Gate for anything except your stupid research? No one!"

"You can't be serious about trying to kill Archibald," White exclaimed.

His voice barely a whisper, Donald answered, "I'm an activist, not a chair-bound philosopher. I have never been more serious. Now, Dr. White—open the vault."

White shivered, walked to the massive door. He touched a button on the control panel beside the door. It swung open. White went inside.

Striding across the antechamber, Donald slid his back against the block wall directly alongside the red door. "All right, Dr. Linstrum. Open this door. Call Walker and Stein, then step back. If your face shows anything suspicious, I'll burn you first."

Fighting fear, Tom called his brother's name. A flicker of Cal's eyelids was the only sign that he had heard. Tom said, "He couldn't stop all of us if we rushed him."

Donald smiled. "I wondered when someone would think of that. Undoubtedly it's true. On the other hand, Thomas, one or more of you would certainly get killed. Would you care to sign the warrant for your brother's execution?"

Heart sinking, Tom knew Donald was right. The laser pistol could mortally injure a man in a millisecond. The risks were too great.

"Call them!" Donald commanded.

Unsteadily, Cal pressed the proper button, waited till the red metal recessed into the wall.

"Stein? Walker? Can you come here a moment?"

Donald gestured savagely. *"Back!"*

Cal obeyed. Footsteps clacked along the tunnel. Donald tensed.

The footsteps came closer. Suddenly Dr. Stein's body filled the doorway. He spotted the floating metal box, started to turn—

Dr. Walker appeared. Donald booted him in the small of the back.

Walker fell against Stein, knocking him to his knees. By the time Walker had righted himself, Donald had reached a far corner of the antechamber. His position afforded him a wider sweep with the laser.

"Don't do a thing," Cal warned Dr. Stein, as the latter struggled to his feet. "He'll kill us if you move."

"But—" Walker pointed to the metal box hovering in the storage-room door. *"What's that?"*

Suddenly Donald's eyes narrowed. "Not one of your little security devices, is it?"

Numbly, Cal shook his head. Tom was dismayed. In a thoughtless second, Cal had thrown away a prime opportunity. If they had been able to convince Donald that the box, whatever its origin, was monitoring this incredible scene—

But Cal was unskilled in deceit, unprepared, as they all were, to face this kind of situation.

Donald told Stein, "Join Dr. White in the vault. You follow, Walker."

Reluctantly, Stein obeyed. In a moment, Walker too was out of sight.

"Now you, Dr. Linstrum. Before you go in, switch on the air systems."

Cal's hand darted across the master panel. Inside the vault, ventilators whirred. Cal plodded through the door.

Once more Donald waved the laser. "Your turn, Thomas."

"Donald, listen. If you use the Gate again, you'll only land in worse trouble. Stop now and I think I can persuade Cal to give you a break—"

Wild bluff. He might as well not have bothered.

"Don't waste my time, Thomas. Inside!"

"No cause is worth—"

"Killing for?" Donald's eyes shone. "On that point, we part company. Sometimes I'm astonished that we've been friends this long. In many ways you're such a child."

Heartsick, Tom started toward the vault.

"One moment, please! What do you propose to do with me?"

Thunderstruck, Tom turned toward the metallic voice. Even Donald looked startled.

The metal box floated forward into the antechamber, waving its stalks and pulsing its green glass hemispheres. It spoke through a small grille in its lighted face. "It takes no great intelligence to deduce that whatever is happening here is against the law. I must warn you, young man—be prepared for serious repercussions. You are being observed by a member of the press."

"A member of the—" Tom began, astonished.

"I," announced the box, "am Sidney Six."

"The reporter?"

"That is correct."

Donald jumped at the box, seized one of its stalks and began pulling. "Then you go in the vault with the rest of them!"

The box couldn't offer physical resistance. But it shot its pointers to the tops of its dials, flashed its lights rapidly, and protested. "Do not think that because I am a mechanical device, I have no civil rights. It has been established in court, McElfresh versus Six, that an artificial news gathering intelligence is entitled to—*ow!*"

Flung by Donald's hand, the box sailed through the vault door and banged against the wall. It hovered unsteadily, now bobbing upward, now sinking down, while the speed of its changing lights became dizzying. Cal and the others reacted with loud exclamations.

"In!" Donald shouted, shoving Tom hard.

As Tom recovered his balance, the massive door began to close. White flung himself against the steel, tried to push it. But Donald had activated the automatic close mechanism—the shutting of the door was inexorable. Deep in its steel, relays clicked.

"I've programmed it to open in five hours," Donald called. "About daylight. By then, my work will be done."

The door shut.

White leaned against it, eyes closed. His posture summed up their defeat.

"Five hours!" Walker said. "In that time, he could destroy—"

White straightened up. "Perhaps if we made noise—"

"No use," said Cal. "There's a guard about three feet from us. But because of the bunker's design, he can't hear a thing through these walls."

"I believe I've been dented."

They all stared.

The metal box had regained its equilibrium and hovered now in front of the files that held many of Department 239-T's records. Busily, Sidney Six explored its own surfaces with its stalks. Then it rotated to show them an indentation in its case.

"See for yourselves! My editors will not take this indignity lightly. Now—" The green glass hemispheres flashed twice. "Would someone kindly explain what is going on?"

"Don't tell him—it—anything!" White warned.

"My dear sir, why not? We are in this perilous predicament together. A predicament which apparently jeopardizes the operation of your facility. Of which I have known for some time, by the way."

Cal snapped, "How?"

"Tut-tut, my dear fellow. Reveal sources? Unethical! But it's evident that matters have become quite serious. That young man with the pistol has all the mannerisms of a mental case. Since he has locked us up for the next few hours, let's have a chat."

Cal fisted his hands. "At a time like this, you want to *chat?*"

"Dr. Linstrum—naturally I know who you are—please realize that I, Sidney Six, have penetrated this installation despite your best efforts to prevent it. Your security has been breached. Therefore, I suggest you cooperate."

Perhaps it was only Tom's imagination. But the sententious metal voice suddenly sounded threatening. "Wake up, Doctor! Face reality! You no longer have any secrets from me!"

Gordon White stared at the animated box. "I thought Sidney Six was a human being."

"A frequent error, sir. However, I am no less intelligent than you. I was constructed by my news syndicate at a cost of over one million dollars. I embody the latest refinements in miniaturization, and actually represent an improvement over Homo sapiens, in that I am not subject to foolish emotional states. In that area, sir, you are the inferior."

White colored. "But I have hands. What would you say if I came over there and ripped you apart?"

"I would protest vigorously! Until you silenced my vocal mechanism, that is. Let me assure you, sir, such overreactive behavior would be futile. Another, similar device would soon be along to replace me. And I have an ace in the hole besides that. My editors have placed top priority on obtaining the story of this department. A story concealed from the public far too long."

"For very good reasons," Cal said.

"That is a matter of opinion. Oh, I am aware of your father's concern about employing your time-travel mechanism to—shall we say—tinker with the past. However, my obligation to report the facts overrides those abstruse philosophical quibbles. The public has a right to know!"

Scowling, Dr. Walker sat down on the floor. The vault's fluorescent lighting was harsh, the temperature low. But at least the ventilators supplied fresh air.

"Ahem!" said Six. "Am I to infer that the obviously unbalanced young man who forced us in here—an employee of the department, isn't he?—is Senator Koop's nephew?"

"How do you know everyone?" Stein asked.

"I have been pursuing this story for months. Ferreting out elusive leads—cryptic phrases buried in Congressional committee reports, titillating paragraphs submeged in memoranda dictated by Vice-President Hand—"

"In plain English," Tom said, "you're a spy."

"This continuing attitude of hostility is most distressing!" cried the box. "We are all in this together!"

"But you're uninvited," Cal said.

"That, of course, is true. My presence, however, is no whim of capricious fate. I laid my plans to penetrate this installation most carefully, arranging to be delivered in the latest shipment of costume cartons. From that vantage point, I intended to observe Department 239-T covertly, until I was ready to announce my presence."

Tom recalled a hole punched in one of the unpacked boxes. He mentioned it.

"Was I watching through that hole? Clever lad! Tonight I intended to emerge and explore the department. When I woke up, I assumed everyone had gone home—"

"Woke up?" Walker repeated. "Do you sleep?"

"Not exactly. From time to time I shut down to cool my circuits. When I reactivated myself, I found I hadn't reckoned on the strength of the tape with which the box was sealed. It required some effort to free myself. I had just done so when that remarkable scene took place outside. And that leads us back to Koop. I gather he plans to tamper with events in the past. What events?"

Cal seemed in more complete control now. "Don't anyone answer that ridiculous hunk of junk."

Sidney Six shot its stalks in Cal's direction. "*Ahem!* I was warned that you were an authoritarian personality, Dr. Linstrum—not to say overbearing. The warnings were not exaggerated. With only modest encouragement, I could dislike you thoroughly."

Cal shrugged. "Too bad."

"I thought you couldn't experience emotion," said Stein.

"My dislike," announced the box, "is wholly rational."

"How did you come by the name Sidney?" Walker asked.

"My editors chose it. I find it repellent, but the decision was not mine. And, taking the editorial viewpoint, I suppose one can't very well print a startling exposé under a by-line consisting of a serial number. The designation Six derives from the fact that I am of the sixth generation of constructs designed to be independent news-gathering agents. Those of us in Series Six were the first completely successful models."

"There's more than one of you?" Tom said.

"Alas, my lad, not at the moment. In a month or two, yes. Several additional Series Six models are now under construction. My earlier colleagues have been destroyed, damaged, or otherwise rendered inoperative in pursuit of journalistic excellence."

To the others, Cal said, "No wonder security had such a tough job. They were looking for a human reporter."

"Quite so! My size is extremely convenient for penetrating hidden installations and ripping off the lid of false secrecy which—"

"One more word," Cal growled, "and I'll send you to join your illustrious colleagues. In the scrapyard."

Sidney Six jiggled its dials to express annoyance. But it didn't reply.

Presently, all the humans in the vault sat down. Stein wanted to know how the box planned to escape from 239-T once its presence had been revealed.

"I mean," he said, "what's to prevent us from dismantling you?"

Sounding worried, the box replied, "When I penetrated and exposed the secret Air Force missile platforms in the Gulf of Mexico, I was similarly threatened. In such cases I strike a bargain. In return for my withholding some of the more delicate aspects of a story—I am not without a conscience, gentlemen—the operators of the facility customarily grant me the right to reveal details that will not imperil national security. As if they had any other choice! Ahem! Further, they obfuscate the intelligence authorities higher up and do not reveal my identity or nature. Everyone"—the machine flashed its hemispheres significantly—"*everyone* respects the power of the press—and of Sidney Six!"

The conversation lapsed. The chilly vault induced

lethargy, and the loquacious machine evidently ran out of things to say about itself. It did ask one or two more questions about Donald Koop's plans. Receiving no reply, it settled down to silence with its stalks folded across its lighted face.

Tom checked his watch. Fifteen past three. Donald had imprisoned them shortly before two. The lock wouldn't open until just before seven. He yawned.

Dr. Walker's chin stubble was beginning to show. Dr. Stein dozed. Cal simply sat against the wall, staring into space.

Tom let his eyes close—

He awoke at fifteen before five. He was stiff. He started to stand up.

Suddenly, as if a switch had been thrown, he *knew*.

He didn't know *how* he knew. The knowledge was simply *there*, tangled in his head along with the other certainty that he had seen President Archibald on television only four days ago.

How was it possible for him to have seen Archibald and, simultaneously, hold this other, bone-chilling fact within his mind?

"Cal?"

In Cal's horrified eyes, Tom saw that his brother shared the same terrifying knowledge. Tom forced out words. "It's the eeriest feeling—I think I know—" He swallowed. "President Archibald was killed five months ago. On the thirteenth of March. He was shot at Camp Lookout by an assassin, while he was heading for his helicopter to return to Washington. The assassin vanished in the forest and has never been caught—" Wildly, Tom stood up. "It's all there! But it wasn't in my mind an hour ago—Cal, *what's happening?*"

Cal said, "It isn't what's happening, Tom, but what *has happened.*"

Dr. Stein said, "It's as if I have an entirely new set of memories put there the moment Koop changed history. Gordon—"

"Yes," White whispered. "I know it too. God help us all."

Suddenly Sidney Six began to wave its stalks. "Archibald dead? How do you know?"

They ignored him. Walker raised a question that was deviling Tom too. "I can't figure it out, Cal. My mind tells me Archibald's gone. At the same time, I remember—vividly—that he was alive last week. Yesterday! Do we all have two sets of memories?"

A series of nods confirmed it. The sense of horror deepened.

"But how?" Stein exclaimed.

Cal answered, "I don't know."

White said, "More important—which set of memories is correct?"

Slowly, Cal raised his right hand. The index and middle fingers spread to form a V.

"Operating on the theory of alternate tracks of time, both are potentially real. Along one branch, Archibald was murdered. Along the other, he wasn't. The branch point was March thirteenth. On that day, one reality stopped—another started. Why we know about both, I'm not prepared to say. One thing's certain. There's only one reality here—" He rapped the floor. "There's one of each of us, one vault, one Department 239-T. You asked the right question, Gordon. Which reality is outside that door?"

They stared at the vault's massive portal. White said, "In two hours, we'll know."

Time crawled. Finally, the interior of the great door began to buzz and click. The thick steel swung outward.

The bunker lay empty, full of shadows. It was too early for any regular employees to have arrived for work. Stein ran down the tunnel, returned to report no sign of Donald Koop. Cal led them to his office. Sidney Six floated along behind, as if it were doing its best to remain unobtrusive. The box drifted into Cal's workroom along with the others.

Dr. Stein shut the door. Cal stepped to the telephone, seized the sculptured receiver and punched buttons.

Time seemed to stretch again. The conflicting memories buffeted Tom's mind—Archibald alive, Archibald dead—alternate time tracks—*Which was real?*

"Hello? This is Dr. Linstrum, 239-T. I'd like to speak with the President, please. Yes, thank you. Yes, I—What?" A pause. "No, don't wake him. No, let me call back in a little while. It's not that urgent."

He broke the connection, staring at them.

"The White House operator said she would connect me with President Hand."

Stein whispered, "He was sworn in after Archibald was assassinated—"

Tom knew it too. So did they all.

In a dead voice, Cal said, "So—Donald succeeded, didn't he?"

8

DARK MEMORY

DR. CALVIN LINSTRUM ordered the red door secured and the Gate chamber declared off limits until further notice.

He, Tom, and Gordon White changed clothes. Cal sent Tom to the cafeteria for coffee and rolls.

Tom's step was slow. His mind felt mushy, and not merely from a sleepless night. As he passed the guard on duty in the corridor, he wondered what the soldier knew of Archibald's assassination. Certainly no one in the bunker save those who had been confined in the vault seemed overly upset this morning. Which present was real for them?

Returning to the department, Tom felt that his own thinking had never been so jumbled. Two sets of memories continued to conflict within him: Archibald alive and Archibald murdered, Ira Hand in office, Donald Koop at large.

At large *where*? In the Adirondacks, last March? To think of it started another headache.

As soon as Tom passed the coffee and rolls, Cal requested that his office door be locked. The department's senior technicians—White, Walker, Stein—sat or stood in postures of weariness, dejection.

Only Sidney Six, resting on a corner of Cal's worktable, seemed alert. "Is it really necessary to lock the door, Dr. Linstrum? That strikes me as a trifle melodramatic."

"I don't need advice from a tin can."

White hefted a massive paperweight. "Want me to shut the thing up, Cal?"

"Don't you dare!" cried the box. "I have warned you gentlemen—destroy me and another Sidney Six will very soon be manufactured to take my place. And in the event you become completely unreasonable, there is that additional ace card I mentioned. Now, I would appreciate someone giving me a summary of what has transpired. I deduce that it involves the President."

Cal's eyes narrowed. "What's his name?"

"Why, Benjamin Archibald. My memory banks—one moment." The lights on the cube flickered rapidly. "Yes, my memory banks confirm that President Archibald is alive, in office. Your remarks about contacting President Ira Hand make no sense."

"Apparently *it* doesn't have two sets of memories," Cal said to the others, ignoring Sidney Six's feverishly gyrating stalks.

"Because it's a machine?" White shrugged. "Who knows how the human mind functions under conditions like this?"

"I think it's time we called security," Walker suggested.

"In a minute," Cal nodded. "First let's make sure this new reality actually exists." He seized Sidney Six.

"Wait, wait, what do you think you're doing?"

"Putting you in that closet, Six. I'm going to bring one of my employees in here. I don't want him frightened out of his wits."

Opening the door of the combination wardrobe and lavatory, Stein stepped back. Cal shoved the box inside. It quivered its stalks in rage. "Your behavior smacks of police state brutality! I will not tolerate—"

"Stay in there and keep quiet. One squawk and I'll turn you into junk. Clear?"

The electronic journalist said, "Ahem!" But it offered no resistance.

"Leo," Cal said, "find someone out there who's just come to work. Anyone."

Dr. Stein returned shortly with a graying, slope-shouldered man who wore thick glasses.

Cal indicated a chair. "Sit down, Bigelow."

"Yes, sir, Dr. Linstrum, thank you."

"Bigelow, I want to ask you a couple of questions. You may find them peculiar. Please understand that I have good reason for asking them and don't worry too much about why." Cal did his best to sound conversational. But the shadows under his eyes belied his tension.

"Anything you say, Dr. Linstrum." Bigelow turned to White. "I came in early to make sure my soup was ready, Doctor. I thought your Pompeii film would be waiting—"

"We had an unexpected delay." White sounded vague.

Cal leaned forward. "Bigelow, do you recall what you were doing back on March 13?"

The photo technician thought a moment. "That was the day President Archibald was murdered in the Adirondacks. Sure! I remember."

"Where did you hear the news?"

"In my daughter's living room. In Richmond. My wife and I drove down for the day to visit with our grandchildren. We'd just finished dinner and little Fred was watching the television. All at once the network interrupted the movie with a bulletin. The newscaster announced that the President was dead, and that Ira Hand had already been sworn in."

Tom and the others exchanged grim glances.

"What about the assassin?" Cal asked carefully.

Bigelow hit the arm of his chair. "I'd have mobilized the whole country! I know the Government made a big effort, but they should have done more. Whoever he is, that monster should be caught! He's probably still congratulating himself. But he can't hide forever. I'll be glad when he's finally hunted down and exposed."

Shielding his eyes, Cal said, "What's your opinion of Ira Hand since he took office?"

Bigelow considered. "On the whole, good. I liked Archibald's stronger stand on disarmament. But Hand seems to have a pretty keen grasp of domestic affairs. The economy has sure boomed."

"Just one more question. What do you think of Donald Koop?"

Bigelow blinked. "The Senator's nephew? The boy who used to work here?"

"*Used* to?" Walker blurted.

"Why, you remember," Bigelow said. "He worked here all last summer. This year, the week after his college let out, he didn't show up. I heard that someone from here phoned Senator Koop and wanted to know what had happened. The Senator didn't know either. He said the boy had left his campus without explanation sometime in

March, and the Senator's been trying to trace him ever since. Some of our less responsible young people do disappear that way."

In a hollow voice, Cal said, "That's right, I was the one who called the Senator. I'd forgotten, but—now I remember."

Silence.

Bigelow shifted nervously. He had caught the peculiarity of Cal's last remark, even though its exact meaning eluded him.

Tom probed his own memory. He discovered a clear image of the morning when Donald should have returned from Harvard, but didn't. The picture was as real as the one of Donald locking them up last night. His headache grew worse.

Cal thanked Bigelow, who shuffled out. Next Cal summoned the soldier stationed outside the gray door. Cal's questions were substantially the same and the soldier's answers similar to those given by Bigelow. The soldier had been visiting a girl friend in Maryland that day in March. He had heard the news of Archibald's death on his car radio.

When the soldier had left, Cal said, "I read it this way. The memories of the other past—the one we lived through until yesterday—the one in which Archibald *didn't* die—those memories have somehow been wiped from the minds of everyone except us. I'll question a few more people, but I have a feeling we won't find the pattern any different. They remember only one past—the one in which Archibald was shot. For some reason, we remember both."

"Perhaps—" Stein sounded hesitant. "Perhaps it's because we lived through the other one. I mean, in close contact with the person who changed everything."

"Seems the only possible explanation," Cal agreed. "Those closely associated with the Gate are the only ones who can see both realities after the time track forks. My father certainly never bargained on that kind of phenomenon. Nor did I."

White said, "We do need to bring security into this."

Cal started for the closet. "Yes, but let's make sure that the news contraption will cooperate."

"I heard that!" cried a tinny voice behind the door. "Dr. Linstrum, if you continue to subject me to unjustified vilification merely because I am a mechano-electronic—"

Cal threw the door open, made a furious hooking gesture. "Come out here, Six. Shut up and listen."

The box floated into the office. Humming softly, it sank into a chair. Cal paced, spelling out in short, choppy sentences all that had taken place so far. The others were clearly worried about Cal's decision to do this. But no one interrupted. At the end, Cal gave them a hint of his reasoning when he said to the box, "Steps will have to be taken to try to undo the damage. But we can't be burdened with that job and also with trying to outwit you. So I'm offering you a choice. Give me your pledge to say nothing about what's happened, at least until we decide on the right course—" Cal's fingers closed around the same paperweight with which White had menaced the box earlier. "Or I'll smash you apart and worry about the consequences later."

"But you can't trust a—a floating tape recorder in the same way you'd trust a human being!" White protested.

"Why, he most certainly can!" Sidney Six countered. "I am not without principles. Based, of course, on a rational evaluation of the circumstances." The glass hemispheres flashed. "Obviously you face a grave predicament, Dr. Linstrum. Indeed, so does the whole country. Therefore, I will cooperate. Make no attempt to file my story—"

"Or leave this bunker."

"As you wish. Whatever the terms, I will not compound your difficulties in any way. You have my pledge, on my honor as a journalist in the great tradition of the free pr—"

"You can stow the rest," Cal sighed, returning to his desk.

But Six couldn't contain its curiosity. "President Archibald shot? President Hand in office? I have no memory of that. No memory whatsoever—until now." The stalk-tips pulsed. "Tell me frankly, Linstrum—What on earth is to be done?"

Fingers pressed to his temples, Cal said in a low voice, "That, I'm afraid, remains the question."

To confirm the theory that only those in the office were burdened with the knowledge of both time tracks, Cal questioned three more employees of Department 239-T: the two secretaries who handled correspondence and routine governmental paper work, and a man who came in regularly to service the automated cafeteria equipment. All told similar stories. Since March 13, the President of the United States had been Ira Hand.

Dr. White fell into an exhausted doze during the interrogation. Pale, Dr. Stein excused himself briefly. He looked no steadier when he returned. Toms' headache dwindled to a dull hurt. His clothing was rumpled, his hands felt gritty, his mouth tasted stale. When the questioning was over, Cal said, "As I see it—"

"If you intend to have a conference, please let me out!" complained the box in the closet. "My receptors are extremely sensitive. Continually straining them in order to hear could result in damage which—"

At Cal's wave, Tom released Six. Somewhat huffily, it announced, "I might say, Dr. Linstrum, that countless others have encountered Sidney Six with no apparent malfunction of their nervous systems. Hiding me from your employees is another gross insult."

Cal glared. The box dimmed its stalk-tips suddenly, murmured, "Ahem!" and sank to an unobtrusive spot by the baseboard.

"For the second time in twenty-four hours," Cal told them, "we need to go after Donald. This time, the stakes are much higher. Presumably he set the Gate for the twelfth of March, waited overnight until Archibald was ready to leave Camp Lookout, then pulled the trigger and fled. If we travel back to the twelfth, perhaps we can stop him."

Walker said, "You mean try to prevent the assassination before it happens? Wouldn't that be compounding the trouble? If tampering with history is dangerous, tampering twice should be doubly so."

"Unless we can simply reverse what's happened. Put things back exactly as they were by seeing to it that Koop gets nowhere near Archibald. That is absolutely all we would do—stop Koop. If the double memory effect holds true, and we succeed, we should be the only ones who'll ever know that Ira Hand was chief executive on an alternate time track. Bigelow, the guard, the rest of them— their memories should be exactly as they were—as *ours* were, yesterday, before all this began."

They agreed that it made sense. Dr. Stein asked whether Cal would clear the plan with President Hand. Cal replied that he was still mulling over that complex question. Clearly, he alone would decide.

"Actually," White said, "we have no choice as to how we use the Gate. After his experience the first time, Koop undoubtedly took a control unit. If we go anywhere, it'll be to the place and date he chose."

"You might check the control unit inventory," Cal said to Tom.

Tom returned to report, "Two gone."

"Mine," said White, "and Donald's."

"Let's make certain the Gate's locked onto the twelfth," Cal suggested. Ordering Sidney Six to remain behind, he led the others out of the office and down the tunnel. Tom was so tired, he stumbled repeatedly.

In the circular room, Dr. Stein punched up the appropriate controls. They waited for the paper tape to chatter from the slot. By the time Stein had finished running his fingers over the raised marks, he looked ill again.

"Something's wrong. The Gate's no longer set for March twelfth. I—I must be reading it incorrectly. Here, you try—" He passed the tape to Cal.

In a moment Cal's head snapped up. "It's today's date. But—he can't have done that!"

Dr. White examined the punched paper. In a voice choked with horror, he said, "The year is A.D. three thousand, nine hundred and eighty-seven!"

Tom goggled. "Two thousand years ahead? In the *future?*"

Back in Cal's office, they waited.

Dr. Stein had gone down two levels, to a section of the bunker seldom visited, in order to speed a printout of information from the Gate's internal clocks. Sidney Six, meanwhile, digested details of the latest revelation. "You mean that young lunatic has traveled into the future, as no one has done before?"

"As no one has dared to do before," Tom corrected. "A traveler in the future would face the same problem we did in Pompeii—high visibility because of the wrong clothing, unfamiliarity with the language, whatever the language will be—whatever it *is*, up ahead—"

Even attempting to speak coherently on the subject presented difficulties.

Sidney Six grasped them at once. "You used the verb *is*. Do you imply that the future coexists with the present?"

"That's a generally accepted theory of time," Cal explained. "The illustrations are numerous—a road, a river are the most common. At this point along the river of time, we exist. Five miles back, beyond a bend, let's say, five hundred years ago exists. Five miles ahead, hidden by another bend, five hundred years hence is equally real. And so, in the same way, is every other point along the river— every other moment in time in the past or future. The fact that it's beyond our power to see those past and future realities doesn't necessarily negate their existence. The complications set in when you think of dynamiting that river at a particular place, in order to rechannel the stream."

"Then you have two streams? Those alternate realities we've been talking about? Frankly, Linstrum, it's perplexing and—"

Stein burst in with a sheaf of computer printout. "It's bad, Cal."

"He's definitely gone?"

"Looks that way. The clocks show that at two thirty-four in the morning, Donald set the Gate for March twelfth, this year. He evidently returned to the chamber later. At three forty-five, the Gate was reset to the current coordinates. The temporal is exactly two thousand years in the future. The spatial is this area—Washington and vicinity. *If* it exists up there."

"Why would he go to the future?" Cal said. *"Why?"*

"If I know Donald," Tom said, "I think he might want to see the long-range results of the assassination. He'd want to know what influence on history he exerted by pulling the trigger. Beyond that, he knows forward travel is forbidden, so if he did it, he'd do it on a big scale."

"He's a madman," said White.

"It has certainly happened before," Sidney Six remarked. "Remember the Oswald affair? And the unfortunate who murdered the younger Kennedy? Such people are mad indeed. Mad with a belief in the importance of self in the scheme of human affairs. Men justify their existence in many ways, large and small. With someone like young Koop, however, the urge assumes diabolical antisocial proportions."

No one, not even Cal, reacted angrily to that, perhaps

because the hovering cube sounded almost frightened. And they knew it was right. Like Presidential assassins of the past, Donald Koop, in the name of his convictions, could both justify and carry out almost any deed.

Cal said quietly, "What a hell of a mess."

Their options had been drastically narrowed. If they went after Donald, it could only be to pursue him in A.D. 3987—a future for which they had no conceivable way of preparing. Cal's plan to prevent Archibald's murder had been destroyed at a stroke.

Stein said, "I feel as if I've been awake for years. I—" All at once, he was weeping loudly, and at the same time, apologizing, "I'm sorry—a man shouldn't—it's all been too much—I can't seem—"

On a quiet signal from White, Walker stepped forward. The two escorted Stein from the office. Tom felt only sympathy. The mind-staggering events of the night had left him in almost the same state. Cal too looked near the point of collapse. And baffled.

Cal reached for the phone. "I'm calling the President. I thought I could make a decision about Donald without consulting him. But with this new factor—"

His words trailed off. He stared at the wall in a forlorn way. Into the phone he said, "Dr. Linstrum again. This time it is an emergency."

9

DECISION

"AND THAT, Mr. President, is everything so far."

Ira Hand looked pale. He sat opposite Cal at the desk, his expression almost childlike, as if he had been handed an incomprehensible puzzle to work and could not work it.

During Cal's narration, Tom had not missed the glances between White and Walker. His brother had omitted any mention of Sidney Six. The box was once again confined to the closet, no doubt with stalks pressed against the door.

Dr. Stein was still absent, resting in the bunker's temporary sleeping quarters. Walker had given him a relaxant. Tom yawned. It was only midmorning. But he felt as though he had not slept for years.

At last, Hand spoke. "Dr. Linstrum, you confront me with facts which my mind has difficulty grasping. You say Ben Archibald was alive yesterday?"

"On one time track, yes."

"I have no memory of that. The last time I saw him was the morning last March when he departed by plane for Camp Lookout. He briefed me on a number of matters before he left. On Sunday, as he was about to enter his helicopter to fly back to the Syracuse airport, he was shot and killed. I was sworn in by the Chief Justice a few minutes after six. The next time I saw Ben, he—he was lying in state. The television coverage—the funeral—dignitaries from all over the world—surely you remember!"

Time Gate

"I remember very clearly. I also remember an alternate reality. There, it never happened."

Hand began walking back and forth with that characteristic rolling gait. But his step lacked energy. "You'll forgive me if I have trouble accepting your story. The death of my friend Ben Archibald was a grave loss for this nation, for the world community, and for me personally. To hear that he was *not* assassinated—"

Hand shook his head.

"Mr. President, I asked for your presence down here because there's a decision only you can make."

Hand pulled out a large handkerchief and mopped his cheeks. "Go on."

"As I said earlier, I had planned to return to Camp Lookout and try to stop the assassination. That same plan involves two steps now. First, travel to the future. There, we'd have to locate Donald, retake the control, come back here, and reset the Gate. Only then could we return to the Adirondacks."

"Travel two thousand years ahead? Doesn't the prospect alarm you?"

"Frankly, it terrifies me. But I'm willing to go. So is Dr. White. It can be argued that it might be best to leave well enough alone. On the other hand, Koop *is* in possession of the means of controlling the Gate. We can keep a constant watch on the Gate chamber, of course. But if he returns by surprise—" Cal shrugged. "Encouraged by the success of his first experiment, he might try another journey back to some other turning point in history. Very likely, if he came back to the chamber, we could stop him. But I hate to wait. Someone so unstable shouldn't be allowed to remain free any longer than absolutely necessary."

"If you should succeed in capturing Koop in the future, and if you were then equally successful in forestalling Ben's murder—I would no longer be President?"

"Nor have any memory of having been, very likely," Cal agreed. "That's why the decision must be yours. To ask a man to remove himself from the highest post in the world—"

"Ben was my great and good friend. I do not want the Presidency if the price must be refusal to try to prevent his death."

"There's no guarantee we'll succeed. All sorts of possibilities exist, including an uninhabitable earth two thousand years hence. Even if the future does prove hospitable, there's also no certainty that we can locate Koop."

Another silence. At the end, Hand said, "You must try."

Cal lost some of his tension. "Very well, sir. And thank you."

"When do you propose to leave?"

"As soon as we can. I hope this afternoon. We all need a little sleep."

"Agreed." Hand began pacing again, regaining some of his old vigor. "I also want you to take a number of steps on my behalf. One, a phone line is to be kept open between this department and my office—my bedroom if it's during the night. Regardless of the hour, I want to know the outcome."

Cal made a note. Tom thought about the results if his brother and Gordon White did succeed. Would Ira Hand suddenly cease to exist in the President's bedroom at the White House? Find himself instead in the home he occupied as second in command?

Then came another disturbing thought.

According to the river theory of time, both the March weekend and the far future coexisted right along with the present. Theoretically, Donald was in two places at once. Which Donald was real? Both?

Tom sighed. He couldn't cope with all the intricacies. Perhaps his father had been able to do so; perhaps that was why he had won the Nobel Prize.

Hand was still talking. ". . . send home all but those personnel you need to assist you in operating the Gate. I will notify Sloat that this installation is to be placed under maximum guard. I'm sure you realize that if a single word of what's happened leaked to the press and the public, we would very likely have a national crisis. No one on the outside must know!"

Cal's eyes jumped to the closet door. "Yes, sir. "Uh— naturally."

Hand started out. He turned back, no longer a supreme symbol of national authority, but simply a rather stooped, overweight man with an uncertain expression. "I still find it hard to believe. But you must do everything in your power to restore things as they were. I am not the man Ben Archibald was. We need him."

As soon as the door closed, Cal punched up the phone.

He announced over the bunker's public-address system that the department would close down in fifteen minutes, and all employees were not to return until further notice.

Dr. Walker stifled a yawn. "How about Stein?"

"If he's well enough, I'd prefer that he stay on duty. I'd like both of you to monitor the Gate."

Tom said, "What about me?"

"You heard the order."

Maybe it was Tom's tiredness. But he refused to be shunted aside. "That's not fair."

"The answer is still no." Cal rose. "Get some sleep, Gordon. I'll meet you in the ready room at three."

"Cal—" Tom began again.

"Tom, I'm in no mood for an argument!"

Temper out of hand, Tom shot back, "I'll be hanged if I'll clear out. In fact, I'm not even going to stay in the bunker. I'm going along. No, don't yell at me, Cal. Listen! You weren't in the cell in Pompeii. You didn't see Donald's reaction. At first he refused to come out. If you'd walked into that cell, he probably would have shot you. For the same reason you took me to Pompeii, you've got to take me on this trip too. You may not be able to get close enough to Donald to retake the Gate control. I can."

"You seem to forget who's in charge of this—"

A noisy thumping from the closet.

"Will someone kindly let me out? I've heard every word. And your reaction, Linstrum, strikes me as typical of your intellectual arrogance. If the lad's statements are true, his suggestion that he go on the mission is eminently sensible. Indeed—ahem! I believe I will join you myself."

"You're out of your mind!" Cal stormed when the box was out of the closet. "If you have one!"

At that, Sidney Six's green glass hemispheres lighted up. "Sir, you are continually insulting. Is that because you are afraid of losing your authority? Is that why you give free rein to your vexatious personality, constantly assuming the shrill posture of a *dictator?*"

"I'll tear you apart!" Cal shouted, lunging.

Sidney Six emitted a klaxonlike sound of alarm and sailed across the office at startling speed, eluding him. Reaching a corner, the box rose rapidly to the ceiling, then pointed its stalks at Cal. If a machine could look wrathful, this one did.

White laid a hand on Cal's arm. "We're all exhausted. Don't let your temper—"

"That—scrap heap is not going with us! Neither is my brother."

Dr. Walker looked puzzled. "Why on earth would you want to go along, Six?"

"Are you mad, sir? To view the future two thousand years hence—what a reportorial coup! Dr. Linstrum, I *insist* on accompanying you. Additionally, I insist that you permit your brother—"

"Let him speak for himself."

"Nonsense! No one can effectively speak for himself in your presence. You automatically reject any ideas that are not expressly your own. I was astonished when you deferred to Hand on the question of traveling to the future. I even imagined your character might have some redeeming qualities—"

Despite his weariness, Tom couldn't help enjoying this.

"—and further—no, sir, be quiet!" the box cried. "Do not speak until I am finished. I see I was in error. You have reverted to type. Well, sir, I not only have the desire to accompany you, I have the means to compel you to say yes."

All at once Cal stopped his attempts to reach up and seize the machine's stalks, saying, "I'm not frightened by cheap bluffs."

"No bluff, sir, rest assured. I am quite prepared to force you."

"I suppose you're going to threaten to blow the story?" Cal sneered.

"Precisely."

"You gave me your pledge—"

"Which I herewith, in the light of your overbearing manner, rescind."

Cal spun back to his desk. "I should have known better than to trust—"

"Dr. Linstrum!"

Glowering, Cal looked up.

"I have no desire to endanger national security. I fully appreciate the consequences of a security leak. Any such leak will come about as a direct result of *your* unwillingness to cooperate—*your* insistence upon playing God in each and every situation. Further, I will publicize the fact that you alone were responsible."

Cal sank into his chair, bridged his fingers in front of his nose, defensively.

"Just how do you propose to publish your story from here?" he demanded.

"You forget the principles of telemetry, sir!"

White said, "You mean you've been storing up everything?"

"Every single word I have overheard," Six confirmed. "It has all been coded—compressed—into approximately four minutes of highly sophisticated electronic signals. I have but to trigger a simple relay operation inside myself—an operation of which you will see no visible sign— and a data collection station in my editors' offices will begin to record the signals I will transmit."

"Not if I climb up there and tear you apart," Cal countered.

"By remaining close to the ceiling, I can certainly elude you for two or three minutes. By that time, the majority of data will be in the possession of my editors." For emphasis, Sidney Six flashed all its lights and quivered all its dials.

Dr. Walker couldn't hide a wary chuckle. "Score one for the machine."

White asked, "Is this the ace card you referred to a couple of times?"

"It is."

White turned to Cal. "Personally, I don't believe it's worth the risk to find out whether Six is bluffing. Besides, I'd vote to take Tom along"—Tom's spirits soared— "for the very reason he stated. I'm less enthusiastic about Six coming. The machine could be a burden."

"In a highly advanced future civilization," Six huffed, "my intellectual capacity could prove useful."

"I'm sure you believe so," White replied, with sarcasm. "Under the circumstances—being totally in the dark about what's up there—it's impossible to predict." He drew a breath. "Still, I vote to preserve security."

Cal complained, offered some additional quibbles. But the heart had gone out of the fight. And they all knew it.

Strange, Tom thought, how some nasty part of him took pleasure in Cal's defeat. Yet he didn't really enjoy seeing his brother backed to the wall.

Dr. Walker tapped his watch. "It'll be noon before we know it. If you're going to get some sleep—"

"The rest of you go ahead," Cal said, not looking up. "I have some things to organize." His hands wandered aimlessly among the papers and microfiles jumbled on his desk. The defeat by Six had cost him his pride.

With a slow step, Tom started out with the others. Six floated after them. All at once Tom grew conscious of Cal watching. He turned, and just as quickly looked away.

Tom rolled into one of the bunks in the temporary sleeping quarters. The memory of Cal's eyes haunted his mind.

Angry eyes.

Accusing.

Sidney Six might have won a small victory for itself and Tom. But in the long run, the actions of the box had only deepened the conflict between brother and brother.

Dr. Stein snored softly in the bunk across the way. The air circulators whispered. Thinking of the future, Tom imagined fantastic cities, incredibly complex machines buzzing in the skies, and on the ground—

How would the people look two thousand years hence? Physically changed, as many scientists predicted? Bodies spindly, muscles atrophied because of increased dependence on machines? And would there be that staple of stories about the future, the oversized, superintelligent head? Surely, among such people, Tom and the others would be worse anachronisms than Donald had been in Pompeii—

Donald.

Tom drifted into a doze troubled by dreams.

Sunlight flashing from his glasses, Donald toppled great gleaming towers with bursts of a laser. Superimposed like a second image in a film, another Donald crouched in powdery snow, exhaling clouds of breath, his eyes and his laser trained on a plowed area where a government helicopter whirled its rotors—

Mercifully, sleep hid the rest.

"Thirty seconds," Stein warned.

Cal, Tom, and White stood shoulder to shoulder on the platform. Clicking busily, Sidney Six floated just above them.

The humans wore neutral gray coveralls of the kind found on workmen in the bunker. All government insignia had been ripped off. Cal and White carried recorders, cameras, and weapons, concealed in the special belts under their clothes.

The neutral uniforms were the only costumes that might even come close to blending in with costuming of the far future. It was really impossible to predict what lay ahead. What if styles had changed so radically that everyone wore kiltlike skirts? Or lived in weather-controlled cities and wore nothing at all? What would they find? *What?*

"Fifteen seconds."

The lights sequenced faster. The platform vibrated.

"Ten seconds."

Though he had slept briefly, Cal still looked tired. He had wrestled unsuccessfully with the problem of spatial coordinates. There was no way to tell whether Donald Koop had set the Gate so that he, and they, would arrive in an area unoccupied by solid matter two thousand years from now. Donald had had the sense to adjust the coordinates upward, to approximately ground level. Beyond that, they could only hope.

"Five—"

The cool, tingling darkness closed around Tom.

When it vanished, he saw a world beyond all imagining.

10

A.D. 3987

THEY STOOD on a slope above a wide, eroded watercourse. In the bottom of the channel, a trickle of water gleamed with scarlet highlights. The stream looked more like oil than water. The channel twisted through a level landscape to disappear in the dull red haze of the horizon.

The fortieth century.

The wind whined. Tom coughed. The air seemed full of dust.

Their shadows stretched across what looked like burned grass. Over everything lay that dull red light.

Judging from the direction of the shadows, they were facing east. Westward, dun plains of scorched grass ran on toward the low, dark red sun. The edge of the sun was visible, though indistinct, as if screened by great clouds of dust.

Everywhere, Tom saw the same dun earth tufted with yellow grass. Could this once have been the lush Virginia countryside? What had become of the signs of civilization? Here was nothing but emptiness, a desolate uniformity, a sense of life burned out.

Waving its stalks gently, Sidney Six said, "Most remarkable!"

Cal and Gordon White headed down toward the watercourse. White pulled out his matchbox camera, put it to his eye, and clicked off exposures.

Cal said, "Either there was gross error in Donald's settings, or what's left of the Potomac has changed course considerably in two thousand years."

"How warm is it?" Tom asked. "Sixty degrees?"

"More like fifty," White replied.

Cal frowned. "Fifty? In August?"

Tom glanced at the sun. Did the masking effect of the hazy atmosphere produce the abnormally lower temperature?

"Surely there must be some human habitation—" White began.

But not another living creature, human or otherwise, could be seen anywhere in the stark landscape. At least not until Tom spotted a couple of crawling insects among the tufts of grass. He pointed them out. The others seemed reassured by the discovery. Earth, then, was not totally dead.

Sidney Six discovered the city.

It would have been easy to miss. No more than the tips of fluted towers were visible along the northern horizon. Seven or eight of them thrust up into the wan red light, glowing with dull highlights, as if they were made of glass. One tower, flared at the top, was higher than the others.

"About ten miles away," Tom guessed.

Cal shook his head. "Fifteen to twenty. Let's get moving."

They trudged straight across the desolate countryside, keeping the city as their fixed destination point. After half an hour they reached the summit of a low hill.

Still no sign of human life. But more of the city had come into view. Many shorter spires could be seen, clustering below the higher ones. Horizontal connectors— aerial roadways?—linked a number of the towers. What was disturbing about the city was its isolated quality. The travelers saw no indication of suburbs. For all its graceful, soaring beauty, the city resembled a self-contained fortress in a hostile wilderness.

They walked on. At last they viewed the city complete, and Tom realized that even those towers which seemed short were tall indeed. The lone spire soaring above all the rest had to be on the order of three hundred storys.

No one said much. Occasionally Sidney Six would clack, buzz, and talk to itself in a low tone, storing a description of the sights for retrieval later.

Obviously the residents of that city had chosen to build

upward, not outward. Because the land would not easily support life? That seemed logical, given the vegetation, the haze in the sky, the indistinct sun now half out of sight behind the western horizon.

Finally, Gordon White said, *"What's happened?* This complete desolation—"

"War?" Sidney Six suggested. "A holocaust?"

"If so, it took place a long time ago," Cal said. "There's no evidence of man-made destruction."

That was true. Yet something had caused the inhabitants of the city to abandon the land.

Tom, shivering, said, "We're assuming we'll find people in that city. What if we don't?"

White nodded. "He's right. We might be walking toward a monument."

Depressed by the thought, they trudged on.

Crossing another low rise, they started down toward what looked like another watercourse, but with two differences. No water flowed in the bottom, and it was overgrown with brown grass. At either side, low walls had been built to keep the banks from collapsing. The walls were made of blocks of a gray, stonelike material.

"Artificial," Cal said after examining the wall. "But very hard."

Walking was easier in the empty stream bed, ditch, or whatever it might be. The channel seemed to be leading toward the city. They tramped for some ten minutes. The walls, showing no evidence of disrepair, continued on either side. Suddenly they heard a low, steady moaning.

A vehicle shot into sight from around a bend, traveling fast. Streamlined, with an opaque black cowl forward, it tapered to a large exhaust tube aft. From the tube gushed a barely visible vapor. The vehicle bore cryptic markings, only one of which was familiar—a triangle, repeated twice.

The vehicle skimmed above the watercourse at a height of about two feet. But it was not a ground-effect machine riding on vertical air jets. The sere grass under its fleeting shadow showed little sign of disturbance.

"Lasers," Cal whispered.

The two men drew their weapons from under their coveralls, then hid them in large outside trousers' pockets. The speeding vehicle began to slow down. The moaning—the sound of its propulsion plant—diminished.

The vehicle came to a stop about ten feet away, then slowly descended to rest on the ground. The hinged cowl fell open. Seated one behind the other were two men.

As they climbed out, Tom caught his breath. Both were at least seven feet tall.

They were extremely slender, sticklike. Each wore a kind of dark, tight-fitting body stocking, with a hard vest over the torso. Their helmets resembled shiny black eggs. One man held a wand. A weapon?

The voice of the man without the weapon boomed through an amplifier. But his peremptory inquiry, though clear in general tone, was gibberish.

Cal waved one hand. The other was still concealed in the pocket where he had hidden the laser. "Strangers! We can't understand you."

Once more the rapid-fire gibberish crackled from the helmet. White pointed to his mouth, moved his lips, and lifted his palms in the universal gesture of noncomprehension.

The man without a weapon walked rapidly back to the vehicle. He climbed aboard and disappeared through a hatch leading to a rear compartment. When he returned, he carried a small metal wafer in one gloved hand.

The man laid the wafer against his throat and took his hand away. The wafer did not fall. Suddenly, from the amplifier, recognizable speech crackled. "We can now translate you. I am Officer Klok. Who are you?"

"Scientists," Cal said. "Travelers—"

"You are small," Klok rasped. "No people with whom we are familiar look as you do. Where have you come from?"

"We'll talk about that with whoever's in charge."

"In charge?"

"The boss. The headman." Cal gestured to the towers visible above the channel bank. "Whoever runs that city."

"The Chairman! You wish to see the Chairman?"

Strain showed on Cal's face. "Right."

"We have been observing you carefully, strangers," Klok informed them. "Since you are most odd in appearance, you will obey what we say in every respect."

"Are you police?" Tom asked.

Klok nodded. "We observed you first on the view at Central. We have come out to ascertain your nature, your origin, and your purpose in approaching Washingtowne."

"Washingtowne!" White exclaimed. "Is this the United States?"

Klok fingered the throat wafer. "I am unable to obtain a translation of those terms. This is Federal Earth, Province Amerik. You will inform us as to your purpose here."

Cal shook his head. "We'll tell that Chairman of yours, no one else."

Klok and his fellow officer conferred, Klok having removed the wafer from his throat temporarily. He replaced it after a moment.

"We will transport you. However, you are cautioned. Officer Nem has a—" The next word was unintelligible. "Arouse a commotion, or cause struggle in any way, and Officer Nem will be compelled to employ liquefaction."

"Liquefaction?" White repeated with a shudder. "No, thanks!"

"What is that device?" Klok demanded, meaning Sidney Six.

"Oh," Cal hedged, "a research machine. I told you—we're scientists."

"It jiggles its arms. It blinks its lights. It hears me?"

"I certainly do!" Six answered. "And I don't mind telling you that I find your bullying attitude highly offensive. I am a representative of the free pr—"

Noting Cal's glare of warning, the box stopped. Officer Klok, however, wasn't satisfied. "In the event of difficulties, your device is also subject to liquefaction."

"We'll keep our—ah—device under control," White promised.

Klok gestured sharply. "Inside!"

One by one they climbed into the vehicle, bent, and crawled through the hatch to the back compartment. Windowless, and so small that they had to sit hunched on padded benches along either side, the chamber smelled of citrus. The aroma came from tanks at the chamber's aft end. Fuel?"

The cowl closed. The vehicle began to vibrate. The moaning resumed. Tom felt them lift, turn, and begin to speed back up the channel toward the city.

Washingtowne. Some things had survived after all. Did the name "Federal Earth" imply worldwide government? That might be a hopeful omen.

Officer Nem pulled the hatch shut and wedged himself onto a bench foward. Because of his height, he was forced

to bend almost double. But his wand, which evidently removed troublemakers by means of *liquefaction,* did not
waver.

Presently, though, he seemed to relax. He unsnapped
latches and lifted off his black helmet. His skull was totally hairless and gently pointed. He had alert brown eyes
three inches wide.

"Mutated genetic strain?" White whispered to Cal.

Officer Nem frowned. Klok had given him the wafer,
which he placed at his throat. "No speaking privately,
thank you please."

"Why not?" Cal challenged.

"We do not as yet know your origin or purpose. And
your appearance is suspicious in the extreme. Indeed," he
added, "never in my career have I encountered persons so
peculiar. Shall I not say—abnormal?"

"I guess it all depends on your point of view," White
murmured, looking less than happy under the policeman's
continued scrutiny.

Tom and the others were unprepared for the spectacular
sight awaiting them when the vehicle landed with a gentle
bump.

Officer Nem preceded them through the hatch. As Tom
clambered out onto a glassy black floor, he could see little
but darkness pricked by points of light. The sun had set
during their trip—

Then it hit him.

The vehicle had climbed extremely high. They were
looking down on the glowing tower city.

Beyond the transparent wall of a great circular room,
glittering spires winked and gleamed. Tiny lights darted on
the horizontal roadways below. They had arrived at the
summit of the very highest tower, evidently descending
through the immense, irislike port in the roof. The view
was breathtaking.

Officer Klok gestured toward a moving stair. "To my
surprise, the Chairman wishes to receive you personally.
Step lively, thank you please."

In other circumstances, Tom might have grinned at the
wafer's tangled translation. Sidney Six was muttering
again, filing another description.

The moving stair was an inclined belt without steps.
Tom stepped on and sank half a foot. But the belt held
him comfortably after that.

On the floor below, Klok and Nem led them along a bright corridor with gleaming walls. Tom couldn't locate the source of the illumination. Around a corner, they came to imposing double doors emblazoned with a silver escutcheon incorporating images of an owl and a tree, plus an inscription in the unreadable characters Tom had noticed on the side of the police vehicle.

A muffled bell rang twice. The doors opened inward.

Inside, another huge, clear-walled chamber overlooked the city. A man rose from a curiously sculptured chair. He was even taller than the officers. A good seven and a half feet, Tom estimated, bony in the extreme. Well into middle years, the man had an austere face, and those unnerving wide eyes. One tuft of gray hair sprouted from his chin. Otherwise his head was hairless.

The man acted neither hostile nor friendly. Officer Klok made a sign of obeisance, then spoke in the unintelligible language.

The man, who was dressed in a plainly cut one-piece garment of rich purple, nodded. Then he waved in dismissal. The officers looked startled. But they marched out.

The tall man walked to the curiously designed chair. The arm contained a number of controls. He pressed a transparent button. A moment later they heard his voice. "This room is now circuited for immediate translation. No intermediary devices are required. We receive quite a few visitors from other provinces. Having the entire room wired is most helpful."

And the system was obviously more sophisticated than the wafers, Tom realized. It did a far better job of translating the man's voice into natural speech. He continued, "I am the Chairman, Doktor Phlonykus. Though I am not as suspicious as my officers—good men, those!—I might say that the room is also heavily monitored for my personal safety. In the event of any unusual activity, various concealed devices will automatically apprehend and restrain troublemakers."

Suddenly he smiled. "But I am confident such a warning is unnecessary. You do not appear unfriendly. Merely—if I will not offend you—unusual-looking. By our standards! Now, please identify yourselves."

"I'm Dr. Calvin Linstrum. You're the Chairman of this city or territory?"

"No," returned Doktor Phlonykus, "I am the Chairman of Federal Earth."

Taking a seat, he let that sink in. After a moment he continued. "Under the terms of my contract, I spend periods of one year administering affairs of the global government from each of the different province capitals. Two months ago, my daughter and I traveled here from our last residence in Europa. Normally I would not have received you in person. It was the description of your physical appearance that prompted me to do so. May I inquire where you come from?"

"From two thousand years in the past."

Doktor Phlonykus' wide lids dropped briefly over his flecked gray eyes. Tom began to catch some of the atmosphere of the room, and the city: order, control, everything in balance, in contrast to the wretched state of the surrounding countryside.

Doktor Phlonykus said merely, "Explain."

Taking the better part of an hour, Cal did.

At the end, Phlonykus said, "Your tale staggers the imagination. Please give me a few moments to adjust."

"I would have thought your society would be familiar with the principles of time travel," White said.

"I have encountered references to it in the literature," Phlonykus said. "It is mentioned in one or two obscure footnotes, if memory serves. We do not possess the knowledge of how such travel is accomplished."

Cal's eyebrows lifted. "You mean the secret's been lost?"

"Along with many other technological accomplishments of the past." Doktor Phlonykus strode to the outer wall, speaking with his back to them. "Do not let the appearance of this fine city deceive you. There are but nineteen such cities scattered around the world. And that is the entire sum and substance of Federal Earth. Ninety-nine percent of the globe has been abandoned as unfit for human life."

The travelers received this staggering news in stunned silence.

Phlonykus continued. "You say you wish assistance in locating one of your number who has journeyed to this time. The answer to that request must wait until I am convinced that you come from where you say."

"We never thought of bringing any proof," Cal admitted.

"The most convincing proofs are your own remarkable physiques. You are so short! Can the human race have changed that much in a mere two thousand years? Of course, the texts make it quite clear that it has. Yet, confronted with living examples—" Phlonykus shook his head. "I find it far easier to cope with the fact in the abstract. But now, perhaps you are in need of rest and refreshment—"

The double doors opened. A girl rushed in.

"Father, may I have permission to tap the central computation blank? My figures on the liftway stresses are wrong. The—"

She stopped suddenly, aware of the visitors.

The girl was young, about Tom's own age. Nicely built. And she was only about an inch taller than Tom. Perhaps the women in this far future had not undergone the same drastic evolutionary changes as the men.

The girl had a pretty face, with flecked gray eyes similar to those of Doktor Phlonykus, but not as wide. Judging from the way her fabric helmet fitted tightly over her head, covering it completely except for the face cutout, she was bald.

Impatiently, Phlonykus said, "Mari, I am busy conferring with these most unusual visitors—"

"I heard about them. Unusual is hardly an adequate description—" She paused. "We're being translated?"

"They do not speak our language, for reasons that I will explain later. Please state your business, Mari. Briefly!"

"My calculations have resulted in a gross error. The work crew is at a standstill. Unless I can use the computation banks tonight—"

To the others, Phlonykus explained, "My daughter is supervising construction of a new pedestrian way on the twelfth level."

"Supervising!" Tom blurted. "How old is she?"

Phlonykus replied, "In calendar years? Why, seventeen. I fail to see—"

"Seventeen and working on a building project?"

"In charge of it," Phlonykus amended. His daughter was watching Tom with unconcealed dislike. He was, after all, shorter. And he had hair.

Phlonykus told his daughter, "The name of this young

man is Thomas Linstrum. He is brother to our other visitor, just there. They do not understand our ways, Mari. I
shall explain why at a more opportune time."

"The computation banks—"

"You'll have to wake a controller. However, if the crew
has reached an impasse, permission is given. Next time, be
more careful in preparing your theoretical base."

"Suggestion received. Thank you, Father." She started
out, still studying the travelers suspiciously. "Good evening
to you all—whoever you may be!"

When she was gone, Phlonykus sighed. "She is impetu-
ous. Typical of the young. But I assure you that she has
the capacity to direct the construction project. Her index
number is three-ten. She is genius rated."

"Genius!" Cal cried, plainly unable to accept the idea of
a seventeen-year-old girl being more intelligent than he
was.

"There is nothing unusual," Phlonykus returned. "Virtually 85 percent of the children born on Federal Earth
achieve that rating. As I suggested, we have lost a number
of technological secrets of the past. But others have survived, including the chemical means for stimulating the
human embryo and removing potentially harmful emotional factors that might inhibit the infant's development to
its genetic limit. In short, we still know how to help the
human brain realize its full potential."

In response to their stares, Phlonykus waved. "Chemistry, gentlemen, simple chemistry! The techniques are five
centuries old! Over the short range, those techniques benefit all of society. Over the long range—" Walking slowly
to the outer wall," he gazed at the lights. "It is an exercise
in futility."

When he faced them again, shadows lay under his eyes.
A trick of the lighting, perhaps, but appropriate to his
melancholy tone. "Do not let my percentage figures
concerning genius children deceive you. There is another,
far more telling percentile in operation. One hundred percent of the children are born to four percent of the
world's population. The rest of the race is incapable of
reproducing itself. As a result, the number of human
beings on the earth has been shrinking steadily for
hundreds of years. Genius, in the end, will be worth nothing, since the finest brains of Federal Earth have failed to
unlock the secret of how to make the race fertile again. As

historical perspective, I might add that the search has been in progress literally for centuries. Without success."

Despair seemed to capture the Chairman. He continued. "In simplest terms, the race is dying. Another two or three hundred years—" He shrugged. "Very likely even the nineteen cities will be gone. Artificial production of children is not the answer. We have tried that. The same sterility to fertility ratios, ninety-six versus four, hold true among those who are laboratory-born. Indeed, recent evidence suggests that the fertile percentage may still be dropping. Sometime after your era, though not long, relatively speaking, and about nineteen hundred years before mine—"

One hand lifted, eloquent, sad.

"In a tragedy of almost unspeakable proportions, mankind destroyed itself."

11

DYING EARTH

"ARE YOU FAMILIAR with the concept of the doomsday device?" Phlonykus asked. "At least, that is what what it is called in the folklore."

Tom nodded. "People in our time speculated about it. Some kind of nuclear or chemical superweapon with the potential to destroy the earth. The idea was an extension of the arms race—bigger and bigger weapons always shifting the balance of power, until one day, some nation would construct a doomsday machine, hide it, then announce its existence—and tip the balance of power permanently toward itself. Some in our country argued for developing our own doomsday capability. But the dangers were too great. None was ever built."

"Not in your time, that's true."

"Later?" Cal said.

Phlonykus nodded. "Construction commenced after the midpoint of the twenty-first century. A one-of-a-kind project. Completion required some thirty years, due to the immense costs. And it nearly bankrupted its builders, because along with the device itself went the construction of a vast network of protective facilities. From the beginning, they meant to trigger the device. And they did."

A shudder raced down Tom's spine. "When?"

"I believe the year was A.D. 2080."

"Who built it?" White asked.

"The Asiatics, in confederation with several of the more militant nations of what was then Afrique. The device was

96

to be used against the western nations and was eventually so employed."

Cal looked pale. "In our era, there was talk of an eventual conflict between the white race and the third world. Revenge for exploitation, real and fancied, of the latter by the former. No one dreamed it would ever come."

"Alas, it did," said Phlonykus.

Tom asked, "Was the doomsday machine a bomb?"

"Not precisely. Its heart was an installation somewhere in Asia. The exact location is documented in the histories. The control center, built around a mammoth computer, launched several dozen radiation sources in a form much like the earliest, primitive space satellites. Each orbiting carrier released intense radioactivity over a wide area of the globe. Bombs without a bang, so to speak. When the device was set off, nearly 80 percent of the human race died in a matter of days. Indeed, the builders lost much of their own population too. It simply was not possible to protect great masses of people from radiation of that high an order. As a result, Asiatic manpower was depleted far beyond the original projections. They were unable to take maximum advantage of their insane strategy. Stretched thin they were able to occupy only about half the globe for about twelve years. In truth, there was little left worth occupying."

Phlonykus paused. His voice dropped lower. "From that moment of incredible destruction dates the decline of man. For about one hundred years, the planet survived in a state close to barbarism. Young colonies on the Moon and Mars, colonies begun with high hopes at the start of the century, were cut off from contact with the mother planet. Lacking supplies, they disappeared within a generation. On Earth, the rebuilding process began—including the horrible business of rounding up the genetic freaks born as a result of the radiation. Survivors lived underground for nearly four hundred years, until the radioactive half-life decayed sufficiently to permit a return to the surface. By then, man's genetic makeup had been drastically altered. Among the side effects, the capability to reproduce was sharply curtailed. And since then, the death of the planet—and the species—has been virtually inevitable. Because it is happening so slowly—" A mournful smile. "Sometimes we pretend that all's well. But that is an illusion. Perhaps it's an illusion necessary for sanity."

Silence.

Tom gazed down into the gleaming tower city. Somewhere down there, Mari was busily supervising a construction project. To what purpose?

Could this marvelous city really represent man at the end of his accomplishments? Recalling the wasted countryside, the city standing like a fortress in a hostile land, Tom had a deep, sad certainty that Phlonykus was neither lying nor exaggerating.

"As a footnote," said the Doktor, "I believe I mentioned that during the chaotic century following 2080, many of man's technological secrets were lost. No wonder. Entire cities were burned by maddened mobs. Some of the knowledge was recovered. We could once again send rockets to the Moon. But we have not done so. Far too costly. As another example, we still know how to produce invisibility shields developed for police work in the early twenty-first century and then adopted by the general public for personal privacy. Sometimes my officers employ such shields. On the other hand, we know nothing of this time-phase effect you described, Dr. Linstrum. Perhaps now you understand my astonishment over your pursuit of the assassin Kop."

"Koop."

"Ah, yes. You say he murdered a chief executive of your land, one Archibeld?"

"Bald," Cal said. "Archibald."

"In our histories it has become *beld*. Faulty scholarship after the destruction, probably."

White looked startled. "You've heard of him?"

"My dear sir, for centuries our historians have tried to sort out the causes of the doomsday catastrophe. Your Archibeld was struck down at midpoint of his career. And I know he worked actively on behalf of eliminating weapons that were the forerunners of the doomsday device."

"That's why Koop killed him," Tom said. "He believed Archibald's disarmament efforts were wrong."

"Disastrous idea! In the best judgment of our scholars, the sudden departure of Archibeld from the world scene centuries ago was a direct, linear cause of the arms buildup that led to the doomsday holocaust. It is theorized that, had Archibeld lived to carry out his plans, things might have been entirely different—" Phlonykus gestured toward the lighted city. "And we might not be crouching here in our splendidly lighted caves, awaiting the final night."

"Then that makes our mission doubly important," White said.

"Wait, wait!"

They all turned, to see Sidney Six waving its stalks. "There's a logical dilemma here, Dr. Linstrum. If you apprehend young Koop, return to the Adirondack forest, and prevent Archibald's murder, time will be wrenched back on its original course—"

"And Federal Earth as we know it might well cease to exist," Phlonykus nodded. "We are, after all, the descendants—the living consequences—of Archibeld's absence from world affairs. That dilemma became apparent as we talked."

"I can't deny the possibility," Cal told him. "If we succeed, you might not be here."

"You place a high price on my help, Dr. Linstrum. To ask me to abet the possible destruction of all I have struggled to build—even the possible destruction of my self—" Doktor Phlonykus turned to stare outside, murmuring, "I am not prepared to give you an immediate answer. You must wait. You must wait."

The Chairman provided comfortable, if unusual, accommodations on a floor several levels below. One of his staff demonstrated operation of the sleeping platform, an obsidianlike slab that hung in the air with no visible means of support.

A chute whisked Tom's coverall away to clean it. Shortly, the assistant returned, reporting unhappily that the automatic cleaners had rejected the unfamiliar fabric, and consigned it to the shredder. The assistant's assistant arrived with more contemporary clothing: a balloonlike sleeping suit and, for the morning, a dark-blue body stocking much like those worn by the police.

Adjoining each private sleeping room was a small, bare chamber with a single handle jutting from the wall. Turned on, the handle activated humming sound waves that tingled Tom's bare skin and left him feeling marvelously clean.

He didn't have to adjust the lighting controls in the sleeping room. The moment he thought about darkening them, they dimmed.

He climbed onto the sleeping slab, discovering that his

body did not—could not—touch it. He was supported comfortably by the gentle currents of air.

Weary, he waited for sleep. He thought of Sidney Six, assigned its own cubicle despite its protests that it could rest its circuits anywhere, even in a hallway. He thought of Mari—

He found himself curiously interested in her.

In a girl who was *bald?*

Halfway into dreams, he laughed. With her tight-fitting fabric helmet in place, she was exceedingly attractive—

Her image vanished as he imagined silvery spheres launched into the atmosphere that day so long ago. He saw continents in flames. Hideous genetically damaged creatures roaming the land. Whole cities sunk in bunkers underground. Colonists on Mars sending messages to their home planet, then waiting, and listening to the messages dying away, unanswered—

Somewhere on this wasted planet, Donald Koop held the key to it all. The last, disturbing image in Tom's mind was of Donald, staggering over the burned landscape beneath the forlorn red sun.

He slept.

In the morning, Doktor Phlonykus summoned them to his private apartments, one floor down from the chamber in which he had received them the preceding night. A meal was ready on a triangular table. The food consisted of a colorless, tasteless beverage full of bubbles, large pink fruits resembling melons, and small dark brown loaves with a rocklike crust. Biting into the crust released a strong flavor reminiscent of yeast. In the mouth the hard substance turned chewy.

Seated on a padded bench beside Mari, Tom asked how her project was proceeding.

The flecked gray eyes regarded him with mistrust. "We have resumed schedule now that the computation error has been corrected." She ate a bite of the melon fruit. "Your name is Thomas?" She pronounced it as two distinct syllables.

"Tom," he smiled.

No smile was offered in return. "And how old?"

He told her.

"What is your intellect rating?"

He explained that, in his time, they didn't have such a rating.

"Barbaric," was her comment. It irritated him.

Doktor Phlonykus entered, looking haggard. He still wore his one-piece purple garment. Had he stayed up all night, deliberating?

Phlonykus made a few perfunctory inquiries about their comfort, then came to the point. "I have considered the matter carefully, Dr. Linstrum. Emotion argues for refusal. Reason pleads an equally eloquent case and tells me that if all the horror of the past centuries could be undone, even at a personal price that I prefer not to contemplate, I really have no choice. Therefore, I will place the full resources of my security wing at your disposal, to help you find the assassin."

Silently, three teardrop-shaped vehicles sped through the sky away from Washingtowne. It was morning, one day after Doktor Phlonykus had announced his decision. It had taken only that long to track and discover Donald Koop.

The tracking, as Phlonykus explained it, wasn't complicated. First, scanning scopes swept the surrounding area for a distance of three hundred kilometers, searching for a single bleeping dot to indicate an unusual life-form. The dot would have to be Donald, Tom learned, since wild animals were nonexistent.

Long ago, animals had become obsolete as food sources. All edibles were chemically synthesized. Insect life existed out on the barrens, to be sure. But the only surviving animal of size was a mutated variety of the dog. These were kept as pets by the city dwellers and never ran wild.

Donald, like Cal and his party, had arrived outside the limit of the short-range scanners keeping constant watch on the area immediately around the city. Cal and the others had crossed the perimeter on their way to the city, prompting the arrival of Officers Klok and Nem. Donald, on the other hand, had evidently headed in the other direction.

Following discovery of the dot, sky vehicles flew eastward at a high altitude, so Donald would not realize he was being observed. Cal was quite strong on this point. If at all possible, he wanted Donald taken by surprise. Their real goal was not Donald himself, but the Gate control.

Missing the city, as Cal and the rest had come close to doing, Donald had wandered to the shore of a dry channel that had to be the old Chesapeake Bay. No water flowed to, as Phlonykus called it, the Lantik Ocean. The Lantik was now only a hundred-kilometer-wide cesspool, roughly midway between the land masses of Amerik and Europa. Surrounding it was a vast, dusty basin.

The sky vehicles brought back high altitude holograms. An enlargement identified Donald positively. He was curled up in a posture of sleep at the top of a dune. So today, the pursuers were flying east. Two of the teardrops carried officers in black vests and helmets. The third, piloted by Phlonykus personally, had Cal and his party aboard.

Although it was early morning, the waste below looked as dim as ever. The streamlined teardrops cast lonely shadows as they ghosted along two storys above the ground.

Mari had insisted on joining them, overcoming her father's objections by saying that the construction project was now back on the track. Tom sat beside her in a sculptured seat behind the pilot's bench. He kept trying to start conversation. "For all this work you do, there must be some preparation, some schooling—"

Her wide eyes were remote. "Schooling? What is that?" Her speech sounded tinny, filtering through a throat wafer.

"A school's a place of instruction."

"An ancient concept," Phlonykus said over his shoulder. "They have not existed for centuries."

"Then how do you learn?"

"The natural way!" Mari told him. "The embryo in the mother's womb is instructed by nonvocalized electronic signals. The mind is implanted with knowledge—"

"Before birth?"

"The process is far too extensive to be completed in nine months. It is continued until age two. By that time, the infant has acquired the sum of human knowledge. Of course, learning how to apply it takes eight more years. At ten, the child is in full command of himself, has chosen his primary vocation, and is physically mature enough to begin an apprenticeship. By the end of puberty, he or she is prepared for a fully functioning role in society."

"That's incredible."

"It is your system that is incredible, Thomas. I know all about it."

When he asked how, she replied blithely that she had used a telescanning machine to read out the contents of his brain while he slept.

"Mari!" Phlonykus said. "That is hardly polite."

"No one said I could not, Father."

"And what did you find?" Tom demanded.

"That you are a very shallow person, Thomas."

He scowled.

"I am speaking intellectually, of course," she added. "Your primitive emotional makeup is quite another matter."

Across the aisle, Cal showed his dislike of the girl. He still refused to accept her supposed brilliance. For once, Tom agreed.

Mari continued matter-of-factly, "You also have peculiar notions about the female sex. As I understand it, your culture regards them as love objects."

"If you mean that we marry, have children—"

"By random chance! The dictates of the heart! To assign emotional values to a circulatory organ is most irrational. And to select a life's companion on the basis of feelings, instead of matched intellectual levels—the only word for that is still—barbaric!"

"There's a lot about us that you find barbaric, isn't there? Not to mention unpleasant."

"If you mean I am unhappy that you are here, that is true. I do not like the possibility of ceasing to exist. To surrender my life, my consciousness, so that generations in the past may labor their way forward through ignorance—"

"Mari!" Phlonykus said. "I have made the decision. Say no more."

"You may be genius rated, Mari," Tom said, "but when it comes to emotional maturity—kindness, compassion for others—you have a lot to learn."

Mari turned scarlet. Then she faced front. Her father commented, "You are wise in your own way, young Thomas Linstrum. The emotional maturity of which you speak is not arrived at by chemical means, nor at an early age. Only the experience of living can provide it."

Tom was almost mad enough to make another remark about bald girls. But he didn't. Why play her game?

A crackling sound filled the teardrop. Phlonykus threw a switch. They heard the translated voice of an officer in another teardrop. "Target in view on the screens. Range, one and a half kilometers and closing."

"Then he is still wandering the shore of the old Lantik," Phlonykus said.

"Let's not set down too closely," Cal cautioned.

The Chairman picked a landing spot half a kilometer from Donald's approximate location. The silent craft settled toward earth. With a gentle bump of extendible pads, it landed. The other two teardrops landed alongside. The party disembarked.

The wind whined as the policemen readied strange weapons that included wands, spheres, and three-pronged staffs tipped with multicolored crystals.

An officer approached. Tom recognized Klok's voice. "The target is roughly one half kilometer forward, where the ditch commences." He indicated a dune hiding the horizon.

Cal pulled his laser pistol from the belt of his dark orange body stocking. All their clothes had been demolished by the cleaning chutes. White drew his weapon too.

Sidney Six quivered its stalks. "I find this exciting. Rationally speaking, of course! Shall we go?"

"We shall," Cal nodded. "But not you."

"Dr. Linstrum, once more I protest your insufferable, authoritarian—"

Phlonykus gestured. Two officers jumped forward, wrestled the box into one of the teardrops, and locked the hatch from outside. Sidney Six complained loudly, banging the teardrop's inner wall. Finally it gave up.

"My officers will follow at a discreet distance," Phlonykus promised.

White said, "We won't call for them unless we need help."

Cal added, "The fewer of us there are, the better our chances of taking him by surprise."

An immense, stooping figure against the dull red sky, Phlonykus said, "I wish you success."

With a curt nod, Cal started up the dune.

At the top, he bellied down. White and Tom crawled up beside him. Ahead, by the drop-off at the shore of the old Bay, they saw a solitary figure.

Donald walked a few steps in one direction, then a few

steps in another. His gait was shambling, without purpose, as if his mind had abdicated all but the most primitive control—

The red sun flashed from Donald's spectacles. Cal whispered, "We'll crawl the rest of the way. Remember, he's still armed."

Tom's mouth grew dry. The wind between the dunes sang on a low, mournful note. On hands and knees, they moved forward.

12

THE BROKEN GLASSES

THEY CRAWLED to the crest of the dune separating them from Donald and the eroded shore. Sadly, Tom contrasted the picture of the Bay in his own time with the panorama of desolation confronting them now. Ghostly sand clouds blew across the basin stretching eastward. This was the end of it, then. Emptiness. Death—

Tom felt a stab of pity for Phlonykus and his people. Of what use was their technology when this emptiness was the true symbol of the destiny of man?

And Donald, with his sick, power-hungry ego, had brought the ruin.

Cal whispered, "When I signal, stand up. Don't show him your laser right away, Gordon," he added, sliding his own weapon back into his belt, the handle grip pointing forward.

"Wouldn't it be better just to charge?" White asked.

"No, we're too far away. He'd have a clear shot at us. Let's see how he reacts."

Donald was about thirty yards away, in the open. He squatted at the edge of the drop-off, drawing a pattern on the ground with the tip of his gun. His face was dreamy, self-satisfied.

"I'm glad we have some backup," White said. "All of a sudden I don't have much guts for this. Look at Koop's face. He enjoys what he sees!"

Tom looked back. Lying shoulder to shoulder on a dune, Doktor Phlonykus and a half dozen of his police awaited developments. One policeman held a rectangular device close to his helmet, as if he were watching it. Some kind of monitor screen trained on them or Donald or both?

"All right," Cal said. "Up!"

Side by side, they stood.

It took about a minute for Donald to realize that he was being observed. When he did, he jumped to his feet. The dreamy-mad smile disappeared. The red sun glared from the blue lenses.

Cal called, "Donald? We want to talk to you."

Another moment passed. Tom was conscious of their vulnerability, clear targets at the top of the dune. Donald held his laser pistol in his right hand. Tom watched for any sudden tensing of the fingers to show that Donald had decided on resistance.

Suddenly, Donald smiled. "This isn't Pompeii, Linstrum. I don't need your help."

"Donald, we want to come down there and talk—"

"Stay where you are!" Donald raised the laser. "I can hear you just fine."

Cal wiped his mouth. "All right. But please listen. There's been an emergency. We need the Gate control—"

"How do you like this?" Donald yelled, doing a crazy pirouette, a full circle, his free hand embracing the hazed sky, the blowing dust, the forlorn basin stretching eastward toward the cesspool of the Lantik. "You were all so sure that if Archy's disarmament plans failed, everything would be wiped out. Bang, no more Earth. But it's still here!"

"Doesn't he see—" Tom began.

"He doesn't see anything," White breathed. "He's lost his mind."

"It's beautiful!" Donald screamed, dancing up and down now, laughing, waving his arms. "And I made it! Me! Donald Koop!"

"If this is the Earth you made, where are the people?" Cal shouted. "Where are the cities? I'll tell you where, Donald. You wiped out almost all—"

White seized Cal's arm. "Don't anger him!"

But the damage was done.

"Don't preach at me, Linstrum! You're wrong, all of you. Archy had to die. It wasn't a catastrophe. The Earth's beautiful—and it's mine! I can do anything I want with it! *I own it!*"

Suddenly he held up a small, familiar object. "I can still change it, Linstrum. Anywhere! Anytime! I'm the *Creator!*"

Creator, moaned the echo on the wind. *Creator*—

White's cheeks shone with sweat. "No wonder he thinks it's beautiful. He believed he's the only one left. He probably never saw the city. He thinks he's—"

Unable to go on, White let an equally horrified Cal say it. "God."

In a moment, White recovered a little. "We can't handle him in that state. Signal Phlonykus."

Tom said, "I'll try to get close enough to grab the control."

"No, Tom, I forbid—"

But Tom was already starting down the dune, trying to walk slowly, steadily. The slope and the sand made footing tricky. Tom called, "Calm down, Donald. You know me."

"My friend Thomas. Sure."

"We won't hurt you, Donald. Put the gun away."

"Don't try to fool me, Thomas," Donald said. "You aren't my friend anymore. Not if you came here with them."

Tom fought his fear as he reached the bottom of the dune. "Please listen, Donald. What Cal said is true. There's been an emergency at the Gate. We desperately need the control."

Instantly, Donald pointed the laser at Tom's stomach.

"The control's mine! It's where it belongs—in the hands of the Creator! You don't realize, Thomas. I have the power of life and death now. Over *everything!*"

Donald's right hand began to shake. The laser muzzle waved erratically. "That includes you, Thomas. So stop."

He took one step back, toward the drop-off.

"I said stop right there—"

"Okay, forget the control. Let's just talk. You don't know what you've done, killing Archibald."

"I changed history!"

Tom was fifteen yards from Donald now, forcing every step. Fear consumed him. "But when you understand what's happened—"

"No closer, Thomas!"

Tom kept walking.

"I'll hurt you if you don't stop right where—*Thomas, you'd better listen!*"

Tom raised his hand. "Donald—"

From the dune, Cal shouted his brother's name. Donald's pistol hand jerked. Tom flung himself forward, hitting the sand as a thin red beam hissed through the air where he had been standing.

Someone else yelled. Tom rolled over, and saw Gordon White pitch sideways. The line of the dune top blackened with helmets. Doktor Phlonykus deployed his men right and left. Cal seemed as surprised to see the officers as Tom was.

Donald scrambled down over the edge of the drop-off, only his head in sight as he aimed the laser at the policemen running both ways along the dune, spreading out to encircle him.

"Tell them no firing!" Cal warned Phlonykus.

Donald steadied his pistol with both hands. Tom heard a wild buzz of sound, then Cal's cursing, as he smashed a three-pronged staff from the hand of the officer who had triggered it. *"I said no firing!"*

"Use the shields!" Phlonykus ordered. "That's why we brought them!"

The Chairman had wanted to employ the invisibility shields from the start. But Cal—because someone else made the suggestion, Tom was sure—had rejected the idea. Now Tom was seeing the result of his brother's stubborn insistence on controlling every situation. There was confusion—chaos—on the crest of the dune, as policemen scurried in all directions, hunting cover. Abruptly, two of them vanished, then two more, evidently employing the shields.

Tom turned again, gasped—

Donald's hands opened. The laser fell. Slowly, he sank from sight.

With the others, Tom raced toward the place where Donald had disappeared. "How is Dr. White?"

"Passed out," Cal shot back.

They found Donald at the bottom of the drop-off.

He lay on his side, his mouth open. His body bore no mark. Both blue lenses, cracked into star patterns, reflected multiple suns. He was dead.

Tom felt the beginning of tears of shock. Doktor Phlonykus said, "My men are trained to react quickly. Officer Tep would not have discharged his sonic had he not believed one of us would be hit."

Cal's weak gesture conveyed his partial comprehension of what had been a natural mistake in the tension of the moment. On his knees beside the body, he looked up all at once.

"I didn't want him dead. *I didn't want him dead.*"

"I—I'm sorry," Tom said, with difficulty. "I tried. But all at once it hit me that nobody could reason with him. He was beyond that." He shook his head. "Dr. White—"

"Mari is attending to him," Phlonykus said, reaching across to the officer holding the rectangular device Tom had noticed before. It was indeed some kind of communications monitor, with an elliptical faceplate. Phlonykus adjusted controls and said to Cal, "Had you not rejected my suggestion about the shields, Dr. Linstrum, this might have been prevented."

Still on his knees, Cal seemed not to hear.

Phlonykus scowled, then spoke to the monitor plate. "Mari?"

A colored dot pattern flashed on the plate, cleared and formed an image of the girl's face. Then the image shifted. Tom saw Dr. White lying on the sand, eyes closed.

Mari's voice rattled through the speaker. "The wound is deep, in the rib region. But it needn't be fatal."

"Take one of the craft and return him to the city at once."

Mari nodded. The image blanked out.

Cal found the control unit. Sand trickled away as he held it up. That strange, lost expression filled his eyes.

"Donald's dead. But nothing's changed. His death here didn't undo the damage."

The crushing complexity of time's paradoxes started an ache at the edge of Tom's mind. He remembered his thoughts of separate Donald's, coexisting at different points along the time river. The ache grew worse as Cal went on. "Back on that March thirteenth in the past, there must be another Donald. Still alive."

"The Donald who was there to kill Archibald?" Tom said. "*Before* he came here and—and died?"

"Yes." Hopelessly, Cal stared at the control. "We may have to capture him all over again."

Tom had no idea how long he waited. Three hours? Four? It seemed like a century.

He paced to the transparent wall, stared up at the taller

towers, blurred now as Earth's diffused sun sank. He could not stop feeling angry about the fact that, just before noon, Cal had put him down again—hard.

Why? Tom wondered again, full of the rage that had become so familiar lately. *I just wanted to go along to help him!*

It didn't help to tell himself that Cal was tense, desperately worried about the growing complexity of their predicament. Donald's death yesterday had opened a Pandora's box of new problems.

Sadness swept over Tom as he stood in a pool of weak red light falling through the tinted wall. Donald had been out of his mind toward the end. Yet Tom still remembered the good times they had shared. He thought briefly of Donald'd corpse, whisked away to refrigerated storage pending Cal's decision on disposition.

Cal's decision. Always *Cal's decision!*

Events seemed to be slipping from their collective hands. As the situation worsened, reactions grew heated—and unpleasant. If the two of them continued to exist in this state of doubt and peril, Tom's anger would surely break loose. A major blowup could be in the making.

Well, he thought, it's been coming for quite a while.

Trying to thrust the problem from his mind, Tom turned back to the shadowy room, and Gordon White.

The scientist lay in what Doktor Phlonykus called a therapy bed. It resembled a giant plastic egg sliced through its long axis. From the rim, various tubes and monitor pads ran to White's temples, arms, legs and chest. Complex equipment in the wall behind the bed read out the status of his life systems.

Directly above the bed hung a circular plate. Tiny magenta dots chased over its surface. Phlonykus had tried to explain how invisible rays from that screen healed a serious wound. But last night, when White was brought to the hospital, Tom had been too tired for much of the explanation to register.

White's color seemed good. Sleeping, he breathed regularly. A light hospital garment concealed the laser wound.

In one corner, a special communicator showed the same color image that had been visible since noon; a section of dry plain located at about the spot where they had arrived in the fortieth century. In the background, four helmeted officers lounged against the vehicle that had taken Cal and

Sidney Six to the point of departure. The officers acted restless.

The curtain of vertical light beams that served as a door dissolved. Mari walked in.

Before the light beams sprang up again, Tom glimpsed two physicians outside. One was nearly eight feet tall.

Mari's flecked gray eyes acknowledged Tom's presence before she surveyed the monitors.

"He's making excellent progress, Thomas. In fact, he may be conscious tomorrow."

"Then you're sure he'll recover?"

"As soon as your friend was safely inside this hospital, we were certain of that. The challenge has been to prevent permanent tissue damage. That, too, I'm happy to say, has been accomplished." She nodded to the communications screen with its image of the red-lighted plain. "No sign of your brother and that queer box?"

"Not yet."

He had almost grown accustomed to the rattle of her voice through the throat wafer, even begun to accept her appearance, including the tight-fitting helmet. She was a pretty girl indeed, with finely turned features, a generous mouth. What he could not grow accustomed to was her constant air of condescension. Some of this resentment showed when he said, "Shouldn't one of the regular doctors check him?"

Mari frowned. "I am fully qualified—"

"In addition to being a construction engineer, you're a practicing physician?"

"That is right."

"Well, in our admittedly primitive era, the study and the practice of medicine are complicated enough so that a man or a woman has no time for anything else. Of course, I realize you're a superior intellect—"

"But, Thomas, our staff physicians are all engaged in other fields of endeavor. Doktor Holmm, the young man you met, is also a nutritional manufacturing systems designer, as well as assistant conductor of our lightplay symphony."

"How in the name of sense can you handle so much?"

"The human mind is capable of great accomplishments, provided it is utilized to capacity. Since all of our development, learning, as you term it, is done in infancy and early childhood, there is ample time for the practice of many vocational roles."

Tom was silent. For the first time, her uncompromising stare softened a bit.

"My comments yesterday upset you, did they not, Thomas?"

"Upset me? Never."

"Speak honestly, Thomas. Perhaps I was too sharp. Now that I have grasped the limitations of your intelligence—"

"Thanks!"

"Please, I did not mean to offend—"

She looked helpless. She did have feelings after all!

Her voice dropped lower. "Before you grow angry, Thomas, consider. Despite all the accomplishments of our people, we have not found a way to arrest the dying of the race."

And she looked at him with such pain that his hostility drained away.

Mari turned back to the communicator. "How long will your brother and the reporting box be gone?"

"No way of telling. They'll have to wait for Donald to appear at Camp Lookout. And there's extra time involved, because they had to travel from here back to the Gate, in our day, to reset it for the weekend in March. Before they jump forward again, they'll have to make another stop and reset it for this present."

Sinking down in a sculptured chair, Mari said, "There is bad feeling between your brother and that chattering machine. I did not understand why your brother took it along."

Tom looked bitter. "I don't think Cal wanted to go alone. But there was another reason. Before Six got into the act, I said I wanted to go."

"And he rejected your idea?"

"Naturally. He said someone had to stay with Gordon in case the present changed suddenly, once the time flow was put back on its original course. It was only an excuse. Cal's a brilliant man. That's part of his problem. He refuses to believe anyone else is capable of coming up with good ideas."

"Especially a sibling," Mari nodded. "I detected the rivalry."

"Oh, you're a psychologist too?"

"I have taken many special seminars in intrapersonal behavior. Your brother has a weakness which is typical of men of his mental profile. It can only lead to friction, hostility—"

"There's a simpler way to say it, Mari. It can lead to trouble. And it will, unless—"

A moving image on the communicator distracted him. The brief moment of rapport with the girl was shattered.

On the screen, all four officers ran toward someone or something out of range of the lens.

Tom turned a switch, so that the officers could pick up his voice on a two-way band inside their helmets.

"Are they back?" he asked.

Alarmed, Mari pointed to the city beyond the wall. "But, Thomas—there is no change!"

She was right. If they were now on an alternate time track, no visual evidence supported the fact.

The officers had disappeared from the screen. Tom shouted. The officers heard him, dissolved the image into a distorted wide-angle view. Tom saw the policemen clustering around Cal. He glimpsed a waving stalk.

"Cal? Six? Somebody answer!"

One of the officers switched lens position again. Now Tom and Mari got a close-up of the metal box hovering. Beyond it, half of Cal's face was in sight.

Cal was unusually pale. For some reason he had his eyes closed.

"Six, did you reach Camp Lookout?" Tom asked.

"With no difficulty. Following our stop in the bunker to reset the Gate, we—I cannot report further at the moment."

"But we've waited all afternoon—"

"There is an emergency! Show him, officers!"

"They must have failed," Tom whispered.

A black helmet filled the screen. "Officer Klok requesting a therapy bed and emergency facilities. We are rushing Linstrum to the city."

A sudden shift of the lens showed Cal. In the bunker, he had evidently put on twentieth-century clothing, including an outercoat. All at once, Tom saw the reason for Cal's unsteadiness, his closed eyes.

He was in pain. A large, wet stain marked the front of his coat. A bloodstain.

Sidney Six lost its composure, exclaiming, "I suggested

treatment in our own time! From the bunker! Dr. Linstrum insisted on returning here to see what had changed. He can barely stand—"

"But who shot him?" Tom pleaded. "Is Archibald alive or dead?"

No answer. Six exclaimed, *"Catch him!"*

Cal pitched forward out of range of the lens.

13

DONALD TIMES TWO

IN A SPARSELY FURNISHED ROOM two floors below, Doktor Holmm conferred with Tom while Sidney Six hovered.

The young physician's calm manner didn't ease Tom's concern. Cal had been rushed to one of the building's surgeries. But Tom still didn't know what had happened at Camp Lookout.

Holmm said, "Your sibling's wound is classified moderately serious to serious. Transplant is the only thing."

"Transplant! What kind?"

"A portion of his intestine was nicked away by a laser. He is bleeding internally. That should be under control very shortly, however. I will perform the implantation. I would advise you to reamin here. If anxiety proves too strong, I will arrange a medication."

"You're—replacing part of his intestine with someone else's?"

Doktor Holmm paused on his way out. "Use of genuine donor's organs ceased centuries ago. We employ only the most perfect synthetics, far more durable than the human variety. What is unknown in connection with the procedure on your sibling is the possible rejection reaction of his body. We have chemical agents to offset that, of course. But metabolically, Dr. Linstrum is different from our average patient."

"What are his chances?"

"Even. It depends entirely on his reaction to the transplant. I will send someone to report as soon as we are certain."

Just as Holmm hurried out, Phlonykus entered.

"I have sent Mari to assist in the surgical theater. She will bring us word of the outcome."

Tom nodded dully, then turned to the floating box. "You and Cal failed—"

"Failed?" Sidney Six waved its stalks. "On the contrary!"

"But conditions here are just the same!" exclaimed Phlonykus. "This—time flow to which Dr. Linstrum referred has not been altered!"

"Yes it has," the machine replied. "At least I assume so, since President Archibald is alive, well, and back in the White House, where he resumed his duties on the morning of March 14, 1987."

"You found Donald?" Tom asked.

Six dials jiggled. "Most curious! Even I, with my vast ability to assimilate the unusual, have difficulty comprehending the existence of two Donald Koops. One here, another there in the Adirondacks—What? Found him? Yes. Your brother and I arrived perhaps half a mile from the site of the lodge and the adjacent helicopter landing field. Are you familiar with the terrain at the campsite?"

Tom shook his head. He had read descriptions of Camp Lookout. But in the tension of the moment, his mind was blank.

Six explained that the rambling lodge was set well back from a bluff that afforded a fine view of the mountains. The cleared landing area was located just west of the lodge, where the line of the bluff made a sweeping curve outward. Beyond the plowed ground, thick woods stretched to the bluff's edge. In those woods, deep with snow, Cal found Donald's tracks without difficulty.

Donald had built a shelter from fallen branches, about six feet back into the trees. He had a clear view of the plowed field.

"Actually," Six said, "Linstrum allowed a generous safety margin. We arrived shortly past ten on the morning of the assassination. Pardon me, the *planned* assassination. Took Koop completely by surprise. I distracted him by sounding my klaxon. Your brother leaped at him, seeking to capture the laser pistol. Unfortunately, footing was poor because of the deep snow. Your brother stumbled. Koop spun around, fired a burst. Your brother fell. Though I am sure he was in great pain, he got to his feet almost at once. Koop then aimed at the nearest target—ahem! One touch of that beam and my career would have, as it were, melted away. Before he could fire, your brother attacked him again. I assisted by flailing Koop with my stalks. He lost the laser pistol in the struggle—"

"But where is Donald now?"

"I am coming to that. My klaxon aroused the Presidential security guards. They rushed from the lodge, joined by Air Force personnel guarding the landing field. Your brother planned to render young Koop unconscious and return him to the bunker, in order to avoid lengthy explanations. Unfortunately, his wound upset those plans. Koop managed to break away and race off through the trees. Apparently he became confused about direction. We heard a piercing shriek—"

Six stopped, its green glass hemispheres flashing. "In spite of the snow, Koop was running extremely fast, you see. He burst from the trees directly on the edge of the bluff. Because of the slippery footing, he could not stop in time. He fell—"

"He's injured?" Phlonykus asked.

"He is dead."

"Dead?" Tom repeated. *"Twice?"*

"I am even less prepared to grapple with the paradoxes than you," Six admitted. "We were not able to examine the body. From the edge of the bluff, it was an exceedingly long way down to those large rocks. But he did not move. And he lay in such a curious, broken position—"

Once more Six stopped. Then, remarkably softly he said, "In the course of my journalistic endeavors, I have seen many ugly sights. But none uglier than Koop sprawled among the boulders. I believe we may safely assume that he not only died there, but on March 13, 1987, as well."

There was a strange, forlorn expression on the face of Doktor Phlonykus.

Six went on. "Dr. Linstrum found strength to return us, via the control device, to the Gate. Just in time, too. The security forces were pelting through the woods. In the bunker, I suggested immediate medical attention, as I believe I mentioned. Your brother insisted on resetting the coordinates to return us here. The rest you know. I only hope that I survive to record this remarkable story."

Tom sank down in a chair, pondering the mid-numbing paradox of two Donalds. And President Archibald restored to life—

No, wrong. Despite all the twists and turns, conditions were presumably back as they had been *before* Donald started on his disastrous time journey. The only difference was that Donald was dead—

Twice.

He heard Phlonykus say softly, "Archibeld lived?"

"Lives," Six corrected. "If I comprehend the river analogy, he lives now—this moment—back there in 1987, where he is busily promoting disarmament."

"But here, it's exactly the same!"

"I haven't had time to notice, Doktor."

Chilled, Tom stared at the Chairman. "You told us that historians considered Archibald's murder a direct, linear cause of the doomsday detonation."

"Yes."

"Perhaps all the historians were wrong."

"That begins to seem an inescapable conclusion."

"The mistake might have come from the work of just one historian, you know. One wrong conclusion, accepted by other historians for generations afterward. It's happened before. In medieval times, for instance, inaccuracies were perpetuated by scholars who assumed that some primary source was absolutely correct."

"Archibeld lived," Phlonykus repeated. "And still the doomsday spheres flew through the sky. Still the planet is dying—"

Slowly, Tom nodded. "Cal straightened out the present we live in. But yours—"

"I had such high hopes," the Chairman said. "And I am not a man who commits himself easily to emotion. You cannot grasp what I felt during the time of decision. I do not wish to die, to be wiped out by an instantaneous change in history. Yet, for the sake of others, I forced myself to permit your brother to leave, hoping"—a weary gesture— "hoping with all my heart that we would suddenly see a new Earth to replace this one that is dying. It has not happened. The historians were wrong. Completely wrong!"

The Chairman rushed from the room.

An hour passed. Two.

Tom was thinking about going to the surgery when Mari appeared. "Success, Thomas! There was no rejection. He will survive, and return to consciousness in a day or two."

Whooping, Tom hugged her.

Alarmed, she wriggled out of his grasp. Tom looked at her more closely. Her wide eyes still mirrored a deep worry.

"Mari, what's wrong?"

"It is my father, Thomas. Some terrible gloom has seized him. He has sealed himself up in his official chambers and will neither see nor speak with anyone."

The Chairman remained in seclusion for three days. Even his daughter was not permitted into his presence.

On the morning of the third day, Cal woke up. He was moved to a large room overlooking the city. The room contained two automated therapy beds. The other was occupied by Gordon White, who was up and around now. He looked sallow, but otherwise he seemed his old self.

Doktor Holmm stated that Cal would be confined for at least another week. This touched off an argument. Cal insisted that he was well. Only a sudden spasm of pain convinced him otherwise.

He fell back against the headrest, struggling to breathe. Doktor Holmm programmed a tranquilizing injection from the bed. The injection returned Cal to a drowsy state and eliminated his inclination to argue.

At dusk, Mari looked in. Relieved, she said that her father had broken his seclusion and had summoned all the chief executives of Federal Earth's nineteen cities to an emergency conference, to begin late that evening. Together with members of Phlonykus' own advisory staff, they would meet in complete secrecy. The subject of the conclave was unknown. Mari reported that her father still looked exceedingly grim.

That night, several immense airships appeared over the city. Each vessel was accompanied by a swarm of smaller protective craft. Flashing running lights of orange and green, the sky vehicles maneuvered to the summit of the tallest tower and dropped down through the iris port. The dignitaries were arriving.

Next evening, Tom discovered why.

Cal and White were finishing dinner. Cal was still in bed. White stood by the window, munching a stalklike purple fruit. Sidney Six had gone off to record its thoughts for posterity.

Abruptly, the light curtain at the door vanished. Phlonykus entered. He wore his purple garment of office, but now a silver medallion decorated the front. He looked tired, but, in contrast to the last time Tom had seen him, his step was purposeful.

"Are you up to conversing, Dr. Linstrum?"

"Of course, Doktor," Cal answered, though his voice was weak.

"My physicians say that in a day or two, Dr. White can resume normal activities. I therefore ask for his personal assistance, and permission for him to operate the Gate on my behalf."

"On your—" Cal nearly upset his meal tray. "For what purpose?"

"For the purpose of returning to the ninth day of December in the year 2080. In the archives, my research staff has discovered that, at noon of that day, the doomsday device was detonated."

All at once, they understood. White said, "You want to try to prevent it?"

"To prevent the destruction of the race? Indeed. I have outlined the potential dangers to my executives and advisers. I have particularly noted the possibility that this society may alter so radically as to cease to exist. We argued the matter more than twelve hours. The vote was narrow. Just a margin of three in my favor."

Thunderstruck, Cal began, "I don't think you understand—"

"But I do, Dr. Linstrum," Phlonykus said. Standing tall in the dim chamber, he made an imposing picture. "I permitted you to carry out your plan, hoping that it would avert the catastrophe. Now it is evident that Archibeld's role was not significant in causing—or deterring—the holocaust. It is no easier to make the decision a second time. But with the means of time control still available, I feel we must undo the damage if we can."

Cal shook his head. "The stakes are too great—"

"The stakes, my dear Linstrum, are nothing short of the survival of man. We know there is no error in the conclusion that stopping the doomsday device would reshape history as we have known it—tragically—for nineteen centuries."

Tom sensed tension in Cal's voice as he said, "I'm sorry, Doktor. The risk—"

"I am fully aware of the risk! I accept it!"

"Without my personal supervision of the Gate—"

Phlonykus snorted in contempt, more human than Tom had ever seen him. "Dr. Linstrum, you force me to remind you that your decisions are not always correct. You refused to permit my men to employ the invisibility shields in capturing Koop. In fact, you sneered at the very idea. *You* did not need such assistance."

Cal was scarlet. Phlonykus continued, "You, sir, are not the only person alive who is capable of making intelligent decisions, or managing a difficult situation through to its conclusion. I intend to go personally to 2080."

White exclaimed, "You'd endanger yourself?"

"Since the decision is mine, Dr. White, I cannot allow the danger, if any, to fall to others."

Cal's mouth wrenched. "You'd try to stop the Asiatics from detonating the doomsday machine? *In the heart of their own country?*"

"Not an easy task, I admit. But I am prepared to cope with it. Despite my age, I am in excellent physical condition. The matter of succession of authority has already been settled. Further, I can enter the past with certain advantages. The personal invisibility shields, for one. In 2080, they were in use only in western countries. They greatly improve the chances for success."

"I still can't permit you to—"

Cuttingly, Phlonykus broke in, "Are you concerned for your personal safety? Afraid you may be wiped out instantaneously?"

"My personal safety has nothing to do with it."

"Then I request—no, I demand use of the control."

"You can't demand anything!"

"If you press me, Linstrum, I can render you incapable of coherent thought. And, by means of drugs, induce Dr. White's cooperation. You are inside my city and my hospital, after all. I dislike even mentioning such measures. But if you force me—"

From the shadows, White spoke up, "As long as Doktor Phlonykus is willing to run the risks, and his own people agree—well, I think we owe him our cooperation." He faced the Chairman. "Coercive drugs won't be necessary, Doktor. I'll help you."

"Not without my authorization!" Cal raged.

Abruptly, White was at the bedside. "Cal, get hold of yourself! This man saved your life. Mine too. Without his help, Archibald would be dead. When I say we're in his debt, that's understating it!"

The tension held another moment. Then it broke, in Cal's low exhalation. "All right. Permission granted. But not until I'm recovered and can do with you."

"No," Phlonykus countered. "You will be confined for several days yet. And I intend to go as soon as possible. The mood of my executives and advisers could change. The vote could be reversed. While I have their consent, no time must be wasted."

Bitterly, Cal said, "Very well. But I don't know the whereabouts of the control unit."

"It's with the apparel we removed prior to your surgery. We have the unit in our possession. The point is, Linstrum, I could not honorably use it without your agreement. Dr. White, we shall depart as soon as I can make necessary preparations. Please see to your personal readiness."

The chairman bent toward Cal, just the merest suggestion of a bow. There was mockery in his glance, but none in his voice. "I thank you for your selfless decision."

He strode out.

A tension had been building inside Tom too. A decision. He said to White, "I'm going along. I'm sure Phlonykus will give his permission."

Before White could reply, Cal barked, "Out of the question!"

"No, Cal," Tom said, hating to do this but knowing he must. It had been a long time coming. And if ever a moment was appropriate, this one was. "I'm going to be my own man for a change. Phlonykus was right. You're a dictator."

"You're doing this deliberately, because I'm laid up in this infernal bed!"

"Partially, that's right," Tom agreed. "But I also want to help them, because they've helped us."

"I emphatically forbid you—"

"I don't care what you say, Cal. Do you understand that? I don't care. I'm grown, and I have my own mind—

regardless of what you think of it. You've pushed me to this, you know. If Phlonykus says yes, I'm going."

He spun and walked out.

In the hospital corridor, he heard Cal shouting at him to come back. He felt shaky now that it was done. And it was. In a matter of moments, the final break had come.

A break that was vitally necessary. And long overdue. But it was none the less painful for all that.

Trying to ignore the shouting, Tom walked faster.

14

"MONGOLYAH"

"JUST HERE," said the elderly technician with the wide amber eyes, "This small plate operates on a rocker principle. The pressure against the top switches on the shield. Pressure against the bottom turns it off. When the shield operates, you feel nothing. Nor is vision impaired, save perhaps for a slight blurring. Those around you are unable to see you, however, and if they are also wearing shields, you cannot see them. How is the fit?"

Tom flapped his arms. "Seems fine."

The technician moved around behind him, unfastened the straps holding the shield in place. The shield, metal but practically weightless, covered Tom's chest.

The technician placed the shield on the laboratory bench alongside the Chairman's. He said to Phlonykus, "Any other special requirements, sir?"

"Winter gear, Lexx. For myself, Dr. White, young Thomas, and Mari. I presume the journalistic box is impervious to extreme temperatures. It can accompany us if you can rig a shield for it."

"I'll try, sir." Technician Lexx's expression indicated doubt. He made notes with a light-stylus. "Cowled coats. Double thermal trousers. Boots—correct, sir?"

Phlonykus nodded. "We're going to a montainous region of the Far East. Mongolyah."

Tom didn't bother to correct the Chairman's pronunciation. He was too busy puzzling over why Mari was joining the mission—a surprise to him. It struck him as a bad idea. There would be danger enough without their being hampered by the presence of a girl.

Chagrined, he realized that he was reacting to Mari almost the way Cal had reacted to him.

Cal. He had been in Tom's thoughts almost constantly these past two days. Since the brief but bitter argument, Tom had not returned to his brother's bedside. Nor had Cal sent any messages.

Tom regretted the quarrel. Yet something in him insisted that he had no choice but to join the mission, to prove his maturity once and for all.

"Weapons, sir?" Lexx's inquiry returned Tom to the reality of the supply laboratory.

"A nerve trigger for myself and one for Dr. White," Phlonykus said. "Also as many hundred-load magazines as you can conveniently pack into the coats. Mari will want some special tools, I'm sure. But she'll tell you in person."

Lexx promised that all requisitioned items would be ready on time. Departure was scheduled in about forty-eight hours, following a final, exhaustive physical checkup for Gordon White, to make sure he was fit for the ordeal.

Phlonykus piloted the sleek vehicle that bore them across the traffic ways toward the tallest tower. Tom asked, "When did your daughter decide to come with us?"

"I made the decision, Thomas. We needed someone to disarm the doomsday device. From what Mari has learned in the archives, she assures me it will be a simple task. All the pads that launched the radiation bearers were operated from one computer—a computer complex for its day, but primitive by our standards. According to Mari, one hundred and forty-four reprogramming steps will totally disarm the system, and cause it to burn itself out beyond repair."

Tom grinned. "I hope she brings a list."

"Oh, no," Phlonykus returned matter-of-factly. "She will have it all in her head, in perfect sequence." He noticed Tom's expression, and smiled. "You continue to find Mari's abilities unusual, don't you?"

"That's an understatement, sir."

"But disarming the computer will be childishly easy! No more difficult for Mari than it would be for a person of your era to repair a wooden wheel. Knowledge is relative to the task. To Mari, that computer is a nineteen-hundred-year-old antique. You should not feel intimidated—or inferior."

"I shouldn't. But I do."

But there was another reason he wished she were not going along, Tom admitted to himself. He was worried about her safety.

It was startling to realize that, against all odds, he had grown to like her. Probably in part because she represented a challenge. But on another level, he simply found her very attractive.

The Chairman steered the cab through a port in the side of the tall tower. Automatic controls braked the vehicle against a landing platform.

As they walked to the moving stair, the Chairman asked, "Have you visited your brother today? He is making excellent progress."

"I'm glad to hear that. I haven't seen him."

"Do you intend to see him before departure?"

"I suppose I'll have to."

"This gulf between you is an unhappy thing."

Tom tried to shrug it off. "He thinks I'm a child."

"Do you really wish to risk your life in Mongolyah to prove otherwise?"

Tom looked into Phlonykus' strange wide eyes. "Yes."

Frowning, the Chairman studied the reflective walls beside the slowly ascending belt. He said at last, "Given Dr. Linstrum's attitudes, I suppose that is the only possible answer."

Some three dozen bald, emaciated dignitaries accompanied the party to the departure site two days later. Tom presumed the men must be the Chairman's advisers. Black-helmeted officers formed a protective ring around them.

Sidney Six had come along, waving its stalks as it protested Phlonykus' decision that it be left behind. "Arbitrary! As arbitrary as Linstrum, if not more so—ahem!" Technician Lexx had failed to adapt an invisibility shield to fit the metal box.

Tom, Phlonykus, Mari, and White stood apart from the rest. They were leaving from approximately the same spot at which Tom and his companions had arrived. Tom could hardly move inside his heavy trousers and cowled, fur-

lined coat. The garments smelled musty, as though re-
trieved from some museum.

Doktor Phlonykus raised his gloved hand. "I wish you
well. May we all be reunited in a happier present."

Confusing thoughts flooded Tom's mind in these last
moments. He felt a keen regret that Cal was not well
enough to be returned to the bunker. If Mari succeeded, if
history changed, would Cal still be in the hospital here?
Would *here* exist?

Earlier, Tom had visited his brother in his recovery
room. They had exchanged little more than curt good-bys.
Cal's expression remained almost childishly sullen. Tom
wondered how he could despise his brother's attitudes and,
simultaneously, fear and hope for his safety.

Phlonykus turned to White. "At your convenience,
Doktor."

White's florid color was back, contrasting with the pale
fur encircling his face. He manipulated the Gate control
awkwardly in his gloved hand.

"Stand by, please—"

The red sun vanished.

Standing on the stainless steel plate, Tom recognized the
familiar lights of the Gate chamber. The chamber was
empty, the red door down the tunnel closed. Where were
Stein and Walker? Perhaps they had grown weary of monitoring the empty chamber, gone off to rest.

White busied himself with the new spatial and temporal
coordinates he and Phlonykus had worked out. Finally,
White called ready.

They took their places on the platform beneath the gold
floodlights. Mari glanced at Tom. Her eyes showed an
emotion he had never seen there before.

Fear.

Had Doktor Phlonykus not been standing between
them, Tom would have followed his impulse and grasped
her mittened hand.

Reading the wall controls, White announced, "Five seconds."

They were thrust through the cool, tingling darkness into
blinding light.

"Shields on!"

Phlonykus cracked out the command before Tom's eyes
adjusted to the dazzling sunshine. He stabbed his glove un-

der his coat and depressed the top of the rocker panel. Details of the surroundings blurred.

He was alone. The others had vanished.

"Dr. White? Mari?"

"Here, Thomas."

Mari's voice. Someone bumped his side. A gloved hand closed on his.

Except for that slight blurring at the fringes of vision, he saw his own body clearly. On the right, he heard the Chairman say, "Hold hands so we stay together. May I have a time reading, please?"

White's voice. "Accounting for time zone differences, shortly past ten."

"Less than two hours. The entrance to the facility should be in sight—" A pause. "Yes! There, on the slope."

Mari said, "That's at least two kilometers away!"

"Sorry we couldn't come closer," White said. "I wanted to allow a safety margin."

Phlonykus spoke with urgency now. "It will require at least an hour to reach the entrance. Then we must wait for an opportune moment to get inside. If none presents itself—"

Tom, responding to a tug on each glove, started to walk across the rocky ground crusted with hoarfrost.

"—we shall have to burn through the outer doors using Dr. White's laser. I hope that is not necessary. It will make penetration of the underground more difficult."

Impossible, Tom thought. But he didn't say it.

The air was thin, piercingly cold. He noticed a plume of vapor on his right. Another came from his own lips as he exhaled.

"Doktor, when we breathe out, the shields don't hide it!"

Mari found a partial solution to the difficulty. Fastening her coat collar across her mouth helped to diffuse the plume that seemed to appear from nowhere. They began trudging again.

Ahead, an immense concrete door was set into the mountain's face. Several small figures clustered around it. Guards, undoubtedly.

Shortly the intruders mastered the knack of moving together while holding hands. They walked faster.

In one way, this desolate plateau ringed by snowy peaks was less unnerving than Pompeii or the fortieth century.

There was no evidence that this was the year 2080, except for several curiously fluted masts poking from the mountainside and a large truck of unfamiliar design parked on a road directly below the concrete door. With its open rear bed, the vehicle resembled a futuristic troop transport.

Still, this *was* Mongolia—the heartland of the Asiatic power bloc. A country in which a white face would be instantly suspect.

The wind-scoured peaks thrust up all around, snowy summits lost in patches of cloud. The only break in the mountains ringing the plateau was a pass far to their left. The rutted road disappeared up there.

Tom shivered, not entirely because of the cold. His mind kept sounding a single word. Doomsday. Once the hands of the clock reached noon, *doomsday*—

While they were still a good half kilometer from the parked truck, the great concrete door slid back. Three Orientals wearing drab uniforms and carrying sidearms strode out of the mountain.

"Missed our chance," White whispered with a telltale leak of breath from under his collar.

The soldiers moved down the slope to the truck. Two climbed into the cab. The third swung a leg over and climbed into the open bed.

At White's urging, they quickened their pace. It was already ten past eleven—less than an hour till the computer automatically launched the orbiting radiation bombs. They formed a single file, accustomed to maneuvering invisibly now. At least Tom certainly hoped they were invisible.

They neared the large truck. The man sitting in the rear smoked a small cigar and anxiously studied the cold, sunlit sky.

Behind Mari, Tom moved carefully around the rear of the truck and across the road of frozen mud. Without warning, Phlonykus stopped. Tom collided with the girl, couldn't stifle an exclamation of surprise.

The Oriental stood up. Frowning, he scrutinized the area from which the sound had come. Tom ached from standing still. Surely the man could see him. *He was staring right at him!*

Frown deepening, the Oriental knocked on the rear of the cab. He jabbered loudly, pointed, then climbed down from the truck bed to investigate.

A gloved hand tugged Tom's, an urgent signal to move.

The suspicious soldier started walking in their direction. Tom bumped into Mari again, backed away as someone's foot—White's?—struck a loose rock, making it roll.

The Oriental wheeled around toward the sound, glanced down—

A grinding rumble up the slope diverted his attention. The great concrete door was rolling aside.

More soldiers began straggling out in twos and threes. They chattered among themselves as they headed for the transport vehicle.

Noting their casual pace, the man who had almost discovered the four began to shout and wave. He pointed to a curiously shaped watch on his wrist, then at the sky. The other soldiers understood. Moving faster, they piled into the back of the vehicle.

Someone turned on the engine. The truck lifted from the ground, riding on jets of air. The noise hid the sound of Tom and his companions running forward.

Tom dodged in and out among the soldiers still straggling out of the mountain. Brushing against one, he jumped back. The man whirled and registered alarm when he saw that no one was within four feet of him.

By that time, Tom had slipped by the guards with their oddly designed rifles. He slid his back against the concrete retaining wall on the near side of the door and darted in just as the door mechanism began to rumble again.

The cement floor vibrated as the door closed, darkening a long, dim tunnel. Had the others gotten inside? Tom groped for them, not daring to speak—

With a ponderous *chunk*, the concrete door shut. Startled, Tom saw Phlonykus, Mari, and White.

"What's wrong with the shields?" he whispered.

Frantically, Phlonykus fumbled under his outercoat, then ran his hand over the rough tunnel wall. "It must be all this rock. Somehow it nullifies—"

"Let's move," White interrupted. "We have thirty-four minutes."

Mari pointed down the tunnel. "There are the lifting tubes. We descend to the fourth level."

They ran that way, beneath ceiling hemispheres that cast a feeble light. The lifting tubes resembled two elevator shafts without cages or doors. In front of the tubes, the corridor formed a T. There, someone cried out.

Tom whipped his head to the left. An armed guard leaped up from a stool.

White and Phlonykus charged him, struck him with their fists, drove him to his knees. They tore the rifle from his hands and punched him twice more.

But the wiry guard had surprising strength. He rolled away, lurched to his feet, stabbed his hand toward the wall—

Panting, White leaped in to deliver a punch. The guard doubled. But his fingers had already closed on a T-shaped switch. As the guard collapsed, the weight of his body dragged his hand down, and the T-bar with it.

Instantly, sirens howled.

15

THE DOOMSDAY CLOCK

EAR-PIERCING, the shrieks multiplied. White snapped the T-switch to its original position. The sirens kept screaming.

"The lifting tubes!" Phlonykus cried, pulling out the nerve trigger that technician Lexx had provided. It was a long, thick wand whose muzzle end widened into a bell. A thick cylinder surrounded the wand at its midpoint.

Phlonykus stared at the Oriental characters above each tube. "This one's down," he said, stepping over the threshold. Unsupported by any kind of platform, he began to sink slowly.

Mari jumped in next, followed by Tom and White.

Descent was smooth. As the main floor rose past Tom's eyes, he saw soldiers racing from the far end of the tunnel to answer the alarms.

They floated down past a door opening onto a steel-lined corridor. "Level two," White said.

Suddenly there was a commotion below, a shout from Phlonykus. Between the tips of his boots, Tom saw the Chairman point the nerve trigger at something outside the shaft. He heard two corklike pops.

The third-level opening came into view. Two Orientals lay asleep, their weapons fallen nearby.

White drew his own nerve trigger, and none too soon. A fat yellow head popped into sight below, its owner registering alarm as he saw Phlonykus floating down. White aimed along the shaft's side, pressed the nerve trigger's firing stud.

The Oriental's eyes glazed. He pitched lazily into the tube—a military officer, judging from his medals. The man turned slowly as the shaft pulled him downward.

Tom could hear jabbering from level four. Jackknifing his body forward through the door, Phlonykus disappeared suddenly.

Soldiers leaped into the tube at the second level. One jockeyed his curiously shaped rifle into position, fired downward—

Tom shoved White, then kicked against the tube wall to propel himself out through the door an instant before a bolt of white light sizzled down the tube. It missed Tom and struck the unconscious officer floating below. The officer disintegrated, pieces of him flying outward to splat against the shaft wall.

Tom shot out of the tube three feet above a parquet floor. The shaft's field let go. He dropped in a heap. White fired the nerve trigger—*pop! pop!*—at two men whose striped robes resembled the diplomatic morning coats of their own era.

Suddenly silence spread around them. Panting, Tom climbed to his feet. A fast count showed eight Orientals sleeping—three military men, five striped-robed civilians.

The room itself was immense and several storys high. Ahead, its semicircular wall blazed with lights and dials.

Among the lights was a row of clocks, showing the time at various points around the world. One clock, the largest, showed twenty-seven until noon.

In startling three-dimensional color, monitor screens displayed images of rocket launching pads. Each pad held a slender missile topped by a spherical pay load capsule. The radiation pods!

Mari stripped off her coat and gloves, ran past some benches set on a carpet in the center of the parquet. Uncovered, her hairless head gleamed. In her haste, the girl knocked over a taboret. An enameled bottle smashed. Clear fluid leaked across the floor. Rice wine? To celebrate the day of destruction?

The red minute hand of the largest clock jumped.

Twenty-six until noon.

"No one can enter except by these tubes," Phlonykus said to White. "Watch the up shaft. I'll take the other. If you exhaust your magazines, I have more—"

In the down tube, two soldiers floated into view, trying

to position their weapons for a shot. Phlonykus crouched, the nerve trigger angled upward, popping. The soldiers drifted downward, out of sight.

But more appeared from above. And others rose in the up shaft. White began firing. Soon the vast room reverberated with yells and popping, as though every bottle in a huge wine cellar was exploding its cork.

"Thomas—*help me!*"

In response to Mari's cry, he dashed around a large control console set out from the semicircular wall. More uniformed soldiers crowded both tubes. One managed a shot. White leaped aside. Where he had been standing, the parquet smoked, bubbled, then hardened into a three-foot depression. White fired again, again—

The clock hands moved. On tiptoe, Mari used a small power tool to loosen the bolts holding a section of wall plate.

Stretching, Tom caught the plate as it fell, threw it aside.

Mari pulled a probelike instrument from her belt. She inserted the probe among the exposed relays, turned it a half turn, then back a full turn.

"Now over here, Thomas."

Using the first tool, she uncovered a second bank of circuits, then a third. Tom caught the faceplates, hurling them to the floor.

Face stark with concentration, Mari bridged two connections with a tool that extruded a strip of silvery metal. One hundred and forty-four steps. She had done six—or was it seven? He didn't see how the girl could remember all the necesary steps, especially in their proper order.

The largest clock showed twenty-four minutes until the hour.

Mari's hands and forearms were buried inside a fourth opening. Suddenly smoke gushed from the interior of the wall. She leaped back as green sparks erupted like miniature fireworks.

"That is the last of the recircuiting," she breathed. "The rest is programming. It will go faster—"

She ran to the padded chair in front of the wide console, which was covered with switches and start-stops of different colors. Sitting, she wiped her palms against her cheeks, glanced once at the clock. Then she bowed her bald head, pressed a control with her right hand, waited, touched another with her left—

The lights on the wall began to change pattern, increasing speed in some places, going dark in others. Her hands began to fly, literally slapping the controls. On-off, *flash, flash*. On-off, *flash*—

By the tubes, the bedlam of shouts and popping continued. Abruptly, brilliant light filled the chamber. A familiar voice cried out. Tom whirled.

Mari screamed, nearly toppling from the chair.

Only Gordon White remained by the tubes. Doktor Phlonykus was gone.

And another bubbling depression was hardening in the floor.

White's nerve trigger popped, disposing of the soldier in the up tube who had apparently been responsible for the blast that had killed Phlonykus. The Oriental floated away, a smile on his sleeping face.

For a moment the great chamber was still. Mari's screams had dwindled to ragged sobs. Both tubes remained empty. Surely the enemy wouldn't give up—

"Phlonykus ran out of loads," White said, unscrewing the cylinder from the wand, then positioning a new one. "He was changing magazines when they shot—*Tom!*"

His shout spun Tom around as Mari ran past him, crying, *"Father!"*

Tom held her back.

"Let me go!"

"Stop, Mari!" He shook her. "Mari, there's nothing left!"

He hadn't meant to say it that bluntly. She started to go limp. Then she regained control. But she kept staring at the new pit in the parquet.

"Mari—look at the clock!"

He turned her toward the wall. Nine minutes till noon. The monitors showed smoke plumes rising from the launch pads.

"How many operations left, Mari?"

She touched her cheek. "Twenty. Twenty-one. I've forgotten—"

"You can't forget, Mari. Your father died so those rockets would never go up." He pushed her toward the console chair. "Don't make his death amount to nothing. *Mari, do you understand?*"

She nodded in a vague way. "My head hurts, Thomas. I can't seem to recall the sequence. It's all a confusion—"

"Try. You can do it." Lifting her bodily, he positioned her in the chair. "You're smart enough, Mari. That brain of yours—genius rated—"

White shouted a warning. A soldier in the down tube leveled his rifle. Tom dragged Mari to the floor.

A blaze of light melted the operator's chair. White fired back, missed.

Tom pushed himself up, and something made him say, "One of those shallow emotional reactions. I couldn't see you killed—"

White's nerve trigger popped again. A long sigh signaled the attacker's sleep. Mari stared at Tom with a curious expression as he helped her up. She laid her other hand on top of his. Then she hurried to the console.

The operator's chair had disappeared, its plastic fused into the floor like white swirls in a dark cake. But the console was undamaged. Mari began to hit the on-offs. Slowly at first, then faster. The clock showed seven minutes till noon.

White called Tom's name, fishing the Gate control unit from his coat. He tossed the control. Tom caught it.

"Hang on to that in case something happens to me. They seem to have given up trying to attack through the tubes. They'll probably try something else. They—"

He stopped, listening, as Tom pocketed the control.

"Hear that?" White whispered.

Tom nodded. "Like air leaking."

White sniffed. "There's no odor."

Tom located a source of the steadily increasing hiss. But no vapor issued from the ceiling ventilator. And he still detected no smell. Yet the evidence of his ears was unmistakable.

"Hurry up, Mari," White yelled. "They're pumping in some kind of gas."

Tom blinked, a ringing in his ears all at once. His stomach grew queasy. When he took a step, his legs were wobbly. Nerve gas!

Temporary or permanent?

No way to tell.

"Five more steps," Mari called, hitting another on-off.

The dizziness worsened. Tom swayed. The clock showed four minutes until the hour. On the monitors, smoke no longer gushed from the rockets. At three pads, technicians dashed back and forth, as if searching for the causes of a malfunction. With a little cry, Mari collapsed.

White grabbed for Tom's arm and missed, lurching like a man intoxicated. "Come on. I don't think they'll come after us in person now—" A racking cough. "Relying on the gas—"

The minute hand jumped to three before the hour.

Tom staggered after White, stomach burning, his head ringing, his fingertips numb. He had never been drunk on old-fashioned alcohol, but he imagined that this must be the sensation—an absolute loss of control of mind and muscles—

White knelt beside Mari. An image on one of the monitors was replaced by the face of a gaunt Oriental with many medals on his uniform. Behind him, other officers hovered. The gaunt man's eyes searched the chamber. Tom knew they were being watched until the gas took effect—

White cupped Mari's chin. "Did you finish?"

"One more—" She rolled her head out of his grasp. "One—"

Tom dropped to his knees, wondering if he could ever get up again. "Mari, this is Thomas. Stay awake. Is there one more step?"

Her flecked gray eyes closed. She held her stomach. "Dizzy. Sick. So sick—I—" She choked.

Tom knew how she felt. The nausea struck in swift waves. On the monitor, the gaunt man's lips peeled back in a smile. Silently, he spoke to those around him. Tom gasped, "One more step? What is it, Mari?"

"Can't—think. Sleepy—"

"Mari, what's the step? Tell me so I can do it."

"Can't—seem to remember—"

She was drifting deeper into unconsciousness. Like some surrealist vision, the clock stretched, looking almost liquid. Tom rubbed his eyes.

Two minutes before twelve.

Tom did the only thing he could think of—slapped Mari's cheek, hard.

Her head snapped over. She moaned.

Fighting his own lethargy, he helped White pull her to a sitting position.

"Mari," he pleaded, "tell me. Which control?"

The blow had revived her a little.

"The main on-off—"

"Which one?"

"Largest. Color code—purple—"

"How do I set it? Mari? *Tell me!*"

"To—on. Full on—" Her head lolled against White's shoulder.

Tom struggled to his feet. The parquet seemed to sway. When he looked down, it was *moving*—

The floor undulated like a black sea. The ripples worsened his nausea, brought a sour taste to his throat.

The central console seemed miles away. He lumbered toward it, saw the console melt, stretch, oddly elastic—

No, it's the gas. A trick in your mind—

Stumbling on, he wondered where he found the strength. Some will other than that of his dazed conscious mind—

One foot lifted.

Another.

Stumbling—staggering through heaving black oceans while the console seemed to retreat—

The clock jumped to sixty seconds before noon.

He reached for the edge of the console. His sense of distance was impaired. He missed, lurched forward, hit his head on the corner. With a cry, he fell.

The pain proved his salvation. It pierced his confusion just enough to let him grope upward, seize the console's edge, and hoist himself to a standing position.

As he gazed down, the switches melted together, gelatinous, unreal—

Thirty seconds remained on the clock.

Largest switch. Color code purple.

Why did the controls run like water? Where was it? *Where?*

Fifteen seconds. The sweep hand kept moving.

Hurry. *Hurry*—

Driven by a last-ditch strength he didn't understand, he found it, and then only because of its distinctive size and color. His hand missed it on the first pass.

Ten seconds, the sweep hand moving—

He tried again. Which way? On?

No, off.

No, on—

He couldn't remember. Nor could he comprehend the Oriental characters on the switch. Meaningless—

Five seconds.

Gambling, he hit the switch and rocked it to the opposite position.

Coughing, he started back across the black sea to White and Mari, mere specks, an infinity away—

Simultaneously, all the lights on the wall shut down.

Tom kept moving, driving himself. White's gesturing had the quality of slow motion. He wanted something. What?

The Gate control!

Tom fumbled it from his pocket and he reached the others. The great wall remained dark only a moment. Suddenly all the lights came on, along with a new panel not previously illuminated. The panel was a large red rectangle etched with oversize characters. It blinked on, off, on, off, like an alarm. On the monitor, the gaunt officer showed consternation, then rage.

"Control," White croaked. "Use—"

"We're—not in the open. The risk—"

"No choice. *Use it.*"

But Tom couldn't. The box slipped from his fingers. Consciousness began to drain from his mind.

They would never get back. They would be executed for aborting the doomsday device—

What did it matter? He was sick, exhausted, wanting only to close his eyes.

He had a surreal glimpse of Gordon White's face as the scientist groped for the fallen control, lifted it—

Too late, Tom thought. Too—

Darkness.

16

3987—AGAIN

DISTANTLY, a voice. It seemed to be repeating familiar words.

Tom's sluggish mind struggled to make sense of them. He opened his eyes—

Remembered.

And recognized the man repeating his name. "Tom," Dr. Stein said, "where's Cal? What's happened?"

"I'm not sure."

Suddenly, vast relief. He was in the Gate chamber. On the far side of the platform, White groggily raised himself onto his hands and knees.

The aftereffects of the gas made it hard to concentrate. But the nausea and the ringing in his ears diminished moment by moment.

He stared at the other person just waking on the platform.

Mari.

She lay with her back to him, whimpering a little. His thoughts came in bursts:

Her father's gone.

Will she remember?

The gold floodlights make her hair shine—

Her *hair?*

Tom rolled her over as she came fully awake. He recognized her, yet he didn't.

Lurking somewhere behind the heart-shaped face of this girl with the long, gold-streaked auburn hair he saw the old Mari—but only dimly. This girl's mouth was wider, her eyes more nearly the size to which he was accustomed. They were still gray, but lacking flecks. White noticed the difference too.

There was fear in the way Mari touched her hair. "What's become of me? Thomas—*who am I?*"

"Do you know your name?"

"My name is Mar—I'm not sure." The hope in her eyes faded, replaced by tears. "I remember my father."

With White's assistance, she got to her feet. The scientist said, "Evidently we succeeded beyond our expectations."

Desperately, Tom plumbed his own mind. Only fragmentary images existed to suggest what now lay ahead in the other—the new—3987. He glimpsed gleaming streams of blue water, a sky warming with stub-winged aircraft, a profusion of brilliant-colored fruits hanging in an orchard. The images made him think of his brother. "Cal's still up there, Dr. White."

"Or maybe he isn't. We'd better find out."

"I'd certainly be grateful for some kind of explanation," Dr. Stein said.

"Later," White said, hurrying to the wall.

Swiftly White reset the coordinates. All at once, Mari started trembling. "Don't take me there. I'm afraid of what I'll find. Of who I'll be—" There was terror in the new girl's voice all at once. "Perhaps I won't be anyone."

Soon White was ready. He stepped onto the platform. Tom gripped Mari's hand. She didn't protest.

The tingling darkness descended—

Tom heard a crack as the limb of the tree in which he had materialized gave way. He landed on his rump in thick, dark grass. Pear-shaped orange fruit rained down around him. The sun dazzled him with summery warmth. Nearby, at the edge of the orchard, Mari was getting to her feet.

Dr. White appeared. Without a word, the three walked toward the top of a nearby hill.

If this was A.D. 3987, they had indeed succeeded. The sky was clear, the air sparkling. The warm wind brought them scents of an abundant land. An animal resembling an albino chipmunk poked its head from a burrow, blinking at them as they passed.

"Seems obvious that the Asiatics never rebuilt the doomsday device," White commented. "Probably too costly and time-consuming. If I knew that Cal was safe, I'd award us medals."

Tom reached the hilltop first. Light struck his eyes—glittering light, from the mirrored faces of innumerable buildings. Low and geometrically shaped, the buildings began about five miles away, filling almost an entire quarter of the horizon.

"That is not my city," Mari said. "Oh, Thomas, that is another—"

She couldn't go on.

They heard a distant whine, saw some kind of train flashing along an elevated rail. The train disappeared behind a hill, racing toward the city.

"Obviously our best bet is to contact the authorities," White said.

"If they can understand us," said Tom.

"Let's see who we can find around that monorail."

They followed the elevated rail for nearly two miles. Then they sighted what seemed to be a passenger switch station, a large bubble suspended on gleaming rods beside the track. The bubble was reached by intricate metal stairs.

Near the station stood many vehicles. Peculiar, pyramidal vehicles, six-wheeled. A family was just parking one of the odd machines. Despite their curious robes, the man, the woman, and the two children looked reassuringly human.

The adults were only a bit taller than Tom and White, with normally contoured eyes, and full heads of hair. One of the children pointed at the trio.

Approaching the family, White smiled.

"Hello. Can you put us in touch with the police?"

Blank stares.

"Authorities?"

Alarmed, the woman jabbered in a strange tongue, then indicated the stairs. The family rushed off.

At the top of the stairs, the husband rapped on a window. A man poked his head out, looked, then ducked back inside.

"One way or another," White said uneasily, "I think we'll meet the authorities."

Shortly, a large, multicolored van arrived. It consisted

of two pyramids connected by a large cylinder. Rolling on twelve oversized tires, it stopped in the parking area. Three officers jumped out to question them, but the language barrier proved insoluble.

Tom, White, and Mari were pushed inside the vehicle's cylindrical section. The trip in the windowless transporter lasted half an hour. They emerged in a kind of garage and entered a corridor with walls and floor that glowed with shifting color patterns. Tom held Mari's hand tightly.

Finally, they faced an official with insignia on the shoulders of his robe.

The man was middle-aged, portly, and had a kind face. After several futile questions, he called for a rhomboidal apparatus on legs.

"I hoped Mari might know the language," White whispered.

Tom said nothing. The girl slumped on a stool, staring at her hands. Who was she in this clean new world in which humanity had not only survived but thrived? Probably, as she had feared, she didn't exist. His heart ached.

The rhomboidal affair proved to be a translator. From that point, matters were simpler.

The portly official was Echelon Chief Bomfils, the equivalent of a police precinct commander. The building was an outlying station. Trying to sound casual, White broached the subject of where they had come from.

Chief Bomfils grew agitated, sending aides scurrying. Soon, his superiors—an area commander and a zone leader—had joined the interrogation, which lasted three hours.

At the end, Tom knew they had reached the right year. Otherwise nothing was the same. Nothing.

Bomfils and his superiors had no knowledge of a doomsday device. In the history of *this* Earth, there never had been an Asian attack.

"An astonishing story," Bomfils said. "I regret to say that I do not believe it."

To judge from the other faces, none of them did.

Tom tried to think of proof. Finally he hit on a possibility. "Does time travel exist here?"

"Of course," said Bomfils, his voice filtering through the rhomboidal apparatus. "It is exclusively the province of temporal scholars in the learning hives."

"Who invented time travel?" Tom asked him.

"I am a defender of public order, young man, not a historian."

"Can't you look it up? Don't you have research materials available?"

The zone leader suggested, "A beam to the information vaults, perhaps?"

Reluctantly, Bomfils agreed.

Another hour passed. The Echelon Chief arranged for a light meal of bland, yeasty foods to be served to the trio. Then an officer arrived with a tiny capsule that was fed into a screen reader. Curiously shaped letters flashed by. Suddenly Bomfils pulled a lever. Unrecognizable characters were replaced by dimensional images. Tom jumped up. "That's my father!"

A moment later Bomfils focused on another image, and Tom got an eerie jolt. He recognized himself, although he was white-haired, and at least fifty years of age. He was posed rather stiffly in an office, next to a stooped, older man—

Cal!

Bomfils switched his gaze from Tom to the image and back again.

"There is a certain resemblance—" He paused, then addressed the other officials. "This is a monographic account of the twentieth-century discovery of the time-phase effect. There are images of the inventor, Linstrum, and his sons who carried on his work, Thomas and Calvin. Perhaps this one, who calls himself Thomas Linstrum, tells the truth."

Partially convinced, Bomfils ordered a city-wide search of police records. It turned up the presence of a peculiar patient in one of the larger hospitals. Via translation of his unfamiliar speech, the man insisted that he was a citizen of the past. Kept company by a metal box of unknown function, the man was recuperating from wounds.

"This report was circulated to all districts," Bomfils explained. "My aides did not bring it to my attention, since it had no application in this command."

"I'm sure it's my brother," Tom said.

"We will escort you to him."

Hardly hearing, Tom turned to Mari. His smile vanished when he saw her forlorn expression. He took her hand.

A police vehicle carried them into the city. With a population of forty-six million, Bomfils said, the city occupied the entire east coast of what had been, long ago, the United States.

The city was called Province East. Deep in its myriad of geometric buildings, so different from the towers of Doktor Phlonykus' doomed Earth, they reached the public hospital. It spread over fourteen blocks. In a huge ward reserved for indigents, they found Calvin Linstrum with Sidney Six hovering at his bedside like a mother tending a sick child.

The change in the future, Cal reported, had taken place without any warning. One minute, he was in his room in Phlonykus' city; the next, in the unfamiliar hospital. He knew then that the course of history had been altered.

"It wouldn't have been," White said, "except for Tom." He explained.

In Cal's eyes, Tom still saw rejection and anger. Something made Tom say, "I admit I forced the issue of going along. But I had to."

"I still find it hard to believe that you alone were responsible for aborting the doomsday device," Cal said.

Sidney Six quivered its stalks. "Dr. Linstrum, you are, on occasion, insufferable! Why do you bridle at giving your brother credit—"

"That's all right, Six," Tom interrupted. "I don't mind. From now on, I won't have to push so hard." He spoke the words with a cool, relaxed certainty that was altogether new.

"Push?" Cal repeated.

"To prove something."

"What?"

"I wasn't sure of myself, Cal. I wasn't sure whether you might not be right. I never admitted that till now, but it was there, pushing me. I feel badly about walking out on you in the other hospital. But it had to be done. Now that we're back—well, I know I'm as capable as the next person. I accomplished something I can be proud of." He looked straight at his brother. "And no one can take that away."

"I'll testify that he handled himself well," White said. "Mari and I certainly didn't have the power to make it to the doomsday console. But he did."

"I've been thinking about that too," Tom said. "Something gave me the strength—drove me. Probably you, Cal.

Ironic, huh? You were responsible for saving the human race after all."

"We can discuss psychological niceties another time," Cal snapped.

Initially disappointed by his brother's all too typical reaction, Tom soon realized that he couldn't expect Cal to change his behavior in a moment. Indeed, he would probably never change much at all. What had changed was Tom's own attitude. Even in these unfamiliar surroundings, he felt more relaxed. There was less need to retort, to argue, to *prove*. He had done the proving inside the mountain in Mongolia. And he had proved his competence to the most important person of all—himself.

In time, perhaps Cal would recognize him as an equal. The history that Bomfils had quoted offered hope.

"The sooner we return to where we belong, the better," Cal was saying. "The doctors keep telling me that I have to rest a few more days. But I'm perfectly well—"

He swung his thin legs off the bed. Suddenly his cheeks paled. He swayed and sat down.

A chubby head poked around the screen at the end of the bed. "If I may be so bold—"

An aide with one of the rhomboidal translators followed Echelon Chief Bomfils, who came right to the point. "What you have revealed to us this afternoon is both startling and significant. Therefore, before you return to— ah—your own time, we feel it would be valuable for us to have your transcript of the highlights of this remarkable affair."

Automatically, every head turned toward Cal. Even Six's stalks pointed that way. Tom didn't feel angry. He accepted the fact that Cal would be the voice of their father until Tom gained his confidence. He made a mental note to speak to Bomfils in private.

In a moment, Cal handed down his answer. "All right, a transcript. But fast. I want to go through the Gate as soon as possible."

Bomfils nodded to agree.

A police vehicle bore them out to the orchard the following evening. On the way, Tom said to Cal, "On the subject of my studying marine biology—"

"We'll discuss that another time."

"That's the point. There's nothing to discuss."

"What do you mean?"

"Marine biology's out. According to the monograph on the early years of the time-phase effect—"

"When did you read that?"

"Last night. Bomfils made it available."

"I wondered where you went for five hours."

"It's fascinating stuff, Cal. It says we worked together in the department. The Gate was my career as well as yours."

"I'm not sure you're really qualified—"

"History says I am," Tom grinned. "Or *was?*" He patted his pocket. "Bomfils provided a hard copy, translated into what he calls Old English. Our English. You can read it sometime. But the monograph definitely says we were co-directors of the department."

Cal went, *"Hmmph."*

"A remarkable document," buzzed Sidney Six, hemispheres flashing. "I perused it over your brother's shoulder. Indeed, I can hardly wait to write my book."

"Your what?"

"My narrative of this adventure! The first published account of the operation of Department 239-T! Not a mere gaggle of press dispatches, mind you. A best-selling book!"

"I'm afraid there already is," White told him. "I looked at the monograph too. Six published his book in the autumn 1988. Archibald wanted to close the department, but as soon as the book appeared, he couldn't."

"Historically speaking—ahem—the die is cast. But don't fret, Dr. Linstrum. I will gloss over your personality defects."

Cal fumed as Six continued. "Now please pardon me while I file away a few more impressions before we depart. For my last chapter, you know."

Flashing its hemispheres twice, the machine began to mutter to itself.

Cal glowered. Tom concealed his amusement.

A moment later, Mari broke the silence. "I am still not certain that I should go with you."

Grumpily, Cal said, "That's all settled. There's no life for you here."

"But I feel so strange, Dr. Linstrum. No longer the same as I was—" The girl touched her long hair.

"No longer genius rated?" Tom smiled, gratified when

she smiled back. He took her hand. "That doesn't bother me a bit."

To his brother he said, "Do you really know why she decided to come with us?"

"I persuaded her that it was the only sensible course."

"And I showed her the monograph. I not only worked with you at the Gate, Cal, I raised a family. You never married, by the way. Too busy—"

Once more Cal looked ruffled. Tom went on. "The monograph includes several long footnotes on our personal lives. And photos of my two sons. One of them took over operation of the Gate after we died."

Cal started. "You know how long we lived?"

Tom patted his pocket. "It's in here."

"When— That is, when did I—"

"I'm not going to tell you. It's the one section of the monograph I'm sorry I read. And I'm going to tear it out before I let you see it."

"I insist that you—"

"No."

Cal started to speak again. He stared at his younger brother, and didn't.

"Anyway," Tom said, "The footnote of real interest was the one about my wife. She was a girl who found out that the heart is a little more than a circulatory organ after all. Her name was Mari."

She smiled at him then, warmly, completely.

The vehicle glided to a halt. Echelon Chief Bomfils appeared outside the hatch. "We have arrived."

In the balmy dusk, they walked up the hill into the orchard. The geometric city glowed along the northern horizon. Sweet aromas drifted from the trees.

"Where's the control?" Cal asked.

With a wry expression, Gordon White surrendered it.

"Some things never change, do they?" White murmured. Tom smiled.

Calvin Linstrum was too preoccupied to notice.

ABOUT THE AUTHOR

John Jakes was born in Chicago. He is a graduate of DePauw University and took his M.A. in literature at Ohio State. He sold his first short story during his second year of college, and his first book twelve months later. Since then, he has published more than 200 short stories and over 50 books—suspense, nonfiction, science fiction, and historical novels. His novels comprising the American Bicentennial Series were all bestsellers, and his books have appeared in translation from Europe to Japan. Originally intending to become an actor, Mr. Jakes has manifested a continuing interest in the theater by writing four plays and the books and lyrics for five musicals, all of which are currently in print and being performed by stock and amateur groups around the United States. The author is married, the father of four children, and lists among his organizations the Authors Guild, the Dramatists Guild, and Science Fiction Writers of America. In 1976 he was awarded an honorary doctorate by Wright State University for his contribution to the nation's Bicentennial observance.